W9-BYW-039

THE CHASE

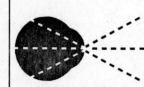

This Large Print Book carries the
Seal of Approval of N.A.V.H.

THE CHASE

DIANN MILLS

THORNDIKE PRESS
A part of Gale, Cengage Learning

RIVERHEAD FREE LIBRARY
330 COURT STREET
RIVERHEAD, NY 11901

GALE
CENGAGE Learning

Detroit • New York • San Francisco • New Haven, Conn • Waterville, Maine • London

GALE
CENGAGE Learning

Copyright © 2012 by DiAnn Mills.
All Scripture quotations, unless otherwise indicated, are taken from The Holy Bible, New International Version®, NIV®. Copyright © 1973, 1978, 1984 by Biblica, Inc.™ Used by permission. All rights reserved worldwide.
Thorndike Press, a part of Gale, Cengage Learning.

ALL RIGHTS RESERVED
Any Internet addresses (websites, blogs, etc.) and telephone numbers printed in this book are offered as a resource to you. These are not intended in any way to be or imply an endorsement on the part of the publishers, nor do we vouch for the content of these sites and numbers for the life of this book.
Thorndike Press® Large Print Christian Mystery
The text of this Large Print edition is unabridged.
Other aspects of the book may vary from the original edition.
Set in 16 pt. Plantin.

LIBRARY OF CONGRESS CATALOGING-IN-PUBLICATION DATA

Mills, DiAnn.
   The chase / by DiAnn Mills.
      pages ; cm. — (Thorndike Press large print Christian mystery) (Crime scene: Houston)
      ISBN 978-1-4104-4980-1 (hardcover) — ISBN 1-4104-4980-7 (hardcover)
   1. Murder—Investigation—Fiction. 2. Child abuse—Fiction. 3. Houston (Tex.)—Fiction. 4. Large type books. I. Title.
   PS3613.I567C53 2012b
   813'.6—dc23   2012017070

Published in 2012 by arrangement with The Zondervan Corporation LLC.

Printed in Mexico
1 2 3 4 5 6 7 16 15 14 13 12

Beloved Doe and those who would not
let this child's death go unsolved.

NOTE TO READER: Some dramatic license has been taken with regard to FBI procedures. Any errors in accuracy are the author's.

CHAPTER 1

Present day
June
Kariss had fulfilled all her dreams but one by age thirty-five. Most women would bask in such a claim, but not Kariss. The one mountain yet to climb beckoned her to strap on hiking boots and make her approach. The peak held her in fascination, and failing meant losing everything she'd ever gained.

Her heels clicked along the marble flooring of the Marriott hotel's lobby adjoining Houston's Intercontinental Airport. Ten minutes early for her appointment with her literary agent and she could use the time to make sure her responses to Meredith were gracious and resolute. A mouthful for sure.

Sinking into a plush chair, she took a deep breath and waited. With all of her prolific abilities, why couldn't she respond with words that relayed her passion for this story?

But now she had the opportunity to convince Meredith of her sincerity. A little encouragement went a long way when calling up the powers of inspiration and creativity.

Right on time, Meredith Rockford slipped into a chair across from Kariss, sipping on a cup of tea, no doubt Earl Grey. Dressed in a black traveler's knit jacket and pants, the only color emitting from Meredith was her crimson lipstick.

"You could have texted me that you were early," Meredith said.

Kariss smiled. "Just got here. Did you have a good night's rest?"

Meredith lifted a brow while taking a sip of her tea. "My head is killing me. I had to fly from New York to Houston. Arrived late and had to cancel our dinner appointment, and you ask me if I slept well?" She set the cup on a table in front of them. "The only thing that will give me a good night's sleep is for you to abandon this ludicrous idea of changing genres."

Kariss valued integrity above all things, and she refused to lose control. "Please understand I have given this writing project considerable thought. I need a break from writing women's fiction. I'm not discounting what you've done for my career, my friends who continue to write women's fiction, or my faithful readers. But I have a deep need to write a suspense novel."

"You rehearsed your spiel very nicely, but let me give you the facts: you, Kariss Walker, are about to commit publishing suicide. Changing genres in the middle of *New York Times* bestselling status means starting all over."

"I was hoping you'd champion my goals."

"My goal is to make sure my writers and my agency make money while ensuring the publishing community has quality writing projects." She crossed her arms. "*After Sunrise* has held the number two slot for three months. *Always a Lady* sold over six hundred thousand copies along with a sweet spot on the bestsellers list. You write women's fiction. Period. Not suspense. Your ratings are going to plummet like an avalanche."

Kariss uncrossed her legs and allowed her arms to lay limp at her side. How much more open could she be? "Ten novels in five years is a bit much, don't you think? Suspense intrigues me. Remember the eight years I spent reporting evening news on Houston's Channel 5? I have more ideas than I will ever have time to write."

"It won't work. Your readers want sweet stories about women. They'll drop you tomorrow if you switch to suspense. Now send me the proposal for the next story. The one we chatted about in New York will do nicely. You're the only writer who can convince the reader that the main character isn't just a story, but a human life."

Meredith started to stand, but Kariss gestured for her to stay. "Please hear me out. Deep inside me is a well of passion for stories that burst onto the suspense scene. These are real and happening in my city. One in particular touched my heart several years ago and has never let me go. I cannot *not* write this. It doesn't matter that I don't have a contract. If one of the big six doesn't want to publish it, I'll self-publish."

"If you do not adhere to the demands of the publishing world, your actions may dissolve our representation of your work."

Kariss moistened her lips. "I am fully aware of the consequences."

"Are you? You may never publish again." Meredith retrieved her cup of Earl Grey and left the lobby.

Kariss gathered her purse and laptop before leaving the hotel. She had two hours until her appointment with Lincoln Abrams, special agent in charge of Houston's FBI. Five years had passed since she'd linked arms with law enforcement agencies and enlisted public support to help find criminals. Excitement with a twinge of apprehension grabbed hold of her senses. If only her agent held the same enthusiasm about her writing a suspense novel. Maybe if she knew the real reason why Kariss wanted to protect children . . .

This story meant more than all the six-figure checks combined. In five years, no one had solved the crime stalking her, and she didn't possess the skills to smoke out a killer. But in her novel version, the perpetrator would be brought to justice.

Drinking a double espresso, his breakfast of choice, Tigo drove through the seedy neighborhood off South Main in Houston, looking for the dark green van last seen at the shipyards speeding away with two hundred and fifty grand of stolen AK-47 rifles.

The area looked deserted except for the battered vehicles matching the twisted and dented people who hid behind their weapons and bravado.

Some residents were simply poor and trying to eke out a living. Why they stayed made no sense. But those weren't the ones Tigo wanted to question. He needed Cheeky and his gang of Arroyos behind bars for gun smuggling. Add to that the identity of the dealers who were selling them weapons, and he was a happy man. Houston ranked as Mexico's largest gun supplier, and Tigo intended to drop that stat like a live grenade.

He drove slowly, studying each peeled-painted house for signs of rodents. He didn't really expect a tattooed gang member this time of the morning, but he also knew they could tear through a door at any moment ready to blow him to pieces. He risked the encounter and hoped they were sleeping off the previous night. His appointment was critical to draw out those who continued to break the law, one important enough for him to break the rules and work alone. He'd long ago given up trying to figure out if he wanted credit for the arrests or if he didn't want to endanger another agent. Probably both.

The gangs living here counted coup on law enforcement types.

Tigo eased to the curb next to a bungalow with boarded-up windows. Turning off the engine of the twenty-year-old Toyota minus the fender and hubcaps, he waited for his guest and drank the espresso.

A toddler pushed open the door of a house across the street. Wearing nothing but a diaper, he carried what looked like a rag

14

— probably a substitution for his mother. The reality of the kid's future yanked at Tigo's thoughts, along with the likelihood of him already being an addict. How long before he was dealing and carrying a piece?

No one else ventured from the neighborhood. But Tigo couldn't wait forever. Linc wanted to see him about something. Glancing at his watch and rolling down the window, he gave himself fifteen minutes.

Candy was ten minutes late. Maybe she'd overslept, since her career kept her occupied at night. But the olive-skinned beauty had always been prompt, especially when the extra money didn't touch her pimp's pockets. She seemed to sense Tigo's drive to nail the gang, but he refused to psychoanalyze that. She claimed to have the information he needed to close down the Houston operation, including names of arms dealers and details about those dealers raising prices on their weapons.

Five more minutes passed, and the espresso cup lay crumpled on the passenger's seat. Candy wouldn't have left him waiting without a call. Lately she'd grown bolder . . . maybe too bold. After all, meeting here at seven-thirty had been her idea. Late nights ate up her earning power. She claimed his presence looked like a john leaving, and the neighborhood slept until noon.

Tigo punched in her number. Four rings. "This is Candy. I'm busy right now." A giggle followed the sexy voice with a Hispanic accent. "Leave a message, and I'll get back to you."

He wasn't stupid enough to leave a message.

They'd met five times, and he believed each one raised the bar on their trust. She wanted to leave her sordid life, but she needed money until she landed a respectable job. Even asked for the name of a shelter. Said her two kids would have a better future. That had suckered Tigo in. Now suspicions about her motives called him a fool.

Tigo fired up the Toyota, muttering the language of the area. At the end of the block, two Hispanics wearing black T-shirts stepped into the street carrying assault rifles, their muscled forearms tattooed with gang symbols, their shaven heads etched deep with crossbones. Tigo spun the car, tires squealing. The smell of burned rubber invaded his nostrils.

At the other end of the street, two more armed men straddled his path, matching the MO behind him. Both had sidearms tucked into the front of their jeans. *Great.*

He headed straight for them. In his quest to singlehandedly stop this gang, thinking a prostitute would take an exchange of money for info, he'd allowed pride to overrule logic. He deserved to have that engraved on his tombstone.

The man to the left in front of him lifted his rifle and fired, shattering Tigo's windshield and narrowly missing his left shoulder. In return, Tigo grabbed his Glock from the passenger seat, tossed it into his left hand, then fired into the man's chest, sending him sprawling backward onto the street.

Another bullet whizzed past the top of Tigo's head. The men behind him were chasing after him. Tigo stomped the accelerator and headed straight for the remaining man on the right. Tigo might have fallen for a classic fog job with Candy, but he still had a few tricks to save his neck.

With the next outburst of fire, he sliced the morning with a pain-filled cry. The man on the right hesitated, giving Tigo the break to send a bullet flying into his chest.

Candy had either set him up or she was dead.

CHAPTER 2

Kariss zipped along outbound Highway 290 to the FBI office on a sun-bathed morning, clearly a good omen for her new writing project. She admired the fluid precision of her silver Jaguar XKR convertible, barely six weeks old. Its dynamic sound system rivaled a concert hall, and she imagined a tuxedo-dressed conductor ushering Bach into action. She detested the statements that people deserved this or that, but this car was definitely worth the sticker price. Of course, if Meredith made good her threats, Kariss would be selling the Jag in a heartbeat.

Traffic on the inbound lane merged bumper to bumper. Another reason for living inside the loop and working from her condo. She'd go nuts if she faced this every day. However, today her destination was worth any price.

Mentally checking what she needed once

she reached the FBI office, she pushed aside Meredith's insensitive attitude toward her goals. Her agent would change her mind once she read the first chapter of her suspense novel — and the book's dedication.

She'd like to add some romance and the grit of a heroine who was not afraid to help solve a crime. The storyline was a little vague, but after today the detailed plotline should fit right into her spreadsheet — a writing technique she hadn't used before. In the past her books were straightforward and pretty easy to write. All she needed to do each morning was take her place at her computer and work through the plot in her head.

Taking a deep breath, Kariss envisioned the exclusive book signings and TV interviews. Admittedly so, she was hungry to make this work.

A late-model green Toyota sped alongside her on the left. At the car's speed, it must be shaking. How did a vehicle that beaten up stay on the road? Her attention swept to the driver, a Hispanic man, and for a brief moment their gazes met before he cut directly into her path. Slamming on her brakes, she stiffened. What a jerk. He'd nearly caused an accident.

She reached to palm her horn, but the

driver looked like the type who might whip out a gun. Great for her novel, but not for real life. He sped down the highway, weaving in and out like her granny's knitting needles.

"You'll get yours." She turned up the radio, still shaken but certain HPD patrolled both sides of the road. Some people didn't deserve a driver's license.

Taking a drink of her Starbucks mocha latte, she eased into the right lane, maintaining her speed at the posted limit of sixty miles per hour. The make of her car kept her on the radar of overenthusiastic police officers. No time for a speeding ticket today.

A police car whizzed by, red light flashing, and she laughed. Sure enough, he had Mr. Toyota in his sights. By the time she passed the police car, both vehicles were chummy at the side of the road.

Kariss turned right onto West 43rd toward Houston's FBI office, her fury over the driver who'd cut her off dispersing. She parked in the designated visitor area and snatched up her laptop and purse with a goal to whiz through security. Her fingers tingled at what lay ahead. Oh, the glory of story.

A sign inside security stated no laptops. Why hadn't she remembered that stipulation? Back when she frequented the FBI office, she hadn't needed her tool of the trade.

She pasted on a warm smile. "I have an appointment with Special Agent in Charge Lincoln Abrams. He won't have a problem with my laptop."

"Yes, ma'am. I still need to scan it and you."

"Then I can take it with me?"

"When I'm finished."

She'd planned an early arrival, knowing the paperwork required before her appointment. Her foot tapped against the concrete of the security's floor. *Patience. You're not a one-legged tap dancer.* Twenty minutes later she sat in the reception area, her paperwork completed, her laptop resting in its pink sleeve beside her.

"Miss Walker?"

Kariss hurried to the receptionist. "Yes, ma'am. Is Mr. Abrams ready to see me?"

The woman smiled. Her black jacket and pants radiated power as her dark eyes narrowed with authority. "I'm sorry. Mr. Abrams has been detained for about forty-five minutes. Would you like to wait?"

Kariss hid her disappointment. Linc held a prestigious position, filled with responsibility and unexpected interruptions. "I'll wait. Thank you." She did have downloaded emails to answer, and she hadn't touched the marketing plan for the new novel.

Nothing could snip her excitement for this writing project.

Tigo's neck stung along with his pride for getting pulled over by one of Houston's finest.

"You're late." Linc Abrams settled back into his chair and steepled his fingers, just like he used to do in college during study groups — when he was right. A file sat on his otherwise cleared desk, empty except for his computer and pictures of his wife and teenage son.

"Got a ticket." Tigo flashed a smile and took a chair across from Linc's desk. His watch registered forty-nine minutes past the scheduled meeting time.

"Flying like a speed demon again?"

"Something like that."

Linc leaned in, his dark-brown gaze calculating yet not unfriendly. "Were you solo this morning?"

"Why would you ask that?"

"I know your habits. Your methods give a whole new definition to *furtive.*"

"Is that a compliment?"

"Not today. I got a report from HPD. Firefight involving the Arroyos and an unidentified driver of a green Toyota." He pointed at Tigo's face. "The giveaway is your bleeding neck."

"I should have driven the speed limit." They danced this kind of interrogation on a regular basis. Next time Tigo would stop to treat the cut. "I was there chasing a lead."

"Nearly lost a friend this morning and all you can say is you were out chasing a lead?"

"This case is driving me nuts while the gunrunner trade escalates."

"We're a team, remember? Who gave you the info? Candy?"

Tigo chuckled. "That's three questions in a row."

"Congrats. You can count. Next time remember 'two,' as in you and your partner, Ryan."

Adrenaline continued to flow. Or rather, it dripped like the blood trickling down his neck. "I work better alone, but I'll watch my rear —"

"You'll take Ryan. The far-reaching effects of these gangs and cartels will get you killed. You were disguised today?"

Tigo nodded. "Okay. I'll do what it takes. I've worked Operation Wasp for a long time, and my patience is running thin. We're being tipped off about some of the Arroyos' transports, and we don't know who is set-

23

ting them up or why."

"Humor me here and answer my questions."

"Questions two and three are the same. Yes, it was Candy." He shrugged, still fuming with what had gone wrong this morning. "She didn't show."

"Good reason. HPD found her dead after midnight near her corner. Throat cut."

He clenched his fist. "We know Cheeky had her killed. I suppose they're bringing in Bling?"

"Looks like a classic. She ticked off her pimp once too often."

Tigo blew out an exasperated breath. "She either sold me out or the Arroyos caught on to what she was doing. Or both. Can I get some coffee?"

"Sure. Looks like you need it — and a Band-Aid. By the way, you had another appointment thirty minutes ago."

Tigo flipped open his Blackberry. He had his schedule memorized. "I don't think so."

"Get your coffee. Do something with that neck. And get back here. We need to talk." Linc stood and walked to the window. "Bring me a cup too."

Less than ten minutes later, Tigo lowered himself into the "think" chair, his reference to the other side of Linc's desk. Coffee in hand, he breathed in the aroma. Not the savory South American beans he ground each morning, but right now he needed the caffeine. His last birthday had pushed him into the backside of thirty, and it was catching up with him.

"I can't take on another case until Cheeky is arrested. Between the drugs and gun smuggling, I want the Arroyos stopped."

"I agree, but no choice in this one. It's more of an assignment than a case."

Tigo didn't like where this was going. While taking a sip of the bitter brew, he considered the ways he could negotiate out of this. Gang warfare and gun smuggling were his top priorities. "Why don't you tell me what's going on?"

"I need a favor."

Tigo maintained his composure, but his nerves seemed to grind. "What kind?"

Linc rested his hand on the file before him. "Do you remember about five years ago when Kariss Walker worked as news anchor for Channel 5?"

"I do. She was influential in enlisting public sentiment for many of our cases as well as HPD's. Never met her. Why?" Had the woman turned up dead?

"She's been writing novels since then. *New York Times* bestsellers."

"Suspense and thrillers?"

Linc shook his head. "No. Women's fiction. I've only ever glanced through her books, but Yvonne reads them. She thinks they're well done."

"What does she want from the FBI?"

Linc scratched his jaw. "I owe her, Tigo. Remember how she helped me infiltrate a drug ring by encouraging public support? Right after that I received a promotion."

"So the agency is indebted. But you're not answering my question."

"I'm getting to it. Kariss wants to write a suspense novel. She's requested permission to use a cold case, one she reported on and investigated. The second request is she'd like to shadow an agent."

A shot of heat raced up Tigo's neck and into his face. "Oh, no. You're not asking me to babysit a woman who wants to be a faux crime fighter."

"In fact, I am. A Memorandum of Understanding has been drafted and already gone through our legal department. She understands the confidentiality aspect of FBI protocol."

"So you and Miss Walker have been discussing this little arrangement for a while?"

Linc blew out a sigh. "Yes . . . we have. When she's finished with her book, I'll also need you to review the material for accuracy."

The day continued down the drain. "Where does our media coordinator fit into this?"

"You'll both meet with her later. She'll explain the guidelines before you sign the MOU."

Tigo rubbed his temples. His neck throbbed, and the coffee tasted like dirt. He'd had better mornings digesting sand in Saudi Arabia.

"Tigo, I wouldn't ask if I had time to help her myself."

"Is this your discipline measure for my independent investigations?"

Linc attempted to mask a laugh. "Hadn't thought of it in those terms, but it sounds good."

Tigo owed Linc for his own position at the FBI, although this stretched the boundaries of years of friendship. "How long will this take? She just needs to gather facts, right? All I need to do is pull the investigation report from the file, right?"

"That's three questions."

He shouldn't have gotten out of bed this morning. "Lay it on me."

"Three months max. Right now I'd like for you to change clothes before meeting her. She's waiting downstairs in the reception area. I have a few things to discuss with her first. Then she's all yours."

Tigo frowned. He didn't want to come within fifty feet of the woman. "If I'm to help her gather data for a cold case, why does she have to shadow me?"

Linc hesitated, and in that moment Tigo realized the worst was yet to come.

"She wants her book to be authentic, and we want the FBI to be well represented. She's going to press you for protocol and details. Keep her away from obvious danger but let her accompany you and Ryan on minor calls. You'll need to read her manuscript for content."

"Any other good news?"

"Her book will be based on the last case she reported before leaving the station. You worked on the case — Cherished Doe."

Oh, he knew that case well . . . "She picked a hard one."

"I agree. She'll be your sidekick for the next few months. I haven't told Ryan. Thought you could handle it."

This day had turned from bad to worse.

CHAPTER 3

Kariss attempted to sit still, but patience had never been one of her virtues. A sign in the waiting room stated visitors were prohibited from accessing the Internet. She'd responded to emails, but without connectivity she couldn't send the dozen messages. Neither could she post to Facebook or Twitter or read the latest marketing blogs. Once she passed Linc's inspection, she'd ask about using the Internet. Why hadn't she brought her Kindle? At least she could read the manuscript her publisher wanted her to endorse.

Of course that could change.

After rereading her female protagonist's characterization workup for the new novel, she played with scenes. Although Cherished Doe remained a mystery, Kariss hoped to write an ending that moved readers to be more aware of the children around them, to nurture and guard the world's most precious treasures. Adults were responsible to protect children from abuse and neglect, and she'd fight anyone who claimed otherwise.

In the deepest part of her heart, the area where compassion should balance with justice and mercy, she nursed the thought of helping the FBI solve the outrage. In her reporting days, crimes against the public kept her glued to a case until the authorities were able to bring in the offender. But this atrocity haunted her, as if she hadn't done enough to help the authorities identify the child. The lack of evidence had festered into a poison, causing her to shove aside mercy for vengeance. She wanted the killer found.

Kariss was hungry for a new adventure, ready to sink her teeth into a challenge above all other challenges. But what differentiated this new height was the passion for a situation she couldn't right, only bring some semblance of justice to. Depending on what the day held, Kariss could later drive to the south side of town and the Pine Grove apartment complex to see if something rattled her memory. Something everyone who'd investigated the crime had overlooked.

The sound of a man's deep voice caught her attention. Linc entered the reception area. Neither his six-foot-tall frame nor his average build commanded attention, but the way he carried himself did. Confidence filled the room, as though the very air around him stepped aside. Intelligence poured into his speech and warmth radiated from his dark eyes, more so than when they'd worked together five years ago.

He reached to shake her hand and smiled. A true friend. She'd definitely use Linc in her book.

"Good to see you, Kariss. It's been a long time."

The thrill of what was happening bounced into her response. "Yes. Too long. Congratulations on your promotions. You deserved them and more."

"Thanks. Sorry for the delay. Had an urgent matter to address."

"Of course. That's your job. I've been busying myself." She gestured around the room. "The new headquarters is impressive."

He grinned as though taking ownership and walked to the glass-enclosed display case. A history of Texas' Juneteenth Day filled the area, commemorating the date in 1865 when slaves were freed by the Emancipation Proclamation during Abraham Lincoln's presidency. African American achievements in a historical timeline proclaimed Linc's heritage. His mother must have known her son's future when she named him Lincoln Abrams.

"We want the public to work alongside us, and this is one way to show we value them as well as our city, state, and country. We change the display monthly."

Kariss observed the tintype pictures, then moved on to the artifacts and the progressive involvement of the African Americans in Houston. She hadn't been aware of how her city's culture, business, and politics were shaped by these hardworking people. This was Linc's world and a reminder of the precision in which he carried out every aspect of his life.

"Are you ready for a tour of the new building?"

"Absolutely."

Linc gave her a thorough tour, but she expected no less. He allowed her just far enough inside the glass doors of the restricted areas to whet her enthusiasm, then ushered her on to the highly sophisticated workout room. As special agent in charge of the entire Houston FBI operation, Linc knew every detail of the building.

They entered his massive office, open and airy with floor-to-ceiling bookcases. Kariss seated herself on a russet-colored leather sofa, and he joined her on a matching chair.

"Linc, how is your family?"

"Good. Ron is a senior this year. Planning to major in political science at Rice. And Yvonne is busy with her volunteer projects and teaching two days a week at Rice."

"Please tell them I said hello. I'd love to see her and Ron."

He walked to his desk and picked up two photos, then handed them to her.

"Yvonne looks stunning as always. Oh, Ron has grown."

"We're so proud of him. Do you remember his rebellious stage in junior high? Well, he made some changes, and we survived." He replaced the photos and returned to his seat.

She recalled Ron's run-in with the police and his parents' subsequent drug intervention. They were survivors. "I'm really glad for all of you."

"You were there. Hey, your career took a leap when you resigned from Channel 5 and began writing full time. Yvonne tells me you're always on the bestsellers lists."

"I try." She pulled her latest release, *After Sunrise,* from her computer sleeve. "I brought this for her."

He studied the cover then flipped it over to read the back. "Thanks." He opened to the first page. "She'll appreciate your personalizing it for her."

"It's the least I could do for old friends. Linc, I'm grateful for your help on my new writing project."

"We want the public to know we're on their side. Solving and preventing crimes works hand in hand. You're in a position to help us achieve that goal."

She thought about the case she wanted to use. An active and aware community diminished the occurrences of crime. "Will Cherished Doe ever be solved?"

"I'd like to think so. It would have to be a joint effort with HPD to reactivate the investigation. Is that the case you still want to use for your book?"

"Definitely. I want to write this novel so the ending reflects a solved case. Any chance of opening it back up?"

He pressed his lips and laid her book upside down on the table separating them. "Those of us who've worked Cherished Doe have not given up — not the special agents involved, Detective Montoya at HPD, the Texas Rangers, or myself."

His passion to solve the child's murder laced every word. Kariss's throat tightened with the reality of the case's unfortunate status. "Maybe something will turn up soon."

He nodded. "We can hope and keep our eyes open. You've been assigned to a good agent. He'll allow you to view what is appropriate in the file and ask questions."

"Does he have any problems with a writer following him around for the next few months?"

He nodded his head. "I'd be a liar if I didn't warn you."

"No enthusiasm, huh? Then why him? A female agent would be fine." They could be girlfriends, chat about the challenges of being a female agent.

"Special Agent Santiago Harris is one of the best. Perhaps *the* best. That's why I want you to learn from him. You indicated a desire to show authenticity, to learn from an agent who has a reputation for being relentless in solving hard cases."

She did need someone sharp. Oh, she could win Special Agent Harris over. Give him a copy of her latest release — her books had won national acclaim after all. Acknowledge him and his contributions to her research. Gush over his helpful attitude while giving TV interviews. Even fashion the lead agent after him. "I trust your judgment. This book may launch a whole new series featuring the FBI."

"We aim to please. Are you ready to meet him?"

Kariss stood, gathering her purse and laptop case, now minus *After Sunrise*. She should have brought two copies to appease her assigned agent.

In the hallway Linc pointed to the right. "He's waiting for us. Tigo —"

"Special Agent Harris?"

"Yes, he goes by Tigo. He's a bit nonconventional. I can say that because we went to college together." He chuckled.

Wonderful. Her book was taking form. "Does he do much undercover work?"

Linc stopped in the hallway and faced her. "Yes. But you are not to accompany him on those missions or ask about his current case. His work takes him into dangerous areas of town — restricted for you. Those places can get you killed. I haven't forgotten a few of your antics in chasing down stories. Don't even go there."

She'd see if Tigo would rescind that stipulation.

"Is this clearly understood, Kariss? I see the wheels turning in your head. Let the reality of a murder investigation play out in fiction, not on your epitaph. Your research is through Tigo. Our media coordinator will meet with you two for the signing of the Memorandum of Understanding. She'll also detail your limitations."

"Of course. Whatever I learn or discover is confidential." She smiled and tapped her foot. What an adventure. She might never write women's fiction again.

They continued down the hallway and stopped at a cubicle, where a dark-haired man talked on a phone with his chair turned away from them. His hair touched his ears, slightly longer than she expected — probably because of undercover work. A few moments later, he ended the call and faced them.

Her heart leaped like the turbo in her Jaguar. *Surely not.*

Blood trickled through the man's Band-Aid and onto his shirt collar. He might be dressed in a sports coat and jeans now, but she recognized his face. He'd been the one who'd cut her off on the highway.

CHAPTER 4

Tigo cringed at the blanched look on the woman's face. Dressed in a light-green silk pantsuit, she didn't fit his expectations of a successful writer. Not sure what he expected. Kariss Walker . . . Sounded like a cowgirl or a country-western singer. Oh, but she was hot — tanned skin and lips that looked ripe for kissing.

She frowned. *Great.* This day had just gotten worse, and it wasn't even noon. *Suck it up, Special Agent Harris.* He stood and reached to shake her hand, offering his most charming smile.

"We meet again. This time under more pleasurable circumstances." The encounter on Highway 290 might have been to his advantage, considering the bandage on his neck. After all, he'd been wounded in the line of duty. Sort of a red badge of courage.

The woman lifted her chin. Sassy. He preferred submissive. Dark, tousled hair clung to her shoulders and framed huge, pecan-colored eyes. She might be a challenge, but he could persuade her to forget this ridiculous idea of following him around like a puppy.

"It's a pleasure, Special Agent Harris. Or shall I call you Tigo?"

He detected the sarcasm and continued to smile. "My friends call me Tigo. You must be Kariss Walker, the prolific writer?"

She stiffened. Hadn't anyone ever taught her how to read body language other than a corpse? "I am. And we'll be friends, now won't we? Or does that depend on who needs to get to the FBI office first?"

"You do have good-looking wheels."

"What am I not getting?" Linc said.

Tigo swallowed a smirk. "Miss Walker and I crossed paths this morning."

She tilted her head. " 'Crossed' is subjective. But it happened before he was pulled over for a speeding ticket."

Linc coughed. "Now this is beginning to make sense."

More like someone had cursed Tigo's morning. "I owe you an apology for my —"

"Reckless operation?"

She was good. Feisty. Probably spoiled by her fame and fortune. The Jaguar stood as

proof of her success. "I had an appointment."

"With me or my longtime friend, Special
Agent in Charge Abrams?"

"Both."

"Look," Linc said, "if you two got off on
the wrong foot, this arrangement might not
work."

With a tilt of her head, Kariss flashed an
award-winning smile at Linc. "Oh, I'm
excited about working with Tigo. This
morning is the past. I'm over it and ready
to open my laptop, ask questions, and take
notes." She shifted her laptop and studied
Tigo's face. "I understand my research has
to occur in and around your busy schedule,
so just give me the guidelines." She peered
closer at him. "Do you need another Band-
Aid? The two you have sticking there aren't
doing the job."

Did she think he couldn't take care of
himself? "It needs a few stitches."

Kariss hurried at a fast clip to the elevator.
Why had she worn stilettos? Keeping up
with Tigo had led to another workout. First
the MOU had to be signed and now this.

"The med center's off campus." He
pressed the Down arrow, and she noted his
Buzz Lightyear watch. If not for her nieces

and nephews, she wouldn't have recognized the *Toy Story* character.

"No problem. Linc told me. My car or yours?" she said between breaths.

"Mine is quicker."

She'd already witnessed that.

"Sure you don't want to stay here?"

"I want the whole experience. One of my characters might need medical attention, and this is an excellent fact-finding mission."

He stepped into the empty elevator and then pierced her with his gaze. But she would not be intimidated. "Make sure I'm not one of your characters."

This guy definitely thought highly of himself. "Why not? Looks like you're Linc's favorite. Or is it least favorite?"

"I'm beginning to wonder."

If Kariss wanted the inside scoop on the work of an FBI agent, she'd have to make the first move. "We've gotten off to a rough start, and I know I'm not on your list of favorite assignments."

He smirked. "Linc tell you that?"

"He indicated the possibility. What can I do to make this easier, other than quitting or requesting another agent?"

"I haven't a clue."

She laughed lightly. The elevator opened,

and they stepped out. "I have no intention of giving up my writing project because you view me as a hindrance to your work."

"All I ask is you don't get in my way."

"I wouldn't think of it."

Tigo continued at the same lightning speed toward the rear of the building. He and Buzz did have much in common. How could one man walk that fast with blood oozing onto his shirt collar? Maybe pain kept him moving.

Through the glass doors, she viewed the employee parking lot. He opened the door and waited, impatience etched across his forehead.

"Is the jog for my benefit or yours?" She struggled to control her breathing.

"I'm in a hurry. Lots to do." He pointed to the car that resembled a castoff from the junkyard. She might use it in her story. "Is that your normal transportation?"

"You don't like the tank?"

"Oh, it's fine." She grimaced at the spider-web effect of the shattered windshield, which looked like a bullet had sailed through. Other similar holes sank into the car's side. "I know this is not your ride of choice. What's your other vehicle?"

He opened her door. The ragged piece of metal protested. "Most days I drive a truck.

But there are three other tank-types available for my use."

Made sense. He'd already jumped from the image of a professional who worked a case from a phone and computer to a . . . Well, she didn't know yet. Buzz Lightyear's phrase "To infinity and beyond" slid across her mind.

She eased onto the ragged seat and hoped her outfit wasn't destroyed by the open springs and dirt. "Were you on a stakeout this morning?"

"Possibly." He slammed the door and walked around the front of the car. Ruggedly handsome, but his condescending and ripply sarcasm reminded her of an ex-boyfriend. Very ex. She'd killed him off in a tragic accident in her third bestseller.

She composed herself before he started the engine. "Did you get what you went after?"

"Since I didn't go after a bullet, the answer is no."

"Is dodging bullets your normal method of gathering information?"

He wrestled the gear shift into reverse, obviously throwing his frustration into the process. "Have you counted how many questions you've asked since we started this ordeal?"

"Ordeal?"

He moistened his lips and backed out of the parking place. "I will answer one question of your choice if you promise you won't ask one more thing until my neck is stitched."

"Okay." She should have understood his pain could make him surly. "I'm sorry. Here's my last question for now: how much of your investigative method involves dodging bullets?"

"Too much."

"Thank you. I believe the next few months will be exciting." She gave him her best smile.

He groaned, and she didn't ask if his response was due to the wound in his neck or her presence.

"I can bring Starbucks every morning." She'd seen that done on a TV show.

"Venti, black."

"A pastry?"

"That's a question, but I'll give you a break. Blueberry scone once a week. Preferably Wednesday."

"It's a deal." She'd found his weakness.

"Here's an assignment for you."

He'd be a great character. "Bring it on."

"See if you can muzzle your enthusiasm until we're on our way back to the office."

Kariss bit her tongue to keep from laughing. This was not at all what she'd expected. But it would be worth any price.

CHAPTER 5

"Do you realize your file is bigger than any other agent's?" Dr. Nguyen shifted his focus from Tigo to the open folder. "More stitches. Two broken arms. One hospitalization after you decided to scale a twenty-foot fence. Need I go on?"

"I'm working on a record." All Tigo wanted today was an opportunity to eradicate gun smugglers and those who sold them weapons. And in the course of a few hours he'd been shot, received his second speeding ticket in three months, been introduced to a woman who would drive him to drink, and now had to endure more pain. He also wondered about a tooth that seemed to be giving him a problem, but he didn't have time to see his dentist.

Dr. Nguyen stepped forward to examine him. "Let me guess how this happened. I'm writing a book, you know."

Not another one.

"Patching you up reminds me of a war zone." Dr. Nguyen chuckled.

"I'm glad my wounds are your comic relief."

Once Tigo received the five stitches and what he needed to keep the wound clean from infection, he took a deep breath and headed back to Kariss Walker, his new assignment. More like a shackle. She wouldn't be riding shotgun with him when he needed to follow up leads. But she'd be waiting at the office to pester him with questions.

A blast of reality blew into his thoughts. A male writer would most likely ask as many questions and get under his skin too. But maybe he could share a few of his exploits and chase this woman away, back to the world of the rich and famous. He stifled a laugh. Linc had shown him the back of Kariss's book. Her tag line read "Real Women, Real Issues." She had no clue about the actual work involved in solving a crime.

"Ready?" Tigo smiled with the intent of convincing her of his sincerity.

"I am." She closed the lid of her laptop. "I've been writing my questions."

His mission went into take-charge mode. "Good idea. Then we can tackle them all at once."

She eyed him suspiciously. "What's the change? Pain meds?"

"I thought I'd give you a rundown on why I was in the middle of a firefight this morning."

Her dark eyes widened. The reaction he needed. "I'll tell you in the car. No point in boring anyone else with the details."

"Great. Can I record you?"

"I'd rather you simply listen." Once in the car, he began, adding a few colorful touches that stretched the truth but served his purpose. ". . . that's when I realized I was late for my appointment with Linc."

"Twelve gang members after one agent. I'm amazed you escaped with only a bullet grazing your neck."

"I was motivated."

"Why didn't you fire a warning shot before it got deadly?"

"FBI agents don't fire warning shots. That's only in the movies and isn't practical."

"Wow. I'm so lucky."

Whoa. That's not the reaction he needed. Before noon, he wanted to make calls to find out the particulars of Candy's death and work on his next lead. He slid into a parking spot and turned off the engine. "My nearly getting killed is lucky for you?"

She startled. "I mean I'm fortunate to learn from your expertise. I'd love to hear about your disguises. How many do you have?"

Tigo sensed defeat creeping over him, but he rarely ran from a challenge. "Because of what I do, there are those who'd like to gun me down. Gangs don't play touch football. We could be together at lunch, and your life would be in danger."

"Not any more than getting cut off on the highway."

Did she have a flippant remark for everything? Time to put his skills into the next gear. "My point, Kariss, is your desire to write this book might get you killed."

She shifted to face him. "Cowboy, trying to persuade me to give up my research only reinforces my determination. Let's start over with your story. This time you can begin by telling the truth." Her gaze bore into his, steady with a spark of humor. "I believe you had a few problems this morning, and by not mentioning a partner you're indicating your little incident was probably not sanctioned by FBI protocol. My question is, how many guys did you really upset? Even fiction heroes don't take on a dozen gang members singlehandedly. Only stubborn women."

She crossed her arms before continuing. "I'm not stupid, Tigo, and I resent your implication that I'm not smart enough to see what you're doing. My goal is not to make your life miserable but to conduct research effectively and professionally. So suck up your male ego and realize you're stuck with me."

He'd met his match, and she'd won the first round.

An hour had passed since Kariss and Tigo had returned from the med clinic to the work cubicles assigned to each agent. She studied the man seated at the desk before her, the FBI agent with a bandage on his neck. She hadn't decided if she liked him. He'd fed her a line of trash as though she were a schoolgirl idolizing a rock star. But like heroes and heroines in a novel, she wasn't giving up one of her character traits. She understood danger and what it meant, but though she hadn't been involved in anything more life threatening than driving in six lanes during rush-hour traffic since she'd quit being a reporter, she had the intelligence to know when to back off from the opposition. Like the past hour.

What did impress her was the autopsy photo of Cherished Doe on his desk. Like her, he hadn't been able to forget.

Tigo rubbed his face. Paperwork must drive him nuts. When he'd told her he needed to document what happened this morning, she decided to work on characterization for her hero, who was decidedly Special Agent Santiago Harris. Hmm. He had an interesting combination of names. She'd have to find out about his heritage. He had yummy-colored skin, reminding her of a man she'd met once in Cozumel. Huh. That line would look better in a novel.

Twenty minutes passed before he scooted back his chair and left the area. How she'd love to get her hands on that report. Maybe he'd feel like talking about the Cherished Doe case when he returned.

She let her fingers fly with the hero's description, filling in the previous blank areas with eye and hair color, height and weight, body build, and distinguishing physical features. She closed her eyes. Tigo had coffee-colored eyes, deep with intensity, and his thick black hair begged to have a woman's fingers combing through it, feathering her touch around his temples —

Kariss caught herself. This was a suspense novel. She couldn't think thoughts like this. Different descriptions, priorities . . . *Focus, Kariss. Venture into a world where the resolu-*

tion of a story means a crime's been solved and characters change and grow into better people.

So she added the description "ruggedly handsome" and considered his skills and abilities. She'd add more details as she learned from the men and women of the FBI.

Tigo returned in a better mood. He stood at the entrance of his assigned cubicle — which was a decent size, but with the extra chair Kariss felt crowded.

"Hard at work?" he said.

Kariss gave him her full attention. "I'm in the prep stage, forming my characters."

"Keep at it. I have a call to make. Do you mind waiting outside my little office."

She offered her sweetest smile and grabbed her laptop. "All right. I wouldn't want to get in the way of FBI business."

For half a second he scowled, but then quickly masked it with a nod. "Anything you hear is confidential. We're working on getting you a cubicle of your own. Possibly the one to the right of mine." He scooted her chair into the hallway.

With his back to her, he punched in a number. She wasn't going to tell him about her acute sense of hearing. Fingers poised, she waited. Although the conversation would be one sided, she could get the gist of what was being said.

"Hey, Ricardo. I understand candy was found last night."

Candy was a code name for drugs. Kariss wondered where the drugs had been found.

"Unfortunate, any way you look at it. Did you pick up bling?" Tigo leaned back in his chair.

Was *bling* a code word or a person?

"A man like you doesn't believe everything he hears."

Silence.

Tigo chuckled. "Sure, I can do lunch tomorrow. What can you tell me now?"

Several seconds passed with Tigo listening. He grabbed a notepad from his desk and jotted down a few things. She'd love to get her hands on that too.

"Thanks. I'll see what I can find and get back to you. I'd like to talk to the guy too." After ending the call, he wrote a few more items, then whirled his chair around to face her.

"Do you have time to discuss the cold case now?" she said.

He held up a finger, wrote something, and placed his notepad inside a drawer. He patted a file and looked up. "Hey, Ryan."

Kariss turned to see a thin man dressed in

a black shirt and khakis standing behind her.

"Heard you were busy this morning. Sorry I missed the action."

"News travels fast. Hey, I'd like you to meet Kariss Walker. She's a writer who'll be observing us for the next three months."

Ryan reached out his hand, and she met a kind face . . . that held a sparkle of mischief. "Ryan Steadman. Pleasure to meet you. Are you a journalist? Doing a feature on wild FBI agents?"

"Not exactly. I'm writing a suspense novel, using one of your cold cases."

Not a muscle moved on his face. "Tigo here is the best agent for your kind of research."

"Linc said the same thing."

"He has good stories, and I'm sure he'll tell you all of them." Ryan nodded at Tigo as if encouraging him to dive into another heroic venture.

She didn't want another ego blast. "I've already heard one."

"They get bigger and better."

This time Tigo laughed. Good to know the man had a sense of humor.

"Tigo," Ryan said. "I need to talk to you later about our informant."

"Sure thing. Around two o'clock will work."

Kariss hoped to be privy to that discussion since she'd been denied access to the phone conversation with Tigo and Ricardo. He had to be the same Ricardo who'd worked on the Cherished Doe case. She turned to Tigo. "You have clearance to give me information for my story."

"We can discuss the file over lunch."

"I wasn't aware of the time."

He tapped his left wrist, right over Buzz Lightyear. "Check your watch."

"I don't wear one."

Obviously bewildered, he shrugged. "Why? Hard to find one to match your outfit?"

She ignored his gibe. "I can't find one that will keep time. I have too much electricity in my body."

He laughed. "Did this happen before or after you started writing fiction?"

If he was setting the stage for the next three months, she'd better be prepared. "I've always been this way. For some reason my body generates more static electricity than other people. I'm sure you've felt it."

"Right from the beginning."

Clearly annoyed but refusing to show her irritation, she cleared her throat. "There isn't a medical term for my condition, but I assure you it's documented. I use my phone to check the time."

"I'll remember that. Any other quirks I should be aware of?"

She considered a response, but why bother? "If I think of something, I'll let you know. Why Buzz Lightyear?"

"Fits my mode of tracking down bad guys."

" 'To infinity and beyond'? How does an FBI agent develop an appreciation for an animated character?"

He chuckled. "Ryan's son is a big Buzz fan. I was playing basketball with him and Ryan when he compared one of my shots to something Buzz would do. So I became Uncle Buzz, and of course I had to complete the MO."

"That one I believe."

"You can populate your story with it. How about Mexican?"

What? His nationality?

"I know a great restaurant close by where we can talk about Cherished Doe. I remember you worked at Channel 5 when the child was found, but we didn't have the privilege of meeting then."

"I reported on the case and enlisted public support. It happened the last two weeks I was there."

"So you have a personal stake in it." He stated his response as though summarizing why she wanted to write the book.

But he had no idea how deep her passion for this story . . . or why. "I've never been able to erase the little girl's autopsy picture from my mind."

"I understand your desire to make a terrible crime right. If that is ever possible. It doesn't bring the child back. Neither will writing a book in which her killer is brought to justice."

"But it might make a reader aware of a potentially dangerous situation and act instead of react."

"Optimistic thought. I've tried working on this case many times, and the outcome is always the same. Dead end." His features shadowed. He cared about this case too. "I'll repeat what I know Linc has already told you. We have nothing to go on."

"Except hope."

"Hope is worthless without a lead."

She refused to reconsider her plans. She simply had to learn to think like Tigo, like a pragmatist.

CHAPTER 6

Kariss dipped a chip into salsa while forming her words to Tigo. The two had been civil to each other since leaving the office for lunch. Linc had served her well by assigning her to Tigo, although the agent could use a few lessons in manners. Her growing list included the way he dipped chips into salsa like he was panning for gold.

Some women would find his crusty edges appealing. But not Kariss Walker, suspense writer. She'd use most of his traits for her hero, but she'd polish his attitude.

Obviously the case involving gangs and gun smuggling had his attention and priority. Maybe she'd do better sliding into his good side with that approach. "How much time can you allot me while working the weapons case?"

He poked his chip into the hotter bowl of salsa. "How long will it take you to conduct your research?"

"I could review the files this afternoon. See about a new angle —"

"There aren't any."

She braced herself. "I want to talk to the HPD detective who also worked the case, Ricardo Montoya."

He nodded. "I can put you in contact with him. Good guy. I talked to him this morning. He's never been able to let the case rest either. Tough situation. A man or woman is murdered and it's regretful. The authorities want the killer found so others can be safe. But a child is a different matter." The lines across his forehead softened. "An adult can fight back. Possibly escape. Not so with a helpless child."

He still had passion for the case.

"I never understood why the FBI was called into a police matter."

He leaned back and peered at her. Was he evaluating her intelligence? "Our assistance to local police agencies falls under 'police cooperation' in our guidelines. Congress gives us authority to assist and provide resources to local police agencies in situations like this, even if the case isn't our jurisdiction."

She started to pose her next question, but he held up his hand. "Pulling out resources for another investigation is a waste of the bureau's manpower and time. It doesn't make sense. Show me new evidence, and I'll be the first one on it."

Which was exactly why she intended to visit the crime scene this afternoon.

"But sometimes cold cases are solved by reviewing evidence already presented."

A wisp of anger crossed his features. "I know my job. The Cherished Doe case is not about rules or stipulations or feelings. The case is cold because that's what it is. Write some violence into it, add some sizzle, and let your story spin."

She wanted to say things a lady shouldn't utter. "I'm writing the story as it happened."

"Good luck."

The server walked up to their table and voiced caution about their hot plates. The few moments' reprieve gave her time to step back from her emotions. She clearly understood Tigo's position, and debating the FBI's findings only alienated her from those who had much to teach her. She had to put aside his insults and play on his macho image.

"I apologize for my comment a few minutes ago. You're the pro. I'm the spectator."

"All right."

"You're a problem solver, right?" she said.

"I thrive on solutions. But I've done the

research, searched through the flimsy evidence, and examined the press conferences — including your TV report — and nothing has persuaded me to reopen the case. I even contacted the various clinics in the area the body was found to see if they had record of a little girl requiring a breathing tube. Nothing."

"Although our differences keep us at odds and will continue to do so, I want you to know I respect your work and your commitment to the FBI."

His gaze met hers, and she saw a hint of respect. "Maybe your perception of character comes from your study of human nature, which must be essential in writing fiction." He studied her for a moment, and she hoped he was finally seeing her as an intelligent person. If he'd read her novel, he'd see a plotline that showed characters involved with real-life problems.

"I'm sorry we didn't meet when I worked at Channel 5."

"That might have helped . . . the awkwardness."

"We both want Cherished Doe's killing solved. My method is a story. Yours requires cold, hard facts."

He tapped his finger against his glass of iced tea. "I'm not a calloused agent who can box up violent crime into cold-case status without a sense of failure. On the other hand, the weapons smuggling currently has my priority."

"Can't you do both?"

He pointed to her plate. "Your food's getting cold."

She held her breath, anger tingling her fingertips. The last time someone had told her to eat, she was ten.

From the way Kariss sliced into her spinach enchilada, Tigo had accomplished his purpose of successfully diffusing her thoughts of rehashing the case.

Pouring hot sauce over his refried beans, he pondered the situation of earlier this morning. Candy was at the morgue. Tigo regretted her death for several reasons — one honorable and one selfish. Her kids were seven and eight, a little old for the system to adopt out. He'd met them once, a boy and a girl. Sweet kids. But the relatives were probably of the same caliber as Candy. Tough break.

The second reason was her ability to provide information about the Arroyos.

The more time that passed, the more guns made it across the border into the hands of cartels. He and Ryan could talk this afternoon. Figure out the next series of moves. Jo-Jack had served them well before Candy entered the picture. His leads had brought about arrests and drug raids. But could he find out what the gun smugglers were doing?

Linc had given permission for Kariss to be privy to the conversation, taking notes and asking questions. Tigo questioned the logic of her presence. Not that he thought she might sell them out, but the Arroyos had methods of forcing people to talk . . .

No. He'd gone into left field with those concerns. Kariss was safe. With his disguises, no one in his undercover work suspected him of being an agent — except Candy. She could have been forced to reveal his name, which meant this morning's firefight might be the beginning of more.

He studied the writer, who'd left a lipstick stain on her water glass. Why did women put the stuff on only to leave it somewhere else? Like a trademark . . . or a tattoo. For a moment the Arroyos' crossbones tattoo popped into his head.

Tigo shrugged and dug into his food, finishing long before Kariss took more than a few bites. Pushing his plate aside, he opened the Cherished Doe file, although he didn't need a refresher. But it made him look like he was on her side.

The rumble of angry voices to his left grabbed his attention. A lovers' spat. She accused him of cheating. He claimed the woman was his wife. Tigo glanced at Kariss, who was drinking in the scene like an investigative reporter. Hmm. Her old role blending with a new one.

He pulled out his Blackberry and googled her name. Time he found out a little more information about his new appendage.

"I can take this in a to-go box," she said.

"No problem. I'm checking on something." He added a smile to reassure her.

His first stop was her website. Whoa. *New York Times* bestseller, just like Linc said. Endorsements from high-profile writers. Huge awards. And two of her novels were being made into movies. Clicking on her bio, he read about her success and awards. She held a prestigious position in the publishing world and supported new writers. The blurb said Kariss had been a homecoming queen, and her parents still lived in Texas City.

"You must be reading something serious." She took a sip of water.

"I am. I'd share it with you, but it's not appropriate."

Later he'd conduct a background check,

find out where she went to school, her majors, and everything else from there. Never hurt to know all about your opponent. "So you were writing during your stint at Channel 5."

She tilted her head, a smile lifting the corners of her mouth. "You were googling me, weren't you?"

Laughter rumbled in his throat, and it had everything to do with being caught. "I was."

"I hope you're pleased with what you've found. I work hard to get my point across."

"I am. Quite an impressive site. Promotion and marketing must be a fun part of your job."

"At times. That part of my writing is difficult, so I let my publicist direct it."

"What part do you like?"

"The actual writing after I brainstorm about the women in my novels."

"What caused an attractive woman like yourself to write fictionalized stories about real issues women face?"

She lifted her chin, "I don't exploit women's feelings, if that's what you're insinuating. I entertain, encourage, and inspire them to make a courageous stand in their lives."

"Touché. Okay, let's talk about the contents of this file. That is, if you're finished eating."

She pulled out a notepad and pushed away her half-eaten lunch. "Fire away."

"In short, I don't think there's anything here that you haven't seen before." He handed her the file and watched her leaf through it. Emotion swept over her face, and she blinked. He well remembered his own reaction to Cherished Doe. But the contents in her hand were all she'd get from him.

"You're right. I have all this information. Guess I'll need to write the story as I originally intended. Make up the ending."

Relief swept through him. Now to ensure she received a crash course in "How to Be an FBI Special Agent in One Week."

CHAPTER 7

Kariss drove south on I-45 toward the side of Houston where Cherished Doe's body had been found. Authorities assumed the little girl had lived and died there. Years had passed since Kariss had driven into Pine Grove Apartments, but the dilapidated community — broken windows, ragged children with empty eyes, and gang-like clusters of mostly male youth — brought back the intense longing to find answers.

The clump of pines still stood with their secret. She parked her car and stared into the trees, wondering what those who were trained in investigations had missed. This setting, the poverty and crime, was where she'd place her characters.

Who allowed you to starve to death, little one? I can't rest until your sweet body has a name and a reason for your suffering.

The need to experience the area moved her to exit her car. She was alone. There was no one to harass her. Smells of sewage met her nostrils along with a suffocating odor of desperation, and she rubbed the lower part of her back. She heard a child laugh and wondered how long before that was stifled.

"¿*Mamacita, que haces aquí?*"

She turned to see who'd called her a sexy lady and asked her what she was doing there. Five Hispanic teens gathered around her car. The one talking looked to be about sixteen years old, shirtless, his jeans hanging below his boxers.

"A little girl was found dead here over five years ago," she said in Spanish. "The killer was never found. Do you remember, because —"

"You don't belong here."

Right, but she did crave answers.

The chuckles of those who'd stepped closer alarmed her. They circled her Jag. What good did keyless entry do when she couldn't reach the door? And her cell phone lay inside the console.

"Nice car."

"*Gracias.*" She moved toward her vehicle with the understanding that showing any fear fed into their intimidation.

"Where are you going in such a hurry?"

"I need to get back to work."

"I could put you to work." He glanced back at the others and laughed.

"No thanks. I have a boss who gets angry when I'm late."

"He won't mind."

She maneuvered her fingers over her keys and the button that would allow her to climb inside her car.

Suck it up, Kariss. You should have known better.

Her brothers had always instructed her to use her head and not show fear. But there were five of these guys. She eyed the leader and drew in a breath meant to calm her scattered nerves. Somehow she managed to walk to her car and face him. At least he didn't have gang markings. She pressed the keypad and the car chirped.

"I think she wants to leave," he said. "Makes me wonder if she doesn't like our company."

He opened her door, and for a split second she feared he planned to take her car. Instead he gestured her to slip inside. She brushed past him, the smell of marijuana wrenching at her stomach. He grabbed her jaw as she passed, forcing a sickening kiss on her mouth.

"You're lucky this time. All we want are your money and credit cards. Next time I'll

69

want more than a kiss."

She reined in the panic firing into her bloodstream. "But I want something too. Inside my purse are my business cards. If you hear of anything about a case called Cherished Doe, the little girl who was found dead, call me. I'll pay for good information." She steadied her gaze into his. "Good information, not trash."

His eyes narrowed.

"Do you read English?"

"I'm not stupid," he said in perfect English.

"Good. When you charge something on my credit cards, I'd hate for you to get caught."

He reached for her purse and smirked.

Kariss drove out of the apartment complex with the reality of danger alerting her from the top of her head to her toes. In her rearview mirror, she could see the teens laughing. She'd been lucky.

The police officer who came to her aid after she phoned 9-1-1 from a convenience store lectured her for fifteen minutes about being in the challenging district of Houston driving a Jag. In his words, "Be glad he stole your purse and not your life."

It took an hour for her to make the necessary calls about identity theft. Fortunately, the address on her ID displayed a post office box and not a physical address.

Kariss drove home less enthusiastic about her writing project than that morning. The obstacles in the way of success left her feeling defeated before she even began. Not enough to call it quits, though. Absolutely not.

She took a deep breath. The problems today were simply roadblocks, and writing suspense meant she'd have those and more to deal with — including overcoming stubborn, driven individuals like Special Agent Santiago Harris and her literary agent, who opposed her dream of writing a suspense novel.

Although Linc was an old friend, he might have assigned her to Tigo to deter her writing project. But it hadn't worked. The Cherished Doe case, the one so dear to her heart, was no more solved than five years ago. She needed to find an angle that would persuade the FBI and HPD to reopen it. The authorities who'd tweaked every aspect of this case were brilliant, trained to bring criminals to justice. She could dialogue with the best of them, but finding something to warrant their further attention had her baffled.

She adjusted the air-conditioning in her

car. Too cold. But not her attitude.

The rest of this week she'd work on building a positive image with Tigo and Ryan. All the while she'd look for a flaw . . . something that begged to be investigated. Contacting HPD detective Ricardo Montoya and picking his brain made perfect sense. She remembered him from her Channel 5 days. They'd talked extensively then about Cherished Doe, and she was sure he'd remember her.

How could she climb higher in Tigo's approval ratings? He resented her questions, and he had his own agenda with his current gun-smuggling case. She'd show him. When this book hit the *New York Times* bestsellers list, he'd eat his words. And appreciate her expertise.

Tonight she'd do her homework and develop a new strategy to win Tigo to her side. Or at least cause him to rethink Cherished Doe.

She'd research gun smuggling and the Arroyo gang. At least she could listen to Tigo and Ryan with some knowledge about the situation and chip in a worthy comment when appropriate. This afternoon's conversation between the two agents had divulged little except their current informant had been found dead, and a man by the name of Jo-Jack was a candidate to provide information. Their talk about Jo-Jack bothered her — buying people for information seemed calloused. Especially when an informant could be killed. She sighed with the reality of law enforcement work. Informants understood the danger when they put themselves into commodity mode. She'd seek one out to get his viewpoint on Cherished Doe.

She definitely wouldn't be making any more trips to Pine Grove Apartments alone.

"How is she?" Tigo stepped into his mother's bedroom, his heart and mind fixed on her pale, sleeping form.

"Not a good day, sir." Natalie, the young nurse, tilted her head. "I gave her something to help her sleep."

He nodded. Lately his mother had more bad days than good. The cancerous tumor on her kidney combined with the weakened condition of her stroke-ridden body meant she had only weeks or possibly days left.

Every day she was hooked up to a dialysis machine.

Every day he expected the dreaded call that she no longer breathed.

Kissing her forehead, he gestured at the

door for Natalie. "Can we talk for a moment?"

In the hallway, with the door to his mother's bedroom closed, Tigo faced the inevitable. "Natalie, I want her remaining days to be pain free."

"We're doing everything possible to ensure she's comfortable." Her eyes filled with compassion.

"I'm concerned you can't tell when she's hurting."

"I assure you that we nurses, who are giving her around-the-clock care, can tell if she's uncomfortable. Her blood pressure elevates and the lines on her face deepen. Of course, we administer her medication in a timely fashion."

"Please make sure she has the strongest available. I'll call her doctor in the morning to see if her pain medication can be upped. I don't give a flip about addictions or if she's sleeping."

"Yes, sir. I —"

"Tigo. 'Sir' makes me feel like I'm at the office instead of my own home." He smiled. "You and the other nurses are doing a fine job. Ignore my bad moods. This is . . . It's hard to watch my mother suffer. I'm helpless, and I'm angry." He glanced at the door leading to his mother's room. "Sometimes you get the worst of it."

"I understand. Many times I believe the end days are harder on those viewing their loved ones suffering than the patients enduring the struggle."

"Suppose you've seen it all. I dread the day one of you has to call me." He swallowed the lump in his throat. "Guess I'm selfish, wanting to keep her alive when she has no quality of life. She was always so active. Never one to give in to sickness."

Natalie said nothing. Not that he expected her to.

"She's a fighter," he said. "Just like she's fought every ordeal of her life."

"You're right." Natalie offered a faint smile. "At times I feel like she's telling *me* not to give up."

"That's my mom, a little powerhouse. And we can't allow any doctor's report to dictate her progress or deterioration."

"Well said."

"Her faith is strong, but where is her God in the midst of this?"

"He's with her, helping her be courageous."

"You're Christian?"

She nodded. "I couldn't take care of Mrs. Harris or any other patient without my faith."

"Thank you." Tigo's verdict on God was still out, but he respected those who found comfort in Him.

"Your neck?"

"Work hazard. Five stitches. Mom will love the story."

A few hours later, while Natalie took her evening break, Tigo sat at his mother's side, holding her limp hand. Loneliness enveloped him . . . the familiar pang of wishing he had someone. A dog might help. But his dedication was divided between his mother and his job. When would he have time for anyone or anything else?

He glanced at the crucifix above his mother's bed, remembering the many times she'd taken him to church. Praised him for being an altar boy and urged him to pray. What good did her piety do her now?

"What a day, Mom. Nearly got myself blown away trying to play the big FBI agent who could single-handedly bring in Cheeky Lopez. Remember him? He's the leader of the Arroyos. How many times have you warned me about my pride? Looks like I need to listen."

He wished she'd squeeze his hand or even move a finger. Instead her mind and body were paralyzed, trapped between the effects of the stroke and cancer and the medication that allowed her to endure it all. Maybe she heard him, and he made sure nothing was said in her presence that he wouldn't say if she were coherent. At times he could envision the feisty woman telling him he wasn't Superman or reminding him he had a partner.

"I have a new sidekick for the next few months. A woman writer. A real nuisance, but drop-dead gorgeous. Problem is I don't know how to get rid of her. I did a background check. Learned she's from Texas City and the youngest of six kids — three sisters and two brothers. Dad's a retired oil worker. Both parents are active in church, a rather conservative denomination. I'm sure they're proud of their daughter and her achievements." He paused. "I'd like to explore who she is and what makes her a super-achiever. She worked at a day care during high school and in the summers between college sessions."

He considered that aspect for a moment. "She must've loved kids to return to that line of . . . torture to finance her education. She's obviously intelligent. Received a Jessie H. Jones scholarship and attended Baylor on a full ride. Nominated for a Fulbright. Graduated summa cum laude with two majors — communications and Spanish.

Passed on grad work and took a job with Channel 5. Soon rose to news anchor on prime time. She did that well for a few years and won awards for her reporting. Took a few daredevil chances to find the truth."

He paused to consider some of the things he'd learned about her reporting days. "She successfully talked a young girl down from jumping from a ten-story office building. Another time she approached a day care that was under investigation for hiring workers without conducting proper background checks. And because of her appeal to the public, several crimes were averted. Anyway, she quit to become a writer. Quickly earned *New York Times* bestselling status. That's impressive — I've got to hand her that. But I feel like I'm babysitting. Fiction is not my thing, and it would be so much easier if she'd go back to writing about women, writing about things she already knows."

He patted her hand. "Sure could use some of your wisdom with this one. She's writing about the Cherished Doe case. You know how I feel about bringing that little girl's killer to justice. You instilled in me the importance of making sure kids are protected. Wish I could do something. Anyway, Linc's given this woman permission to follow me around while she learns the art of being an agent. Sure messes up my investigation of the Arroyos and their gun smuggling."

As much as he wanted to go deep undercover, the idea of leaving his mother alone during her last days was heartless. Some would argue that she wasn't even aware of his presence. But he'd know. She deserved more . . . so much more.

His cell phone rang and interrupted his thoughts. The caller ID read "Candy."

"Hola," Tigo greeted in Spanish.

"Dulce le llamaba mucho," a man said.

"We're friends. Of course she called me a lot." This was either Candy's pimp or whoever had killed her. Tigo had learned Bling had been released when he coughed up an alibi.

"Tell me your name, and I'll ask her."

"She's dead, so it's not her who wants to know."

"Smart man, but we know who you are."

"I doubt it." Tigo noted a slight lisp in the caller's voice. "Give it your best shot."

The man laughed. *"Usted es policía."* He spat the words and cursed.

Tigo hoped that meant Houston PD and not the FBI. "Wrong. This time you tell me who you are."

"You already know. Watch your back 'cause we're out to get you."

CHAPTER 8

Kariss launched the second day of her FBI research by bringing Starbucks to Tigo. Yesterday, she'd made the offer to bring him coffee each morning, and he'd agreed. Tomorrow she'd bring him a blueberry scone or muffin just like he'd requested for Wednesdays. Her mother always said a good cup of coffee shared with friends was a great way to start the day. However, Mom didn't know Tigo and his dynamic disposition.

Flashing a smile, she held his venti black in one hand and her hazelnut latte, minus the whipped cream, in the other. Setting the cup in front of him, she waited at his desk until he lifted his head from the computer screen. "Peace offering."

He nodded and reached for the drink. "That'll do for the first fifteen minutes." He toasted her. "Thanks."

Ah, progress. If only for a little while.

"Are we off to anyplace special today?"

He chuckled. "Nowhere I can take you."

"Going undercover, I presume. Where?"

"Ryan and I have a couple of gun shops to check out."

She scrunched her forehead, then caught herself. If she didn't stop overusing the muscle between her eyes, she'd have to resort to a facial filler. "Visiting a gun shop isn't dangerous."

"I didn't say where, and I didn't say the business was legit. Nor did I say how many thugs would be watching our every move. However, you could deter them for a few minutes."

"Then I can go?"

"Two words — no way. Nor do you say a word to any of your family and friends about anything you hear or see." He grinned. "I don't imagine you'd be willing to do what it would take to keep the bad guys busy."

"Try me. I can talk big."

"So I noticed." He took another drink. "This will kick me into gear."

"I could take notes."

"Dead issue, Kariss."

The chair she'd used yesterday was missing. "How was your evening?"

"Fine." He'd noticed her looking for the chair. "The cubicle next to me is empty."

He looked tired, which meant he'd probably had a busy night running from bad guys. Or maybe they'd run from him.

"Mine was fine too. I read up on gun smuggling in Houston. How's the 'Don't lie for the other guy' campaign going?"

He eyed her, a give-me-a-break look. "In my opinion, straw men don't give a flip about the feds teaming up with the firearm industry. Gun smugglers and those who help them are interested in what's going to fill their pockets, not billboards and slogans."

"It's a program designed to educate the public and enlist their support."

"Sounds good on paper, but I don't see any of the stats dropping. Maybe if they print their material in Spanish a few grade school kids would take notice."

Ouch, Tigo's cynicism was in high gear. "My point is the good guys might more easily detect a straw purchase."

"In theory." He took a long drink. How did he drink his coffee that hot?

"Guess I'll go to my new desk and make myself at home. When are we leaving?"

He lifted a brow, and she laughed.

"I reviewed the cases you helped the FBI solve. Good investigative reporting."

She heard a little admiration and decided

to freeze the moment. "Thanks."

He studied her, and she could almost hear the wheels spin. "Kariss, what I do is dangerous and I will *not* get you involved. You heard about my little experience with a gang yesterday — with zest. Think about this: the ones involved in Houston's cartels and gangs take on different appearances. The guy volunteering to coach Little League may be dealing thousands of dollars of cocaine. The person you choose to represent your area might be involved in human trafficking. The gal who does your nails could be smuggling weapons. Do you get the picture?"

The understanding of what Tigo and all those involved in the FBI and other law-enforcement agencies did to keep people safe sobered her. "Hard to trust anyone."

"Right. The arrests I've made haven't gone unnoticed. Every time I expose myself is a risk. It's not a question of if I'm on a gang's radar. The question is when will they learn my identity? The arrests made as a result of your TV coverage have exposed your identity to those who might want revenge too."

"I'm aware of repercussions." Her face flushed. "Risk was something I didn't heed. However, I did take a self-defense class upon the insistence of family and friends."

"Do you have a handgun?"

"No. And I don't want one."

"Guns to bad guys are like words to you. They're tools of the trade. So observe me if you must, but it will be on my terms. If I have to look out for you, then I can't do my job, and we both end up in a pool of blood."

She nodded while apprehension seeped through to her bones. "I will not be a liability to you or the FBI."

Kariss knew he'd dramatized his scenario to frighten her, like the previous day. But he made sense. She wasn't naive. Neither did she want to spout that none of the dangers mattered. She valued her life and his. Linc and Tigo had given her boundaries, and she needed to stay within those parameters.

Latte in hand, she took a seat at her new desk. After powering up her laptop, she used her cell to call Detective Montoya. Perhaps he remembered something about the case. She left a message and made a note on her spreadsheet about the contact. She felt weepy. The disappointments from yesterday had crashed her excitement to write the story. Nothing seemed to be going right.

Shaking her head to rid it of unwanted emotions, she pulled up her research file.

Tigo had an idea, one he couldn't toss

85

aside. Kariss's intent of writing Cherished Doe's story had dredged up his frustration at not being able to solve the crime. All the times his mother had volunteered to work with children at church and her genuine love and concern for them had floated back into his thoughts. He opened the cold case file, which he did periodically. At times the case consumed him. Took him to a dark place where mercy had no room. The data had not changed . . . only time. The case had frustrated law enforcement officials long enough.

Tigo's mind whirled. A child didn't enter the world and disappear without touching someone's heart.

Kariss understood the value of enlisting public sentiment in solving crimes. She'd been good at it, and her methods had been successful.

He lifted the phone and contacted Linc's office. Thirty minutes later he quickened his steps to the SAC's office and took a seat on the leather sofa.

He hoped this wasn't a mistake. "I want to talk to HPD about reopening the Cherished Doe case."

"Why?" Linc's irritation was evident by the deepening lines on his brow. "We haven't had any new developments to warrant the time or work."

"I have an idea."

"How much of this is you, and how much is Kariss?"

Good question, but that had nothing to do with why he sat in Linc's office. "Her questions jostled my memory. Got me to thinking about it again." Tigo studied Linc's face. "I've never given up on Cherished Doe. Just ran out of places to run down answers. Honestly, the elapsed time has strengthened my determination to solve the case."

"What's your new idea?"

"I'm suggesting a different angle. What if the FBI, HPD, and Texas Rangers make a last-resort appeal to the media for public support? Show the autopsy picture of the unidentified child. Interview residents at the Pine Grove Apartments again. Representatives from all three law enforcement agencies could hold a press conference. Offer a reward. Talk it up so the whole city is looking for answers."

Linc walked to the window of his office facing Highway 290. Tigo joined him, noting the inbound morning traffic had not thinned. The only sound in the office was the hum of the air-conditioning, although Tigo sensed activity going on in Linc's head.

"I despise cold cases. Makes me feel inept," Linc said. "But we had tons of media coverage five years ago. If we didn't have any success when the case was fresh on our minds, why would now make any difference?"

"Maybe the right set of eyes didn't see it then," Tigo said. "Or maybe someone was afraid to come forward then and now circumstances have changed."

"And you want me to convince HPD of this crazy idea of yours."

"None of us have been able to shove Cherished Doe into a file." Tigo nodded at Linc's desk where he knew the photo of his son sat. "I don't have a son or a daughter. If I did, nothing could stop me from taking good care of them. Adults get themselves into unfortunate situations, but a child has no means to fight back. Especially a little girl who was starved to death."

"You made your point. I'll make a few calls. See what happens. We've never made an effort like this before. If conducted correctly, it has the potential to significantly impact the public to help us find how this child died."

"Thanks. I think it'll work."

"It's worth a shot."

CHAPTER 9

The following afternoon, Kariss sat at the desk assigned to her at the FBI office and played a word game on her iPhone. Whenever plot problems occurred, this was her method of forcing creativity into her mind. By toying with words, the tools of her craft, characters and their situations fell into place.

What she really wanted to do was drive back to Pine Grove Apartments.

Tigo stuck his head around her cubicle entrance just as she added eighteen points to her score. "A press conference has been called for Thursday morning regarding Cherished Doe."

"What?!"

"The FBI, HPD, and Texas Rangers are making a last-ditch appeal to the media in hopes of finding out what happened to the little girl."

Neither the Houston Police Department

nor the FBI had solved the mystery. They'd labeled the little girl's killing as a cold case and tucked the child's scant information into a file labeled "pending inactive."

Glancing at Tigo, Kariss rubbed the chills of emotion rising on her arms. She didn't know whether to turn a cartwheel or shout hallelujah or both. This time the person or persons responsible would be found. She could feel it. A new strategy to find Cherished Doe's killer was exactly what she'd hoped for. She filled her lungs with hope and determination.

"Where will it be held?" she finally said.

"Right here. Our media coordinator is making the arrangements."

Tigo explained how he'd talked to Linc about convincing HPD to enlist the public's help. "Finding what happened to that child is important to every law enforcement official who's ever worked the case. Fresh eyes could make the critical difference." He walked away then turned to face her. "Your interest surfaced a need to try one more time. Thanks."

His gratitude nearly sent her over an emotional edge. "Thanks. I've never heard of reaching out to the media in this manner. And I've been there."

"If it works, then we're onto something

for the future."

"I hope so. My fear is the one responsible has slipped back across the border. That may be a wrong assumption, though — profiling the killer because the child was Hispanic."

"It's a good reason to include the Spanish networks. The law enforcement agencies involved are offering a reward for information leading to an arrest."

"Is there anything I can do?"

"Linc thinks that your attendance at the press conference will show a viable connection with the past and present. Some of the reporters will be your peers."

"Oh, I'll be there." An image of the past, when she'd first reported Cherished Doe, intensified the longing to bring closure to all who were involved. "But I don't want anyone to know about my book project. That sounds self-seeking."

Approval swept across his face. "All right. You might have an ending to your story, and we might have an arrest."

Detective Montoya hadn't returned her call. But she'd probably see him on Thursday. For the first time this week, she felt positive about the case.

By Thursday morning, Kariss's anticipation

about the press conference had swung into high gear. She hadn't tweeted, posted information on Facebook, or informed any of her friends or family about the press conference. But with those self-imposed restraints came two sleepless nights while she waited for Thursday morning. Too many scenarios of what might have happened to the nameless child kept her thoughts spinning.

Last night she'd dreamed about the autopsy picture. In her suspended state, she walked along the pine trees at Pine Grove Apartments.

"Help me," a child's voice whispered.

Kariss ventured toward the sound, and into the canopy of thick trees any semblance of light vanished.

"Help me," the whisper came again, and a faint breeze bathed Kariss's face.

Brush crackled beneath her feet, and she struggled without a path. All she heard was the haunting cry for help. Ahead in a clearing, a faint light poured through from the treetops onto a small form wrapped in a pink blanket. The body moved and frail arms reached out to her.

"I have you," Kariss said, bending to the hard earth. "Hold on tight."

As she reached for the child, a burst of

fire erupted from the woods. Hot flames burned her face and hands, beating her back from the child.

The cries for help grew louder. Then they stopped, and all she heard was the crackle of fire.

Kariss had awakened terrified and found it impossible to go back to sleep. Must the past stalk her forever? Would she ever find redemption?

She had no idea what it felt like to be a mother, but she'd seen her own mother protect and care for two boys and four girls. Kariss's parents had placed their children's needs above their own. Wasn't that what parents were supposed to do? Nurture and grow their children into responsible members of society. Teach them the difference between right and wrong, and instill the value of education. Love them, not hurt them. Feed them, not watch them starve to death.

At nine forty-five, Kariss and many agents made their way ceremoniously to the enclosed area outside of the FBI building. The early June temps were pleasant. The blue sky looked promising, or maybe she was simply reading into the day the hope in her heart. But what Kariss noted was the FBI emblem carved into the stone behind the podium. If any agency could find a way to solve this seemingly unsolvable crime, it was this prestigious law enforcement bureau.

Houston's chief of police stood alongside Linc with Detective Montoya and members of the Texas Rangers. Some of the men and women she didn't recognize, but she assumed they were representatives of Crime Stoppers. Every TV network, radio, and newspaper reporter in the city was poised, camera ready and notepad open. She inhaled the buzz of a story breaking into the lives of Houstonians.

After Linc welcomed the crowd, Chief of Police Blackburn stepped up to the podium.

"Five years ago a female child between the ages of four and seven was found in a clump of trees beside Pine Grove Apartments in south Houston. We named her Cherished Doe because to date her identity and how she died remain a mystery. She wore green pajamas and was wrapped in a quilt, then placed in a purple, flowered bag. Medical examiners ruled the cause of death as starvation. She was discarded like an unwanted animal." Chief Blackburn's gaze spanned the crowd. "On behalf of the FBI, Texas Rangers, Crime Stoppers, and HPD, we implore you to help us find out what happened to this child.

"Note the little girl had a scar on her neck and two on her abdomen indicating a feeding tube. She was of Hispanic descent. I don't understand why the child was not taken to a hospital or a fire department when the caretaker could not or would not provide care. We who stand before you need the media's help to solve this case. Those responsible for Cherished Doe's death must be brought to justice. The message to the public needs to be clear. We will not tolerate abuse of our children. In addition, we are offering a twenty-five-thousand-dollar reward — twenty thousand from the FBI and five thousand from Crime Stoppers."

Kariss studied Chief Blackburn's face. His jaw tensed while he gave the passionate plea for communities to think back to the time of Cherished Doe's death. He asked the media to show the graphic autopsy photos and to interview residents of Pine Grove Apartments. Not a sound came from the reporters, as though each person struggled with their reaction to the horror.

Once the press conference and a Q&A were conducted, the crowd slowly dispersed. Kariss wove through those still mingling in hopes no one stopped her. She wanted to type her notes and observations while they were fresh in her mind.

"Kariss Walker."

She cringed, recognizing a familiar voice. She turned to greet Mike McDougal, a tenacious reporter for Channel 5. A man she'd dated for a brief period — a low time in her life.

"Haven't seen you in ages." He cast a leering glance her way. "You look great."

"Thanks. I saw you're still writing articles and a regular online blog."

"My life, the reporter. You were the one who first reported this case, right?"

She smiled into his deep-blue eyes, his trademark for manipulating the most determined woman. "You have a good memory."

"Thought so. How did a bestselling writer finagle an invitation here?"

"I originally reported it. Guess I'm lucky."

He laughed. "I'm not swallowing that. You must be back in the game."

"Never know." She walked the twenty feet to the FBI office.

"Which station?" He had followed her.

"Does it really matter?"

"So you haven't signed the contract."

"Gotta run."

"How about dinner?"

"I'm seeing someone."

"Coffee? For old time's sake?"

"Too busy." Her fingers touched the door.

96

Detective Montoya stood inside, and she breathed relief. His build reminded her of a bouncer.

"I don't give up easily," Mike said.

"See you later." The urgency to record what she'd heard and seen in the faces of Linc, Chief Blackburn, and many of those in attendance quickened her steps. But first she'd visit with her old acquaintance. She greeted the homicide detective.

"Morning, Kariss. Good to see you here. It's been a few years."

"That it has. Did you receive my message about wanting to chat about this case?"

"I did. Sorry, the work piles up. Do you still want to talk?"

"Let's put it on hold. I called before I learned about the press conference. Hope we all can find the answers."

"You never forgot about Cherished Doe either."

She nodded. "What happened was a terrible wrong. The little girl doesn't even have a name."

"Reaching out to the media is a brilliant move. Hey, I saw you started writing novels."

"Yes. I'm now exploring a suspense novel."

"I don't read much. With your background, why don't you write something everyone would read, like biographies?"

Kariss continued to smile. She'd not change her mind. Today had reinforced her desire to write this book. Some might say it was to further her career by appealing to public sentiment. Meredith claimed she'd lost her mind. But if Kariss faced the truth, her reasons were to eliminate the vile members of society who preyed on children. Was she foolish to think she could make a difference?

Tigo stayed until the media disbanded, like soldiers given a mission. Chief Blackburn had done a good job. He was a man of strong convictions, and his beliefs formed his appeal. Now to see how the media spun a twist on the story. For certain, investigative reporters were on their way to the Pine Grove Apartments, internalizing the press conference and working on how they'd question the residents.

Back at his desk, Tigo viewed some of the agents standing outside their cubicles searching their communication devices to read the reports. He was just as curious, and the evening news could not come fast enough. But all the agents had work to do that had nothing to do with this morning. He was one of them.

After checking his phone messages, he listened to one from Jo-Jack. Perfect. The man must be hungry . . . or needed a fix. Tigo returned the call.

"Hey, Jo-Jack. What's happening?"

"Are you still interested in buying a little information?"

"Depends on what you have."

"What interests you?"

"The Arroyos and guns. Who's buying. Who's selling. The woman's name who's over the mules."

"That could cost you plenty. Heard what happened to Candy, and the word is they're after the one who was payin' for the info."

"What did she tell them?"

"Nothing. They're wastin' anyone they suspect. Two bodies on the northeast side make me nervous. Cheeky gets the job done."

"Nothing new there. What else have you heard?"

"They think her contact was the same man who shot and killed two of them a few days ago."

Tigo wasn't going to admit anything to him. "Could be. Makes me wonder who told them about the arrangement with Candy."

"Not me. I'm not stupid. You'd have me

picked up."

"Remember that. Can't shoot up in jail. Do we have a deal?"

"Let me see what I can find out."

"Don't wait too long. You can be replaced." Tigo disconnected the call and wrote a quick note to Ryan. The two needed to work out their next move. The Arroyos had slit Candy's throat and weren't hiding it. They were after revenge and liked to use intimidation to keep others in line. Tigo would lay low awhile. Get rid of his old disguise.

Tigo frowned at the mound of unfinished paperwork on his desk and the work in his in-box. One of them was an EC, electronic communication report, so he could pay Jo-Jack. He pulled it from the stack and began filling in the blanks. The informant's payment fell under the category of "services rendered." Too bad Tigo couldn't hire someone to fill in the blanks.

He sensed Kariss in his cubicle's entrance, watching his every move. She'd been listening to his side of the conversation.

"What happens now with Cherished Doe?" she said.

"We wait."

"Care to talk about how you feel the press conference impacted the media?"

100

He shook his head. "No point in it. What we need are results." He turned his attention back to the EC. "It went well. Like everything else, the indicator will be in the response."

CHAPTER 10

All afternoon and into the early evening, excitement wove through Kariss. She followed various TV channels on her iPhone and stayed at the FBI office past six o'clock to view the evening news' live feeds. Each station had a unique spin, a heart-wrenching plea for community action. The reporters warned the viewers of the autopsy picture's graphic nature and presented the reward as a way of encouraging those with information to step forward. The theme of every TV story was the atrocity done to Cherished Doe and the reality that she could be a child the viewer might recognize.

Kariss expected someone to call within minutes, and Tigo had warned that an influx of prank calls would have to be analyzed for solid information. But she felt certain that by tomorrow, answers would be available and the case solved.

Over four hours later, the agents who'd

remained at the office buzzed with optimistic comments. Linc, Ryan, and Tigo were among them.

Tigo took a quick look at his watch. "I need to get home."

"Sure." Ryan stretched. "It's been a long day."

"Yeah. I told Natalie I'd be home by nine, and here it is ten-thirty."

Kariss noticed that Tigo didn't wear a wedding ring. He either had a live-in girl-friend or he viewed a wedding band as a determent to his undercover work. What about kids? Since he and Linc were college buds, he probably had a few of his own. Kariss cringed. She pictured Tigo as a no-excuse type of parent. Ah, maybe not. She shook off a twinge of what she recognized as jealousy. An emotion she didn't need or want. Besides, he interested her about as much as a toothache.

That was a lie. The more she was around him, the more she felt a strange attraction.

"See you at seven in the morning," Tigo said to Ryan. "We've got to work out a few details."

She wished she could be a fly on the wall during that early-morning meeting, but she was too tired to ask. Today had been enough to lift her spirits. Soon they'd all know

Cherished Doe's name and how she died, more so the identity of the killer. "Thanks for letting me stay to view the media reports."

"No problem," Linc said. "What happened today in cooperation with the media is monumental. Let's pray it works."

Kariss recalled Linc and Yvonne were Christians, like her family. The mention of prayer worked for them. She didn't find it offensive, just part of who they were. But most people of faith seldom spoke openly about it in the workplace. Not sure how she felt about "witnessing."

She walked to her desk and gathered her purse and laptop. She'd check her phone messages on the way home.

Tigo fell in step with her to the lower hall leading to the parking lot. He held the glass door open. "You were where you needed to be today. Like us, you were there in the beginning and never forgot the case. Thanks for pushing us to give it one more try."

"You're welcome. We all have a stake in identifying the little girl."

"However, don't tell anyone I admitted you were right."

"I'm sworn to secrecy."

He laughed and walked toward his black, sleek truck, an F-250 Ford Lariat.

She appreciated his compliment. Tigo was an enigma. He fit the profile of a TV or movie superhero who cleverly saw what others didn't. But she'd also seen him involved as a team player.

She opened the door to her Jaguar and caught another glimpse of him. Respect for his position settled in her, and she hoped to understand him more over the days and weeks ahead.

Shaking her head, she put aside her analysis of Tigo until she got to know him better. She slid inside her car, the new-car scent reminding her of how much she valued the Jag's performance.

She pulled onto the highway and punched in her mother's number, ignoring the flashing light that reminded her Meredith had called. Dealing with her agent's continuous tirade after such a rewarding day wasn't on the calendar.

"Hey, Mom. Got your message."

"Wanted to say I saw you on the six o'clock news. The camera did a panoramic view of those attending the press conference, and I saw my beautiful baby girl."

"You're biased, but thanks. What did you and Dad think of the media coverage?" Kariss knew with certainty they would be honest.

"Well, I cried. But you're not surprised with my confession since you girls inherited the same propensity for tears. The chief of police did an outstanding job of requesting help from those who were able to enlist public sentiment. I mean, sometimes all I hear is politically correct — what do you call that?"

"Jargon."

"Yes, that's it. I respected the way he worded his appeal. It showed he cared."

"Wonderful. I wondered how the public would interpret the message."

"Reminded me of the church. You know how the body of Christ is unified in purpose, no matter what the denomination."

Here it comes. "I see a similarity. So —"

"We're in a great sermon series. Why don't you join us Sunday, and we'll take you to lunch? Vicki's going too."

Spending time with her sister and her family was tempting. "Mom, thanks, but I have plans."

"What could be more important than feeding your soul and your stomach while being with those who love you?"

Peace and quiet without preaching.

Stop it, Kariss, that's tacky. Disrespectful.

"Would you think about it?" Mom's voice wasn't pleading, only sincere. Kariss refused to criticize her mother's faith. It simply wasn't for her.

"I will. And I'll call Vicki."

"What are you writing now?"

"I'm putting together a story about an FBI agent who solves a cold case. Very much like the Cherished Doe."

"Oh, honey, that will be another bestseller for sure. But are you ever going to write for a Christian publishing house? Those are the only kind of books my friends read."

Kariss's heart crashed into her toes. "I don't think so . . ." Her voice trailed off.

"Oh, sweetheart, I wish I could give your books to my friends. But this one sounds too violent."

"I understand. But some aspects of the crime must be presented to make the story real."

"What about God?"

Please, Mom. "If I wrote for a Christian audience, I'd lose thousands of faithful readers. Those readers pay the bills and allow me to give to worthwhile charities." She refused to say that she'd given much to her parents' church. That wasn't necessary . . . and she'd grown up in that church.

"I think you'd have even more readers. You, Kariss, are a gifted writer. You've been given a special talent. You were born doing things naturally with words that others only wish they could attempt. I love you no matter what you write. So let's end this discussion. Want to go shopping on Friday night? Dad has a meeting, and we could do dinner and hit the mall."

"You bet. I'll meet you at Papadeaux's at six."

Kariss slipped her phone back into her purse, allowing the weight of what Mom really meant to slowly dissipate. Someday she'd return to church, after she'd lived a little. The rules and "Thou shalt nots" were too confining.

Saturday she planned to attend a meeting with the Story Sisters, a writing group that had become her lifeblood. She'd participated for a couple of years and loved to hear about their writing projects and adventures. Seeing familiar faces and sharing about the craft always gave her a perk. She desperately needed encouragement from fellow writers, and the sisterhood would motivate her to convince Meredith that changing genres was a good move. Kariss didn't plan to reveal her writing project to the group. She simply needed to breathe the same air as those who often faced challenges with their writing.

Just as she pulled off the 610 loop her phone jingled again, and she answered before checking the caller.

"Do you mean I actually have the great Kariss Walker, bestselling, award-winning author?" Sarcasm rippled through Meredith's tone.

"I apologize for not returning your call."

"Lately all I get is a recording."

Kariss moistened her lips. "I did my best to explain how I feel when you were here in Houston."

"Useless tripe."

The woman could crumble a cement wall with her cutting tone. "I feel like a redundant fool here, but I don't know how else to communicate my desire to write this novel."

"Try me, because your actions are not conducive to my caliber of writers. The Rockford Literary Agency handles only bestselling writers who adhere to my career plan for their lives. Writers stand in line for my wisdom and consideration for me to represent them. I've worked hard for you in developing a platform, and what have you done in return?"

"Excuse me. I believe you've received a hefty percentage of my advances and royalty checks."

"But you're high maintenance. I had to beg for the country's best image coach to redo your wardrobe, makeup, teach you how to speak —"

Fury danced in Kariss's veins. "That wasn't me. I became a part of your agency because I already had those essentials from my TV days, including a platform. May I suggest you have my file in front of you before you place your next call?"

"Whatever. This call is to inform you that I must have the new book proposal in my in-box within twenty-four hours."

Kariss acknowledged her one and only position. "Then we no longer have a professional relationship. I'll fax the termination of your representation tonight."

"Jo-Jack has given us good leads before." Tigo put his truck into park and shut off the engine. Here in his home's garage, he had a few moments, but he needed to cut Ryan's call short. "The proof will be in what he brings in. He claims that Cheeky thinks he's working against us. Hard to say."

"What are you going to do in the meantime?"

"Play it from the office. Come up with a different disguise. Right now I think they're looking for a cop. No point in wasting time thinking about what information they extracted from Candy."

"Extracted is a good way to put it." Ryan's voice held no humor. The Arroyos beheaded their last victim. Candy had been lucky.

"I . . . I looked into the whereabouts of her kids. Living with another hooker. Foster care looks like the best option."

"You're involved again."

"I owe Candy. Her kids meant a lot to her. You know me, I have priorities. I've contacted CPS to see about a good foster home. And I deposited the cash due her into an account to be used for her kids. Not sure my call did any good, but I tried. I have more than one reason to nail Cheeky."

"Tigo, none of us want your priorities to get you killed. You'd better change your MO before you venture into that snake pit again."

The comment irritated him, though he understood Ryan's caution. "I know how to be careful."

Cheeky paced the floor of the bar, empty this time of day except for Froggie, his lead man. He swallowed a gulp of Buchanan's that only fueled his fury. Two of his men were dead, key men whom he depended on. They had been stupid but fearless, and that's what he needed to keep his organization on top and making money. Candy had already paid for her betrayal, now the *policía* responsible would pay with his blood. But Cheeky had to think his way through his next move, play out all the scenarios. What he did best.

"The man who killed our men," Cheeky said. "Do you have a name?"

"Not yet. Word's out. *Policía,* but I don't know which one."

Cheeky had plans to move up in his world, and his second cousin held a prominent role in Mexico's largest cartel. Loyalty paved the way, and Cheeky had positioned himself repeatedly to get the job done. Not once had he failed. Smuggling weapons for his cousin's cartel ranked high on the list, while he maneuvered wealthy professionals toward his cousin for a web of white-collar crime. Drugs and prostitution brought in its share of profits — all looked good.

Soon Cheeky would have the respect he deserved. His cousin's cartel was observing how he handled the Houston *policía,* the Skulls who bragged about taking over the city, and his own people, all while making millions. The Arroyos understood they eliminated the competition and took risks. No one got in Cheeky's business.

"What do you want me to do, boss?" Froggie said.

Cheeky studied the man who had more guts than brains. "I want this man stopped."

"I'll find him," Froggie said. *"¿Quiero que lo desparezca?"*

Cheeky took another drink. "Do it. Now."

CHAPTER 11

Two weeks passed and the FBI had learned nothing to aid them in solving Cherished Doe's death. Optimism trickled down the drain, and Kariss's hopes fell with her disillusion.

She worked on turning the facts about her book project into fiction by tweaking here and there. Her male hero began looking more and more like Tigo. Acting like him too. But the female agent sent vague messages. Every time Kariss sat her down to interview her, she turned her face and refused to respond. Obviously Kariss had upset her. Stubborn characters could be difficult until the writer discovered their true motivation.

To expand her research, Kariss introduced herself to a woman agent by the name of Hillary Wallace, who was approachable and enjoyed lattes. However, the woman was as closed mouth as Tigo and Ryan when it came to revealing behind-the-scenes information. The problem with Hillary was that she wanted to write a novel too, but she had no skills. None. Kariss enjoyed mentoring new writers, but Hillary's manuscript would take a decade of work. And every time Kariss saw the woman agent, she wanted to know if Kariss had read her latest chapter. That task had become excruciatingly painful. Instead of looking for Hillary, Kariss had begun to dodge her.

In the midst of brooding about no longer having representation by the most prestigious literary agency in the country and the unlikelihood of Cherished Doe being solved, Kariss decided to simply write her novel. After all, a writer best expresses herself when she is in the midst of creating. And Kariss refused to dwell on her current publisher's disinterest in suspense.

Tigo approached her from his cubicle. "Univision scheduled their Cherished Doe documentary for this Friday night."

She'd nearly forgotten the Spanish program. "What time?"

"Ten o'clock and the program repeats at one a.m."

"Have you seen what they've put together?"

"No. But their excellent programming is

why I haven't given up. *Aquí y Ahora* reaches a wide Spanish-speaking audience."

She sensed her heart speeding toward hope again. "These are the people who are most likely to have answers. I shouldn't have gotten so down." She smiled at him. "My optimism is up again."

"Glad it takes so little to make you perky."

Perky? Like she was a shih tzu begging for attention? How could one man be so exasperating? Granted, she'd almost tripped over the edge of self-pity, but being described as perky didn't help.

Tigo saw he'd frustrated Kariss one more time. He wasn't sure what he'd done, but it happened at frequent intervals. Her never-ending chatter hammered against his brain, but he was learning to manage it. Her wit and warmth gave her a few extra points on the personality chart. The news-reporter–turned–women's-fiction-writer–turned–suspense-writer was quite intelligent. That added a few additional points.

Not sure what his point system meant anyway. Why was he keeping score?

And she did bring him Starbucks every morning with a smile. Perky. His description fit, but she obviously didn't think so. He'd ask how she preferred him to describe her, but that might not be smart.

Snatching five DVDs and his noise-canceling headphones, he walked back to her cubicle.

"If you'd like to view the networks' news releases again, you can use my headphones. I have a meeting and a few phone calls to make. Just return them when you're done."

Her dark eyes grew larger. It took so little to please this woman. "Thanks." She cast an admiring glance at his headphones. "I like this brand. And I did want to look at these DVDs with an objective point of view. Perhaps my fiction mind will see a plot thread."

"How's the story going?"

"Feels like a drought."

"Now you have a little time to work on it." And he could work on the string of leads their new informant had provided. Much of it looked bogus, but he wanted to check out a few tips with Ryan before calling Jo-Jack. Now that he had distracted Kariss, he had time — quiet and uninterrupted.

"Don't forget I want to be in on the discussion with Ryan about the gun smugglers."

Tigo inwardly groaned. Not if he and Ryan had their meeting without her knowledge.

Once he'd examined Jo-Jack's leads, including a gun deal supposedly going down on Sunday night, he made his way to Ryan's cubicle, which was on his left side, while Kariss worked on his right.

"Did your wife let you out of the house?" Ryan tilted back in his chair and linked his fingers behind his head.

"That's not funny. I'm going to send Kariss your way. Let you answer her questions."

"Give her a break, Tigo. She's smart."

"Don't I know it. Can't dance around anything."

"She's a writer. Posing questions is how she learns. Be careful. You'll probably find yourself in her next book."

Tigo pointed his pen at Ryan. "She loves bald men."

"Right. You're the one she spends all of her time with. Then she makes notes."

"We've had that talk," Tigo said. "And I told her to keep me out of her stories. Right now she's watching the DVDs of the Cherished Doe press coverage, which gives us time to talk. Teasing aside, it was her persistence that moved me to talk to Linc about reopening the case." He wanted the case solved, not for Kariss or himself, but for the little girl in an unmarked grave. "I hope Univision flushes something out."

"The Hispanic community is family oriented, but they're also loyal to each other. However, I think if anyone recognizes the little girl, they'll come forward."

"And I've got to let go of the case and be patient." He hesitated. "Let me make sure Kariss is behaving herself." Tigo slipped over to her cubicle. She inserted a disc into her computer and adjusted the headphones.

He returned, convinced his and Ryan's conversation would be private. "I wanted to talk to you about Jo-Jack."

Ryan nodded. "All right. What do you think about his information?"

"He thinks we're stupid for trying to stop the Arroyos. He says they have too much money behind them. That we have no idea who all's involved."

"So we're supposed to back off like scared girls?"

"Right. I'm going to call him once we're finished. I texted him earlier, but he hasn't responded. We need a face-to-face. I want to tell him he's useless to us unless he can come up with better info." Tigo tapped his pen on the desktop. "I wish I could go undercover. But not while I'm chained to Miss Walker."

"Why does that make a difference when

most of our undercover work is done at night? Tell her she stays here. It's too dangerous, just like Linc told her."

The night work meant time away from his mother, whose days were numbered. But then. . . . "Now is not a good time."

"All you need are tattoos and a bald head." Ryan chuckled.

"You fit the scenario better than I do."

Tigo considered telling him about his mother's condition. But that was personal. Ryan knew his mother lived with him but not about the cancer. "Still thinking about posing as a buyer. Minimum exposure. With Candy dead, the case isn't going anywhere, and since I don't know what they might have gotten out of her, infiltrating the gang with my old disguise doesn't make sense."

"I'm repeating myself, but a new look has more potential of keeping you alive."

Tigo grinned. "Before I commit to that, I'd like to listen to a surveillance recording made when Candy was alive. The background noise was definitely a bar, and I'd like to do a sound recognition on the voices. I want to narrow down the location."

Tigo sensed Kariss standing behind them. "I thought you were viewing the press coverage. You couldn't have viewed all of those this quickly."

"I noted the differences from each station. I wondered if your and Ryan's discussion was off limits."

"It is. But I need to listen to something. Go ahead and fire questions at Ryan while I locate a recording. Makes him feel important."

"Never mind. Nothing personal, Ryan, but I have plenty of work to do."

She handed Tigo the headphones, and he returned to his desk. After adjusting them, he pushed in the DVD. Although the picture played, no sound came through. He ejected the disc and tried again. Same problem. Yanking off the headphones, he tossed them on the desk.

"Problem?" Kariss peered at him from the doorway.

"Did you have any trouble with the headphones?"

"No. Maybe it's your —" She drew in a breath. "If they aren't working, it might be my fault."

This woman would be the death of him. "Why? What happened?"

"Remember I told you about my problem with wearing a watch?"

He squinted. "Are you telling me that you just destroyed my headphones because of the 'too much electricity in your body' syndrome?"

"Possibly."

He stood, fighting back the continuous annoyance. "Don't you think it would have been courteous to tell me this before you used them?"

"Honestly, Tigo, I forgot. I'll get you a new set."

"Gee, thanks, Kariss. But your generosity doesn't help me now." His cell phone rang. No name read across his caller ID. This had better be good considering the mood he was in. He pressed on the connection. "Santiago here."

"It's Jo-Jack." The man's raspy voice sounded like he needed to clear his throat.

"Hold on a minute." Tigo hurried out of his cubicle and into the empty hallway. "What have you got, because so far nothing you've given me has been worth a dime."

"But this is," Jo-Jack whispered. Was the quiet tone for Tigo's or Jo-Jack's benefit? "Took me time to find out what I wanted. But it was worth it. Got a dealer's name."

"You made the same claim last Saturday."

"But this guy operates out of a fancy office in the Galleria. Lots of connections."

"Who?"

"How much is it worth to you?"

"I paid you plenty for bad information.

Give me the name, and if it pans out, then we'll talk about more business."

"Can't talk right now. Too many people around. Meet me at Candy's corner at two-thirty."

"Where are you calling me from?"

"Pay phone. Lost my cell."

"That's the cost of doing business. Get another phone. Text me if you remember the name."

"All right. What I have is good. Be here. It's worth it."

Tigo slipped his phone back into his pocket. Playing games was not his style, and for all he knew Cheeky had put Jo-Jack up to the call. But he'd been reliable in the past, and Tigo needed a break.

CHAPTER 12

At two-thirty p.m., Tigo and Ryan drove to Candy's old corner and parked on the opposite side of the street. Since Tigo's tank now had a wanted sign, he'd picked up a fifteen-year-old Chevy Impala to drive to this part of town. Both men wore torn jeans and T-shirts, but Tigo had added glasses and a baseball cap. He exited the car and nodded at Jo-Jack across the street.

Tigo scanned the area before stepping into a drugstore and heading to the magazine section, right where he could see the overhead mirror displaying who entered the store. He picked up a sports magazine and pretended interest. Jo-Jack joined him. Tigo could tell by the smell — a mix of a dirty body, bad sewage, and Snickers bars.

"Were you followed?" Tigo pretended to read the magazine with one eye on the store's mirror.

"I'm smarter than Candy." Jo-Jack turned

a page of a magazine. "She stopped respecting the Arroyos."

"Is that what happened to her?"

"She got too sure of herself. Thought the FBI could save her."

Guilt attempted to nail Tigo for Candy's death, but he shoved it away. She knew what she'd been getting into. "What about you?"

"As I said, I'm smarter. And I need the money."

"What do you have for me?"

"The man you're looking for goes by the name of Bat. He and Cheeky do a lot of business."

Must be a supplier. "Got a last name?"

Jo-Jack shrugged. "Hey, I risked my neck to get this for you. I should have more after the weekend."

Candy had spoken about Bat, but Tigo hadn't been able to dig up any more information. "Okay. We're in business. Do you know who's tipping us off about Arroyos' transports?"

"No idea. I just know the Arroyos are out for blood. There's a contract out on the man Cheeky was supplying info to."

"No surprise there."

Tigo left the store and joined Ryan in the car. Five minutes later, Jo-Jack slid into the backseat and they drove to the next intersection. After Jo-Jack signed the EC form, Tigo handed him one thousand dollars in an envelope. He hoped this informant stayed alive.

Friday night, Kariss sat on the sofa with her cell in hand waiting for Univision to broadcast *Aquí y Ahora*. A half-eaten container of Moose Tracks ice cream sat on a plate in front of her. She watched the clock. The Cherished Doe documentary would be presented as the last segment of the program.

Her heart slammed against her chest until she closed her eyes and willed herself to calm down. If she were a praying woman, she'd talk to God about bringing the right people to view the program tonight.

The story opened in a playground setting. Children played on swings, a small boy climbed the steps to a slide, and little girls squealed their delight on a merry-go-round. The sound of laughter mingled with "Mommy, look at me" and "Push me, Mommy."

One mother stood alone with her back to the TV camera. She held onto a stroller where a little girl sat watching the other children. The camera didn't capture the little girl's face, only the back of her head.

The male narrator talked about the world's most precious treasures — children — and the sacrifices made to ensure they were healthy, happy, and safe. The program continued with an interview from Detective Montoya and his accounting of the Cherished Doe case. Two mothers from the Pine Grove apartment complex expressed their horror surrounding the little girl's tragic death.

The common response from the interviewed mothers and Detective Montoya centered on the question, "Why didn't the mother take the child to a hospital/fire station/Catholic Charities/CPS for help?"

Graphic shots filled the screen with a plea from Detective Montoya for any persons who had information about the unsolved case to come forward. The FBI's number flashed on the screen along with information about the twenty-five-thousand-dollar reward.

When the program concluded, Kariss considered driving to the FBI office to be near the phone lines. She doubted if her security status allowed a late-night visit, but she wanted to be there. Univision's coverage of Cherished Doe had been a sympathetic appeal to the Hispanic community. The men and women interviewed had appeared shocked that the identity of the little girl and the person responsible for her death were still unknown.

But all she could do was crawl into bed and trust that Tigo called her in the morning with good news. Keyed up and emotionally drained, she lay awake with the autopsy picture of Cherished Doe fixed in her mind.

Tigo worked the phones the night *Aquí y Ahora* broadcast Cherished Doe. The program aired at ten p.m. and then again at one a.m. Three calls came in around ten-thirty, but the people offering obscure information were obviously more interested in the reward than helping to solve a crime. At 1:07, one of the phones rang, and Tigo answered it.

"I know who the little girl is from *Aquí y Ahora,*" a man said in English with a Hispanic accent. "I've seen the program twice tonight, and she looks like my niece."

"Thank you for calling." Tigo gestured for a tracer and secured another agent's attention to listen and record the conversation. "Sir, what's your name?"

"Gilberto Olvera, and I'm an American citizen."

"Why do you believe the little girl on tonight's program might be your niece?"

"Her looks and her medical condition. I'm not interested in the reward. I only want to bring forth this information for my brother's sake, the child's father. I hope I'm wrong, but it doesn't appear so."

"Where is your brother?"

"He lives in Mexico, and his name is Xavier Olvera. If I'm correct, the little girl's name is Benita."

"Was she in your care during the time of her death?"

"No. Five years ago when my brother was deported, his wife and child still lived here in Houston."

"We'd like for you to come in and talk to us."

"I can drive there now. I won't be able to sleep until I know for sure that this is my niece."

"We can pick you up, so —"

"Sir, I called you. I've given you my name, my brother's, and my niece's name. We've been on the phone long enough for you to trace me. Give me the address of your office, and I'll be there within thirty minutes."

Tigo trusted Gilberto's words and nodded to the agent recording the call. "All right." He gave the address. "An agent by the name of Tigo Harris will meet you at the entrance of the office. In the event you

129

change your mind, we'll find you."

"I gave you my word. If Benita is the little girl found dead five years ago, that concerns me."

Gilberto disconnected the call. Tigo breathed in and studied the agents beside him. He didn't know whether to celebrate or be cautious. But Cherished Doe might be Benita Olvera, and the little girl who had starved to death might have family who cared about her. He rubbed his face, conscious of how this case had affected him differently from so many others. Other cases were adults and the few children involved in violent crime had identities. Cherished Doe didn't even have a proper tombstone. "I think we're onto something. We could have the answers before sunrise." He turned to the agent tracing the call.

"We traced the call to Gilberto Olvera on the southeast side of town."

For Tigo, the caller could not get to the office fast enough.

CHAPTER 13

Kariss had just drifted off into a deep sleep when her phone rang at six a.m. When the ringtone of Jerry Lee Lewis's "Great Balls of Fire" alerted her the third time, she grabbed her cell off the nightstand, her hand trembling from being wakened. Calls this early were never good news.

"Kariss, this is Tigo. Looks like we've identified Cherished Doe."

Fully awake, she sat up in bed. "Wonderful! How did it happen? Who called the office?" Her heart sped alongside the internal fuel racing through her veins. "You have a name and how she died?"

"We think so. Her father is in Mexico, and we're working on having him brought here to make the official identification of the little girl and for questioning."

"Do you think the father killed her?"

"He couldn't have. The little girl's death occurred while he was in Mexico."

"What about the mother?"

"The information about her is vague." He yawned. "I've been here all night, working on pure adrenaline. Too keyed up to head home. Anyway, I thought you'd want to know."

"I really appreciate this. I know you're tired, but I have so many questions —"

"I understand. We got a call at 1:07 from a man who claimed to be Cherished Doe's uncle . . ." Tigo told her about the call and Gilberto Olvera's arrival at the FBI office twenty minutes later.

"So what's next?"

He yawned again. "Want to have breakfast? I could tell you what happened during the questioning."

She tossed back the coverlet. "Where do you want to meet?"

"There's an IHOP fifteen minutes from the office. Say forty-five minutes?"

"I know right where that is." Tigo hung up before she had time to ask any more questions. She headed to the closet and reached for her jeans.

A tingle in her stomach reminded her of the news. Cherished Doe had a name! Slipping her feet into sandals, she grabbed her cosmetic bag. Oh, yes, her laptop needed to go with her. Did the media know about the

132

call made to the FBI? Was anyone in custody?

Although Kariss arrived at the restaurant ten minutes earlier than the scheduled time, Tigo was already at a booth drinking coffee. He waved her over. For a man who'd been up all night, he looked good. But when she scooted into the booth across from him, she could see how bloodshot his eyes were.

A server approached and filled her cup with steaming-hot coffee. They both ordered omelets — his filled with everything imaginable and smothered in cheese, and hers filled with mushrooms and tomatoes.

"Tigo, tell me what happened when Gilberto Olvera arrived at the office."

"Linc and I showed him the autopsy photos, and he identified Cherished Doe as his niece, Benita Olvera. Her father is his brother, who was deported to Mexico a little over five-and-a-half years ago."

"Shortly before the child was found."

"Yes. Gilberto confirmed that the little girl was born with a physical condition that required a feeding tube, and she was alive when her father, Xavier, left the U.S. He even gave us the name of the doctor who was treating her."

"Another lead."

"We learned later that the doctor is now

practicing in Denver. He can't give us much more information than Gilberto, except for the date of the last time he treated Benita."

"But the little girl starved to death. Are you thinking the mother is to blame?"

"Not sure at this point. We have more questions than answers."

A cold, snakelike sensation curled up Kariss's spine. "Where's the mother now?"

"Good question. Gilberto hasn't seen her in a few years, but he heard she entertained men. Last address was the Pine Grove Apartments."

"Let me guess. Agents went to question her early this morning, and she doesn't live there anymore."

"You got it. Another family occupies the apartment she used to live in, and the resident manager has never heard of her. Right now, we're arranging to get the father here." He paused and she caught a glimmer of compassion. "Gilberto called him from our office. I talked to him for a few minutes, and he was . . . upset. He's been sending his wife money for the care of their child for five years. Naturally, he sent it to a post office box."

Kariss cringed. "She took the money even after the little girl was dead? How could she be so cruel?" She remembered Chief of

Police Blackburn's statement about the child being discarded like an unwanted animal. The words mirrored her thoughts. "She starved her own child instead of taking her someplace where qualified people could care for her?"

"It looks that way, but we don't know the whole story. We're looking for her." Tigo leaned across the table. "Take a deep breath and relax until we learn the truth. Maybe the mother isn't involved. Who knows? Maybe she met the same end as her daughter."

Kariss took a drink of orange juice. "You're right. I'm jumping to conclusions. My fiction mind is working overtime. When will the father arrive?"

"As soon as the paperwork is completed and arrangements made."

She flexed her fingers to ease the tension in her body. The answers were so slow in coming, but she wasn't the only one needing to understand what happened five years ago.

Benita . . . what a pretty name for a sweet angel.

Tigo opened the blinds to his mother's bedroom and let the morning sunshine stream across her bed. Her eyes were closed in a drug-induced sleep that allowed her to escape the pain. She wouldn't want it this way. How many times had she told him that in the event she was terminally ill, she didn't want to be drugged? No sleeping while death stalked her door. It would keep her from experiencing life to the fullest. But Tigo couldn't bring himself to endure the torment in her eyes and the cries from her lips.

Forgive me, Mom. I love you too much to watch you suffer. For my conscience's sake, I'm insisting on strong pain medication.

His dear mother, Francisca Harris, an Argentinean immigrant who'd earned her U.S. citizenship and raised him alone after an ugly divorce. She'd become a high school Spanish teacher while struggling through the woes of having a deadbeat ex-husband who never paid child support. Money was always tight, but she made sure Tigo wore the best clothes and had the advantages of every American child. She was the strongest woman he'd ever known, and now she was reduced to sleeping her remaining days.

He kissed her forehead and took her limp hand, noting the peacefulness in her face. How long had it been since he'd seen her dark-brown eyes with their mischievous twinkle or her wide smile?

Ryan's request for Tigo to go undercover went against his vow to spend as much time as possible with his mother. When her body gave in to the cancer, he'd dive deeper into his investigation. His heart told him she'd encourage him to continue his work and stop the gun smugglers.

Tigo yawned, his eyes feeling like they held bags of sand. Although he longed to crawl into his own bed, the satisfaction of identifying Cherished Doe settled in his bones. Easing into a chair, he ran his finger over his mother's veined hands and parchment-thin skin.

"We may have some answers for a case that has haunted me for a long time," he said. "Our Cherished Doe may be Benita Olvera. We'll know soon." He proceeded to tell his mother all that had happened during the night.

Once he finished, he tucked the sheet around her neck, the way she liked it, the same way she used to do for him. She'd told or read him stories during his younger years, and when he learned to read, he read to her. Just as he often did now.

Tigo studied her beloved face and shook his head. The once strong and resourceful woman had taught him how to play baseball, escorted him to church, and helped him see where his teenage rebellion was headed. She deserved so much more. None of which he could give her.

"I'm heading to bed, Mom. The days of staying out all night are fading into memory. It's making an old man out of me." He stood and glanced around, looking for a way to make her more comfortable.

The fresh red roses that she loved were replaced every five days. Their scent filled the room, reminding him too much of a funeral home. Would anyone ever understand his devotion to the woman who had molded him into the man he was today? He pulled a wilted petal from one of the roses and examined the others. Only the best for his mother.

Tigo left the room and nodded at the day nurse, an older woman with kind blue eyes and a warm smile. "She's resting peacefully. I need some sleep, so when you need a break, knock on my door."

"Tigo, I'm fine. Get your rest."

"But you are the one who cares for my mother. I'll expect the knock."

He could blow away a gang member with little remorse or walk into the midst of gun-bearing criminals wearing a disguise. Who would ever think the gruff and tough Special Agent Santiago Harris doted on his dying mother?

Or that the memory of a little girl who'd starved to death never left him alone.

CHAPTER 14

Kariss wondered if today she'd learn what happened that day years ago that ended in a child's death. Gilberto and Xavier Olvera arrived at Houston's FBI office on Wednesday morning for questioning with Tigo and Ryan. She hoped she could meet the Olvera brothers and offer her condolences. But she understood Tigo and Ryan had protocol to follow, and she'd not interfere. Sometimes her assertiveness annoyed them. Yet in her eagerness to honor the child who'd occupied her thoughts for so long, she didn't want to impose upon the agents and the Olvera brothers.

Kariss restrained her compulsion and waited for Tigo to return to his cubicle. What a strange man, so opposite any man she'd ever met. His attention to detail drove her nuts, but she knew he stayed alive because of his desire to constantly fine-tune his methods. That much she'd learned in observing him — all for research, of course. Her respect for him increased, and she longed to call him "friend" if only he'd let her.

Over two hours later, Tigo and Ryan walked to her work area with two Hispanic men. The younger man must be Xavier Olvera. His reddened eyes and splotchy face indicated the emotional turmoil of the morning. Kariss stood and met Tigo's gaze. No glaring, back-away signs met hers.

He smiled and turned to the two men. "I'd like for you to meet Kariss Walker, the woman who originally reported the TV news about Benita. Like many of us here at the FBI, she never forgot the crime," Tigo said in Spanish.

The younger man reached out his hand, and she grasped it. "*Muchas gracias.* My name is Xavier Olvera. Thank you for making sure no one forgot my Benita."

When her heart felt like it was ready to explode, what could she say other than she was sorry for his loss? *"Lo siento por su pérdida."*

The other man extended his hand. "I'm Gilberto Olvera, Benita's uncle. It's a pleasure to meet you. This is a sad day for me and my brother."

She inhaled to maintain her composure

and looked to Tigo for direction. She certainly wouldn't mention that she was writing a book about Benita. At that moment, her story seemed to taint the child's memory.

"Would you like to join us for a cup of coffee?" Tigo said. "When I told Xavier about your role, he wanted to tell you his story."

"I'd be honored." She couldn't imagine the man's emotions nor fathom how she'd feel in his situation, but she'd offer her support.

Tigo led the way to a small lounge area where the four gathered around a table. While he poured coffee, Kariss spoke to Xavier about his journey to the United States, including Gilberto in the conversation. The brothers' rigid bodies indicated their distrust and grief. But her ability to speak their language appeared to ease the men's demeanor.

Tigo encouraged Xavier to tell his story, and Kariss sensed the request was two-fold: a courtesy for her benefit and a chance for the two agents to listen for any discrepancy.

"I was in Houston illegally," Xavier said. "My wife and I came here to have a better life. Gilberto talked about the many opportunities, and I thought I could find a way to be a citizen. Running from those who'd send us back wasn't right." Xavier placed his hands around the coffee cup, as if Styrofoam were his anchor.

"Delores is my wife's name. She was . . . very beautiful. Benita had her eyes." He paused, and Gilberto touched his shoulder. "At first we lived with my brother, then we found an apartment at Pine Grove. I worked painting houses, making more money than in Mexico. Benita was born here. Delores gave birth two months early, and Benita was a sick baby. She needed a feeding tube." He pointed to his neck and abdomen where the autopsy pictures had indicated scars. "She started to gain weight and grow stronger. I felt *Dios* was going to make her well. I always said the rosary and lit candles for her . . . and Delores." He took a sip of coffee, then his hands grasped the cup again. A tear fell over his cheek.

Gilberto tightened his grip on Xavier's shoulder. So much love and comfort between brothers reminded Kariss of her own siblings. She glanced away and blinked.

"You don't have to tell me this," she said.

"It's important to me. I'm okay." He offered a grim smile. "The authorities learned I was not a citizen and sent me back to Mexico. So I had to leave my wife and five-year-old daughter here. I didn't want to go, but I'd broken this country's laws. At first my wife called me once a week and told me how Benita was doing. She also learned she was having another baby. Every week I sent money to take care of my family."

Gilberto clenched his fist. "Delores had it sent to a post office box."

Xavier took another sip of coffee. "I sent money these past five years. Delores called me less and less until she stopped. But I thought she was busy working. And although I had no way of contacting her, I never thought she'd let my baby girl die." He breathed in deeply. "She starved my Benita to death. Good parents don't treat their babies this way." The bitterness in his words cut through Kariss's heart.

"Are you sure your wife is responsible?" Tigo said.

He nodded. "I've been thinking about all she said. She complained often about taking care of our daughter. My brother and his wife would have welcomed Benita into their home. They have no children. I know . . . my wife let her die so she wouldn't have to take her to the doctor or buy medicine. Then she could use the money for herself."

Tigo turned to Gilberto. "You mentioned

that you'd seen Delores three years ago. I didn't question you earlier, but this information could possibly help us find her."

Gilberto reached inside his shirt pocket and pulled out a folded piece of paper. He handed it to Tigo. "I wrote down all I could remember since my brother was deported. And I signed my name. From what I remember, Delores moved from their apartment two months after Xavier left. I tried to find her, but none of her neighbors or friends knew where she'd gone. Then three years ago, I saw her at a Fiesta grocery store. She was with another man — not a good man from what I could see. I asked her about Benita. She said the little girl was in a hospital. I asked to see her, but I was told no one could visit Benita but Delores. She told me the doctors said other people could bring germs, make her sicker. I told her my niece needed to know other members of her family loved her. I offered to wear scrubs like the doctors and nurses wore in surgery. She ignored me and left with the man."

Xavier stiffened. "Did she have the new baby with her?"

"She was alone."

Xavier buried his face in his hands and sobbed. Kariss wanted to cry with him.

Instead she drank the bitter coffee. He raised his head. "I apologize. My life and my joy was Benita and the child I've never seen. I pray for them every day."

Gilberto sucked in a breath. "My brother often went without food to send money." He looked into Tigo's face as if the agent had an answer for his brother's plight.

"I understand. But we can't blame Delores until we hear her story. She could be innocent in all of this. She might not be alive either."

Gilberto lunged forward. "I've seen the pictures of Benita. She lied to my brother and stole his money. I saw her with another man. When you find Delores, you'd better keep her away from me."

Tigo thanked the Olvera brothers for their cooperation and promised to keep them informed about the case. The next few days for them would be spent in a flurry of media interviews. Stressful for the two grieving men.

He hoped the FBI found Delores Olvera before Gilberto or Xavier did, or he was positive he'd have another murder on his hands. Both men would kill her without thinking twice.

The Olvera brothers' testimony indicated

Delores Olvera had allowed her daughter to die — a selfish woman who loved money more than her child. Tigo should stuff his own opinion, but he was convinced of the woman's guilt.

He grimaced and rubbed his jaw. His tooth was bothering him again. Great. He'd pop a few Tylenol and hope it went away.

His thoughts turned to Kariss and he walked to her work area. She sat at her desk and stared blankly at the wall. For once she wasn't writing. The pained expression on her face revealed more about her inner workings than any verbalizations would have.

He lingered in the doorway. "Are you all right?"

She nodded but didn't acknowledge him with eye contact. "Writing women's fiction was never easy emotionally. Sometimes the situations in my characters's lives were heartbreaking, but I never expected to feel this amount of agony when confronted with the facts about Cherished Doe."

He pulled a chair next to her. "But you dealt with this reality when you worked for Channel 5."

"Right. I had sit-down meetings with victims and got involved with their problems. Followed my instincts when I felt there was more behind a story than what was on a piece of paper. Studied the facts and deliberated the aftermath. I investigated events and allowed my emotions to create a passion for reporting the stories, but Cherished Doe ripped at my heart." She ran her fingers through her curly hair. "I seem to have this protective nature for children."

He knew the truth about what drove her, but he'd wait for her to tell him. "Is that why you encourage others to learn the facts about child abuse and neglect? I saw the links on your website, and I read the online article about how you mentor kids at women's shelters."

She nodded.

"Tigo, I'm not as strong as you are. The truth about Benita makes me physically ill."

"It should upset all of us. You did well today."

"I was crumbling."

He tilted his head. A strong woman sat before him, and he knew she wouldn't mention the fire. At least not today. "Why did you quit TV work?"

She gave him a pressed-lip smile. "I couldn't keep up with the pressure."

"Station politics?"

She rubbed her palms. "Sort of. Competition is incredible in that field. The need to look youthful, fashionable, sophisticated —"

"Looks to me like you filled those qualifications just fine."

A faint blush crept up her cheeks, and he liked it. Very much. "Thanks. I tried, but I got tired of what I felt was a show. How long before my age stood in the way of my career? Anyway, I longed to write."

"You've had success there too."

She tucked her hair behind her ears. "Are you being a therapist today? Because you were wonderful with Xavier and Gilberto. Now me."

"Don't think so." He should tell her that his probing was more his means of processing life, the need to have all the facts about any given situation laid out before him. But her psyche looked delicate at the moment. Not that he could blame her. "Are you giving up on this project?"

"Absolutely not. I'm simply going to take all of this emotion and pour it into my story. The pros say that a writer's best work comes from personal pain. I always believed that concept and have even taught it to fledging writers. Experience earned through personal stress and grief will always make a better book, no matter how difficult the process." She straightened and reached for a tissue to dab her nose. "No, Tigo. You're not rid of me yet. I have miles to go."

He wasn't surprised. She stood in the way of his work, yet he admired her tenacity. "You know, I had a feeling you were ready to stick this out. Nothing about you says 'quitter.' "

"But I quit Channel 5."

Or did the inability to solve Cherished Doe move her to resign? "I'd call your decision a career choice . . . weighing the options and making an intelligent move. Writing definitely looks more lucrative."

She stretched her neck. "Writing a book is a bit of a gamble. There isn't a formula for a bestseller. It's a mix of skill, luck, the publisher, publicist, and a fabulous platform. I thought I'd take a real cut in pay when I started writing. The stats were not good and book advances are determined by how many books the sales staff projects the book will sell. My first book did poorly, and I failed to earn out my advance. Then the second shocked me when sales skyrocketed. Still not sure why. The publisher went back to my first book and piggybacked on the success of the second one. The sales rose and pulled me out of the hole. But . . ."

"What?"

"I wrote what the publishing house dictated, not what I wanted to write. Things have changed. I'm willing to take a risk to write the book of my heart."

"You've got guts."

"Do I, Tigo? I'm not sure. The future's unpredictable."

"The question is how far are you willing to go to reach your goals?"

"I want to say I'll do whatever it takes."

"Be careful and keep your head up."

Chapter 15

Saturday afternoon, Kariss realized a need to talk to another woman, and that meant her sister Vicki, who listened and responded with wisdom. Their two older sisters were busy with kids and careers, but Vicki always found the time to talk to Kariss. They were best friends too — a rarity that Kariss didn't take lightly. Vicki had recently experienced an unfaithful husband and a painful divorce. Kariss realized she'd shirked her commitment to help her sister work through the many stages of an ended relationship. Much of the lack of interaction had to do with Vicki's lingering hope that her ex-husband would leave his current live-in and patch up their marriage. What Kariss wanted to do to him wasn't repeatable.

She dug through her purse for her cell to call Vicki and grabbed a note from last week's meeting with Gilberto and Xavier Olvera. The anger and frustration sweeping through her were of tsunami proportions. How could she help Vicki when thoughts about finding Benita's mother consumed her? She wanted to be with the investigators who were looking for Delores Olvera, and when they found her, she wanted to find out *why.* A part of Kariss wanted to believe a mother would never allow her child to die.

She eased onto the sofa and curled her feet under her. Rain trickled against the windows, putting her into think mode. She wanted to head back to Pine Grove Apartments, but the teens who'd stolen her purse last time might not be lenient this time.

The moment Vicki answered, Kariss knew she was in her car. Wiper blades swished in rhythm.

"I'm checking in on you." Actually, that was a lie, since Kariss needed to talk to her.

"I'm good. And I was going to call you today. See how you were doing with the new book and the FBI research."

"Slow progress, but it's coming."

"Any more news about Cherished Doe? Haven't heard or seen anything since the media report. Of course I haven't read the paper or switched on the TV in two days. Worked two doubles at the hospital."

Just hearing Vicki's voice had a calming effect. Kariss drew in a deep breath and told her about the Olvera brothers and the FBI's search for Delores.

"How could a woman do such a thing?" Vicki's voice broke. "I can't even imagine."

"I hope the mother has an explanation, and I hope she's innocent. But I keep wondering where she is."

"Be careful, Kariss. The whole scenario sounds dangerous."

"Not at all. Once Delores is found, the ink will dry on the investigation."

"And you can finish your book."

With no literary agent and no publisher. But she'd already determined she was going to find new ones. "Yeah. Sure."

"What are you not saying? Is the FBI agent helping you a jerk? 'Cause if he is, I'll camp on his doorstep and give him a piece of my mind."

Kariss laughed. "That's what I threatened when you found Wyatt with his girlfriend."

"Then we're even. Seriously, is the agent giving you a rough time?"

"Not any more than I expected. He's a good guy. Hard to figure out, but I'm trying. I have to understand his position. He was in the middle of an important case involving gangs and gun smugglers, and suddenly I come along."

"What's he like? A seasoned agent? A Sean

154

Connery sort of guy?"

Kariss giggled and paused to form a description of Tigo. "He's of South American descent with a macho feel. But definitely not my type. He has a reputation for being a rogue. Shake it down with a problem-solving mastermind who zeros in on any inefficiency, and you have Tigo Harris."

"Sounds like an antibiotic."

Kariss laughed, and it felt good. "That's a perfect description. I enjoy teasing him, and he does the same to me. His partner is friendlier, but not as much fun."

"Can you request a female agent?"

Kariss immediately thought of Hillary. "I'm good. Really."

"When is the Gulf Coast Writers Conference? Sounds like you need a break from your research."

Another sore spot. "Soon. First time in years that I won't be attending."

"And here I thought about tagging along like I did two years ago. When is it?"

"July in New Orleans. Hmm, I can only imagine how great it would be to spend the time with you. But the situation can't be helped. This book means so much more."

"But you loved last year's conference in Miami."

"I did, but this year's different. Unless you

want to go in my place?"

"Right. Me who hates crowds and knows nothing about the publishing business. Let's go back to what you said earlier. I want to know more about the FBI agent. I have a feeling there's something you aren't telling me. Sparks flying?"

"Oh, sparks are flying all right, but not the kind you're thinking." Kariss shuddered at the thought. "He has a few good points, and he'll make an intriguing hero. Nothing else. Now tell me what's going on with you?"

"You're changing the subject, but I'll give you a break. On Tuesday I'll be officially divorced for three months, and like an idiot, I keep expecting Wyatt to call."

"Even though he's re-married?"

"He could realize he's made a mistake. We did have eight years together."

Kariss squeezed her eyes shut. "You had an eight-year marital relationship, during which you shared him with other women for over seven years. And he and his current live-in have a baby together."

"That doesn't make me feel any better when I'm missing him. Wishing things were different."

"Just give yourself a reality check." All Kariss had to do was look at her sister's life and she realized her troubles were nothing.

"Another reality check was he took her and their baby to our church a few weeks ago."

Kariss groaned. "Don't tell me that was the Sunday Mom wanted me to go."

"The same."

"I'm the world's worst sister. But then I would have made a horrible scene and humiliated the whole family."

"It was sorta hard to see God in the middle of his show of piety."

Kariss didn't plan to dive into the God thing. "What are you doing this very minute?"

"Driving to Walmart. Do you need something? I used the last of my makeup."

"I have a great idea. Why don't you head my direction, and let's spend the rest of the day together? We can do the Walmart thing. Rent some movies. Dinner. Whatever you want."

"Would love it. But no dinner. Tummy is a little upset."

Kariss's own stomach did a jig. "Please tell me you've had a period."

"Can't. Haven't experienced a tampon since Wyatt spent the night here before the divorce. Four months ago."

Vicki's situation appeared to be growing

steadily worse. "I'm here, you know. Have you been to the doctor?"

"Saw my ob-gyn five weeks ago. Confirmed my suspicions."

"You didn't tell me? How can I help you if you keep things from me? Is everything okay?"

"Yes. No one knows, and I'm not telling Mom and Dad they're going to be grand-parents again until I'm busting out of my jeans. Which won't be long."

Kariss wanted to scream at Vicki. She was a nurse. Didn't she know what caused babies?

"I want this baby, sis. I have a good job, and I'll make it work."

"We'll both make this happen. You know I have plenty of room in this huge condo. You and the baby could have two of the bedrooms and give up your tiny one-bedroom apartment. I've never liked the area. Totally unsafe. When's your lease up?"

"It's on a month-by-month basis. Like my life. Anyway, you're sweet, but I refuse to be a burden. Oh, Kariss, you know how long I've wanted a baby."

Except the timing was all out of whack. "Yeah." She remembered the tearful calls during Vicki's marriage when each month her period arrived on time and Vicki was devastated.

"I believe God had this happen for a reason. Being a single mom is not how I planned my life, but I took a risk when Wyatt came to see me. Dad's a great role model, and Mom's walking wisdom. I'll do my best to love and raise this child."

"Think about moving in with me. I could use the company. Remember all those years I worked in day care? This gal's great with kids, especially babies."

"I'll think about it."

"We'd have such fun fixing up a nursery."

"You're tempting me. And I do want a good home for my baby."

Now why hadn't Delores Olvera felt the same way?

Cheeky demanded allegiance from every person who worked for him, from his lead man to his mules. Or he got rid of them. So when Froggie interrupted his time with Monika, he picked up his .38 Special.

"This had better be important."

"It is, boss, or I wouldn't have bothered you." Froggie didn't move a muscle.

"Did you find the *policía?*" Cheeky nodded at Monika to leave the two men alone, a pity, since the sixteen-year-old knew how to please him.

"Not yet," Froggie said. "I'm working on it. He wears a disguise when he walks the streets."

"I told you I wanted him to disappear." Cheeky watched Monika grab a sheet and whip it around her slender body before leaving the bedroom.

Froggie nodded. "I'm heading out again when we're finished. Took care of one of the Skulls last night."

"I know about that." Cheeky's temper rose. "I gave you an order and it's not done. So why are you here?"

"Jo-Jack's bragged to a woman about knowing our every move. Thought you'd want to know."

Cheeky swore. Jo-Jack sold more cocaine than the others, but he'd gone too far. Needed to learn a lesson. Knew their every move? He'd never make it through Arroyo initiation. "*Ve da le una calentada.* We'll see if he figures out how to keep his mouth shut."

"Don't kill him?"

Cheeky waved his gun in Froggie's face. In the past, Jo-Jack had pretended to work for the FBI, then passed information on to Cheeky. They'd given the *policía* the slip many times because of Jo-Jack. "Are you deaf? I give the orders."

160

Jo-Jack . . . cocky but valuable. Cheeky would spare him this time.

By Monday morning, Tigo came to the conclusion that Delores Olvera was either dead or on the run. Media poured out their support to Xavier, a hardworking man who believed his wife had cared for their ill child when in actuality she'd let the little girl starve to death. A nationwide search had been enacted for the woman. The media climate changed from asking for public support to identify Benita to finding her mother, now a person of interest in a murder. Univision planned a follow-up with Xavier, which would be aired in a couple of weeks.

Tigo settled into detail mode, sending agents back to Pine Grove Apartments to try to jar someone's memory, since five years ago the agents didn't have Benita's name. He personally interviewed the apartment manager and asked for a list of past residents, especially anyone who could have been Xavier and Delores's neighbors. Unfortunately, the manager had been there only two years, and the owner lived in Singapore. The previous manager had not kept accurate records, bringing that part of the investigation to a close. A medical clinic in

161

the area contacted the FBI with Benita's medical records, noting the little girl hadn't been seen by a doctor since Xavier was deported.

Tigo paced the room. Neither Ryan nor any of the other agents questioned him. They knew his habits. Earlier he'd worked out, pushing his body so he could push his mind. But the truth was he had to wait for others to do their job.

Rubbing his palms, he made a decision to work through the mound of papers on his desk. He wondered about Jo-Jack, who hadn't checked in since Tigo had met him at the drugstore. The investigation needed the gun dealer's name who supposedly worked at the Galleria. Tigo had his own lead, an oil-and-gas man by the name of Peter Masterson who had been linked a year ago to a homicide involving stolen guns. Masterson had an alibi and no paper trail. The case had been dismissed. But it might not hurt to pay him a little visit.

Tigo's cell rang. The caller ID read "Unlisted."

"Tigo here."

"This is the ER at Ben Taub Hospital," a woman said. "Joseph Jackson gave us this number and requested we place a call to you. Mr. Jackson would like to see you. He says it's important."

"Why? Is he there?"

"He's been badly beaten and has a knife wound to the abdomen. Are you a family member?"

"Sort of. I can be there in the next hour."

"Better hurry. He'll be going into surgery shortly."

"What is the extent of his injuries?"

"Sir, if you were family —"

"I'm the closest he has."

The woman hesitated.

"Is he dying?" Tigo asked.

"Mr. Jackson has internal bleeding. He's critical but conscious."

"I'm leaving now." Tigo hung up. This sounded legit, but he didn't plan to take any chances and risk walking into a firefight at the hospital parking lot. He called the ER at Ben Taub to confirm Joseph Jackson was being treated. Bingo — fourth floor, critical wound unit. This was the real deal. Jo-Jack must fear for his life or he wouldn't have had a call placed to Tigo.

Glancing at Kariss, he had an idea. Why not invite her to accompany him and Ryan on a field trip to the hospital? She'd see firsthand what happens when someone crossed the wrong people or was seen tagging along with an FBI special agent.

Maybe a long look at Jo-Jack would persuade her to abandon this unrealistic quest. Her book using Cherished Doe had potential, and he wished her well. Her interest in his current case was another matter, one she didn't need to be a part of. Harsh reality, but a good lesson.

CHAPTER 16

July

Kariss sat alone in one of the waiting rooms of the medical center's surgical area and waited. Jo-Jack's surgery had taken over three hours, and he hadn't been moved to recovery yet. Needing a decent cup of coffee, she texted Tigo and told him she was headed to the McDonald's located in the hospital's basement. She didn't want either agent to exit the surgical area and not be able to locate her.

As she took the elevator down, she pondered Jo-Jack's situation. She didn't see how an injured man could survive a knife wound to the abdomen, and the longer the doctors kept him in surgery the less she counted on Jo-Jack's chances of survival. How did people live in such fear and chaos? This wasn't a movie. It was real life. Men like Tigo and Ryan worked in an unsafe environment to ensure the safety of those living in

Houston and the surrounding area. The agents had a tough job, one she didn't want but one she valued.

You'd better suck it up and deal with the reality of crime if you're going to run with the big dogs.

Back in the waiting room now, the bitter coffee left a horrible taste in her mouth that breath mints only temporarily disguised. Her concern for Jo-Jack, a man she'd never met, hindered her creativity and ability to take notes. She closed her eyes. Her parents would pray in this situation, and perhaps she should too.

Vicki's pregnancy had jolted Kariss too. Her sister shouldn't have married Wyatt. He had a reputation of sleeping with women and stringing them along like abacus beads. When the thrill vanished, he dumped them. Vicki had fallen for his lines every time he proved unfaithful. Why the man wanted her to marry him was obvious — he had political aspirations, and Vicki was his arm ornament.

Shaking her head to dispel the many thoughts bombarding her brain, Kariss walked across the room to a window. Outside gray clouds hovered over the city and darkened the room.

The sound of male voices coming down

the hall broke the silence of her thoughts. Two men, both wearing black head bandanas and black T-shirts strolled into the vacant waiting room. Perhaps if she hadn't been privy to Jo-Jack's informant work and Tigo's run-in with a gang, she wouldn't feel so apprehensive. She eased into a dimly lit corner and hoped their visit was short lived.

"He's still in surgery. So what do we do?" one man said in Spanish.

"We'll get our chance."

The first man swore. "I don't like sticking around hospitals. Too many cops here."

"Don't have a choice. We gotta finish what we started. I thought he'd bleed out."

"Let's hope he didn't talk. No matter. He's a dead man for claiming he slept with my sister."

"What about Cheeky?"

"I'll take care of him."

Kariss's heart ached from its incessant pounding. Could they hear her reaction? They were talking murder, and she knew they meant Jo-Jack. Or anyone who got in their way. That meant Tigo or Ryan. Her friends could walk down the hall any minute and get nailed by these guys. She had to warn them . . . Tigo and Ryan carried guns . . . The men in the waiting room must have weapons too.

Heroics weren't on the list of traits required for a writer. But she could text Tigo and warn him. Gulping in air, she walked back into the waiting room to where her purse rested and grabbed her phone and laptop.

2 BAD GUYS N WAITING ROOM
TALKING ABOUT KILLING MAN IN
SURGERY.

She waited and stared out the window while straining to hear any more conversation.

Moments crept by. Finally her cell buzzed with a text.

GET OUT OF THERE.

No problem. She'd simply gather up her things and stroll past the two men. Pretend she didn't understand them and possibly give them a smile and take note of any distinguishing physical features. That made sense. If only her knees would stop shaking so she could move. Holding onto her cell phone, she sensed the men's eyes on her, and again her heart thudded until her chest hurt. The tattoos on their upper arms . . . weren't those gang signs?

Kariss turned around. The open waiting

area allowed her to leave freely, but they would get a clear look at her.

"How long do we wait?" one man said.

"For as long as it takes." The other man laughed.

She caught a glimpse of the scoffer's face, one she sealed into memory. Her unsteady legs moved her on. The clip of footsteps approaching the waiting room sent fear to her fingertips.

Stay calm. The two men on a murder mission have no clue you understood them.

Whoever walked her way might not be Tigo or Ryan though. She was safe unless the terror in her face gave her away.

Tigo and Ryan came into view, and she dropped her phone, its guts spewing over the floor. She caught Tigo's gaze and hoped the stats about nonverbal body language were right.

Her jaw tightened, and she hurried toward them, hoping her terrified gaze alerted them to the men seated behind her. She mouthed "two men" then "not good."

Both agents pulled their weapons, the metal glistening. This happened in other writers' books. Not hers. Not real life. Her pulse sped faster. Ryan pushed her behind him.

The two killers stood and hurried into the

hall, passing Kariss, Ryan and Tigo.

"*¡Detente! ¡Policía!*" Tigo said in Spanish, but they kept moving.

Gunfire pierced the air, and Kariss sank to the floor, paralyzed by horror.

Scuffling.

Tigo's repeated demands for them to stop.

Screams.

Footsteps racing away.

Moments later Tigo's voice drew her back to reality. "It's over, Kariss."

She opened her eyes to blood splattered on the walls and a man's body sprawled facedown on the floor. The sterile surroundings had been contaminated.

"Don't look at him." Tigo's once-firm voice now held compassion. A security guard stood over the man's body. Tigo bent beside her. "Stay here. Do *not* answer any questions about what you witnessed."

She drew in air, determined not to show weakness. Her experience with dead bodies had been through photos. Not this. "Where's Ryan?"

"Chasing down the other guy. I'm going to help."

Kariss slowly stood and faced the security guard. A small crowd formed behind her. A movie script. The good guys always won.

The security guard hurried to her side.

"Miss, are you all right?"

She nodded. Of course she'd be okay. The trauma was mental not physical. Acid rose from her stomach, but she fought it. Tigo and Ryan would find the other man.

Her gaze trailed away from the body then back again. Police officers arrived, probably from the ER, and surrounded the body. All asked her questions, but just as Tigo instructed, she didn't give a statement.

Kariss sank back to the floor and stared at the blood on the walls, the body, and the police officers for what seemed like an hour — or was it simply minutes? A life had been wasted in the name of violence. She shivered. No wonder Tigo invested his time and knowledge to end gang warfare.

Finally the two agents came around the corner. Kariss just wanted to make sure they were unharmed and to hear the man had been apprehended.

"I didn't say anything to them." She hoped her words sounded braver than she felt.

"Good." Tigo nodded at Ryan, who passed them to stand inside the yellow crime-scene tape. "We didn't catch him, Kariss."

"That means I can identify him." She looked into his face, knowing the answer yet fearing his response and the implication.

171

"Yes, it does. They're members of the Arroyos."

Her life now balanced on the same tightrope as Jo-Jack's.

Tigo's job description didn't include babysitting women writers who'd gotten themselves in over their heads in . . . research. But he wanted to make sure Kariss wasn't in shock over what she'd seen. She needed to be escorted from this scene before her face or name was flashed across the evening news. The media would soon swarm the area like flies at a Dumpster.

He left her alone while he wove through the small crowd to Ryan, who'd knelt to examine the body. The dead man's bandana had been pushed back when he fell, revealing the Arroyos' gang sign. "Hey," Tigo said. "I'm getting Kariss out of the hospital."

"Good idea. I'll handle things here and report in later."

Standing, Tigo caught Kariss's attention — obviously shaken, as was evident in her eyes, but in control. She was stronger than he'd given her credit for. He walked to her side and helped her up from the floor. "I'm getting you away from this before the media arrive."

"You mean the vultures?"

Odd response since she'd been one.

They made their way onto an empty elevator. Her face reflected the shock of what had just happened. "If . . . if I'm interpreting this right, by leaving the scene I'm making sure the media can't snap pictures and link me to the crime."

"Correct. I don't think this is your idea of publicity and promotion."

"Thank you. I don't have a death wish either." She patted his arm. "I'm okay on my own."

"Those aren't the words of a fluff writer."

"I've never been fluff. And thanks for getting me out of here."

The elevator door opened to a handful of media types.

"Kariss," said a man who needed a haircut. "How did you get here so fast? That firefight just happened."

She lifted her head, and Tigo could tell by her demeanor that she'd assumed a role. Good for her.

"Hi, Mike. Looks like you arrived too late," she said as she exited the elevator.

The elevator filled behind her, leaving Mike behind. His attention whipped to the closing door and back to her. "You got an exclusive? How do you rate?"

She smiled. "I'm a professional, and I have

my contacts."

"Care to share how you were tipped off?"

"I don't think so." She tilted her head.

"Okay, what network or newspaper? I've done my homework, and no one owns up to bringing you onboard."

"You'll find out soon enough."

"What about giving me your number so we can catch up?"

"We just did."

"Kariss, there's a ton of history between us."

"Leave it there."

Tigo touched the small of her back and kept her moving toward the hospital's entrance. She had history with the Mike guy? Once outside, her body relaxed under his touch, and he removed his hand. She might not feel at ease if she considered the fact that the man she'd recognized could be waiting for them somewhere in the parking lot.

"Tell me the shooting on the surgical floor didn't happen," she said. "I want to be assured I'm in the middle of a nightmare."

"Can't do it. Did you take good notes?"

"That's not funny."

He pointed toward his truck. "I agree. Let's hurry along in case the shooter stayed behind for target practice."

"You mean us, don't you?"

"Exactly."

She quickened her steps. "How is Jo-Jack doing?"

"He'd just been moved to recovery when you texted me. Confirmed the Arroyos had worked him over and sunk a knife into his stomach. Left him for dead. We couldn't get any more information."

"Tigo, I've never seen a real dead body before. Not like what's back there."

"I hope it's your last." But it wouldn't be his last. When the Arroyos lined up their victims like pinballs, he didn't want to end up in their scopes. Neither did he want Kariss alongside him.

"I hope Mike doesn't mention me in his column. At least he thinks I'm a reporter."

"I think you're safe there. Do you feel up to describing the shooter for us? We'll also see if the security camera's footage caught the two men's faces."

"To see if they're in the system?"

"Yes, Kariss." She'd been listening and watching far too many crime shows. "Putting a name with a face and getting out a warrant is smarter than waiting for him to come after you."

"You're rather blunt."

"I have to be. Anything else would have

175

gotten me and other good people killed a long time ago. I'm sorry to have brought you here today. Not one of my best decisions."

"Tigo, am I the only witness?"

"Looks like it. Another one may turn up later."

"How did the two men get past the hospital's metal detectors?"

"Good question."

"This is more dangerous than I thought."

"You've entered real life. Not a crime file or a website."

CHAPTER 17

Stark reality left Kariss numb and frightened. The two shooters at Ben Taub Hospital had avoided the security cameras. The footage revealed nothing. TV reporting had never taken her into this dangerous of territory. She'd never lacked courage, but right now she could use a heavy dose of common sense to see her way clear of this mess.

She closed her eyes to recall everything she remembered about the man who'd escaped the firefight at the hospital. *Firefight.* A word she'd used but not experienced. She sat with Tigo and a woman artist who would sketch a likeness of the shooter from her description.

"Aside from the bandana-covered head and tattooed forearms, he was muscular. He had thick biceps liked he worked out every day." She took a deep breath. "If I give you wrong information, then the wrong man could be arrested."

"An Arroyo initiation means breaking the law, and the man's most likely in the system. So we're good there," Tigo said.

His words soothed her frazzled nerves, assuring her she wouldn't be incriminating anyone who was innocent.

"What else do you remember?"

"His face was rather long for a Hispanic, and he had a scar running down the right side of his face near his ear. His eyes were wide set. No eyebrows. I made it a point to memorize their facial features."

"Smart move. Now we're getting somewhere," Tigo said. "Neither I nor Ryan got a good look at him. Anything distinct about the chin, jawline, or width of the nose?"

"A wide nose. Reminded me of a bulldog."

"Good job," Tigo said. "Did you hear a name?"

"No. They said whoever they were after was still in surgery. And they talked about getting the job done, and the man they were after was a dead man. One of them didn't like hospitals because of the cops. Not sure that's in the right order. I was pretty shaken up at the time. A comment was made about how the victim shouldn't have claimed to sleep with his sister. And they thought he'd bleed out."

"What happened after that?"

"I texted you. Gathered up my things and when I walked past them, I saw you and Ryan."

Tigo turned his attention to the artist's sketch. "Run it through and see what you get."

Kariss watched, fascinated. She'd seen this kind of work on TV shows but had never experienced it. She focused on helping the agents and not her own fear. Had to get past the fiction world she created and focus on reality.

The woman pressed a key, and two photos filled the screen.

"That's him." Kariss pointed to the man she'd seen a short time ago.

"That's a man with a record for leaving no live bodies behind." Tigo sat back in his chair. "He torched a man at a bar."

"That's not comforting. Who is he?" She kept her hands folded in her lap so he wouldn't see her trembling.

"Froggie Diego. Wanted for murder, rape, and armed robbery. He's also the one we believe carried out the beheading of a rival gang member. One of Cheeky's key men."

She sensed her eyes widening, and her pulse began to race. "He . . . he sounds like a horrible man. Does he normally stay on his side of town?"

"He goes where a job needs to be done, and Ben Taub has been the scene of violent crimes more than once. Understand he does what he's told."

"Are you deliberately trying to scare me?"

"Is it working? I've been trying to run you out of Houston since we walked to the hospital parking lot."

He'd nearly succeeded, but she'd never let him know. "I'm fine. I'll simply be aware of the company I keep."

"What if he finds out who you are and decides to make a home visit?"

"I live in a gated community."

"That would never stop an Arroyo."

"I'm not budging."

"Does anything scare you?"

Yes, but it was more in line with a nightmare that mirrored the past. She bit into her quivering lip. "I'm in this for as long as it takes. In my opinion, I'm safer here than anywhere else."

Tigo spent the morning of the Fourth of July with his mother before heading to a special-event detail at Memorial Park. While people picnicked, played games, and waited for a concert by the Houston Symphony to be followed by fireworks, he'd be looking for possible bombs. Ever since 9/11, the FBI attended large events to ensure the safety of the people. Sometimes extra agents were called in from other cities.

Until it was time for him to leave, he'd sit at his mother's bedside, scrolling through secured and non-secured sites that might have any information about the Arroyos' dealings. YouTube had two videos about the gang. One dealt with an execution — a beheading of a rival gang member, a key man in the Skulls. Another was a party where faces were blocked. Lots of talk there, and he guessed Cheeky was among them.

A familiar woman sat in the background. He stilled the frame and confirmed it was Candy, the petite beauty, now gone, leaving two orphaned kids behind. This proved her claims and information had always been right on.

The voices in the video could be used to track down key people. But identifying members wasn't the real problem. The authorities needed to make arrests. The gang members hid like roaches, coming out at night to forage, then scattering when morning broke the horizon. If one of them was being investigated, he went *esconder* — isolated from the others until things settled down.

The Arroyos had declared war on anyone

carrying a badge. Much like the cartels in Mexico.

Candy had been good about wearing a recorder, and the ATF agents had been successful in thwarting a few shipments, but Tigo wanted more. The Arroyos were working with someone who provided guns. Someone who covered his tracks.

Kariss had nearly gotten herself killed in a firefight. She'd held up better than most men. Much better. Although the woman drove him crazy, she had strength . . . and courage. Danger stalked her, but she hadn't voiced it like he expected, although he'd seen the terror in her eyes. He hoped the Arroyo who ran was more concerned with saving his own skin than finding out her name. Tigo cringed at the damage the media could have done. They'd have played right into the shooter's hands with a photo and name.

What about Mike McDougal, the reporter who claimed he and Kariss had history? Tigo wanted to think he'd conjured up that line, but obviously it was true. How close were they? And did he even want to know?

Tigo laid the laptop aside. On holidays, he dwelled more on his lonely existence. That aspect of his lifestyle hadn't changed since he left college. Old friends had families, and he didn't fit. Couldn't have an intelligent conversation when he wasn't married or didn't have kids. Their problems were way out of his zone. None of them were caretakers for aging or ill parents. So he turned down invitations, refused blind dates, and dreaded holidays — grim reminders of his miserable personal life.

He stiffened, as though his mother could read his thoughts. She'd lived the same type of life for him, her every breath for Tigo. She mirrored her belief about children being a gift and a culture's future. He could do no less for her, not because of obligation or a skewed sense of responsibility, but because he loved her.

A text came in from Jo-Jack. The man was scared and wondering where he could go once the hospital released him. Right now police were giving him 24/7 protection. Tigo typed a reply.

THAT'S HANDLED. SAFE HOUSE IN
DALLAS.

At least tucked away, Jo-Jack had a chance of staying alive until arrests were made and he could testify. Except the Arroyos who'd beaten him were probably watching the hospital. Tigo wouldn't put it past any of them to fire on an FBI transport vehicle. The move would need to happen at night. Probably a helicopter lift made to look like a life flight. In essence, it would be.

CHAPTER 18

Monday morning, every vehicle in Kariss's rearview mirror was a potential killer. Her imagination spun in a blur, and her stomach threatened to reject breakfast. She wished her Jaguar was a tank, then she might feel safe. But the flip side — leaving the city — was not an option. She'd never been a runner, and she wasn't about to start now.

A vehicle eased up beside her on the highway . . . a pickup truck filled with Hispanic workers. She gripped the steering wheel as though it could save her from an assailant.

Calm down, Kariss.

The Arroyos had no idea who she was or where she lived. At least she wanted to believe so.

Once she made it to the FBI office, her habit of making a list of what needed to be accomplished for the week amounted to a blank screen on her laptop. She couldn't concentrate on her writing or the questions she wanted to pose to Tigo. Her fears about the Arroyos wanting her dead continued to rise. Maybe her research at the FBI wasn't worth the price, especially if she didn't live to finish the book.

She sipped her latte and peeked around her cubicle at Tigo, who had finished his liquid energy an hour ago. He was on the phone, so she returned to her work area. They hadn't discussed the shooting since the facial recognition event. Neither had she broached the topic with Vicki, who had enough trauma in her life. No one else to talk to about it . . . but herself. That conversation would be funny, except in her writing life too much exposition ruined a good story. Readers skipped it. Their eyes scrolled down to the action.

So she must do the same. Set her sights on the future, the arrests of Arroyos, her novel, and most important, how Benita had died.

Her cell rang, a welcome sound since her mind refused to concentrate on her story. "Unknown" registered on the caller ID. Maybe it was the new agent she'd queried.

"Kariss Walker here."

"Good morning, Miss Walker," a man said in Spanish. "This is Xavier Olvera. Do you remember me?"

She tucked her phone between her ear and shoulder, then pulled up a new document page on her laptop. "Good to hear from you. I saw the media interviews. You did a fine job." She positioned her fingers on the keyboard.

"Thank you. I spoke to Special Agent Harris earlier, and now I realize I need help."

"What's the problem?"

"The FBI and the police can't find Delores. They say she's either dead or hiding. I've looked everywhere too. She's disappeared."

"I'm sure they'll be able to find her. Her information has been sent to law enforcement officials across the country, and the search for her has been a topic of top TV networks, columnists, and reporters. Investigations take time." She minimized the document to reveal her desktop background — a pic of her nieces and four nephews taken at Easter at her parents' farm. She'd scratch at the gates of hell if anyone tried to hurt them.

"I don't care about Delores. I just want to find the child I've never seen."

Kariss had wondered about the child as soon as she'd heard about Delores' claim of being pregnant when he was deported.

"What did Agent Harris suggest?"

"He said there was nothing he could do. Delores could have the child with her or could have abandoned it or given it up. But after what she did to Benita, I . . . I have to know for sure."

"Sir, we don't even know if she was honest about the pregnancy."

"How do you think I feel?"

Devastated for sure. "I don't understand how I can help you."

"You could pressure Agent Harris. Get him to look for my child as well as Delores. Hospitals have records of babies, *verdad?* The baby would have been born around October five years ago."

"But would Delores have used her real name?"

"I believe so. It makes sense that by giving the baby my name, she could prove it belonged to me and get more money."

"But Delores broke contact with you, so your theory isn't necessarily realistic." Kariss cringed. She sounded heartless. "Mr. Olvera, I feel for your loss and the tragedies that have fallen on you. But I think this is hopeless without the help of law enforcement officials. Once they find Delores, they can verify whether there is, or was, a second child."

"You think she killed the baby too?"

"I'm so sorry." Even if she believed Delores had killed both children, would it make any difference to Xavier? But Kariss couldn't bring herself to dump more truth on him. "I think when the authorities find your wife, then you'll learn the truth about both of your children."

"I need your help to find my child. You're the only one I can trust. My brother believes like Agent Harris. They say to wait for the police. They say to wait to find Delores. But all I can think about is the hope of finding my child. *Dios aprieta, pero no ahorca.*"

Weight dug into her shoulders. She understood the saying: God tightens the grip, but he doesn't choke you. Xavier's plea . . . his deceased Benita. "Let me see what I can find out and get back to you. I have your number."

"When?"

No putting off this guy. "Probably this afternoon or tomorrow."

"If I don't hear from you by tonight, I'll call you."

Kariss stared at her phone long after she and Xavier finished their conversation. She understood his concerns. In his shoes she'd feel the same. The years spent working in day care with precious children swept across her mind . . . the laughter, the innocence . . . and the fire. What if he did have another child who was alive? Yes, she'd turn up stones to find a possible child too.

Her first stop was Tigo. She'd talk to him while the situation was still fresh in their minds. If he'd refused Xavier, her chance of enlisting his help was slim. But she'd try. Downing her now-cold coffee, she closed her eyes, allowing her need to help children wash over her.

She wanted to help this man, who'd had his heart ripped open. She wanted to bring joy back to his saddened life. Another child wouldn't replace Benita, but the anticipation brought hope. Maybe in doing so she could redeem her own failings.

She approached his cubicle. "Tigo, got a minute?"

The scowl on his face indicated bad timing.

"I can come back later."

He leaned back. "Now is as good a time as any. I'm leaving for an appointment in a few minutes."

"Investigation not going well?"

"Let's just say I have some extenuating circumstances." Frustration poured into his words.

She slid into a chair near his desk. "Xavier

Olvera just called me. Said he'd talked to you earlier."

Tigo tapped a pen on his desk. Not a muscle moved on his face. Neither did he blink. "So he asked you to help him find a child that may not exist?"

"Yes. And I agree it looks hopeless."

"I suppose you threw in your support, and now you're begging me to pour my expertise into a situation that has no leads?"

Oh, he was in a bad mood. "Not exactly. I'm asking for your advice."

"I'll tell you the same thing I told him: I despise what happened to his daughter and the grief it's caused him and his family. I'm mad as well. I'm angry that the mother has disappeared, and we can't find any leads to track her down. But we can't waste resources. I can't jump into dredging up a child who doesn't have a sex or a birthdate. When we find Delores, we can ask her about the second child."

"That child would be about five years old, his only child. The same age as Benita when she died."

"I'm sorry, Kariss. The FBI can't waste their time on what-ifs. Other law officials are looking for Delores, but we can't look for a child who potentially doesn't even exist. We deal in specific crimes. If in doubt,

191

look at our website. Please, don't bother Ricardo Montoya. He's on case overload too."

She refused to be dismissed. "Can't you see this isn't over?"

"I have reality to take care of. Have you forgotten the Arroyos' mission at the hospital? That has my attention. It's real. People are dying. You were almost a victim, or have you discarded the thought of being at the receiving end of a bullet?"

She shook her head. "No, I remember all of it. Vividly."

His efforts to frighten her weren't wasted, but she'd been involved in the Cherished Doe case far too long to let it ride. "I value your concern, and I also know I don't have your skill and wisdom in this field. But I'll do all I can to help Xavier learn the truth. I'm asking if there is a good place to start."

Tigo leaned forward. "You have the ending to Benita's story. If you don't like the reality of the situation, then write it to suit yourself."

After sending Kariss out of his office to think about his blunt but logical response to Xavier Olvera's pleas for help, Tigo shut down his computer. He'd been curt and should apologize, but she needed to under-

192

stand the world didn't dance to the tune of good people. He hoped he made her angry enough to leave the city until key Arroyos were arrested.

Her safety needled at him. She had a soft heart that he'd seen with this case. And she could make some stupid decisions in the name of caring, like spending time on the wrong side of town where the Arroyos had easy access. Tigo was itching to have her cell phone records directed to his Blackberry, but ethics prohibited it unless she authorized it, and he had a feeling she'd refuse access.

Right now he had an appointment for a root canal. His tooth throbbed like a beating drum, and he refused to take pain meds while working. The dentist — one Tigo hadn't met before — specialized in root canals. The thought sent his blood pressure on an upward spiral. He'd rather face a firing squad. But he'd put off the procedure long enough, and he couldn't hide the pain from other agents anymore.

At the dental complex, he signed in and filled out enough forms to perform brain surgery. His personal dentist had sent X-rays, so all he needed to do was wait — alone and distracted. No one screamed. All he heard was soft music, reminding him of a funeral home.

"Mr. Harris." A woman with perfect teeth smiled from the doorway and escorted him to a chair.

She took X-rays again. And he waited.

A young man stepped into the room, dressed in jeans and a golf T-shirt. This guy, who looked younger than Tigo, couldn't be the specialist.

"Good afternoon, Mr. Harris. I see you need a root canal. We'll get you numbed up and take a look at your tooth." He slipped into a pair of gloves.

Tigo's dentist always swabbed the area with a topical solution before bringing out the novocaine shot. Not this guy.

"Take deep breaths, sir. No need to be nervous. You'll feel a little prick."

It was no prick.

"Sensitive, huh."

Tigo nodded. A lot of good it did.

"Now, before we get started, understand that if this root canal can't be performed, we'll need to extract the tooth. Your dentist will handle an implant." No smile. No understanding.

Tigo nodded. It was an upper-right molar, and he didn't want to part with it. "How long have you been practicing?"

"About six years." He leaned against the

side of the counter, looking like one of the kids in Tigo's neighborhood who threw hoops.

Tigo continued to take deep breaths.

"So what's your nine-to-five?"

No way would he tell him he was an FBI agent. "Desk job."

"All right." He chuckled. "I read your file, Agent Harris. Let's get this done."

While Tigo leaned back with his mouth open, vulnerable to the world, he had plenty of time to ponder the many questions about the gun-smuggling case. The Arroyos were growing bolder and were at war with the Skulls, a rival gang, and rumors had surfaced that they planned to take over the city with the help of a Mexican cartel. They wouldn't make such boasts without those who supplied the weapons, those with means to hide their illegal activities in the heart of Houston.

When Tigo considered the rising crime along the border towns, his determination increased. Although his and Ryan's case looked minuscule in the whole fight against drugs, gun smuggling, sex trafficking, and whatever else bad guys dabbled in, crippling the Arroyos had far-reaching effects. He wanted to nail the gun and ammo suppliers along with making gang arrests.

A huge undertaking, but not impossible.

An hour and a half later, which really was painless after the novocaine, the dentist ripped off his gloves. "Done. Your dentist will see to positioning a post in the root canal, build up the tooth, and take impressions for a crown. Call me if you have any problems."

Problems? How fast could he run?

CHAPTER 19

Tuesday morning, Tigo drove with Ryan to Peter Masterson's office building at eleven a.m. Two agents were posted at the back exit in case Masterson decided to leave his ninth-floor office suite before the interview. He'd been arrested for murder in January, but he'd been released when the only witness died of an apparent overdose. He also dabbled in gun smuggling, according to Jo-Jack. Again no proof. But Tigo had an ace in his back pocket regarding the murder charges — a new witness who would reopen the case.

Masterson's secretary insisted they must have an appointment, and he was booked solid for the next two days. Tigo knew a hidden closed-circuit video feed allowed Masterson to sit in his plush office and observe the conversation.

Tigo smiled at the secretary. "Tell Mr. Masterson that Special Agent Tigo Harris and Special Agent Ryan Steadman from the FBI are here to see him without an appointment."

The blonde, a long-legged beauty, gestured for them to sit down, then excused herself.

"Don't be long," Tigo said. "We know how to find him."

Tigo wasn't in a mood to deal with her or Masterson. The wealthy businessman had shot and killed a gun dealer from El Paso who'd taken him for several hundred thousand dollars. Masterson's girlfriend witnessed the murder. She went to HPD, and they arrested him. Two days later it was Masterson's girlfriend who'd been found dead.

But Tigo had a new angle. A witness had contacted the FBI. Said he'd been afraid to step forward after viewing the media reports on Masterson's connection to his girlfriend's death. But his conscience kept pestering him. Although the testimony was filled with holes, Masterson might be persuaded to assist the FBI in closing down the gun smugglers in exchange for leniency on the murder charge. His list of assets, including an overseas account, ensured him enough cash flow to buy whatever he wanted — except the FBI.

The blonde returned. "He prefers to have his attorney present."

Ryan walked to the door that led down the hall to Masterson's office. "He only needs his attorney when he has something to hide."

She picked up the phone and informed Masterson of the persistent FBI agents. Stiffening, her gaze bore into Ryan and Tigo. "Mr. Masterson will see you. I'll escort you to his office."

Ryan opened the door leading to the man's office. "We know the way."

Tigo thanked her and closed the door behind them. No doubt Masterson had cameras at the back of the building and knew he couldn't escape the questioning.

Masterson stepped into the hallway, dressed in one of his own tailor-made suits, another one of his enterprises. He was also a major stockholder in several offshore oil companies, including one near Africa. Everything was legit, which infuriated Tigo even more.

Masterson smiled and unbuttoned his suit coat. "What brings the FBI to my office today?"

"We have a few questions about some of your friends," Tigo said.

Masterson gestured the two into his spacious office, sparkling with glass and chrome. "I have many friends, gentleman. Please sit down. Can I get you something?"

"No thanks." Tigo said. He and Ryan took chairs facing the office door, and Masterson seated himself between them. "We'll get right to the point. We hear you're doing business with the Arroyos."

"Since when does Cheeky need info about oil and gas? If he has concerns about tax evasion, then he can make an appointment like my other clients."

Tigo laughed. "He needs to make sure he can fulfill his orders."

"I fail to understand what this has to do with me."

"It's simple," Tigo said. "We want Cheeky Lopez. You two conduct business together on a regular basis, and we want to make an exchange."

"I'm not interested. Neither do I know what you're talking about."

"Think real hard," Tigo continued. "We have enough evidence on you to tuck you away for life on murder charges."

"I don't think so."

"Your lady friend wasn't the only one who saw you pull the trigger that night."

Masterson shook his head. "You can do better than that."

"You think we're bluffing? The shooting occurred in the parking lot of the Hyatt at three a.m. on January fifth of this year. You might have thought you were smart using a silencer, but a man on the second floor saw the whole thing. Plea bargaining is the name of the game. You choose. Work with us in bringing in Cheeky and his boys or grow old in prison." Tigo shrugged. "Or death row."

"You're lying."

"Am I? You're willing to risk your life to protect Cheeky?" Tigo stood. "I thought we could work out a deal. Better call your new girlfriend and tell her you won't be home for dinner because you're going to jail."

"This conversation ended when you walked in. Trump up murder charges on someone who's guilty, not me."

"Tell you what. I give you until noon tomorrow to think about your future."

On Friday, Kariss left a note for Tigo that she was meeting her sister for lunch on Westheimer then heading home for the weekend. He probably didn't care how she spent her hours, but out of courtesy she'd keep him in the loop. After all, his quick thinking at the hospital had saved her life. What she hadn't written in the note was her meeting later with Xavier. The fire in Tigo's words about the man a few days ago still burned inside her. The idea of him telling her to leave the situation alone only spurred her on. She'd agreed to meet with Xavier because of his desperate situation. If another child existed, no matter how remote the possibility, then Kariss needed to help.

A twinge of fear sliced into her heart, but she mentally kicked it away. Earlier today she'd wondered if her zeal to help Xavier was a crash course in getting herself killed, since the search for Delores was predominantly on the side of town Kariss should avoid at all costs. Which brought her to a conclusion: Tomorrow morning, she planned a shopping excursion — for a handgun, complete with a training course on how to use it. She needed information about how to obtain a permit, and she had no clue what kind of handgun best suited her. Something small that would fit nicely inside her purse.

Kariss cringed at the thought of owning a weapon. Worse yet, what if she had to use it? But that was the very reason she needed to do research about the best one for her situation. Sort of like buying a car . . . or a new laptop.

She'd considered googling how to buy a

handgun, but that might put her on the FBI's radar. At least that's what her writer friends claimed. Whether it was true or not, she didn't dare risk the wrath of Tigo.

Asking her family for advice meant an endless drill by the entire Walker family, a force that left her scrambling for other options. Rather than lie, she'd keep them out of it.

The members of her online writer's group were scattered all over the country. None of the participants were from Texas and knew her state's laws regarding owning firearms.

She wished there was an app for those needing gun information. But that wasn't the case. So she'd resort to hands-on shopping. She'd written about guns but hadn't researched what might be the best one for her.

If she was going to run with the big dogs, then she needed to learn how to bark.

Vicki was seated in a booth when Kariss arrived at The Cheesecake Factory. She looked healthy, her cheeks rosy. And happy, which Kariss didn't understand.

"You look amazing," Kariss said. "Don't you have morning sickness?"

Vicki moistened her lips. "Every day, but it usually only lasts until ten-thirty."

"Considering the circumstances, I guess

that's a blessing."

"Wyatt didn't think any of my news was a blessing."

The hostess handed them menus, and the server took their drink orders, giving Kariss a few moments to think about her response. She should be more compassionate about her sister's condition, but disappointment in Vicki's dependence on her ex-husband settled in. "Why tell him?"

Vicki startled. "Because he's the father."

"As in he might come back?"

"In my dreams. I've wised up a little. He needs to prepare his bank account for child support."

"I'm glad you're seeing the light. Sis, you don't need him. I'll help you raise your baby."

Vicki took a sip of water and swiped beneath her eye. "Thanks, Sis. I've thought this through. I could eliminate him from the equation. Struggle through the financial aspect of raising this baby. But why make my child suffer because of my stubbornness? One more time he'd be given a license to live responsibility free. It's time he realized his actions have consequences."

Vicki had grown a smidgen smarter.

"I understand your reasoning, but I wish you would have reconsidered. What are you going to tell the child when he asks why his dad doesn't see him? Because you know Wyatt is much too social to get involved with a kid," Kariss said.

"Maybe Wyatt will want to be a father. Can't predict the future. In any event, I'm the mom, and I'll handle it the best way I can."

Kariss propped her elbow on the table and cupped her chin. "I'm thrilled that you're going to have a baby. I just wish the father weren't such a jerk."

Vicki laughed. "So do I. Yet God has given me a gift, and I will rejoice in it."

"Sounds like you went to Wednesday-night church."

Vicki nodded. "Need all the help I can get. Wyatt and his new family weren't there. It ought to be interesting when I start to show. I may need to change churches to keep the gossip down. Hey, how about going with me and the parents this Sunday?"

"Why? Are you planning to tell them then?"

"Yes."

Kariss moaned. "Have I become your backbone?"

"You can write it off as research for your next novel. You know, get into the emotive conflict thing with your characters."

She was already there in many respects. "Okay. I'll do the church and lunch thing on Sunday. It'll be good to see Mom and Dad."

"I appreciate this. Once the news is out, I'm sure they'll be thrilled." Vicki patted her tummy. "The way I've been eating, I'll soon have a bump."

"And we'll be planning a baby shower." Kariss forced enthusiasm into her voice. "In fact, when we finish here let's look at baby furniture. I'm buying."

"You can't go through life paying my way. I have money saved to take care of furnishing a nursery. And I want to wait until I find out if it's a boy or a girl."

"All right. What about maternity clothes? Do you have any?"

"Not yet. I figure Emma and Melanie have some I can borrow."

"Wrong there. Both of them ended that part of womanhood. I was at Mom's garage sale when they deposited them. So, please, can I indulge my best friend?"

"We can look."

Kariss touched Vicki's arm. "I hope you one day meet a guy who'll jump through hoops to prove how much he loves you and my little niece or nephew."

"I only want one man, and he doesn't

want me."

Kariss looked at her like she was crazy. "Your hormones must have kicked in."

Vicki's eyes flooded, then the dam burst. The months ahead would be very hard.

CHAPTER 20

Friday afternoon, Tigo and Ryan planned an extended lunch break to the southeast side of town. A gun shop owner there had had multiple arrests for illegal gun trade, but he also had a smart attorney. Tigo had tried on more than one occasion to get an indictment, but nothing ever stuck. The FBI also suspected him of building hidden units into vehicles to smuggle drugs and guns across the border.

The two agents walked to Tigo's truck, complaining about the one-hundred-degree heat and exchanging stats about the temps attributing to the city's crime.

Ryan opened the passenger side of Tigo's truck. "What makes you think Hershey is going to cooperate with us?"

"I found out a few things about his oldest daughter that we could use as leverage." He slid inside his truck and turned on the engine.

"Like what?"

"She's a nurse at MD Anderson, specializing in pediatrics."

"I don't get it. Has she been arrested?"

"No. She turned away from her family's lifestyle when she was sixteen. Walked into a police station and said she wanted out of her neighborhood. And that was seventeen years ago. Two days ago I learned about a problem at the hospital involving stolen analgesics." Tigo flipped on the AC. "HPD arrested an orderly. Cut-and-dry case, but Hershey doesn't know that."

"And you're sure she's not involved in illegal activity?"

"The last time we checked, she's clean." Tigo drove out of the parking lot. "Worked hard to get out of her daddy's spotlight. Changed her name."

"Have you talked to her?"

"Yep. She doesn't have a thing to do with Hershey. Neither will she associate with him to help us."

"So what's the plan?"

"That he'll do whatever it takes to protect her."

Ryan turned the AC vent his way. "If it's been seventeen years, I doubt the Arroyos know about her. Hershey's gun shop's only been in business for ten."

"Right, and I'm thinking Hershey's proud of her achievements. She's the only one of her family who doesn't have a record. Wouldn't want anything to spoil her career."

"If the Arroyos knew about her, they might put a little pressure on him. Squeeze him for more guns or to cut them a deal on building out units for their vehicles."

"That's what I'm thinking," Tigo said. "Going to bring up the firefight at the medical center last week. The shooter got away, but you shot him in the side. The Arroyos have their own doc-in-a-box and personal pharmacy, but someone has to get them what they need. I'm going to mention her as a suspect for supplying them with meds and see where it goes."

"Got it. By the way, Kariss's ticked at you again."

Tigo didn't need a reminder. "She doesn't handle reality very well."

"Is this about getting her to abandon her research in view of the shooting?"

"Some of it. Xavier Olvera is on a campaign to find his other child. When I told him there wasn't anything we could do without evidence, he went to Kariss. I strongly insisted she not get involved." Tigo paused. "Why would she keep a second child when the first one cramped her style?

My guess is she aborted it."

"Gilberto or Xavier will kill her if they get to her first." Ryan sighed. "Wouldn't blame either one of them."

"I'd sure like to know where she's hiding."

"Kariss's passion for protecting children will get her into trouble if she isn't careful."

"I'm afraid of the same thing." Tigo studied Ryan. "I don't dislike her. She's persistent, and because of her dogged approach to Cherished Doe we have answers. I give her credit for sticking to the case. And after the shooting, she displayed intelligence and control in a tough situation."

"But she's not a trained agent. She's only writing about a case."

"Don't remind me. The problem is she wants to tag along on all our investigations, and she knows that's impossible. She's already in a precarious situation with the Arroyos, and now she wants to be a Girl Scout and help Xavier. Linc's instructions state that she's to stay away from danger. My call. But it seems like we're walking a tightrope here. I thought she'd be safe at the hospital when Jo-Jack was shot, and look what happened."

"I agree. Bothers me too. I checked her file. She took a few risks while working as a news anchor. Good for law enforcement agencies, but a dangerous approach. Remember the drug deal that Linc closed? She not only reached out for public support but also convinced the ex-wife of a dealer to lead Linc to the stash."

"Think about it, Ryan. What if she attempts to help Xavier where he's living with his brother? The search involves the area of town where the Arroyos live and work. That's why I was so rough on her. She needs to climb into her fancy Jaguar and take a vacation — and I told her so."

"Every reporter I've met is all about getting the story."

"I thought novelists stayed holed up in their writing cave, drinking gallons of coffee, existing on fast food, and avoiding the world."

Ryan laughed. "None of that fits Kariss. She's never behaved like that."

"Right. My concern is she'll get too sure of herself. I heard her say she doesn't own a gun, and I'm assuming she wouldn't lie about it."

"Don't even go there. But if she pursues a CHL, there's nothing you can do."

"If I could find a way to stop her from that venture I'd have already done it." Tigo zipped down Highway 290. "Hadn't even thought she'd be stupid enough to arm herself so she could venture into the bad side of town. I can see having a gun in her home, but not in her purse."

"Just try to think like a fiction writer out for a story who might be afraid," Ryan said.

"Don't want to go there either. Would you call the hospital and check on Jo-Jack? I want to move him as soon as he's able to travel."

Ryan punched in the number, and Tigo listened.

"You've got to be kidding. Anyone see him leave?"

Tigo knew exactly what had happened. He palmed the steering wheel and waited for Ryan to end the call. "Our pal left the hospital?"

"Sure did. Sometime between nine-thirty and ten-fifteen. According to the police officer on duty, an orderly wheeled Jo-Jack out of his room and onto an elevator. Great. We make all the arrangements to save his neck, and he takes off. Worse yet, we never got a word out of him. I take that back. He told you a man by the name of 'Bat' was involved. Somebody with money."

"Another hole in this case. Jo-Jack won't last long on the streets. We lost Candy, and I'm afraid it's only a matter of time before we lose Jo-Jack too."

"Unless he has someplace to hide out and doesn't want us to know where."

"But who helped him leave? Maybe he's trying to cut a deal with the Arroyos by feeding us bad information while setting us up." Tigo needed a shot of espresso to give his brain a jolt.

"Do you think he's smart enough to put together a plan like that?"

"He's lived enough years on the streets to know how to make things happen. But needing a fix could make him careless."

Ryan shook his head. "Looks like we're in the market for another informant."

Kariss and Vicki exited the maternity boutique with purchases in hand. Kariss loved what they'd found. She loved being able to help her sister even more.

"You shouldn't have bought both outfits while I was in the ladies' room," Vicki said. "You don't play fair. Never have, as well as I can remember."

"They looked terrific on you. Your colors too." She took a quick look at Vicki's short, curly hair that matched her dark brown eye color. "Pregnancy has brought out your beauty." Reminding Kariss of how Vicki used to look BW — Before Wyatt.

"Thanks. I appreciate it. Hard to imagine myself big enough to wear them."

"We should start a scrapbook, label it 'before and after.' Videos too. Have you made a decision to move in with me?"

"I'm thinking about it. But here's my out. If I start to get on your nerves, then tell me and I'll move."

"We shared a room as kids, and we always got along."

"We didn't have a baby. That brings me to another point. If this works out between us, I'll be able to pay off all my bills, and then the baby and I can move to a two-bedroom apartment. It's important to have a home for my child, not mooch off my little sis."

"We'll see. I know how you feel, and I'd be the same way. Maybe you could live with me until you're able to buy a house. Wouldn't that be grand?"

Vicki shrugged. "Sounds like a dream, but it has a lovely ring to it. I'm hoping Wyatt agrees to child support without taking him to court. That will help."

Kariss bit her tongue to keep from voicing her opinion about the man who'd stolen Vicki's heart then broken it.

Vicki clutched Kariss's arm. "Maybe I'm on hormonal overload, but there's a woman who's followed us for the past two blocks.

Looks like she waited for us while we shopped in the last store."

A twinge of fear crept through Kariss. The Arroyos ranked at the top. "Would Wyatt have someone follow you?"

"You mean to check if I was seeing another man?"

"Exactly."

"It wouldn't surprise me. Or his live-in could have me followed. She might not appreciate her baby and mine being less than a year apart."

Kariss stopped in front of a coffee shop. "I need a latte. Do you mind ordering while I ask the lovely lady behind us what she's up to?"

Vicki's eyes widened. "This could be a coincidence."

Kariss turned to view the woman in question. Black hair . . . Hispanic. Lots of makeup. Rough looking. Maybe Kariss's bravado needed an adjustment. "Trust me, if Wyatt is behind this, we're going to end it right here."

"Then I'm not leaving you," Vicki said.

Great. Now what should she do?

Vicki walked to the woman behind them. "Hey, why is it every time I look around, you're there?"

The woman cursed. "Free country. I go

where I want."

Kariss caught sight of the tattoo on the woman's arm. Possibly a gang sign.

"Did Wyatt send you?" Vicki said.

"Vicki, I'll handle this," Kariss said.

The woman, whose mascara, smeared in the heat, made her look like a raccoon, peered at Kariss. "You have no idea who you two are messing with."

"Oh, really? Want to enlighten us? Better yet, who's paying you to tail us?"

But Kariss did have an idea. Pulling out her phone, she pressed in 9-1 while snapping the woman's picture. The woman grabbed for Kariss's phone, then pushed her onto the sidewalk when Kariss wouldn't let it go and raced away.

"Are you all right?" Vicki's frantic voice stopped Kariss from rising to her feet and chasing the woman.

"I'm good, and I still have my phone."

"Too late for 9-1-1." Vicki's voice trembled.

"Doesn't matter. I got her pic."

CHAPTER 21

Tigo and Ryan drove through a sleazy section of town. Most Houston residents had no idea such degradation existed in their own city. Drugs, prostitution, gun smuggling, human trafficking — name it and it was there along with the smell of greed and desperation. Survival meant gang membership, and the average lifespan for males ranged in the mid-twenties.

"I told my sister what was going on in our city, but she didn't believe me," Ryan said.

"Did you offer a drive-through? Let her see gangs in action?"

"Yeah, but she declined after my wife filled her in on a few of my stories. But I don't tell my wife everything, or she wouldn't let me out of the house in the morning."

"Another reason why I'm not married. Not so sure I could put a woman through my method of solving crimes."

They stopped at a traffic light. Graffiti

covered buildings on both sides. A young black woman walked past, her short, tight skirt revealing every inch of her body from the waist down. A skinny dog crossed the street in front of them.

"I use to think I held the record for slipping in and out of tight spots unscathed," Ryan said. "Then you came on board, and now my adventures look like a weenie's attempt."

"You have a family, and I'm married to risks."

Ryan nodded. "My family means everything to me. My job is to keep their world safe, which means taking risks. Tigo, someday you're going to fall hard, and when it happens, you'll see life from a different perspective."

"So you think I'll step down from my title as FBI's daredevil?"

"No. You'll be worse. It's all about the love of family. That's why I have no problem going deeper into the gangs to end the crime."

"We're a team. Know what? Someday I'd like to train other agents at Quantico. Take what I've learned and show them how to stay alive and bring in bad guys."

"You'd be good. I've seen you work with new agents."

The light changed, and Tigo drove

through, his eyes taking in everything that moved. He wondered if a woman would ever be his motivation instead of his panoramic, save-the-world syndrome. This part of his life and his ill mother were the reasons why he remained single.

"I've been meaning to ask. How's your mother?"

How much did he say? Ryan and Linc were his closest friends, and even Linc didn't know how serious her condition was. "She has days, possibly hours, left."

"Why didn't you tell me?"

"Why burden you with my problems?"

Ryan let out a heavy sigh. "We're friends, and that means we aren't too macho to talk about the junk in our lives. Don't ignore the stats. We all need to vent the stuff that might interfere with our jobs . . . or our judgment."

"Yes, Pops. I'll keep your advice in mind." Tigo understood Ryan's lecture. "Hey, Mom's physical condition has made me jumpy . . . irritable for a long time. I apologize for allowing it to step between what we do. She was a wonderful mother, raised me single-handedly. Her wisdom stopped me from ruining my life."

"How's that?"

Tigo rubbed his chin, understanding Ryan

was being a textbook-perfect partner. "While in high school, I started running with the wrong crowd. Things got worse. I was the guy in charge. Got my rear into trouble too many times. I even looked at getting involved in a gang. Once, while sitting in jail and waiting for her to bail me out, she chose to visit instead. Oh, man, she lectured me for two hours then told me to rot because she refused to post bail. I walked out of there five days later and changed my ways."

Ryan laughed. "Now I know why you're able to think like a bad guy. What'd she tell you?"

"I'll tell you during our next therapy session." His cell was ringing, and he looked at the caller's name. "I wonder what kind of mess she's gotten herself into this time?"

"Must be Kariss."

Tigo chuckled and turned his attention to the call. "What's going on?"

"Somebody's been tailing me and my sister at the Galleria."

"Are you sure?"

"Positive. I confronted the woman, and she threatened me. Pushed me down. She didn't fit the type of woman here. Dressed in black. Nasty looking."

His internal alarms sounded. "Kariss, are

you hurt?"

"I'm fine."

He needed to see her to be sure. Hadn't she been through enough? "Did she say anything?"

"Told me I didn't know who I was messing with. Wanted my phone in a bad way. I think she thought I was trying to call 9-1-1."

"Were you?"

"Uh-huh. And taking her pic. Which I got, along with fingerprints."

"Good job. Are you heading back to the office?"

"I have a few errands to run. I could be there around four-thirty."

"Wait for me there. We need to talk. I don't like this, Kariss. The Arroyos might be on to you."

"The woman could have been someone my ex-brother-in-law hired. My sister is having a few problems with him."

"Okay. Be safe. I'll see you later, and we'll talk about it." He slipped the phone back into his pocket. "Sure hope that was nothing. She caught a woman following her and her sister at the Galleria. But our girl snapped a pic."

"Tigo, Kariss is under your skin."

"Right. Like a splinter."

"Keep telling yourself she isn't wiggling into your heart, and you might believe it."

"You're way off base, Ryan." If and when he was ever interested in a woman, she wouldn't be an over-anxious writer who couldn't stay out of trouble. "We're almost to Hershey's little establishment."

"Go ahead. Change the subject. I'll play. I've been thinking about his daughter. How did she manage to rise above the culture?"

Tigo eased to a stop in front of a building converted from a gas station to a gun shop. Both businesses sold fuel. Windows were boarded, but the Discount Guns sign above the door indicated what went on inside. "I think his daughter was smart enough to see she had no future here. Instead of capitalizing on what area of crime she wanted to earn her living with, she decided to get out."

"Any validity there?"

"Yeah. She's the real deal. Squeaky clean. She has a younger brother who's doing time for armed robbery. Another victim of the whole subculture thing. Before his incarceration, she paid for rehab and counseling and brought him to her part of town. But nothing worked. His DNA spells trouble. When Hershey's daughter isn't working with children at MD Anderson, she's volunteering with kids at her church."

"Someone influenced her."

"A priest. Okay, let's go see how our man feels about his daughter."

The two men exited the car and walked to the gun shop, their sidearms evident in their waistbands. A couple of black men stood outside. No doubt there to defend Hershey's honor. Ryan pressed the call button to release the door lock. When it opened, they stepped into a shadowy area filled with every type of weapon.

"Put your guns on the counter or both of you are dead men. Now."

CHAPTER 22

"Flip on the lights, Hershey," Tigo said. "This is your friendly FBI, and we need to talk. Unless you'd rather we haul you in for questioning." He saw the man standing near the rear entrance. No doubt considering whether to escape or face the agents.

Lights flickered. Hershey took slow steps toward them and laid a rifle across the counter. He couldn't be over fifty-five, but he looked twenty years older. Drugs and hard living had sliced into his face. "What can I do for you? My permits are up to date."

"We're looking for who might be supplying the Arroyos," Tigo said. "Thought you could help us."

"I run a legit business here. You know that."

"Straw men have ways of covering their tracks."

"I wouldn't know anything about that."

"Right." Tigo glanced around the shop to make sure they were alone. "The problem is several shipments of AK-47s into Mexico supposedly came from this gun shop. Got the serial numbers if you'd like to see them."

"Don't know a thing about it. What my customers do with the guns they buy here is none of my business. Now if you'll leave, I have things to do."

Ryan walked around the shop, examining hand guns. "Where's the prices on these?"

"I have 'em in my head."

"I bet that makes bookkeeping a pain."

"I'm a smart man. I have good records. You can check 'em out with a subpoena."

"I think I will." Ryan picked up a 9mm. "Do your customers use their names?"

Hershey scowled. "What do you think? I'd be shut down if I didn't follow the law."

Tigo leaned on the display case. He held more than one ace with Hershey. "I talked to your daughter the other day."

His left eye twitched. "I don't have a daughter."

"Hershey, we know better. Does Cheeky?"

His eyes hardened. "What does my daughter have to do with anything?"

"Looks like the hospital where she works has a problem with someone stealing pain meds."

"My girl doesn't mess with drugs. She doesn't do them or deal them."

"We're thinking she's involved." Tigo refused to release the pressure. "She could route those drugs right through her daddy's gun shop. With the gang activity lately, the Arroyos could use some pain meds."

"Get out of here. Don't be involving my daughter in something illegal. When she left here, she left all of it behind."

"When's the last time you saw her?" Tigo said.

"Seventeen years ago. She thinks she's better than me 'cause she got herself some education. Maybe that's good. Keeps her out of this part of town."

"Oh, does it?" Tigo caught Ryan's eye. "That's not what we heard. Is it?"

"Nope," Ryan said. "Got the warrant for her arrest on my desk."

"What do you want? I have no idea where the Arroyos are getting their guns. Mine are accounted for, and I don't know a thing about missing drugs at any hospital."

Tigo shook his head. "I'd hate to mention her as a person of interest considering who her father is. Makes her look guilty."

Hershey nearly came across the display case. "Keep my daughter out of this."

"Then give us the information we need."

Tigo wanted Cheeky stopped, and he didn't care about the cost.

Hershey's face reddened. "I don't know nothing."

Tigo pressed his lips together and bore his gaze deep into the man's eyes. "Names, Hershey. We'll make sure your daughter's not involved in the drug investigation."

"You mess with Cheeky and you lose your head."

"That's your final word? Think about your daughter. You know . . . we could make this worth your while."

"Get out of my business and leave me alone."

"We haven't mentioned the units you're building to transport drugs and weapons. Guess we can handle that when we return with a search warrant."

Tigo nodded at Ryan, and they walked to the door. *Four, three, two, one.* Tigo touched the door.

"Okay. Okay. But how are you going to explain to those outside that I'm not cooperating?"

"We'll handle it," Tigo said.

Hershey's jaw clenched. "Word is one of yours is on the Arroyos' list."

"What for?"

"Killing three of them."

228

Those bullets had Tigo's name on them. "Then they need to be afraid, don't they?"

"Since when are any of them afraid of cops or the FBI? Right now they're edgy. Looking for revenge. And since someone is letting you guys know when transports are headed across the border, they're losing money."

"Who's Bat?"

Hershey glared into Tigo's eyes. "I've heard the name. Never met him."

"Keep your ears open. We have reason to believe he's supplying guns to the Arroyos. I'm also looking for the woman who's in charge of the mules."

Not a muscle moved on Hershey's dark face.

"Think about helping us, and I'll get back to you. Which is worse? The FBI knowing about your daughter, or the Arroyos?" Tigo nodded and left the gun shop. The two men outside had multiplied to four.

"Any of you know about a triple homicide on the northeast side two nights ago?" One took a step closer, and Tigo drew his weapon.

"Gang style." Ryan pulled his Glock. "Any of you vouch for Hershey?"

They were ready for a fight.

"If you do, phone HPD. There's a reward,"

Ryan said.

One of the men spit a string of expletives. A few minutes later, they were driving out of the hot zone.

"I need to go undercover," Tigo said. "The situation is getting worse. How long before gang warfare here looks like Mexico?"

"I'm ready when you are."

"It's all I can think about. Tough call when my mother's dying."

"What would she have you do?"

Tigo smiled. "You two talking? She'd have me bring in those killers and help stop the flow of drugs, guns, and ammo making its way across the border."

"What's your new disguise?"

"Not sure yet. Want to be my bodyguard?"

"Sure. I've missed it."

Tigo laughed. "Now to get the word out — and the paper trail."

"When can we get started? Or should I ask what SAC Abrams has to say about it?"

"I have to convince him. He wants me to postpone the idea. With three of the Arroyos dead, the gang will be looking for one of us to infiltrate. Even posing as a buyer is dangerous, but I'm willing to take the risk."

CHAPTER 23

"Xavier, your wife probably lied to you about being pregnant. I'm sorry, but it's something for you to consider." Kariss had agreed to meet him at a Fiesta store inside the loop on the southeast side of town. She and Xavier sat in her car while shoppers pushed carts full of bagged groceries to their vehicles. She needed to be honest, even as blunt as Tigo.

"From what I've been told, she did things while living here . . . stole from people . . . had boyfriends." He blinked back his emotion.

Kariss reached for tissues and handed him one.

Xavier cleared his throat. "Although the police, FBI, and Gilberto think a personal search is hopeless, I believe I have a child and he or she is alive." He shrugged. "I'd be a fool not to realize the child might not belong to me. But I can't let it stop my search."

Kariss attempted to separate her feelings from the truth. "If a baby exists, Delores might have sold or abandoned it like she did Benita. I know that's difficult, but we need to be honest and look at the whole picture, Xavier. The authorities will have to find Delores before you learn the truth about your family."

"They don't know where to look."

"And you do? I want to see you united with your child and justice served, but I have no idea how I can help."

"Why were you at the FBI when Gilberto and I came to see the agents?"

She didn't want to tell him about her book project, have him think she was using his tragedy to entertain readers. He'd think she was heartless and cruel when she wanted readers to understand the responsibility of protecting their children. She'd save the topic for another time. "I'm a writer, and I've been spending time at the FBI learning more about their procedures."

"Are you writing about Benita?" The soft tone of his voice urged her on.

"Would that upset you? If it does, I won't write a word." And she meant it. "I didn't know when would be the proper time to ask you."

He settled back onto the seat. Moments ticked by. "I see you care about what happened to Benita. It's fine. I don't read English, but I'd like to know what you say."

"Of course."

"I'm sure you've learned much about the FBI."

"Very little."

"I see. What I want to say is nothing's impossible. I've begun my search for Delores by looking for our old friends. Some still live in the Pine Grove Apartments, but they're afraid to say anything to reporters or police. Many are here illegally. I've talked to one family, and his wife claims Delores stayed at our apartment around two months after I left. She was pregnant when she moved out. She packed up her things and left during the night, even leaving furniture behind. The woman heard Delores say she'd never go back to Mexico. She planned her future after she let Benita die. Or maybe before. Delores is smart."

"She must have felt secure in not getting caught." Kariss chose to ride the conversation, certain she could do nothing to bring Xavier comfort.

"I think so too. I keep asking myself if she still felt safe after the TV show. Would she go to San Antonio or Austin or maybe to a border town where she could slip back into Mexico if she feared arrest?

"At times I think I could kill her with my bare hands." The lines in his forehead read of despair. "I know. Neither of us has answers."

"Any other leads?"

"I'm meeting with a man who lived in the building behind us. He's . . ." Xavier scratched his head. "He spent time in jail."

"For what?"

"Drugs. Fighting. Delores liked him. He told me about her wanting to . . . be with him."

Xavier didn't need to say more.

"Are you afraid of him?"

"No. I don't have anything he wants, and I don't need money bad enough to break the law. We come from the same town in Mexico. Grew up together."

"You've come closer to finding out where she is than the authorities."

"I'm one of these people. They trust me. I understand their fear of the law. From here, I'm going to see Delores's grandmother who lives in a nursing home. But her mind is bad. I hope she might say something that can help me."

"I don't understand why you wanted to meet with me."

"I need everything the FBI, the police, and the Texas Rangers have in their files about Benita."

The case wasn't closed, but it had been a cold case. "I don't know if the information is public since the case was reopened. Let me make a call to find out."

Kariss spent a few minutes talking to Hillary. Asking Tigo about the case would only anger him, and she'd already irritated him once today. When the call ended, complete with Kariss agreeing to look at another one of Hillary's story ideas, she concentrated on Xavier. "Good news. As Benita's father, you can file a Freedom of Information Act request. This will be reviewed by the FBI's legal department to determine what can be released to you, based on the privacy laws. Statements made from living persons may not be released. The agent I spoke to suggested going to the FBI website."

"But the statements made by living people would be the ones I'd need to find Delores and my child." Desperation was woven into his words.

"Possibly. But that's the law. You could search through their website for more information."

"The last time I looked, it wasn't in Spanish." He stared out the passenger window for several seconds. "No one believes my child is alive. They pity me instead of offering encouragement. 'Go back to Mexico. Start your life over.' "

"I'm sorry. I really am. All I can do is point you in the direction of the law. I'd like to help, but what can I do?"

"Please. My stay in this country is limited. At any time, I can be escorted across the border. I must work night and day, and I can't do it alone. I beg of you."

Kariss remembered the years she'd wondered about Cherished Doe's identity. That passion had followed her to the FBI and persuaded them to reopen the case. She recalled the hope after the press conference, and the swirling of rekindled emotion during the viewing of Univision's program. But the thought of investigating anything on this side of town brought a swirl of acid through her stomach. The raw memories about the Arroyos who wanted her dead couldn't be willed away. Yet how could she abandon Benita's little brother or sister?

"I'll do my best. I can't make any promises."

Kariss drove back to the FBI office to talk to Tigo about the woman who'd assaulted her when she was with Vicki earlier. She'd been careful not to touch the phone where the woman's fingerprints were present.

Inside, Tigo sat at his desk. His mood looked to be friendlier. She reached inside her purse and gave him a twenty-five-dollar Starbucks gift card.

"Another peace offering," she said.

He glanced up with a half smile. "I can't take this. Looks like I'm being bribed."

"Would I attempt to bribe a member of the FBI?"

"I'm a pretty good judge of character, and you look guilty."

She placed the card in front of him. "Call it appreciation. I know I'm a real pain, and my enthusiasm gets in the way of common sense."

He settled back in his chair. "I'm rough for a reason. I hope you'll consider a vacation until this is over. You're getting in too deep."

The sincerity in his eyes touched her, and if she allowed logic to make its way from her head to her actions, she'd book a flight out to anywhere. But she'd agreed to help Xavier. "I'll think about it." She reached inside her purse and carefully pulled out her cell. "I'm hoping this provides another lead."

He had a plastic bag on his desk, and she

dropped her cell into it. "Ready to take a walk?"

"Yes. I have some bad news. The pic I took? Well, all I got was her hand."

"That's not so bad. We have fingerprints, and the pic might also give us a clue to her identity."

She sighed. "Good. Amateur detective work is not my forte."

"Glad you understand your professional expertise. What does your sister know?"

"Nothing. She thinks the woman was someone her ex-husband paid to follow her."

His curious look spurred her on.

"Her ex-husband paid her a few visits after moving in with his live-in, and now Vicki's pregnant. His live-in recently gave birth to a child of his as well, which makes the situation very messy."

"I get it." He stood and gestured toward the door. "Let's see if we can ID this woman."

"I'm getting to be a pro at this."

"I'd rather think this is the last time you give information to the facial recognition team."

"Believe me. I hope this woman is linked to my ex-brother-in-law. What she said today could apply to Vicki or me."

The woman's fingerprints were not in the system. Neither did the likeness Kariss gave to the FBI artist reveal a wanted face. Neither did the black rose tattoo on her arm offer any clues to her identity.

A vacation sounded increasingly appealing to Kariss.

"Tell me about this ex-brother-in-law."

She lifted a brow. "Are you going to pay him a visit?"

He laughed. "Do you ever step outside your world of story?"

"This is different. It's my story. Wyatt Phillips is a commercial real estate broker and has actually weathered the recession."

"Where is his office?" Tigo picked up his pen.

"West side, off the Katy Freeway." She pulled out Wyatt's card that he'd given her a long time ago when he wanted her to meet him for lunch. Not sure why she'd kept it.

"Too late to catch up with him today, but I'll introduce myself to him on Monday."

"Is following someone illegal?"

"No. But paying someone to assault another is."

Weary from the stress of the week, Kariss entered her condo, tossed her keys onto the counter, and headed straight to her bedroom, peeling off her clothes as she went. Maybe she should time how long it took her to perform the task when she was so exhausted.

Why am I thinking about this?

She needed to work on her book. But nothing lofty would happen tonight. She didn't have the energy to accomplish anything.

Kariss rolled back the pink-and-white comforter on her bed. This would be a "Special K for dinner and watch a love story on TV" night before she drifted off to sleep.

Wait . . . she needed to check email. She made the trek back to the kitchen for her cereal and to grab her computer from the kitchen table. The agent she'd queried should have responded. With a deep breath, she crawled into bed, the coolness of the sheets lulling her into utopia. Closing her eyes, she tasted the first bite of Special K with pecans. Skim milk of course. She might have to dive into the cookies-and-cream ice cream in the freezer. But first things first.

Her in-box contained the normal spam and fan email. So nice to be loved and appreciated.

There it was. Kariss's heart pounded, and she clicked on the message.

A computer-generated response.

Dear Writer,

Thank you for your interest in Sabrina Literary Group. We are currently accepting email queries only for adult fiction. No fantasy, sci-fi, or speculative-fiction type projects. Do not send attachments or phone our offices.

For consideration by our literary team, include the following in a one-page query: genre and targeted audience, your platform, brief bio, amount of funds available for publicity and promotion, and a three-sentence summary of your book's topic.

If we are interested in your writing project, we will request a completed manuscript for our review.

Allow three months for our response.

Sincerely,
Sabrina Literary Group

Kariss reread the message. Were they clueless as to Kariss Walker's status in the publishing world? And since when did the amount of publicity and promotion funds have a thing to do with a literary agency? She reached for the phone to call. No. Why would she want to embarrass them? Hitting Reply, she typed a brief email indicating who she was and her status on the *Times* bestsellers list.

Within a few minutes, she received the same computer-generated response. What a technologically deficient way to conduct business. She should toss her laptop into the gulf and flip hamburgers for the rest of her life.

Her mother's words marched across her mind. *Pride cometh before a fall.* Had her mother prayed Kariss's career in secular writing would fail? No . . . her mother wouldn't do such a thing.

But her father might.

CHAPTER 24

Saturday morning, Kariss entered the gun shop and immediately captured the attention of an older man behind the display case. The business had been there about a year, and it was clean and impressive. Not at all what she expected — no bald, tattooed fellow wearing a leather vest. The attendant had a full head of white hair and a neatly trimmed beard. Of course, when she thought about it, her dad and brothers were into hunting, and they looked normal.

Working with Tigo had her profiling too many people. She needed to keep her judgment in check, beginning now.

Taking a deep breath, she walked to the counter. "I need to buy a handgun."

"Then you're at the right place." He smiled, revealing perfectly white teeth. "What did you have in mind?"

She glanced around at the shapes and sizes of every firearm imaginable. "I have no idea. Something that's easy to shoot."

"For yourself?"

"Yes. I've never bought a gun before."

"That's why I'm here." He reminded her of a pastor during her teen years. This experience would be a great addition to a book. "I'll show you a few and let you hold them while I explain their features."

"Sounds good." Relief eased her.

He gestured toward the display case. With a smile, he removed a small gun and placed it in her hand. The cold metal signified the possibility of taking another person's life, a way to protect herself or those she loved. The implications caused her to nearly vomit. Her fiction mind sped into overdrive. As a teen, she'd steered away from Dad's rifles, the mere thought shaking her to her toes. So many times since she worked at Channel 5 she'd considered purchasing a handgun and taking the classes to use one properly.

"No need to tremble," the man said. "It's not loaded." His warm blue eyes didn't mock her. "This is a .38."

A .38? In her research, she'd read and written about these. But she hadn't held one. "Thanks. I'm a little nervous."

"No need. Education is the key here."

She looked and listened and held several

handguns until she made her decision, a 9mm semi-automatic Taurus. The name made her feel comfortable, like she was buying a car.

At the counter, she pulled out her credit card.

"I need a little information first," he said, placing a form in front of her. "This needs to be completed before you can make your purchase. Your name, address, and driver's license number will do. And I'll need to make a copy of your Texas driver's license."

"So you need to run a check on me?" Her pulse raced ahead. Would Tigo find out?

"Yes. This goes straight to the Bureau of Alcohol, Tobacco, Firearms, and Explosives. Only takes a minute."

She rubbed the lower part of her back. Of course people couldn't walk into a shop and purchase a gun without completing paperwork.

"Is this a problem?" he said.

"No, sir." She fumbled through her purse for her license. This purchase was to ensure she didn't end up sprawled out on a slab of concrete via one of the Arroyos. Tigo had asked if she owned a gun, and she'd responded negatively. But with all that had happened, she wanted to contemplate the value of telling him.

A few minutes later, the man looked up. "Okay, we're set. Will the gun be stored at your home?"

"Not exactly. I want to keep it in my purse."

"Then you'll need a concealed handgun license."

"Would you explain this to me?"

"A concealed handgun license is commonly called a CHL. If you're planning to keep this on you, then there are classes and testing to complete first. It's a comprehensive procedure. I have the qualifications right here." He reached for a piece of paper and handed it to her.

Kariss glanced up at him and nodded before reading the list of qualifications.

- Be 21 years old. Members and former members of the armed forces must be 18.
- Have a clean criminal history, including military service and recent juvenile records.
- Not be under a protective order.
- Not be chemically dependent.
- Not be of unsound mind.
- Not be delinquent in paying fines, fees, child support, etc.
- Be eligible to purchase a handgun by

completing the NICS check — National Instant Criminal Background Check.

- Complete required training.

Kariss thought Tigo might have issue with the "unsound mind" clause.

At the bottom of the paper were several websites. She'd need to check these out, possibly at the library in case Tigo ran a check on her computer. She didn't know how close an eye he was keeping on her, but he didn't need to know everything she did.

She scanned the list one more time and realized she needed more information about the mandatory class. "What's the required training?"

"The course requires ten to fifteen hours and includes a written examination and a shooting practical."

This was exactly what she'd been hoping for. "What goes on in the workshop portion?"

"Speakers will give you specific instructions and tell stories of their experiences. Then you take a test. Most people enjoy it."

Enjoy it? She'd consider it more research. "Okay. I can handle a workshop and instructions on how to shoot. Is there a cost for the class?"

"Yes. Depends on where you go. I can make a couple of recommendations."

"Good. Then I get my CHL when I pass the tests?"

"Not quite. You must pass both tests with a score of 70 percent or better before you make application. The form is extensive and there's a $150 fee."

"When's the next class?"

"There's one for the written portion next Saturday."

That wasn't bad. "How long does the entire procedure take?"

"If there are no problems, approximately sixty days."

She could be dead by the time she was approved to carry her gun. Was it worth it? She glanced at the 9mm on the counter. A single woman needed to be able to protect herself. That was why she'd taken the self-defense course.

"Is there a way to speed up the process?"

"Not that I know of. The state has laws." He eyed her strangely. "Miss, are you afraid? If you're fearful for your life, I strongly suggest you contact the police."

"Oh, not at all," Kariss replied, sensing his comment fell under a stipulation that might disqualify her from the license. "This is more than what I expected, but safety and marksmanship make sense. How do I sign up?"

Saturday morning, while sitting at his mother's side, Tigo phoned a friend — a prosthetic disguise specialist who'd assisted Tigo the last time he and Ryan had gone undercover. Derek Kyowski was one of the best in the business, and he approached his job like a kid to candy.

Previously, Tigo had used blue contacts, a mustache, and false teeth to achieve his undercover work — and end a drug ring. This time, he needed a facial mask. The enemies he'd made over a year ago still stalked the area of town where he needed to infiltrate the Arroyos.

"Morning, Derek. This is Tigo. I need a facelift."

Derek laughed. "You just made my day. What's the look you're after?"

Tigo glanced around his mother's room where sunlight filtered through the blinds and onto the bed. Peaceful. So against the world he planned to enter. If she were coherent, she'd be listening to every word. He liked to think she still was.

"Gray hair, wiry beard, glasses. I'm think-ing acne scars on the cheeks or something along those lines."

"I can do that. Make a new man out of you. Or rather an old one."

"That's what I need."

"Wanna come in today?"

"On a Saturday?"

"I haven't heard any Tigo stories for a while."

"I could bore you with a few. All cold cases of course."

"I'm writing a book, you know."

Not another one. "Are you still at the same place?"

"I am. Wife is helping out with a new grandbaby, and I could use the company. Why not come on over after lunch? That will give me some time to pull together ideas."

"I'll be there about one-thirty."

Tigo paced the floor, feeling his grin spread until he laughed aloud. When Derek had helped him with a disguise in the past, he'd fooled Linc and Ryan. Imagine the fun he could have with Kariss.

He leaned over the bed and planted a kiss on his mother's forehead. "When I get back, I'll read to you from your favorite Elizabeth Barrett Browning book. Promise."

Promptly at one-thirty, Tigo arrived at Derek's office. An appointment with the widely acclaimed prosthetic specialist was like taking a field trip to a museum — totally fascinating. Derek had a scrapbook of makeup and prosthetic disguises for clients to choose from, along with plenty of pics of those he'd helped. At least July wasn't as busy as other times of the year, like Halloween.

Derek escorted Tigo into his office, and the two men examined the various effects achieved from hair, beard, and glasses.

"Remember the different looks of Jennifer Garner in *Alias?*" Derek pulled up a website that showed the many faces of the actress during the TV run. "Want to go blonde or redhead instead of gray?"

"Maybe balding. I need to look wealthy, mean, and tough."

Derek chuckled. "Figured that." Turning his attention back to the computer, he brought up another site and pointed to four photos. "This one has thinning gray hair, wiry brows, black-rimmed glasses, and facial scars like you suggested. The second one has less hair and a double chin. You could use light makeup and blue contacts on that one. The third changes your ethnicity to more of a Jamaican." He grinned. "We'd need to darken the hands on this one. The last one is an alternate of the first, but I'd add a larger nose and ears."

Tigo studied each one, considering the role needed as a weapon's buyer. "I like the first one, but add the double chin. Gives me a greedy look. I'll team it with an expensive suit."

"Are you soloing this one, or does Ryan need my expertise?"

"I'll have him give you a call. He worked with me last time, and we nearly got our rears kicked."

"When don't you?" Derek settled back in his chair. "Are you seeing anyone?"

"Too busy." Tigo hoped this wasn't about Derek's niece again. "Couldn't ask any woman to put up with my schedule."

"The danger aspect might not be too appealing either. Just thought I'd check. My niece just ended a relationship. But she's a bit high-maintenance."

Kariss Walker was enough trouble without adding another. "If I ever decide to look, it would have to be with a woman who'd put up with my job — and my independence."

"Got it. Now I'm ready for a few stories, fully embellished to Hollywood proportions."

CHAPTER 25

Kariss held her breath as Vicki led up to breaking the news about her pregnancy to their parents. They didn't like Wyatt any more than Kariss did, but their remarks in the past had been less . . . colorful. They were about to learn their next grandchild would inherit some of their ex-son-in-law's genes. That tidbit would sour their stomachs — at Dad's favorite home-style cooking restaurant.

". . . I have exciting news." Vicki beamed, but Kariss refused to go there. "I'm pregnant. You're going to be a Pawpaw and Grammy again."

Dad set his fork beside his plate and stared at the mashed potatoes and fried fish. He met Vicki's gaze and offered a tight smile. Real tight. "I can tell this is something you want."

"Very much so."

"Do I dare ask the father?"

Kariss breathed the closest thing to a prayer she knew.

"Dad," Vicki said. "It's Wyatt's child."

"Figures. Not sure why he brings his new girlfriend and baby to our church. I know we're all sinners, but I don't think he's repented of what he's done to God or you. Does he know?"

"Yes."

Dad played with his napkin. "Those babies will be less than a year apart."

Mom's face was ashen, and she touched Dad's hand. "Take it easy. Vicki knows what he's done."

"Why did you tell him?" Bitterness seemed to crawl from Dad's voice.

Whoa. Kariss hadn't expected that response.

Vicki flashed a helpless look at Kariss, then back to Dad. "I understand your disappointment, but he is the father. I'll make sure Wyatt provides financial support, even if it takes a few trips to court. If he refuses to be a father, then my baby is better off." She lifted her chin, but her lips quivered.

Vicki's gumption brought a smile to Kariss. Her sister could do this.

Dad slowly nodded. "That's all we can ask, sugar. We're here to help you and our grandbaby. You made a mistake with Wyatt."

He hesitated. "Make that two. Maybe he'll 'fess up to being a man. But I doubt it." He paused again, which was his manner of thinking through whatever he had to say. "I'm being blunt when you've already been hurt by him too many times to list. And . . . you don't need any more of my lecturing. So let me say your mother and I will be praying for you and this baby. I believe I speak for the entire family." He picked up his glass of iced tea and toasted her. "You're my little girl, and I'd still like the opportunity to break Wyatt's nose."

Kariss hid a grin. Good old Dad, the man who made sure he was cleaning his rifle when boyfriends came calling. Another reason why she'd shied away from weapons.

Vicki let out a sigh and whispered a thank-you.

"Would you like to move back home?" their mother said. "Goodness knows our house is big enough, and the rural area is a great place for a little one to grow up."

"You're sweet, and I appreciate the invitation. Don't know what I'd do without you," Vicki said. "Kariss made the same offer, and I think I'm going to take her up on it."

"Yeah." Kariss lifted her iced tea for another toast. "My three-thousand-square-feet condo needs company."

"Families stick together." Dad picked up his fork. "Kariss, let's talk about where your life is going without God. Your mother and I . . ."

Kariss drove home on I-45 North from Texas City after filling her tummy with food and her heart with laughter. Dad's wishes about her spirituality were a common additive to any family event, and she'd grown used to it, expected it. And she'd never disrespect him by not giving him eye contact. Her soul was another matter. The God thing didn't work for her . . . hadn't for years. Maybe when she reached their age, faith would make sense. She'd grown up memorizing Scripture, going to church camp, and then youth group. But none of those practices made sense to her after the fire.

She wished her siblings lived closer to each other. A family reunion was coming up the end of August, and the date couldn't come fast enough. No matter what disagreements or misunderstandings a family of her size experienced, they loved each other, and that bond helped them work out any problems.

She found her favorite radio station and listened to smooth jazz while her car whizzed past the others. At this rate, she'd get a speeding ticket and ruin a perfectly good day. She eased on the brakes and pulled into the right-hand lane. The traffic thickened with those returning from Galveston to Houston, forcing her to slow down. She remembered her first encounter with Tigo and laughed aloud. Then she sobered. He had a daredevil side. He'd earned a reputation for getting a job done because of his courage and determination. She'd seen glimpses of it. Certainly a man who'd earned her respect and admiration.

Maybe more, if she allowed her heart to take a dive.

A black pickup followed close behind her. She sped up a little, and it stayed on her bumper. Now what was that about? She moved into another lane, and the truck swerved over with her.

Kariss glanced at her rearview mirror. Two men of Hispanic descent occupied the truck. She'd never been prejudiced, but the events of late had made her jumpy. She changed lanes again. The truck followed.

Her full stomach moved to her throat.

Don't overreact. Think. Use your head.

This wasn't a plotline in a book, but reality. And she'd seen enough blood in real life to know this had dangerous potential.

But she wasn't about to go down without a fight.

Kariss glanced into the mirror again and swallowed hard. The pickup was only inches from her bumper. Did he have his window down so he could shoot at her?

She trembled . . . *Stop it, Kariss. Think like Tigo. Then do it.*

She swerved back into the right lane and pressed her foot on the gas. She'd bought the Jaguar for its performance. Now was the test. The car in front of her loomed closer. She swung into the left lane and back into the right with the black truck imitating every turn of her wheels.

The driver could be looking for some Sunday afternoon fun — see who could outrun the fancy sports car. They could be drunk or high. Or their forearms and bald heads might be tattooed with gang signs and one of their names might be Froggie Diego.

Tigo had become her hero in more ways than one. She'd handle this situation like a pro.

Weaving in and out of traffic at eighty miles per hour, she nearly clipped a Lexus, then another truck. She looked for an exit ramp. Where were the cops when she needed them? She reached for her phone on the passenger side to punch in 9-1-1. But that required her to look at her phone. If she didn't pay attention to the road, she'd lose control of her car and kill herself and someone else.

The traffic slowed and forced her speed to a crawl. Up ahead, vehicles were at a standstill. What now? She cut off a car on her right to get into that lane. The truck couldn't get over, and she stole a moment to take a breath. An embankment separated I-45 from a feeder road. Tigo and her brothers wouldn't think twice about this. She crossed over the shoulder and down toward the feeder.

The Jaguar bumped over the rough terrain and to the road. She tore her gaze from the jarring ride to her phone and pressed in 9-1-1, then held the phone against her shoulder with her head. A crack met her ears. A bullet had shattered the rear window and then ripped into the windshield, not two feet from her head. She gasped. Yesterday's gun purchase lay in her panty drawer at home.

"9-1-1. What is your emergency?"

"Help me. A truck is chasing me, and the driver just fired a shot at me."

"Where is your emergency?"

"I just jumped I-45 to a feeder road near Dickinson." Kariss slammed onto her brakes as she neared a stop sign. The truck had followed her. "He's behind me, and I'm going to run a stop sign."

"We're sending help." The calm voice did little to settle her nerves.

Another bullet cracked the windshield on the passenger side.

"Someone is trying to kill me!"

"We have police cars heading your way from Dickinson. One is in your vicinity."

"The truck's gaining speed." She pressed on the accelerator, ready to barrel through a farmer's fence if it meant getting out of the shooter's firing range.

"Do you need medical attention?"

"Not yet."

"Stay on the line until it's safe to pull over and help has arrived. What's your name?"

"Kariss . . . Kariss Walker."

"Do you know who's following you?"

"No."

"Keep talking, Kariss."

"I hear the sirens."

"Good. Where is the truck now?"

Cars ahead were stopped on both sides of the shoulder, and she feared the traffic light ahead might turn red. She took another glance at the rearview mirror. "It's gaining speed. Maybe —" She gulped for air.

"Maybe they'll hear the sirens and leave me alone."

She sailed through a green traffic light at the intersection where a police car approached from the right side, forcing other vehicles aside. The truck pursuing her whipped under the bridge in a U-turn and headed back south on I-45.

Kariss pulled over onto the right shoulder, noting her white knuckles seemingly attached to the steering wheel.

"Kariss, are you all right?" the 9-1-1 dispatcher said.

"I'm stopped now. I think some police are after the truck."

"Take a few deep breaths. I'm right here until the police arrive."

"Okay . . . thanks."

The phone slipped from her shoulder. How would she explain this to Tigo?

CHAPTER 26

Monday morning, Tigo parked his car in the parking space allotted for guests of Phillips Commercial Realty Company. He hadn't decided his real motive for talking to the owner, except to narrow down who'd followed Kariss and her sister the previous Friday.

Tigo's to-do list had grown to mammoth proportions, and he intended to make this call short and to the point. Inside the office, a middle-aged woman with bright red hair smiled and welcomed him.

"I'd like to see Wyatt Phillips."

"Do you have an appointment?"

"No, ma'am. I'm Special Agent Santiago Harris from the FBI, and I'd like to ask Mr. Phillips a few questions." He showed her his ID, then tucked it back inside his jacket pocket. "This won't take long."

The woman paled. "Yes, sir. I'll see if he can free his schedule."

Did she have something to hide?

She picked up the phone. Her fingers trembled. "An agent from the FBI is here to see you." She ended the call. "Mr. Phillips will be right out. You can have a seat while you wait."

"Thanks. I'll stand."

"My nephew is in the FBI in Dallas. Real nice kid. Smart too. We think he'll go far."

Yes, she was nervous.

Within thirty seconds, Wyatt Phillips appeared in the front office. He had a pretty-boy look about him and a plastic smile. Too confident in his body language. Phillips held out his hand and Tigo grasped it. He followed Phillips back to his office. Neat. Orderly. Soft music playing.

"What brings the FBI to my office? Am I being recruited?" He laughed, but Tigo failed to join him.

"This concerns your ex-wife, Victoria Phillips."

"Has something happened to her?" Not a crease of emotion.

"She was followed by a woman last Friday while in the company of her sister Kariss. When Mrs. Phillips questioned the woman, she assaulted Kariss and fled the scene."

"Sounds like Kariss's problem." His nose twitched, and he scratched it.

"I understand you and your ex-wife have a few issues."

"Our relationship is none of the FBI's business. Would you like to speak to my attorney?"

"I can if it becomes necessary. True, I'm not the least interested in your personal life. But hiring a stalker or a potential killer does make it FBI business."

Phillips's eyes widened, and his face reddened. "Hey. You're out of line. I wouldn't have Vicki followed or hire someone to hurt her. Maybe you need to look into her crazy sister's life."

"We're investigating Kariss Walker's background too." Tigo removed a copy of the sketch made of the woman in question. "Does this woman look familiar?"

Phillips's gaze barely lit on the sketch. "Never saw her before in my life."

"Look closer, Mr. Phillips. I want to make sure you don't recognize this woman."

Phillips took the sketch. "As I said before, I don't know her."

"I'd like to talk to your current wife."

"She's not my wife. She's my girlfriend." He shook his head. "I don't want to drag her into this. We have a new baby. He's fussy. Neither of us is getting much sleep."

Tigo wanted to comment on Phillips's

264

lack of sleep, but swallowed the sarcasm instead. "I need to talk to her. What's her name?" Tigo took a pen and pad of paper from his jacket and studied Phillips's face.

"She doesn't know Vicki's pregnant, and I'd like to keep it that way."

Phillips should have thought about the repercussions of his actions before now. "My intentions are to talk to her about last Friday's incident."

Phillips took a deep breath. "Lissa Montgomery."

"A phone number?"

"It's a cell." Phillips rattled off the information.

"Thank you. We'll be in touch." Tigo left Phillips's office, but he wanted to spend a few minutes with the receptionist.

"What did you say your nephew's name was? The one who's in the FBI?"

The woman took a deep breath, no doubt to compose herself. She gave him good eye contact, told him her nephew's name, and he jotted it down.

"Did you say he worked in Dallas?"

"Yes." Her eye contact remained the same.

"Say, I was wondering if you could help me." He showed her the sketch of the woman. "Have you ever seen her before?"

"No, sir." She blinked.

He handed her a business card. "If you happen to see her, would you give me a call?"

Once in his truck, Tigo phoned Lissa. He assumed Phillips had called her first. Tigo left a message instructing her to contact him by five o'clock today or he'd pay her a visit.

Tigo arrived at his desk at ten-thirty. Kariss had texted him earlier asking when she should bring his Starbucks. He had the woman trained, at least in one area. While driving back from Phillips Commercial Realty, he'd received a call from Ricardo Montoya and learned about Kariss's Sunday afternoon call to 9-1-1.

Kariss Walker needed to be under his radar every hour. If not, he'd be attending her funeral.

"Good morning." She set his coffee on the desk. "Hope your weekend was good."

He glanced up. *Control, Tigo.* He decided to take a gentle approach. After all, since last Friday she'd been assaulted and shot at. Most people would give up this ridiculous venture of researching the FBI.

"Good to see you," he said. "Want to take our coffee to the break room?"

A spark of alarm flashed across her dark-brown eyes. She blinked. "Sure. Do I need to take notes?"

He waved away her question. "I need a break. It's been a long morning, and the paperwork on my desk is depressing."

They reached for their coffees and walked past the other agents. He greeted them while his mind raced on how to approach her police rescue. Once in the break room, he made small talk to relax her. She crossed her legs, her left foot shaking.

"I realize I know very little about you, and here we are working together."

"What would you like to know? After the shooting, you nearly had my blood type." Her voice sounded light, but her lower lip trembled.

"Your life has been rather precarious since then."

"Mildly stated." She took a sip of her latte. "I'm dealing with it. Making changes in my life. I'd still like to have the identity of the woman who assaulted me last Friday. Like you, I think Wyatt or his new wife is responsible."

"I visited him earlier this morning. He denied any knowledge of it, but his secretary acted as though she recognized the woman from the sketch. I have a call in to Lissa. If she doesn't respond by this afternoon, I'll take a ride over there."

Kariss nodded. "I've seen her, but haven't

267

met her. Thanks for handling the situation."

She sounded formal. He opened his coffee and let the aroma fill his nostrils. "For the record, the two aren't married. Your sister might need to know that."

"I'm not surprised. He's a real jerk."

"Tell me about your brothers and sisters. You're the youngest, so start from the top."

She tilted her head and studied him. "Not sure what this is about, but all right, here goes. Craig is the oldest, and he owns a construction company in Austin. Emma teaches psychology at A&M. Melanie is a geologist and works for an oil-and-gas company, also in Austin. Vicki is a nurse, and Conn is in his sixth year of a four-year degree at a junior college."

"Nieces? Nephews?"

"Are you padding my file?"

"Just making an effort to be friends."

Her eyes narrowed. "We've been together five days a week for nearly two months. You dislike your assignment to me, and that's probably a mild term. You'd like nothing better than for me to leave town. Now you decide to be friends? I know better."

He had to give her credit for holding herself together. "A little edgy, aren't we? I thought it was a nice gesture."

"Tigo, you don't do nice gestures. You're

calculating and always working on a problem, but I'll give you what you're asking. Craig has three boys. Emma has one girl. Melanie has one each. Vicki is expecting her first, and Conn isn't married. But he may have a few kids out there. How's that?"

"Are all of you close?"

"Better than average. Vicki and I are more like best friends." She took a deep breath. Why couldn't she simply tell him about yesterday? "Can I dig deeper?"

"Maybe. Depends on what you want to know." She took a drink of her coffee and eyed him. "Tigo, I had a rough weekend, and I have a feeling you're about to lecture me about something. If that's the case, I'd like to postpone it."

"Not this time. Ricardo Montoya phoned me earlier. He told me about yesterday afternoon."

She rubbed her arms.

"Why didn't you call me?" His voice sounded oddly gentle, even to himself. Not his usual method of interrogation.

"I didn't want to bother you. I didn't get the license plate number or see who was in the truck. Just the nationality."

"Haven't we come further than that?" He softened his voice even more. "This is a fed case, and I'm the agent assigned to it. You were dragged into gang warfare and gun smuggling due to my poor judgment. I'm involved, and I want to be bothered."

She glanced away then back to him. "I bought a gun on Saturday. Signed up for a CHL license."

"Carrying a concealed weapon is not the answer. Takes time for the classes, testing, and final approval."

"I know. But I had to do something." She peered into his eyes. "I stopped by the car dealership this morning, and I'm picking up another car today. Putting the Jag in storage until this is over."

"Good move. The Jag is like a moving target. What's the new car?"

"A Prius. I hear they have exceptional acceleration and speed, and with the outstanding gas mileage, I'll still be sailing along when the bad guys run out of fuel."

He grinned. "Smart girl. I don't know any other way to express that I'm concerned about your safety." He studied her for a moment. "Kariss, whether you like it or not, people care about you. If I could force you out of the city until the Arroyos are brought in and Delores Olvera is found, I would. I've even considered having you 'kidnapped.' You qualify for witness protec-

270

tion after all."

For once Kariss was speechless.

CHAPTER 27

"I'm following you to pick up your new car." Tigo's announcement had startled Kariss.

"Why? The dealership isn't ten minutes from here."

"I'll feel better when you're driving a different car."

Tigo's concern for her revealed a tender side, one she'd seen on more than one occasion. He stayed with her until she drove away in a new white Prius, all professional and middle-class.

The man was simply too complex.

In the security of her condo, Kariss couldn't stop her thoughts from spinning from one frightening incident to another. She could leave town like Tigo suggested, but wasn't running a coward's way out? Her mind reverted to writer mode. Her heroes needed to have courage to flee or stand and fight. In her situation she didn't know what was smart or stupid.

Wyatt's girlfriend, Lissa, had told Tigo she knew nothing about the woman who'd stalked Kariss and Vicki. But a person who stooped low enough to pay someone to follow them wouldn't admit to it. Just take note they'd been found out. Kariss hoped the situation wasn't a part of Wyatt's project to intimidate Vicki.

Sinking into her favorite chair, Kariss closed her eyes and rubbed her temples. A dull headache had plagued her all afternoon. No wonder, considering the mess in her life. The option to be placed into witness protection hadn't really registered until today's conversation with Tigo, and now she felt true fright, physically and mentally. She'd like to think this whole experience could be typed into a file titled "Emotive Conflict Research" if she stayed alive long enough to document it. She was distrustful of everyone but Tigo.

Owning a gun and taking lessons on how to use it didn't make her feel safe either. The process of acquiring the skill and license took far too long. Right now the gun lay on her nightstand. She didn't even know how to load it, proving that in a crisis, she'd be dead while she figured out how to insert a bullet. One day soon she'd allow herself a good cry about all of this. Maybe when it was over. Or maybe she'd celebrate and take Vicki on a trip to Hawaii — a survival treat.

Right now, she needed to devote some thought to Xavier's circumstances and shove her own problems aside. Delores's grandmother claimed she didn't have any grandchildren and didn't know a Delores. But the man who'd once lived near Xavier and Delores, the one who'd spent time in jail, said he'd recently seen the woman at a Walmart — alone. Kariss had given the information to Tigo then walked away. After this morning's serious talk, she refused to burden him with the other trauma in her life. She'd figure it out soon.

Think about Xavier's tragedy. That is your book's topic.

Kariss picked up her phone and called the local fire station. "I'm working on a story about a soldier who returns from Iraq and learns his ex-girlfriend dropped their baby off at a fire station. Who keeps records of abandoned children?"

"If the baby's missing, he would need to contact the police or Child Protective Services. When a child is abandoned at a safe haven, the police are notified, then CPS places the child."

She looked over her notes, thanked the

fireman, and ended the call. Her next inquiry went to CPS. She repeated the same scenario.

"The baby would have been placed in foster care. Efforts are made to identify the child, but if there's no identity, then the baby's probably been adopted."

"Given my story's situation, how long is a child in foster care before an adoption can occur?"

"Up to eighteen months."

"What's done to locate the parents?"

"CPS needs time to resolve the legal case and to attempt to find either of the parents. A mother could abandon her child, but the father might be willing and able to take the child or children. If the parents cannot be found, then CPS serves them by publication."

Kariss remembered reading abandoned children notices in the paper while working at Channel 5.

"The process could take six months to a year," the CPS worker said. "Parental rights can be terminated more quickly if the parents never present themselves to the court. Note that children are required to live in the home with adoptive parents for at least six months before the adoption can be consummated."

"Who has the records of abandoned children?"

"We do."

"Are they public?"

"No. Texas CPS records are closed. When the child is of age, he or she has access to their file — why and when the child was taken into custody."

"About how many abandoned child cases do you have a year?"

"I have no idea."

"How often does CPS take these cases to court?"

"Whenever they make their way up the docket. The custody cases are held in open court."

Kariss needed time to internalize what she'd just learned. "Thank you for your time and information." She disconnected the call. Telling Xavier about this latest finding wouldn't be easy. What if his child had been recently abandoned? Was there a way to find out? Without a name, would CPS even take him seriously? Could his child be in a foster home?

Before she ended her search, she'd talk to Catholic Charities, since many Hispanics shared that faith. Glancing at her hurriedly scribbled notes, she quickly typed them into a file.

The doorbell rang, and she rose to answer it. She lived in a gated community, and visitors had to phone for entrance into the complex. Must be a neighbor. "Who's there?"

"Tigo."

She flung open the door to meet his grinning face. He leaned against the door jamb. "Did you flash your badge to gain access here? Never mind. I already know the answer."

He looked entirely too easygoing, as though she expected his arrival. But she wasn't swallowing this ruse.

"You're still upset with me," he said.

"Not upset. Just stressed to the max. Haven't you tortured me enough for one day?"

He chuckled. He really was good looking — if she could get past his analytic personality. "I wanted to talk. Do you have plans for dinner?"

"Is this like the coffee in the lounge this morning?"

"Sort of. I thought you deserved to see a good side of me."

"I've seen it in rare moments, and I appreciate the thought. But I'm not a dinner date." She abruptly closed the door. "Go home to your wife or live-in or whoever she is."

He knocked this time, and she leaned closer to hear what he might have to say. A movie clip swept across her mind, showing a determined FBI agent kicking down the door. "I don't have a wife or girlfriend."

She knew better. "Who's Natalie?"

"One of my mother's nurses."

His mother? How sad. Compassion seized her. "Your mother's ill?"

"Yes. Are you going to let me in?"

"Why should I?"

"To make peace."

"Why?"

"I'm worried you're going to do something stupid. Purchasing a gun makes me uneasy."

He'd gotten his nose into her business once too often. She opened the door and crossed her arms over her chest. "Tigo, in all of your FBI work, haven't you ever had a class on how to communicate with women?"

"Of course. Should I have brought flowers?"

"Yes, and candy."

He continued to grin. "Dinner?"

"Will you answer some questions for me?"

"The best I can."

He was up to something, but staying at home trying to figure out how to help

Xavier depressed her. "Do you have your truck or the new slum mobile?"

"Truck."

"Okay. I need a few minutes to freshen up. Change clothes." Kariss stepped away and let Tigo inside. "Where are we going?"

"Houston's."

She'd make him wait fifteen minutes for spite. This could be a side of him to include in her book. "Would you like a soda or bottled water?"

"Water sounds good." He glanced around the room. "I like the chrome and glass. Not so sure I could keep all the white furniture clean."

"That's why it's a woman's condo."

In the living room, Tigo picked up a DVD on the entertainment center. "This is a good action movie. Credible scenes."

"Once you get past the blood."

"It's a movie."

"I usually cover my eyes."

"Do you always shut your eyes during the bloody scenes?"

Kariss could only imagine his response. "Yes."

"But it's not real." He pointed to the DVD's colorful cover, but she refused to look at the red. "Those are actors. Fake blood."

"It's real to me." She took a breath. "I see it. I feel it. I'm there."

"Then how do you propose to write real-life suspense with FBI involvement?"

"Those parts won't be easy. I'll simply go back to how I felt the day in the hospital. I also have yesterday's chase written into a file in case I want to give a character a heart attack."

"Research has nearly gotten you killed."

"Don't remind me." The visuals kept her awake at night.

He replaced the DVD. "What about the research for your previous books? Women's issues can be difficult."

She studied her newly manicured nails. "The publisher made the request of my agent. They provided everything I needed, except the interviews I conducted."

"How did you get started?"

"I met an editor at a dinner party. He'd seen my news reporting on Channel 5, and it went from there."

"You must write fast."

"I do, which was to my benefit. If you don't have any more questions, I'm going to get ready now." She grabbed her purse to retrieve her makeup bag. "Oh, we might need reservations. My laptop is there to locate the number."

"Thanks. Mind if I check a few other things while I'm at it?"

"Always working, Agent Harris?"

"Sure. I have to be one step ahead of you."

"Knock yourself out."

Once at the restaurant, one of her favorites, they were escorted to a booth. Amidst the dim lighting that she used to think cozy and romantic, she felt vulnerable. Was it the Arroyo thing or being alone with Tigo? If she were honest, she'd say both.

After they'd given their food orders, she pulled out her notepad, the one filled with comments and accountings when she was privy to his and Ryan's conversations.

"How's the gun-smuggling case going?" She clicked her pen and poised it to write.

"Moving ahead."

"How's Jo-Jack?"

"He has a death warrant."

She shuddered at the memory. "So he's not communicating?"

"Nope. Left the hospital without a forwarding address."

"But he was in serious condition."

"Right."

"Do you have another informant?"

"A possibility." He waved at someone in another booth. "We have willing applicants, but their desire doesn't mean they can

281

provide good information."

"How do you find these people?"

"By walking the streets."

"Can you tell me about that?"

"I might someday. My turn. Have you talked to Xavier today?"

"No. But I can assure you he refuses to give up." She took a deep breath. "I called CPS and learned nothing. And I plan to contact Catholic Charities and review newspaper archives. Then I give up. Well, maybe I'll give up."

Tigo nodded. "Wish I could talk you out of helping him at all, but that's like spitting in the wind."

She chose to change the topic. "I have more questions. I've heard some lingo from you and Ryan that I don't understand. I'm assuming it's unique to the FBI, but it would add credibility to my story."

"Bring it on."

"What's FIG?"

"Field Intelligence Group. Helps us analyze information from all sources."

"Can I find out more info online?"

"You can. I'll give you a tour at the office. Should have taken care of that aspect before."

"Great." She peered into his face. He was doing his best to be charming, and he'd given no indication why he really wanted dinner. She started to ask about his mother, but given she was under nurse's care, her condition couldn't be good.

"No more questions?"

She gave her best dazzling smile. "What's candy and bling? Slang for drugs?"

He startled, then shook his head. "Candy was an informant. Found her with her throat cut about the same time you started your research. Bling was her pimp."

"He killed her?"

"The Arroyos took the credit. She'd been giving me info."

The thought shook Kariss to the core. "I'm sorry."

"But since you mentioned it, you might want to spend time thinking about how she ended up."

"I thought the matter was handled until yesterday. I keep telling myself the two men chasing me were drunk or high and simply liked my car. The Arroyos don't have my name."

"But Froggie Diego has your face, and he might have mine and Ryan's."

The waiter brought their food and filled their water glasses. Tigo thanked him. She could almost hear the wheels grinding in his mind, as though he were planning his next offensive strategy.

"What do you want me to do now?" she said. "Because you've gone to a lot of trouble about something."

"Would you consider discussing the situation with a family member? Or boyfriend?"

"I don't want to involve my family, and I don't have a boyfriend. This is a solo project."

"Independence can be dangerous, Kariss. I don't know how much plainer I can be. I feel like I'm talking to a brick wall."

"What do you know that you're not telling me?"

"You already are aware of what the Arroyos do. They steal and murder with no conscience. Right now, they think we're cops, and they don't give up. They're a gang. They work for the common good of the group. It's family. Their goals, behavior, what matters, relationships, and how they cope with life comes from being a member of the gang."

She was a fan of psychology and understood the complexity of human behavior. The things gangs did for power and control were frightening. So she'd stay out of their way. By the end of August, she'd be finished with her FBI research. Then she'd take a long vacation.

After all, Houston was a huge city, and the Arroyos had nothing to do with her story about Benita and how she might have died.

CHAPTER 28

Tigo escorted Kariss inside her condo and drove home convinced she hadn't listened to any of his warnings or advice. He'd gone there with the purpose of convincing her to lay low until the Arroyos were brought in. Unfortunately, she held the trophy for stubbornness.

While she readied herself for dinner, he'd accessed her laptop. He walked an ethical line there, but she'd given him permission.

The folder labeled "Cherished Doe Manuscript" had a first chapter, but he wasn't interested in reading it then. The file "Characters" would be a later pursuit, but the one titled "Notes" had sparked his attention.

She'd duplicated everything in the FBI file about Cherished Doe and made comments in the left-hand column for events that must have importance to her story. He valued her orderly accounting of the press conference and represented media. No fiction there, only details in a well-journaled fashion. Still scrolling, he'd reached the portion surrounding Gilberto's and Xavier's visit to the FBI. Tigo had stopped to analyze a highlighted portion about Xavier.

I don't understand why neither HPD nor the FBI will investigate the possibility of Xavier's child. He's lost one little girl, and my heart goes out to him for a possible second.

Finding nothing else to link her to dangerous activity, he'd moved on to check what websites she'd accessed, hoping to find more information about the newly purchased gun. Typical sites popped up, writing and marketing blogs, thesaurus, a ten-thousand-year calendar — Tigo wondered if she was thinking about writing sci-fi — a reverse dictionary, and fbi.gov. He'd scanned other sites until he felt reasonably certain her purchase of a handgun was precautionary. Again he'd wondered if her CHL would be an asset given the circumstances. He'd have to find out where she planned to take the classes and offer to take her to the shooting range. If she was determined to learn how to protect herself, then Tigo wanted to make sure she developed good habits.

Kariss's tenacity might have gotten her far in the book publishing world, but in the world of crime solving, trudging ahead without a plan was deadly. If the Arroyos were not taken into custody soon, she'd be dead before the book was written. Her persistence reminded him of a few reporters — had to have the story no matter where the scoop led. Well, he'd done all he could to warn her.

Tigo wanted her inside the FBI office every day, seven days a week. He'd gladly bring in a cot. But he couldn't force her to do anything. Nothing in his past equipped him to deal with Kariss Walker — not his stint in the marines, the work in Saudi Arabia, or his FBI training. To make matters worse, she filled too much of his thoughts. He wished she had a wart on her nose or bad breath.

Once home, he spent a few minutes at his mother's bedside. She'd had a restful day, and for that he was grateful. His thoughts eased back to dinner and how stunning Kariss had looked. Did she have any idea what her eyes did to him, or how he'd like to run his fingers through her thick curls?

"Kariss Walker, you're nothing but trouble." He looked at his sleeping mother and addressed his next comment to her. "And you'd like her spunk."

Having his and Ryan's disguises finished

would go a long way to eliminate some of his stressors. The paperwork containing new ID and the past ten years of illegal arms trading in Ecuador were in place for both of them.

Later on tonight, he'd return a call to Hershey. The man supposedly had contact information for those wanting to purchase arms. Tigo trusted Jo-Jack more than Hershey. Hershey had an agenda of his own between gun sales and building out the units for transport. How long Tigo could use his daughter as leverage remained to be seen.

If only he could find Jo-Jack. Where was he hiding? A thought occurred to Tigo. He picked up his phone and pressed speed dial for Ryan.

"I have an idea where Jo-Jack's hiding out."

"Where?"

"Conroe. His hospital records list a brother living there. Last name of Elston. Must be a half-brother. Want to look him up first thing in the morning? I can pick you up around seven-thirty. Drop you by your car later."

"Deal. How'd it go with Kariss?"

"Don't even ask. Can't believe I've let her get under my skin."

Ryan chuckled. "Did she admit working with Xavier?"

"Yes. On a phone basis only. But I know Xavier is motivated, and she doesn't have the heart to tell him no."

"Have you met your match?"

Tigo hoped not. But he had considered picking her up each morning and delivering her back home each evening just so he knew where she was.

Tuesday morning, Tigo and Ryan drove to an address northeast of Houston down a graveled, dead-end road. Surrounded by spindly pines and thick brush, the battered trailer house looked older than Tigo. Weeds had nearly taken over, and a rusted-out Chevy looked like a nesting ground for snakes. If not for two mangy dogs sniffing at his truck, he'd have assumed it was deserted.

Jo-Jack and his brother had fallen on hard times.

Tigo and Ryan exited the truck and drew their firearms. Tigo detected the smell of burning charcoal. Odd, since most breakfasts weren't barbecue.

"Do you smell that?" Ryan said.

"Sausage possibly."

"I was thinking more like someone whipping up a batch of meth." Ryan gazed into the trees as they walked to the trailer's door. "Depends on what's on the menu for breakfast."

"Anything's possible." The dogs followed them and wagged their tales. Tigo pounded on the door. "Mr. Elston, this is the FBI. We have a few questions for you about your brother."

Not even a whisper of a sound.

He pounded the door again. "If anyone is inside, please show your face." He turned the knob. Locked. "Ryan, be my guest."

Ryan kicked in the door. Tigo stepped in, his Glock positioned to fire. In the shadowy area, he smelled rotten food and human waste. His black coffee threatened to reappear. Beer cans, broken furniture, and trash littered the area, while weeds grew up through the floor.

"Mr. Elston, we'd like to ask you a few questions."

The two searched the small area, finding nothing but more of the same filth.

"Tigo, I bet Jo-Jack's been here," Ryan said from the kitchen area. "I've found gauze, bandages, peroxide. Here's some tape too. Ah, a couple of Snickers wrappers."

Jo-Jack's candy of choice.

Tigo and Ryan resumed their search outside where charcoal lay gray-hot in a grill.

"Whoever was here must have seen us pull up." Tigo scrutinized their surroundings. "As hot as it is, living inside would be impossible." He pointed to a dirty cooler and lifted the lid. Bacon, sausage, and hamburger lay piled beside a half dozen eggs. Beside the grill lay a skillet blackened by the coals and paper plates with two forks and a fishing knife.

The dogs attempted to bury their noses in the cooler, but Tigo snapped the lid back into place. The two men scrutinized the thick pines that reached up to a blue sky.

"Jo-Jack, if we can find you, so can the Arroyos. They haven't given up. We can keep you safe but not here. You were badly hurt the last time we spoke, and I bet you need a doctor now." He stared deep into the brush and saw a narrow path. "We're going and won't be back. You know how to reach us. Cooperation with the FBI is the only way to keep you alive."

The only sound greeting them was a mockingbird. A crow flew overhead. Tigo glanced at Ryan. "Let's go. We have work to do."

The two walked toward the truck.

"Wait," a voice called from the thick pines to their right where Tigo had noted the path. "My brother needs help." A bone-thin man stepped from the woods, grasping Jo-Jack around the waist.

A growing stain of fresh blood on Jo-Jack's dirty T-shirt caught Tigo's attention, and he hurried to help. "Call 9-1-1," he said to Ryan.

Tigo met the two men and together they lowered Jo-Jack to the soft ground. "How long's he been bleeding like this?"

"Gets worse every time we move to the woods," the weathered brother said.

"How often do you make the trip?" The ashen color of Jo-Jack's face indicated the end was near.

"An old lady lives at the intersection of this road. She calls whenever someone turns this way. Kids mostly. Head back here to smoke pot." He swiped at his nose.

"She'll be calling. An ambulance is on its way."

Jo-Jack's eyes fluttered. "No. They'll find me."

"Not this time. We'll make sure the hospital uses a different name. Then we'll get you to a safe house like we promised before."

"Leave me here." Jo-Jack sucked in a breath. "I'll be okay."

Tigo lifted the T-shirt. Infection oozed from an abdomen hot with fever. The Arroyos might not need to finish Jo-Jack off. Tigo turned to Ryan. "I've got a first-aid kit in the truck. I'll be right back."

"I'll get it." Ryan sprinted to the truck.

"A clean bandage would be nice," the brother said. "I have peroxide in the trailer."

"He needs more than what we have, like antibiotics and treatment for infection." IVs and possible surgery ranked high on Tigo's list as well, but he'd not frighten the two men.

"I've been worse," Jo-Jack whispered, his words an effort.

"If you don't get help, you're not going to make it. We need you alive."

"This ain't livin'."

He had a point, but not if Tigo had a say in the matter. He stared at Elston. "Did you help him leave the hospital?"

The man nodded. "He was scared of the Arroyos. I've been takin' good care of him."

The infection proved the quality of his care. "Don't do it again, or you'll kill him for sure. Jo-Jack, I need names. Places."

A cell phone rang and the brother answered. "Yeah. We're doing all right. Call me when the ambulance turns this way."

Jo-Jack's eyes closed, and his body lay limp.

CHAPTER 29

Creative people often slid into depression. Kariss recognized the symptoms and had acquired tools to beat off the monster when she sensed it camping on her doorstep. Tuesday morning, the self-talk accomplished nothing. She told herself how lucky she was to share the same disorder as the great masters: Dickinson, Poe, Emerson, Dickens, Faulkner, Hemingway, Melville, Tolstoy, O'Keefe, Gaugin, Michelangelo, Van Gogh, Rachmaninoff, Schumann, and Tchaikovsky. Ah, she had the list memorized.

Analyzing her mood this morning didn't chase the blues away. She should have taken a three-mile run. Eaten a better breakfast than an oatmeal-raisin cookie from Starbucks. Brought her iPod to the office so she could listen to soothing music.

Paralyzing truth seized her. Her stomach curdled. An unbidden memory of Nikki surfaced, and the fire became as vivid as it had been the afternoon it ended a little girl's life. . . .

The fire engine's siren pierced the air and grew louder while smoke billowed from the windows of Little People's Academy Day Care. Children covered their ears. Some cried. Caretakers counted the children in their charge.

Kariss searched through the two-year-olds in her class. "Where's Nikki?"

"With Erin," the lead teacher said.

Kariss spotted Erin beside her sister, who worked with four-year-olds. Nikki was nowhere in sight. She hurried to Erin. "Where's Nikki?"

The young woman's eyes widened. "I don't know. I thought she was with you."

Kariss gasped. "She was asleep and assigned to you while we were outside. Did you leave her alone?"

Erin paled, and reality shook Kariss. She raced to the side door of the day care that led into the two-year-old room.

"Don't go back there," the lead teacher said. "Kariss, stop!"

She ignored the many shouts and flung open the door. Smoke filled the room, clouding her vision and making it difficult to breathe. A child coughed, then screams rose from a cot in the corner.

"Nikki, I'm coming." She grabbed the little girl just as the wall collapsed. Flames crackled and sputtered, raining debris onto Kariss's lower back, burning her shirt and scorching her flesh. She fell with the weight, holding Nikki close to her chest. "Don't worry, sweetheart. I have you."

Suffocating heat stole her breath. Nikki coughed harder. "Lord, save this baby." Kariss still couldn't remember if her plea was uttered or if it was a silent banner meant to reach heaven's gates. All she could think about was protecting Nikki from the flames. The ceiling creaked and gave way. Something struck her head, and Kariss passed out.

When Kariss had awoken in the hospital, her parents surrounded her bed. Her back felt like someone had lit a match to it, and her throat burned.

"You're going to be okay," her mother said. "Don't try to talk."

"How's Nikki?" She didn't care about herself.

Her mother stroked her cheek, like she did when she was a child. Kariss's heart thumped. *No, please, not little Nikki.*

"Honey, she didn't make it." Tears flooded Mom's eyes. Dad took her hand on the opposite side of the bed.

Nikki, my little angel. Pale-blue eyes mirrored the sky and a mass of thick, blonde hair hung to the middle of her back. *That's when I hit the Mute button on God.*

Kariss attempted to shove aside the haunting scene. How many times had she told herself it wasn't her fault? She'd done her best. No one blamed her.

She stiffened her resolve and touched her back where the scar served as a reminder. She placed her trembling fingers on the laptop. Would the overwhelming guilt ever end? Wasn't there a way to redeem herself?

Chapter One

Who can ever forget the laughter of a child?

Chase it away, Kariss. You can do this thing. It won't bring Nikki back, or Benita, but it can bring awareness.

She raised her chin, closed her eyes, and returned to her story. She could do this.

While waiting for Tigo and Ryan, Kariss finished the first chapter of her novel, knowing she'd return to it several times before the book was finished. She'd massaged the facts of the case and begun a fictionalized version of Cherished Doe.

The title didn't grab her.

The hook was lame. But she had four hundred pages to travel alongside her characters before correctly penning that crucial first sentence.

She could not, would not, give up on writing this story.

Tigo and Ryan arrived late morning. Tigo wore a frown, and Ryan's forehead crinkled like a man ten years older. They'd missed an interview in which Kariss was supposed to tag along, unless they'd conducted it before they arrived.

Tigo stood before her desk. Something akin to deep concern emitted from his eyes.

"What's wrong? Is this about the missed interview?"

"We can handle that tomorrow. This is about Jo-Jack."

She didn't like where this was going. "You found him."

"We did. Living out in the middle of nowhere. Infection had set into his abdominal wound, and he died before the ambulance arrived."

How many had to die before this ended? "I'm sorry." The memory of the two shooters in the surgical waiting room made her shiver. They'd ultimately been successful in eliminating Jo-Jack, and now they were trying to find her. "Were you able to talk to him before he died?"

"No. He was afraid. In intense pain. Had no will to live."

She understood giving up. This morning, she'd wanted to pack up and head to the West Coast. She'd write a book that pleased her publisher and her readers.

But a man had just died. If she slithered into the past, then she had no more gumption than Jo-Jack.

She met Tigo's eyes. A man who faced danger like she shopped for lipstick. He was wired so differently from anyone she'd ever met, and he lived in a world foreign to hers.

"I've done enough reading about the gun-smuggling problem to understand how important this case is to you. I know Houston is Mexico's largest gun supplier, and I can only imagine the lives that have been destroyed because of it."

"Cartels in Mexico recruit gangs to help them purchase and transport guns and ammo across the border. They also prey on the innocent."

"You mean they threaten people if they don't help them?"

He nodded. "Kids, desperate fathers who need to provide for their families, and single

301

women are used as mules to drive the weapons into Mexico. The gangs can't do it. They need people who don't have a police record."

"But how do huge shipments of weapons and ammunition get across the border if they're driven in regular vehicles?"

"Several cars and trucks are used, often equipped with hidden compartments, and this method is safer for the gangs. Smaller shipments reduce the likelihood of getting caught. About three months ago, we stopped a car filled with semi-automatics stored in the floorboard. That vehicle was driven by a pregnant woman."

"Aren't weapons available in Mexico? I mean, the cartels are carrying on war there."

"Not the kind or the amount the cartels want. An assault rifle that sells for a grand here sells for two to three thousand dollars there, depending on who has to be paid off en route."

She saw the determination in his eyes. No wonder he wanted to get past finding Delores Olvera. The gangs and gun smugglers had become his passion just like she wanted to help Xavier locate his child.

"I'm sure you'll figure out a way to bring in whoever is responsible." She moistened her lips. "That sounded like a computer-generated answer. I mean you have the skills to stop them. You and Ryan risk your lives so the rest of us are safe."

Tigo offered a slight smile. "You must be in the writing mode. Ryan and I aren't the only ones chipping away at this case. We'll get there." He left her work area, then retraced his steps.

"Your CHL workshop is Saturday, right?"

She nodded.

"I might go too."

"The gun shop owner told me various law-enforcement types often speak to the group about their experiences."

Tigo crossed his arms over his chest. "Not so sure my stories would be entertaining."

Kariss knew different.

He walked back to his cubicle. No doubt losing Jo-Jack to the Arroyos' vicious methods of keeping themselves clear of the law had to weigh on his shoulders. Tigo must have determination in his DNA — that and compassion. The latter was a trait he didn't reveal often, but she'd seen it and felt it.

After lunch, she planned to visit Catholic Charities. Her call to Child Protective Services had nearly defeated her, but she hoped today's meeting would offer more hope.

The problem was the five-year span during which Delores could have given up her baby at any time. The likelihood of an infant being immediately adopted in comparison with a toddler loomed over her. She called Gilberto and asked to speak to Xavier.

"Miss Walker, it's a pleasure to hear from you."

If only she had something to encourage him. "I'm driving to Catholic Charities this afternoon, and I have a few questions."

"Anything, Miss Walker."

"Please call me Kariss."

"Thanks. I'd ask to join you, but I have a few people to see. I appreciate all you're doing to help me."

"I've done nothing yet but give you bad news." She formed her words for what she needed to ask. "Did you and Delores discuss any names for the new baby?"

"For a boy — Gilberto after my brother. That's what I wanted. But considering what she did to Benita and my family, I doubt if she'd have used his name. We didn't talk about a girl. Why?"

"Sometimes when parents abandon their children, they pin a note onto the child's clothing indicating a name. Not much to go on, but I wanted to ask before I had my meeting this afternoon."

"I'm trying to remember if she ever mentioned a girl's name. Benita is her grand-mother."

"What was her mother's name?"

"Delores hated her mother."

"Your mother's name?"

"Delores, like my wife. I'm sorry. If I remember a name, I'll call you."

The search tipped into the hopeless arena, but she refused to sink there again. The logical side of her said to give up, but something urged her on, as though she hadn't looked in the right place. The thought kept her awake at night, and she couldn't imagine how Xavier felt. Optimism had to rule. Catholic Charities might provide wonderful information.

"How are you holding up?" she said.

"Okay. I've been going to every apartment in the complex to see if they remember Delores. Most of them have never seen her. It's been too long. People are friendly and sympathetic, but that doesn't give me any answers."

"What will it take for you to give up?"

"Someone in this city knows about my child. I don't want to think about going back to Mexico until I find the truth. And my time is running out. I don't know how long your government will let me stay here. But I hope it will be long enough for them to find Delores."

"I hope I learn something today. I'll call after I return from my appointment. Xavier, if Catholic Charities doesn't provide answers, we still have one more option through newspaper archives. If nothing turns up there, I'm fresh out of ideas."

"You do what you think is right. But I can't give up. I told Agent Harris that I'd talk to the man who claimed to see Delores at Walmart. See if he'd talk to the FBI."

"Maybe he has more information."

"He's afraid because he's illegal. If he'll tell me about Delores, then I can give the information to Agent Harris."

Xavier's tenacity wove a fresh path of resolve in Kariss. Although the question of what was the best outcome for him often stalked Kariss's most noble intentions. If Delores had deliberately allowed Benita to die, then what kind of abuse could she inflict upon another child?

Taking a deep breath, she realized that someday she needed to explore the Bible again. Who was God really, and did He care what happened on this chaotic planet?

CHAPTER 30

Cheeky punched in Froggie's number. Ever since he'd escaped the *policía* at the hospital, he'd been frozen until the pressure eased up. Cheeky had pulled the gang in tighter, examining his people for signs of disloyalty. He had no more answers than before, and Froggie was the problem.

"Meet you downstairs in thirty minutes." He clicked his phone shut and headed for the bathroom. Froggie'd screwed up twice. No matter they were *compadres.* Twice was too many times. Cheeky pulled out his .38 and set it on the sink beside his Rolex while he brushed his teeth. He had Froggie's entire family working at Falcon Lake — illiterate and doing exactly as they were told. It no longer made any difference that Froggie's parents were his godparents. They all needed to go.

Monika wrapped her arms around his waist and kissed his back. "What can I do for you?" she whispered.

"You're doing it." He smiled into the mirror after catching sight of hers. She had a perfect body, and he couldn't get enough of her. "I'll make reservations for dinner tonight. That place you like downtown."

"*Gracias.* I'll wear something nice."

"You always do." He turned and kissed her, allowing his hands to roam where they wanted. "I have some business for the next hour or so. Can you take a shower or something?"

"Sure." She slid her hands from his shoulders and trailed her fingers down his chest.

He picked up his phone and called a man he could trust. "Be here in one hour. Got a job for you."

When Froggie arrived ten minutes late, the fury in Cheeky grew. He walked onto the patio and Froggie followed. "Where have you been?"

"My girlfriend wouldn't let me leave." Froggie's smile didn't match his face. "Sorry, boss. *La regué.*"

Cheeky glared and walked to the edge of the patio that looked out onto a manicured lawn and a crystal-blue pool. "You did more than mess up. You failed me. Years ago I thought we were so close that I couldn't fight you." Cheeky lifted his gun to the man's head. "You've lost your value." He swore and pulled the trigger. Pieces of flesh and blood spattered his clothes. He laughed and spit on what was left of Froggie's face.

An hour later, his new lead man arrived while Monika hosed down the mess on the patio.

"Froggie's gone," Cheeky said. "Paulo, you have a promotion."

"Yes, sir." Paulo was taller than Froggie and had wider shoulders. He talked with a lisp, but that didn't stop his fists or his trigger finger.

"His family lives in Falcon Lake. Make them *desaparecen*."

"Anything else?"

"Kariss Walker. *Ella es propietaria de un Jaguar,*" he said, rattling off a license-plate number. "Find the car and you find her. Follow her and see where she lives."

"Get rid of her and the car?"

"Not yet. I want to talk to her first." The *policía* who'd infiltrated them was still alive, and Cheeky needed that man dead. Better yet, he needed both of them as examples of the Arroyos' power.

Cheeky massaged his left shoulder. He hadn't used his chainsaw for a long time.

Kariss left the FBI office and climbed into

309

her Prius. The little machine didn't have the powerful engine of her Jaguar. Yet she felt oddly secure in the hybrid.

Zipping south to downtown Houston, the memories of last Sunday's clash cut into her heart, raw and relentless. And when those thoughts began to fade, she remembered Jo-Jack. Had he kept a careful watch in every direction in case an Arroyo discovered where he hid? She didn't want to live like that. Jo-Jack felt the same way.

Her attention flew from one mirror to the other, but traffic was mild. The day glistened with beauty, the sky filled with soft billowy clouds that looked as though they held dreams. Kariss willed her spirit to feel the same whimsical hope.

Once downtown, she made her way to Louisiana Avenue, getting lost twice because the one-way streets kept turning her around. Navigation skills were not her specialty, even with the GPS app on her phone. The highrise buildings, the different architecture, and the varied people always held her attention. She passed a homeless woman pushing a grocery cart. Such a contrast against the professionals who filed by without giving the woman a second look.

Finally Kariss parked and walked to the building housing Catholic Charities. She strode into the offices and hoped her desperation didn't seep through the pores of her skin. The woman in charge of foster care was dressed in a light-green suit and flowered scarf. She smiled, and Kariss supposed those in need found the woman easy to talk to. Kariss explained Xavier's situation, calling attention to Cherished Doe and the father's frantic appeal.

Sadness met Kariss's gaze, and the woman hesitated before speaking. "Miss Walker, I'm sure you realize how futile your search is. You have no date of birth. Neither do you have the sex of the child. The father has given you an approximate birthdate, but we don't know if the mother delivered in Houston or somewhere else or not at all."

"I know this looks hopeless. But Mr. Olvera has already lost one child, and I want to believe another one exists. The idea that the mother might have disposed of it as well is devastating."

The woman stood and closed the office door. "If the child is alive and is a girl, the mother could have sold her into sex trafficking."

Kariss hadn't considered such degradation. Didn't want to imagine it. "Delores allowed Benita to starve. She could probably be cruel and selfish enough to sell her child, couldn't she?" She glanced into the woman's face. Compassion met her through gentle eyes. "I guess this isn't a time for naïveté."

"I'm so sorry. I can see you feel for the father and his plight. The case is sad. Broke my heart when I watched the media reports. But I don't see a way for us to help you."

"Are your procedures for abandoned children the same as Child Protective Services?"

The woman walked back to her desk. "Unlike the safe havens in our city where children can be abandoned, our gates are locked at night. A child could be left outside, but I don't recall it ever happening."

The familiar sinking feeling settled into Kariss. "What about your housing for pregnant women?"

"There is a possibility within those units. Our women live independently, and we don't monitor them. If a woman doesn't answer her cell phone or something is reported that warrants our attention, then we check to make sure everything is okay. Sometimes a woman in our system gives birth then disappears, leaving her baby behind. That's rare, because we work with our mothers to give them the tools they need to be good nurturers and providers.

We help them attain job skills and life aptitudes and teach them how to handle difficult situations. In some instances prepare them to give up their baby for adoption."

"What happens when a mother in your facility abandons her child?"

"We wait six months and then go to court for due cause. During that time, we do everything possible to locate family members, and the mother might return. Counseling is available for all concerned. After we have exhausted all means to find the child's family, adoption procedures begin."

"Do you have records of these children — when they were abandoned, the race, the approximate age?"

"We do. But in Texas, the records are closed."

"I understand." Kariss thanked the woman. Just as she'd thought, the search for Xavier's child had nearly reached an end. "Do you have any other suggestions?"

"I wish I could help you. Please tell Mr. Olvera that if his child was left here, he or she has gone to a good home where a family wanted a baby to love and cherish."

Kariss forced a smile, disappointment seeping into her emotions.

"At this point, Miss Walker, that's the best news I can offer."

CHAPTER 31

Wednesday morning, Kariss watched Tigo at his desk. He appeared to have worked through the varied emotions of losing Jo-Jack yesterday, so she chose not to bring up the matter. Instead she made her way to the squad board, which was a huge bulletin board, labeled "Operation Wasp," where the agents could view pics and names of key people in the gun-smuggling case. New information had been added, and she was curious about the content.

Cheeky Lopez's picture in a glossy 8×10 was posted on the left-hand side of the board labeled "leader of the Arroyos." Other pics followed — one of them was Froggie Diego, and she shuddered. The gang signs matched. Each pic had the member's real name and his list of crimes. Empty spots held names like "Bat" and "man with a lisp," and "woman mule-overseer." Candy's and Jo-Jack's names had been crossed out.

A black man by the name of Hershey must be a new informant, but it looked like he might be involved in illegal gun-running too.

Kariss sensed Tigo standing beside her. "Ryan and I have an interview at eleven if you'd like to sit in."

"Great. What's the topic?"

"A man claims to have overheard a conversation in a parking garage that might lead to information about the gun smugglers."

"Where's the parking garage?" Kariss loved the idea of using this information in her book. She'd been collecting research for what she hoped was an FBI series.

"The Galleria."

She startled. "Sounds like a strange locale to me. What would Arroyos be doing there?"

"The Arroyos aren't the only ones involved in gun smuggling. We need to pick apart his story to see if he has other motives. A good reason for you to listen to the interview. No questions. Just take notes and follow our lead."

"I get it. White-collar crime. Do you think he may be lying or have another reason to make this claim?"

"You're getting smarter." He nodded, and for a moment she felt like a little girl who'd just earned a gold star.

"I have two great teachers."

"How far along are you in the book?"

"One chapter. Lots of notes."

"That's one chapter more than I'd have written."

"My process on this one is a little slow. Weighing the truth. Changing facts to protect innocent people. And weaving in fiction." She watched Ryan enter his work area. "Wish I could do something for him. He doesn't drink coffee or tea, and he eats entirely too healthy."

"Bring him one of your books."

"Great idea. I have one inside my desk drawer."

"Go ahead. I need to talk to him about the interview. We'll swing by to get you."

She walked back to retrieve the book and realized she needed to make sure she spelled his name right. Her gesture had to wait. Picking up her iPod, she swiped the screen to her word game. She formed a word and added fifteen points to her score . . .

Tigo tossed a paper clip onto her desk. How long had he been observing her? "What are you playing?"

Pleased with her score, she glanced up. "Word Family. It's like Scrabble."

"How many players?"

"Just me."

He laughed. "What kind of game is that?

No competition."

"It increases my vocabulary."

"Right. You probably use a website to build your words."

Her eyes widened, pretending innocence. "Are you insinuating I'd cheat?"

"Just as I thought." He pointed to her iPod. "Why don't you play a war game? Wouldn't that put you into the mood for your book?"

"I like this one. Do you play?"

"No, but I'm aware of the game."

"I'll take you on." She tilted her head. "Unless you don't think you can handle my skills."

"Miss Writer, I'll teach you words you never imagined. I give 'intellectual' a whole new dimension."

"Deal." She'd show him the importance of a writer's greatest asset. She pressed New Game, sent an invite to Tigo, and dragged the screen's tiles into place. Her first word was *divas*. Double word score for eighteen points.

Thirty seconds later he played his tiles — *driven* for fourteen points.

She'd already proved who the better player was.

Arnold Bates arrived promptly at eleven.

Dressed in a dark-blue silk suit that must have equaled Kariss's condo payment, the middle-aged businessman appeared confident. Perhaps too confident. And a bit arrogant . . . with calculating gray eyes. Perhaps she'd been around Tigo too long and his problem-solving nature had begun to rub off.

Despite Bates's disagreeable first impression, she hoped he had solid information for the agents.

After Tigo and Ryan introduced themselves, Tigo turned to Kariss.

"This is Agent Jenson. She'll be taking notes during our discussion."

Bates reached out his hand, and she grasped it. "Pleasure to meet you, Agent Jenson."

She hid a smile, appreciating the perk.

The four met in an interview room and took seats at a rectangular table. Tigo, Ryan, and Kariss sat across from Bates. She wished she could ask questions, but that had been forbidden. Did they think she'd interrogate their interviewee?

Tigo crossed his legs and took on an unassuming position. She noted the body language he used to put the man at ease. "Mr. Bates, we appreciate your willingness to come forward with information that has the potential to solve a crime."

Bates folded his hands on the table. "I feel it's my civic duty."

"Tuesday afternoon you called our offices and stated you'd overheard a conversation in the parking garage of your office building on Monday morning."

He nodded. "Not sure why the conversation took place there instead of a private meeting area. The more I consider what transpired, the more nervous it makes me." Mr. Bates didn't flinch a muscle.

She jotted down *doesn't appear nervous*.

"Why don't you begin by giving us your occupation and why you were in the parking garage?"

Mr. Bates peered at Tigo's face. Again no emotion. "I run a company out of a suite of offices at the Galleria in the Premiere Building — an insurance company on the tenth floor. Been there four years. I had a meeting over midmorning coffee, which was why I happened to be in the garage that time of day. Normally I'm working."

"What time was it?"

"Ten thirty-five, on Monday. I remember checking my watch on the elevator."

Tigo smiled. "What did you see?"

"Two men standing at the tailgate of a pickup. Both dressed casually —"

319

"What do you mean 'casually'?"

"Jeans. Button-down shirts. Baseball caps."

Why was Tigo zeroing in on the men's clothes?

"Long-sleeved or short-sleeved?"

"Long."

A peculiar detail for Tigo to note. The temps outside had been nearly one hundred this week. Certainly not long-sleeved weather. Did he think Bates was lying?

"What nationality?"

"Hispanic."

"What color were their shirts?"

"I don't remember. White, I think. What does that have to do with anything?"

Kariss would ask Tigo about this later as well.

"Every detail brings us closer to finding the men." Tigo gestured for him to continue. "What happened?"

"One of them said they were tired of taking orders from a man just because he had money. The other said the merchandise was worth the price and doubled the investment. The first man said the last shipment went straight to Mexico with no hitch."

"Did they refer to each other by name?"

Kariss studied Tigo's face. He could win an Oscar for his stoic performance. Ryan appeared intense, his attention on taking notes. They were playing a role for Mr. Bates's benefit. She quickly noted Tigo's question.

"No. I would have remembered." Mr. Bates moistened his lips. "Then I heard what I felt was information the FBI needed. The second man said the shipment of assault rifles from Chicago was expected August 17. The first man said Cheeky asked for a dozen of their best drivers."

Kariss concealed her recognition of the gang leader's name.

"Who's Cheeky?" Tigo said.

"I thought you'd know. Sounded like the man was important."

"We'll look into it. Did they say where the rifles would be delivered?"

"Someplace off the Buffalo Speedway. I didn't hear the rest of it."

Kariss kept her attention on her notes. This was her city, her home. Not a scene of horrendous crimes.

"Where were you in proximity to the two men?"

"On the other side of my SUV. I was hidden from their view."

Tigo toyed with a pen, just as she'd seen him do so many times in the past when he was thinking through a matter. "What else was said?"

"Nothing worth repeating. They were hungry. Planned to get something to eat."

"Did they say where?"

"No. One of them wanted breakfast."

"Do you remember any other details?"

Bates appeared to ponder the matter. "Nothing I can recall. To be perfectly honest, I was shaken up. One man got into the truck, and the other got into a dark-green SUV. As they drove by, I ducked so they wouldn't see me."

"Lucky for you. What make of vehicles?"

"Chevy Avalanche, black, and the SUV was a Lexus." He frowned. "I failed to get the license-plate numbers. I was afraid."

Kariss remembered when the sight of two Arroyos paralyzed her.

"No problem. Mr. Bates, you've given us valuable information. Was anything else said about where the transfer would take place?"

"No."

"What language were they speaking?"

"Spanish. I'm fluent."

"And you're positive you weren't seen?"

"Yes. Think about it, Agent Harris. I'm alive to tell you about it."

No expression on Tigo's face. "Were the men armed?"

"Not that I could see. I assumed they had

weapons since their conversation revolved around them."

"What about gang signs?"

She'd assumed the two men were Arroyos. For sure she'd be a lousy investigative reporter without the facts.

"None."

Ah, their clothing and baseball caps would have hidden those signs.

Something about Bates's story bothered her, as though everything he'd said had been a script. She wondered if her doubts could be her fiction mind on an adrenaline rush.

"Who owns the Premiere Building?" Tigo said.

"Peter Masterson."

"What kind of a relationship do you have with Mr. Masterson?"

"I pass him now and then."

"You're not friends?"

"Only acquaintances. I see him occasionally at social events. We support many of the same charities."

"Do you have a relationship with any of the other tenants in the Premiere Building?"

"No. I'm a busy man. What does this have to do with the conversation I overheard?" Annoyance dripped from Bates's words.

Kariss had been under Tigo's questioning

before and could relate to Bates's irritation. But Tigo always had a plan.

"Clearly we don't want to take any more of your time than necessary. We need to establish your relationship with those in your building. You've relayed valuable information that could be linked to gun smugglers and gang activity. Since the conversation occurred in the parking garage, that could mean one of the tenants is connected to a serious crime."

Bates stiffened. "I'm not stupid, Agent Harris. I came here because it is as my civic duty. In providing the FBI with what I witnessed, I'm risking my life." He swallowed hard. "I have no idea who the men may have seen or if their meeting occurred in the Premiere Building. I apologize for my abruptness. The incident has left me a little edgy."

Kariss noted his reddened face looked more like "furious" than "a little edgy."

"I understand." Tigo turned his attention to Ryan. "Should we let him take a look at a few pics? See if he can pick out a face?"

The insurance man from the Galleria couldn't identify a single Arroyo. He stated they were too far away and had had their caps pulled over their eyes.

After Kariss gave Tigo her notes, she

returned to her desk, leaving the two agents alone to discuss the interview. Had Arnold Bates spoken the truth? One thing for sure was he knew a name: the man Tigo wanted to arrest.

CHAPTER 32

After Arnold Bates left the FBI building, Tigo and Ryan walked to the break room to discuss the interview.

"What do you think?" Tigo said. "How'd you read him?"

Ryan opened the door. "I want to know why he contacted us. A man of his caliber knows what's going on in the city, and that includes Masterson's activities. His arrests and indictments should make Bates suspicious of anyone in the building. No logic there."

"Or he doesn't want to name Masterson, and that's why he came to us. The fear factor. Could be the prospect of a firefight between the FBI and the Arroyos in his place of business makes him anxious."

"Why not move his company to another location?" Ryan shrugged.

"Bates might be tied to a lease." Tigo slid a dollar into the vending machine for a bottle of water. "Sounded like his lines were rehearsed. And he didn't come across as the concerned-citizen type either." He glanced at a bag of peanuts in the vending machine. "Want something?"

"No. I'm good."

Tigo twisted off the water bottle cap. "Bates's money buys him whatever he wants. No reason why he couldn't buy his way out of a lease."

"So the question is why did Bates seek us out? If Masterson suspected that he contacted us specifically about gun smuggling, he wouldn't think twice about getting rid of him. But . . ."

"What? Spill it, Ryan. Are you thinking Masterson sent him? Because that's what my gut's telling me." He waited for Ryan to voice his thoughts.

"One of the things that Candy told us was the Arroyos were in a standoff with their supplier about money," Ryan said. "Masterson could be using Bates to leak information to set them up. He's been paid, and there are plenty of other smugglers who will buy his guns and ammo."

"Do you think there's a link between who's tipping us off about transports and Bates's visit today?" Tigo said.

"I need more information before making

that stretch, like a connection between Bates and Masterson."

"Let's put a surveillance team on Bates and see who he's keeping company with. I'd like to check the latest reports on the team assigned to Masterson."

"I'll run both requests through the FIG."

"I'll get a background check done on Bates and a list of his clients along with phone records." Tigo took a long drink.

"Remember Jo-Jack gave you the name of Bat," Ryan said. "Could be Bates."

"He's low-class in a high-class suit. His body language danced with manipulation. I wonder if he buys his clothes from Masterson's line."

"One way to find out. That would link them."

"We're going to get these guys," Tigo said. "I can feel it."

"How about putting a little pressure on Hershey to set up our boy. I'm anxious to pull this together."

Nailing Masterson had been on Tigo's priority list for a long time. Bates could be the man to make it happen. Add Masterson and Cheeky to the group and the FBI could significantly cripple gun smuggling in Houston.

Tigo walked outside so he could check on

his mother. Sweat beaded on his brow in the ninety-eight-degree heat, and the humidity was every bit as overwhelming.

"Hi, Natalie. Just checking in. When I left this morning, Mom's blood pressure was extremely low."

"It's risen some. We're getting her ready for dialysis, and she'll see the doctor afterward."

"Good. Thanks." He disconnected the phone and stared out at the parking lot. Between the helplessness of Mom slipping away and the intricacies of gang warfare, his mind spun like a Category 5 hurricane.

Alone in his work area, Tigo did a background check on Arnold Bates. He wanted to digest every word for possible answers linking him to Masterson's operation.

Bates did well. House in River Oaks. Married to old money. A daughter in college. Belonged to an Episcopalian church. He owned other investments under a corporation called Cardinal Ventures, and those drew Tigo's scrutiny — a coffee-bean company with plantations in Brazil and Tanzania, petroleum products from South Korea, and East Indian furniture . . . all perfect fronts for smuggling arms and ammo. Another area of investigation. He picked up his phone and called the FIG.

"I need a full report on Cardinal Ventures' companies. Owned by Arnold Bates. Feed it back to my Blackberry."

While he waited, he picked up his iPhone and checked to see Kariss's latest word in their ongoing game. He was ahead by twenty points. Ah, *dexter* on a triple-word score was forty-two points, giving him a huge lead. If he kept this up, they'd be tied two and two.

An hour later, he took a look at the FIG's report. Cardinal Ventures looked squeaky clean. He pulled up Masterson's file and scrolled through his national and international holdings. Time to dive deeper.

Kariss decided to talk to Xavier in person about what she'd learned at Catholic Charities. He chose the McDonald's near the Fiesta where they'd previously met. He also requested she accompany him to the nursing home that housed Delores's grandmother, Benita Martinez. Although he'd visited the older woman previously, he thought she might reveal information this time that her mind hadn't been able to unravel before. Kariss agreed since she needed to give him more disheartening news.

The late afternoon had McDonald's

crowded with high school kids — hungry and noisy. A booth full of boys sat in front of Kariss. When one of them stuck French fries up his nose, then ate them, she was ready to leave.

"Xavier, it's so loud in here. Can we take my car and drive to the nursing home now?"

"Yes, these kids give me a headache."

She laughed, remembering her younger days and the trouble she'd gotten into.

The nursing home was a ten-minute drive. Poor Xavier, exploring every corner more than once to find his child . . . a child who might not even have been born or belonged to him.

The brick building housing the elderly looked in better shape than Kariss expected. The modest grounds had two crepe myrtles blooming in dark pink flowers, and purple and white petunias bloomed in flower beds along both sides of the facility's entrance. She parked her car and gave Xavier a reassuring smile. If only they could find useful information . . . But she had her reservations.

The moment Kariss stepped inside the nursing home, she detected the faint odors characteristic of most nursing homes — urine and aging bodies. Difficult to remove the smells, even the cleanest of facilities had trouble dealing with the problem. This one was spotless. Kariss had once done an investigative report about several of Houston's nursing homes, and she'd seen every caliber of staff and housing. In her opinion, Delores's grandmother was receiving excellent care, which caused Kariss to wonder who paid for it.

Kariss and Xavier greeted everyone in Spanish, and he asked permission to see Benita Martinez. They waited in the visitor sitting area while an attendant took a wheelchair to the woman's room.

The tiny woman with smooth, tanned skin and white hair smiled at Kariss and Xavier. "I wondered where you two had been. Did you bring the cookies?"

Xavier took her hand. "I forgot them, Grandmother. I'll remember cookies the next time. What flavor would you like?"

"Lemon." She sighed. "I was looking forward to them. Delores brought me chocolate ones yesterday."

Kariss peered into Xavier's face. This mention of Mrs. Martinez's granddaughter had to surprise him since last time she hadn't remembered Delores.

"That was nice of her." Xavier patted her hand. "Did she visit very long?"

"Not really. She had errands."

"Grandmother, I'd like for you to meet my friend Kariss."

Mrs. Martinez tilted her weathered face toward Kariss. "Why aren't you dating a good Mexican girl? Aren't they good enough for you?"

Xavier continued to pat her hand. What a kind man. "She's not a girlfriend. Just a friend."

Mrs. Martinez covered her mouth. "Excuse me. I didn't mean to be rude. It's a pleasure to meet you, my dear. Will you remind Xavier to bring me cookies the next time you come to see me?"

Good. She was coherent enough to recognize Xavier. "I will," Kariss said. "Tell me about your granddaughter Delores."

"You don't know her?"

"No, ma'am. Just through Xavier. Did you say she brought you cookies yesterday?"

Mrs. Martinez glanced away and then back to Kariss. The light in her eyes dulled. "She brought me a box of candy and stayed all afternoon."

"Did you eat all of them?" Kariss understood the woman's disoriented mind, but truth could surface through the cobwebs.

Benita laughed lightly, a sweet sound. "I bet you'd like one. The cherry creams are my favorite."

"Oh, I like chocolate all the way through. And yes, I'd love a piece."

Mrs. Martinez turned to Xavier. "Please be a nice boy and get the box of candy from my room. It's in the drawer beside my bed."

Xavier excused himself to find an attendant.

"Tell me about your granddaughter." Kariss felt like she was taking advantage of the woman's mental health, but solving a horrible crime meant seeking out information. Still, guilt crept through her. "How often does she come to see you?"

Mrs. Martinez brightened. "She comes every day."

"Does she bring her children?"

"Delores . . . I don't think so. Someone keeps them for her." The woman reached out for Kariss's hand and gave her a light squeeze. "I told Anna that we couldn't cook for all those people unless we had help. What were they thinking?"

Kariss listened and commented when necessary as Mrs. Martinez touched on one subject and then another. The woman talked with childlike enthusiasm about a picnic along the river and then changed the discussion to a concern about money to pay the rent. Xavier returned carrying a bag of cookies. Chocolate. Could it be Delores had brought them?

Xavier handed Mrs. Martinez the cookies. "The residents are not supposed to have food in their room, so we had to search. The bag was found in the back of a drawer. But I didn't find any candy."

"Are they stale?" Kariss's hope rose as she uttered her words.

"Of course not." Mrs. Martinez reached inside the bag.

Xavier swallowed hard, visible emotion rising to the surface. "Soft and fresh. I want to believe Delores brought them."

"She did," Mrs. Martinez said. "My granddaughter knows how to please this old woman. Would you like a cookie? I have plenty."

Xavier swiped a single tear. "No, thank you, Grandmother."

Kariss echoed his response while her thoughts raced with what they'd learned. Xavier's frantic search could be near the end . . . finding out what really happened to little Benita.

"I should watch the parking lot for the next few days to see if Delores stops by," he said.

Kariss stood and walked behind Mrs. Martinez. She placed her hands on the woman's shoulders. "The FBI needs to have a couple of agents on site," she whispered. "I'll tell Tigo." The same question bothering her earlier rose in her thoughts again. "Who pays the bill here?"

Xavier sighed. "I have no idea."

"That's important. If you'll sit with Mrs. Martinez, I'll find out."

"But you'll be back?" the woman said.

Sweet lady. "In a few minutes. Xavier is with you." When this was over, she'd come back to visit her . . . and bring lemon cookies.

Kariss walked to the director's office and knocked on the open door. A short, middle-aged woman whirled around in her chair. "Excuse me," Kariss said. "I'm here visiting Benita Martinez. Can you tell me who pays her bill?"

"Why?"

"We want to make sure she continues to receive excellent care. If the person responsible for her finances isn't able, we want to help."

"I see." The woman opened a file cabinet and leafed through the files. Pulling one out, she lay it on her desk. "I'm sorry, but I don't have a name. The bill is paid each month in cash. Sometimes a woman hands us an envelope with Mrs. Martinez's name on it, and other times I find the envelope on my desk."

"How strange. Delores told us that she paid it during her visits."

The woman's smile did not quite reach her eyes. "Oh, Delores does see her grandmother often. Such a kind woman." She hesitated and glanced at the folder. "Delores does pay her grandmother's bill. She asked me to keep her payments secret, but since you already know, there's no reason for me to hide it. I've often wondered why Delores wouldn't want others to know of her generosity." The woman closed the file. "She seems like the type who would want her good deeds to remain a secret. She's such a dear."

She's a potential killer.

"She was by yesterday. Brought us chocolates, and I'm afraid we ate them all." She smiled and shook her head. "Our residents are not supposed to have food in their rooms, but I close my eyes when Delores brings her grandmother treats."

"I'll be sure to keep your secret. What days does she visit?"

"Never the same. Like an angel, she comes unannounced."

That thought curdled Kariss's stomach. No murderer was an angel. "Does she bring her children to visit too?"

"She's always alone. I was unaware she had little ones."

More bad news for Xavier. Tigo needed to know about this immediately. "Thank you so much. Let me give you Xavier's information in case Mrs. Martinez needs something." She reached inside her purse and found Gilberto's phone number. After jotting down the information for the woman, she stepped outside into the parking lot.

Tigo's phone went straight to voice mail, which meant he was in a meeting or a tight situation. "This is Kariss. I have some information about Delores Olvera. Could be a good lead. Call me when you can."

She rubbed her arms to stop the chills in the ninety-five-plus-degree temperatures. Xavier's persistence may have paid off. Her phone rang, and she snatched it from her purse.

"What do you have?" Tigo said, his voice formal as though agitated.

"We have a lead on Delores." Kariss relayed the conversation with the nursing home director. "She was here yesterday."

"I'll get agents stationed there immediately. We need to see the nursing home's records too. Good job, Agent Walker. You might have to change your profession."

She laughed, releasing the stress of the day. "Xavier is the persistent one. I'm afraid the child he's looking for doesn't exist, but he refuses to give up."

"Sad, but realistic. Have you gone through newspaper archives yet?"

"That's on the schedule for tomorrow. If the search dead-ends, then there's nothing else I can do. I'll not be back to the office until afterward. Will you miss me?"

"Do you really want to know?" He chuckled. "Can't believe I'm saying this, but I feel better when you're here. Which reminds me, your presence on the southeast side of town is not smart."

She glanced around at the peaceful surroundings. "Yes, sir. I admit I prefer to write about crimes than live them. The blood is pumping, and I'm having a hard time not thinking about being shot at."

" 'Caution is the beginning of wisdom.' "

Her father would have had another version of that from the Bible. "I'm taking Xavier back to his car, or rather Gilberto's car, in a few minutes."

"Call me when you're heading home."

How sweet. He did have a few admirable qualities about him. "Are you playing body-guard?"

"Somebody needs to. You have a knack for being at the wrong place at the wrong time."

Unfortunately, he was right.

CHAPTER 33

After leaving the nursing home, Kariss drove Xavier back to McDonald's. They needed to talk about what they'd learned, and she needed to tell him about her experience at Catholic Charities. But the information learned at the nursing home buffered the discouraging news.

Teens still lingered outside the restaurant, and a few of them looked like they could be trouble. She pointed to a strip mall across the street. "We could talk there. I'll drive through and get us something to drink."

After grabbing two iced teas and maneuvering the traffic, she parked the car and kept the engine running for the air-conditioning.

"I'm ready to hear what you've found out," Xavier said. "I didn't ask when we left the nursing home, because you looked like you were thinking." He laughed. "You are sometimes funny. So serious. Do you ever have fun?"

She hadn't considered entertainment lately. Xavier's comment was unusual considering his plight. "I have five brothers and sisters. When we get together, we all have a good time."

"Gilberto and I have six brothers. Our poor mother said the rosary a lot. My father had a furniture store, and he insisted we have some education."

"I'm glad you have family. Are your other brothers in Mexico?"

"Yes. Only Gilberto was wise enough to apply for entrance into the U.S. I've already completed my paperwork for the same. No matter how long it takes, this is where my little girl is buried." He shrugged. "If I have another child, I'm not so sure I'd want to take him or her back with me. I know many of my people got here without following the law, and Delores and I did the same. But I want to do things the right way."

Kariss could only smile a response. She had no idea what it was like to live in Mexico or raise a family there. Media reported horrendous living conditions.

"*Dios* has the answers," he whispered.

"By the look on your face, I see you have hope." She'd once had that same faith. "I have a lead on Delores. The director at the nursing home said she has been paying her grandmother's bill in cash. She also visits there frequently."

He smiled and nodded. "At last we have something to go on. Have you contacted your friends at the FBI?"

"Tigo is sending agents to the nursing home now. The director will tell Delores about my questioning."

"Once we're finished talking, I'm going to return Gilberto's car and walk to the nursing home. I'll stay close enough to watch the parking lot."

"No need to walk. I'll drive you there. But you won't have to stand vigil with the FBI sending agents there."

"I can't wait at Gilberto's and do nothing. What if she arrives and has the child? It's too big of a risk."

"What will you do if you see her?"

He stiffened. "You shouldn't ask. My first thought would be the child. If Delores was alone . . ."

Kariss nodded. The image of Benita's autopsy picture flashed through her mind.

"Did you ask the director if she brings a child?"

"She didn't even know Delores had children."

He glanced out the car window, his face a

mass of battle scars. "You had something else to tell me."

"Catholic Charities can't help us. Not enough information."

He looked at her. A muscle twitched below his right eye. "Remember my friend, the man who grew up near me in Mexico and lived in Pine Grove Apartments?"

"The man who'd been to jail?"

"Yes. He claims he can help me find Delores."

"Xavier, we talked about him before. He could get you into trouble. Today gives us a better lead."

"I'm a smart man, Kariss. I know some very bad men in Mexico. Cartels that do terrible things to people. I've lived among killers for a long time, and I know how to be safe."

"Just be careful. We learned more about Delores today, and the FBI is moving in to apprehend her. What if your involvement with a criminal ruined your chance at citizenship?"

"Sometimes I think I could meet my own death easier than learning Delores killed this child too. I want something to live for."

His last statement brought back her longing to see Xavier's effort reap him happiness. "Would you give me your friend's name so Agent Harris can check him out?"

"What would that prove? If he's wanted, then I lose my source of information."

"Just think about it. See if it makes sense to you. This man —" Someone banged on her car door. She whirled around. A Hispanic man pressed a gun to the window, a man she'd never seen before.

"Get out of the car," he said in English.

She looked into his face, memorizing every hardened feature.

"I said, get out. Just you. Turn the car off."

"What did he say?" The sound of Xavier's voice shook Kariss to her senses.

"He said for me to get out of the car." She reached for the door handle, fearful he'd pull the trigger and shoot both of them if she didn't.

"I'll go with you."

"No." The door opened. "His business is with me."

Kariss never took her eyes off the shooter's face. She exited the car into the heat, and the man stepped back. "What do you want?"

"I think you already know."

He didn't have gang markings, but that didn't mean he wasn't one of those who wanted her dead. "I have no idea what you're talking about."

He aimed his gun at her chest.

Think, Kariss. Do something.

A siren filled the air, snapping the shooter's attention and giving her enough time to slam her palm into his wrist. He dropped the gun and it fired, creasing her left shoulder with what felt like a mosquito bite.

The man cursed, and the siren sounded closer. She kicked his gun, and he took off running. A police car raced into the shopping strip, sirens blaring, and stopped in front of her car. One police officer took off after the shooter on foot, while the driver hurried to her side. Kariss watched the shooter race across the street and jump into a car near the McDonald's before speeding away.

Only when the first police officer backtracked to her side did she notice her ragged breathing and the stinging in her shoulder. Xavier had removed his shirt and dabbed at her shoulder. Odd, she hadn't noticed him get out of the car.

"Ma'am, are you all right?" a young police officer said.

She blinked. He'd asked the same question three times. She reached to touch her shoulder and saw the blood on her fingers. "I might need a doctor." Xavier handed her his shirt for her to press against her shoulder.

"Yes, ma'am. I've called 9-1-1. An ambulance will be here shortly. Do you know who assaulted you?"

"I have no idea." But she could guess.

"Can you describe him?"

"My mind's hazy." She'd give the shooter's description to Tigo and him only.

"What about the gentleman beside you?"

"He doesn't speak English."

"My partner speaks Spanish."

"I'm sure he didn't see the man."

The police officer studied her. Doubt crested his eyes, then he glanced at her Prius. "Looks like a carjacking. You were lucky. Quick thinking."

"Yes . . . I suppose I am."

"You must have taken a self-defense course."

She nodded. "Never thought I'd use it."

"It saved your life."

Her shoulder throbbed. "How did you get here so quickly?"

"We'd just finished responding to a call at Fiesta's when we saw the crime in progress."

She took a deep breath to steady herself. "Did you say you called an ambulance?"

"Yes, ma'am."

"No thanks. I'll drive myself." Her last experience at a hospital nearly got her killed.

"That's not advisable. You could be in

shock." He looked at Xavier. "Can your friend drive you?"

"No, thank you," Kariss said again. She wiped the perspiration from her forehead, then realized the same hand had blood covering it.

"Is this gentleman a part of the problem?"

"Absolutely not."

"Are you sure, ma'am? We're here to protect you."

"He is a good man. Innocent of what just happened. I assure you."

"All right. I can't let you drive, and you need medical attention."

"It's not necessary."

"Is there anyone we can call?"

"Yes, sir. Special Agent Tigo Harris of the FBI." She closed her eyes as emotion and pain threatened to overtake her. "I have his number."

CHAPTER 34

Tigo drove to the address where Kariss waited with an HPD officer. The police called the incident an attempted carjacking. But Tigo knew better. The Arroyos were not giving up. Getting rid of the Jaguar hadn't made a difference. Could this be about Xavier? He'd have to think about that angle . . . Xavier, Delores, and Kariss.

He pulled into the strip mall where the crime had taken place and exited his truck. Crime-scene tape roped off the area around Kariss's Prius while media vans hovered like vultures. Tigo's attention flew to the dark-haired woman sitting on the curb beside the police car, holding a cloth to her shoulder. Blood stained the left side of her white blouse. An ambulance was parked there, too, but none of the paramedics were working on her. Odd, since she obviously needed medical attention. Xavier stood next to her.

Tigo wanted to find out what the two were

doing at that location when she was supposed to be driving back home. He saw a reporter push his way past the crime-scene tape to Kariss, and Tigo hurried after him. She didn't need the media obtaining a statement and flashing her name and face across Houston. Tigo recognized the reporter as the man who claimed to have history with her. Mike McDougal. What had she ever seen in him?

Tigo flashed his badge at those hovering over Kariss. "FBI, move aside, please. This is a crime scene, and you can be arrested for interfering with an investigation."

McDougal refused to budge.

"Sir, I asked you once to step away."

The reporter had a cocky look about him, and he still needed a haircut. "I'm talking to Miss Walker."

"Looks to me like she needs medical attention, not an interview."

The sight of blood staining her shirt made Tigo furious. This wasn't Kariss's fault. He'd allowed her to accompany him and Ryan to the hospital to question Jo-Jack, and now the Arroyos were after her. This jerk McDougal knew her name and would splash it across the front page.

"Sir, I'm Special Agent Tigo Harris." He shoved his ID in McDougal's face. "I'm asking you one last time to step aside."

The reporter stepped back and aimed his camera.

"No pictures or I'll have to confiscate your equipment."

The police officer cleared his throat. "You heard the agent. Or would you like me to arrest you?"

McDougal backed away, then frowned at Tigo. "Hey, I saw you with Kariss at the hospital. What's going on?"

"None of your business, and I suggest you leave her alone. I've had enough." Tigo bit his tongue to keep from saying anything that could put Kariss in danger. Neither she nor the FBI was in the market for unneeded publicity.

"Looks like you have more than a professional interest in her," McDougal said. "But I'll honor the FBI." McDougal took several steps back from the crime scene.

Tigo turned to the police officer. "Thanks for what you've done. What happened here?"

"An apparent carjacking. We spotted the crime taking place. Unfortunately the man responsible fled the scene. Miss Walker refused the paramedics' help."

Tigo stared into Kariss's pale face. "Are you okay?"

"Just my shoulder."

"Why not let these people patch you up?"

She shook her head. "I . . . I just want to get away from here."

He understood. He wanted her safe and out of view too. "I'll take you to get it looked at."

"I don't want a hospital. Someone could follow us."

Fear had wrapped its clutches around her. "We'll talk about it along the way." He turned to Xavier and greeted him in Spanish. "Are you all right?"

Xavier nodded. "Miss Walker did a brave thing. She knocked the man's gun from his hand."

Kariss handed Tigo a bloodstained shirt.

"Use this until you have a bandage," he said, handing it back. Later he'd find out more about Kariss's heroism, after her shoulder was bandaged. His heart had taken a dip with her, and he wanted her free from pain. "Where can I take you?" he asked Xavier.

"I'll drive myself. My brother's house is not far from here. Miss Walker needs to see a doctor."

"Great. I'm going to get Kariss medical attention immediately then."

"I saw the man who assaulted her, but I've

never seen him before."

"I'd like to talk about the events leading up to the attempted carjacking. Possibly have you help us identify him. Can I reach you on Gilberto's phone?"

"Yes, sir." Xavier stiffened. "He didn't want the car. He wanted Miss Walker."

Just what Tigo suspected. "What were you and Miss Walker doing? She called me from the nursing home. Said she was heading back to her house."

"We parked here to talk."

Later he'd find out what the topic of conversation had been. "A unit has been dispatched to the nursing home. We're close to finding Delores. Thanks to you."

Xavier nodded. "Call me and I'll tell you all I know. The police have already questioned me."

Tigo turned to study Kariss's face. She was pale, her eyes dilated. He'd pelt her with questions after a trip to the hospital — no matter how much she protested going. This time he wouldn't leave her side. "Let's go."

She clutched her upper arm. Blood dripped through her fingers. "What about my car?"

"We'll pick it up later." He took her arm

and linked it in his. They walked toward his truck.

"I'm sorry. Didn't know who else to call." Although she attempted to sound strong, the fear in her eyes told him otherwise.

"You were wise to call me, Kariss. This will be okay."

"I was afraid you'd be angry."

"Don't think so."

"Good. Now we both have battle scars." She smiled, but her lips trembled.

He wanted to lecture her. Shake her. "We've been lucky. I think today was an experience you can use in your book."

"I'm better at writing about painful situations than experiencing it."

He helped her inside his truck. "How bad is it?"

"I could lie and say it's nothing. But I'll do my best not to bleed on your truck."

"As if I care." He started to close the door, but she held out her hand.

"Tigo, I memorized everything about his face. And he wasn't the shooter from the hospital."

"That's my girl." The words were spoken before he realized what he'd said. Closing the door, he hoped she hadn't paid attention. Once inside, he started up the engine and lowered the AC.

"Thanks," she whispered. "I'm miserably hot."

"Sure it's not your shoulder?"

"Hmm. Could be. I didn't want to give the officer any information. Was I right?"

"You handled the situation just fine." He cleared his throat. "Kariss, I told you hanging out with me was dangerous."

"Too late. I'm already there. Can your doctor at the med clinic fix me up?"

"I'm taking you to the hospital. That gives us more time together."

"So is this a date?"

He wished it was. Maybe when this was over. "Kariss, we'd kill each other."

"We're headed there now. Thanks for getting Mike out of the picture."

"No problem."

"We dated for about four months once. Definitely not one of my better choices. He told me he needed a thousand dollars to help his sister pay for his five-year-old niece's medical expenses. She had juvenile diabetes and was getting progressively worse, or so Mike said. I gave him the money, then he bragged to a couple of other reporters about betting the money at the races. No sister and no niece."

"I'm sorry." One more reason why Tigo didn't like the guy.

"Just wanted you to know."

He glanced her way. "Lean back and close your eyes. I want you to think one more time about taking a vacation. Give us time to bring these guys in. You could relax and write without looking over your shoulder."

"No thanks. I'll be more careful."

For the first time, he was glad she had a gun, even if it was at her condo. She'd look real good taking a gun class on Saturday with her injured shoulder. A real war machine. "I hear you have a few mean moves."

Her eyes were closed. "Self-defense. One of my characters had to learn it, and the best way to write about it is to do it myself."

"Why am I not surprised?"

Kariss wanted to cry. Her shoulder hurt, and she didn't want anyone touching it. But what choice did she have? How did Tigo endure this on a regular basis? After receiving medical care, including five stitches, Tigo drove her to the office. She wanted to take pain meds and go to bed, but that would come after she helped him ID the shooter. After all, earlier he'd called her an agent.

She learned the man who had accosted her was in the system.

"We have his fingerprints on the gun,"

Tigo said. "He won't be on the streets for long."

What about Cheeky and the others the FBI were seeking? she wondered. She'd have that conversation when she felt better.

"I'm taking you home." His announcement came like a command.

"I'm concerned about my car. I'm afraid if it's left overnight in that area, it'll be gone."

"Okay. I'll send a couple of agents after your car," Tigo said. "We'll park it here."

"How will I get to the office in the morning?"

Tigo ran his fingers through his hair. "I saw the type and dosage of your pain meds. You'll sleep till noon tomorrow. But call me when you wake up so I know you're okay."

How sweet. "I'm wondering if I should go to the media with this. You know, make a statement about someone being after me because that person thought I'd seen a crime."

"Not a good idea. You'd be giving your name and background info. Perfect for an assassin."

She cringed, but Tigo was right. "I hate being helpless."

"Let us handle the Arroyos. You came here to get a story about Cherished Doe. Go

357

home. Get some rest, and work on that next bestseller." His words were sincere, which was exactly what she needed.

After insisting she take a couple of pain meds, Tigo drove her home. They stopped at the security gate of her complex, and she gave him her code to enter into the keypad.

"Write down those numbers," she said. "Never thought I'd be doing this, but I want you to have them. Just in case."

He pulled out his ever-present notepad and jotted down the numbers. "What about your blood type and social security number?"

"Those are private." Oh, her bed sounded good. The meds were doing the trick. "Hey, what did you say to Mike McDougal?"

"Told him you and I were seeing each other and not to mess with the FBI."

"You didn't."

He chuckled. "I *implied* the situation."

"Better hope today doesn't make his blog."

He groaned with another realization that he'd let his feelings for her affect his professionalism. "I agree." He parked his truck in the visitor area. "Can I have your keys?"

"I'm not an invalid. I can make it inside my condo."

"I have a feeling I might need to carry you."

"I'm not that bad." She forced her eyes to stay open and handed him her purse. "Side pocket. I could use the help. You know the drill — for research."

CHAPTER 35

Wednesday morning, Tigo worked at his desk. Kariss hadn't called, and he was certain she'd not be into the office the rest of the week.

He clicked on the fingerprint report from the man who'd shot Kariss. Lucky Perez had done a three-year stint for robbery and was linked to Arroyo gang activity. The man must be working on his initiation. Now she'd upset two men who wanted her dead. Tigo printed the man's pic and information.

He walked to the squad board and pinned the new findings. One more face. One more name in Operation Wasp. He and Ryan were working on a weapon's deal with Cheeky where they'd offer guns cheaper than their current source.

Soon he and Ryan would have them nailed.

Tigo walked back to his desk and saw an

email from the FIG regarding Arnold Bates's client file. He clicked on the attachment and scanned the list, recognizing a few names and businesses, all of which he'd have the FIG check out.

Tigo whistled. Phillips Commercial Realty Company was listed. He found Ryan at his desk. "Have you seen Bates's client list?"

Ryan stood and stretched. "Haven't checked email for the past thirty minutes. Who's on the list?"

"Wyatt Phillips."

"The one who was married to Kariss's sister?"

"The same. Is this a coincidence, or is there more to the story about the woman who assaulted Kariss?"

"How does our resident writer manage to keep both feet in trouble at all times? I mean, look at the size of this city!"

"Does make me wonder about a few things. What do you think about taking a look at Phillips's phone records?"

"Go for it. What do we know about his girlfriend?" Ryan said.

"When I drove out to her and Phillips's house, she was cooperative. Expressed her regret to Vicki and Kariss. Apologized for not being available when I called. Thought it was a prank call." Tigo huffed. "Right.

After I just talked to Phillips."

"If Kariss hadn't been approached by a woman who offered vague reasons for following them, I wouldn't mess with Phillips or his girlfriend. But something's not right. I want the woman found so we can question her. If this is about a man who's trying to dig up dirt about his ex-wife, then fine. But if the woman was really tailing Kariss, that's another matter."

"It will be interesting to compare Bates's and Phillips's phone records."

"Makes sense to me," Tigo said. "Oh, I received a call from Derek Kyowski. Our disguises will be ready in a week."

Kariss surfed through TV channels before drifting off to sleep. Her shoulder throbbed, but that would soon fade into oblivion. No way could she drag herself to the FBI office. She barely had the strength to make it to the bathroom. Writing this suspense novel had gotten way out of control.

Her laptop lay open on the bed beside her. She'd attempted to title the novel again. The list consisted of: *Cherished Doe, Red Greed, Never Forgotten, Dark Greed.* Today wasn't monumental in the creative department.

She'd subscribed to a website that allowed

her to search through newspaper archives. Nothing about abandoned children fit Xavier's situation. Weariness crept through her body, and her shoulder slowly numbed.

Her cell rang. She saw the caller was Tigo and muted the TV.

"Did you miss your Starbucks?"

"I figured you wouldn't make it in today, and I picked up one myself."

"Checking up on me?"

"Of course. Wanted to make sure you were resting."

"Trust me, I am. Just took another pain med, so I . . . might drift off while you're talking."

He chuckled. "I have that effect on women. I shouldn't have bothered you, so I'll ask a quick question. Have you ever suspected Wyatt Phillips of criminal activity?"

She lay back against the pillow, her mind beginning to fog. She swallowed hard and focused on her response. "Immoral, yes. Criminal, no. He isn't smart enough to weave that intricate of a web. Thinks with his . . . Never mind. Vicki caught him and his present girlfriend . . . together at their house. A criminal mind would have shown discretion and intelligence."

"Is this the sister talking or the medicine?"

"Both. But he does like his money. When Vicki left him, he hired a lawyer who somehow proved Wyatt was penniless." Her words slurred. "His financial records show the real estate company had taken a beating during the recession, and their home had a huge second mortgage."

"What about their joint savings and checking accounts?"

"Disappeared. Vicki didn't have the money to hire an attorney who could investigate the situation. She packed up her belongings and moved to an apartment. The house sold in a few weeks. And . . . and his girlfriend bought a home for them in The Woodlands."

"I've been there. Pretty impressive for a woman serving tables. I'll need to check that out. Interesting. Say, how long ago was . . ."

Kariss couldn't stay awake any longer. Neither could she muster the words to speak.

CHAPTER 36

By Friday, Kariss had cabin fever. As much as she loved her spacious condo, she missed people. Tigo had delivered her Prius last night, and he'd given her orders not to drive while taking the pain meds. Today she vowed not to take any of the little white pills.

But she needed a heavy dose of something other than herself. She'd immersed her energies into helping Xavier and had come up with nothing. She was writing a book with no one to represent or publish it. Every thought turned inward. Depressed, she needed to center on a project that didn't deal with crime and greed. That meant her parents or one of her siblings. Self-centered people didn't make good contributions to society, and she intended to leave a legacy. She picked up her cell to call Vicki for a lunch date. Her sister worked the afternoon shift at the hospital this week and might want to talk about her pregnancy or Wyatt.

After setting a meeting time of noon, Kariss realized she had two hours to figure out how to explain her shoulder. Even her shirt couldn't cover the bulkiness of the bandages.

The two met at a popular French restaurant close to Vicki's apartment. Her sister looked a little green, not at all like her normal peaches-and-cream glow. They stood in line to place their order. The delicious aroma of delicate pastries and fresh bread filled the air.

Kariss took a second look at her sister. She needed to be in bed. "We don't have to do this. We can go someplace quiet and talk, or reschedule."

Vicki inhaled and slowly exhaled. "I'll be okay. It's wearing off, and the baby needs to eat."

"At what expense?"

"I'm the mother, and it's my job to make sure proper nutrients are available to my baby." She smiled weakly.

"You're right, and here I am making inappropriate remarks. Why don't you find us a table, and I'll place the order?"

"Sounds good. I'd like a bowl of soup. Whatever looks good, but not dairy based. Kariss?"

Here it comes. "When were you planning

to tell me about your shoulder?"

"Oh, I can right now."

"Go for it. I've gone through a dozen scenarios in the last few minutes."

Kariss blinked. "I was jogging, and a cyclist hit me."

"He must have run over you."

"It was a she." *Kariss, you need your mouth washed out with soap.*

"When did this happen?"

"Wednesday." That part was true.

Kariss placed the order and learned it would be a few minutes before they were served. She found her sister sipping on water. "I hate this for you. I thought the throw-uppies were over. Can't you take something to stop the sickness?"

"The doctor prescribed medication, but I'm concerned how it might affect the baby."

"Isn't it FDA approved?"

Vicki nodded. "I want the best for this little girl."

"It's a girl?"

"A pink and frilly bundle."

"Wonderful. Now I know how to shop. What names do you like?"

"I'm thinking Kendal."

"Nice. How are you spelling it?"

"K-I-N-D-L-E."

Kariss startled. Being pregnant had shaken

367

more than her sister's abdomen. "Why not Nook or Apple or Sony?"

Vicki cringed. "Hadn't thought of that. Guess I'll not be creative in the spelling."

Kariss touched her sister's hand. "You can spell your little girl's name any way you want. I don't even care if you name her after Grandma."

"Myrtle?"

They both laughed.

"I want to take you up on your offer to move in."

That made the whole week worth it. "Fantastic. When?"

"Is a week too soon? My rent's due in two weeks, and I wanted to be out by then."

Kariss's mind raced with the thrill of helping Vicki through the pregnancy and with the baby. "Perfect. What else is going on?"

"I heard from Wyatt."

Just the sound of his name soured Kariss's stomach. "What's he up to?"

Vicki pressed her lips. "He wants a paternity test."

"Oh, he's priceless." She had a mental picture of their dad taking off after him with a cleaned shotgun and his worn Bible.

"Can't believe he'd even think such a thing." Vicki wiped her perspiring forehead. "Especially since he'd been to see me more than once."

"He was unfaithful, and he wants to believe you'd stoop to the same level."

"I was wavering about the amount of child support payments, but his latest accusation has pushed me over the edge. He wiped out our bank accounts, and now he can make a few deposits for the sake of his child. I'm going for all I can get. I think his live-in must be pressing him for the paternity test. Blonde and Sexy must see dollar signs floating out the door."

"I'm glad you've gotten smarter about him, but I know it hurts."

"This gets worse. He called me while I was on my way here. Wants to talk about the whole pregnancy thing, so I asked him to meet with both of us. I hope you don't mind."

Kariss wanted to stand on the table and dance. "I love the idea. No way is he going to browbeat you with me glaring daggers into his baby blues." She paused, thinking through what she hadn't revealed to her sister about Wyatt. "He came on to me a few times before and after you separated."

Vicki blinked. "I'm . . . I'm not surprised. The more I think about this baby, the less I'm thinking about him. New me, huh?"

"That info will keep me from slapping him

in the face."

"Restrain yourself. He just walked through the front door."

Kariss refused to look at Wyatt until he seated himself at their table. She nearly exploded in laughter. The fifteen-year age difference between Vicki and Wyatt had never been a huge issue, but now his face looked as smooth as a baby's rear. Botox must be a way of keeping his new wife happy.

"Vicki, Kariss, it's good to see you," he said.

"Wish I could say the same." Kariss tilted her head. "How many vials of Botox did it take to smooth the plowed lines in your face?"

He smiled. "Glad you noticed. Looks like you've had a little accident. Trip over your ego?"

Ouch. He'd gotten her good.

He focused on Vicki. "You're looking a little green."

"Thanks. Look, Wyatt, I have no intentions of swapping who looks the worst here. All I want to know is what you have to say. Kariss and I would like to enjoy our lunch."

"I'll make it brief. I'm willing to pay for your indiscretion so we can go on with our lives."

"I have insurance to pay for the baby, but there's a deductible. My attorney will draw up the papers for child support."

He reached for her hand, and she snatched it back. "Your girlfriend would not approve. You've touched me for the last time."

You go, Vicki.

"I think you've misunderstood my meaning. I'll pay for an abortion. That will end the problem, no matter who's the father."

Vicki stood, her face crimson. "Why, you disgusting piece of trash." She picked up her glass of ice water and tossed it in his face. "Get away from me, you filthy pig."

Wyatt wiped his face with a paper napkin. "You are sadly mistaken if you think I'll pay one dime to support your brat. I have a life, and that doesn't include every-other-weekend visits or contributing to your diaper fund. I already have one kid to support, and that's my limit. Here I thought we could get back together, but this proves your irrational attitude."

Kariss clenched her fists to keep from tossing her own water at him, along with her hand across his face.

"And you've just proved how selfish you really are. My attorney will handle our communications, and I'll send you the bill for the paternity test."

Wyatt scooted back his chair and stomped away from them. Kariss thought he was leaving the restaurant, but he headed for the bathroom. People seated around them stared.

"Do you want me to go after him?" an older man said. "It'd be my pleasure."

Vicki's gaze flew from him to the bathroom. "I'm tempted. But I think hurting his cash flow will be my best move."

"I was ready to toss my Dr Pepper at him," a young mother said. "Hope your next relationship is an improvement over this one."

Vicki smiled. "From now on, it's just baby and me." She sat down, her hands trembling.

"Are you okay?" Kariss said.

"Tummy is whirling." She lifted her chin. "For the first time, I stood up to him. Can't believe it."

"And a grand job you did too. Daddy would be proud."

She giggled. "I'm a little embarrassed, but I feel good at the same time."

"Wyatt's the one who made a fool of himself."

"How could I have been so blind for so many years? Now I sound like our parents. Next I'll be quoting Scripture."

"In this instance, it fits. You were blind, and now you see." Kariss smiled up at the server as he placed the food before them and offered to clean up the spill.

"This is cause for celebration," Vicki said. "I'm a new, independent woman, about to be a mother."

"And you're moving in with me."

The figure of a man sitting at a table across the room caught Kariss's attention. She met his stare, and she remembered where she'd seen him before. He was Arnold Bates, the interviewee from the FBI office, the man who'd had gun smuggling information for Tigo and Ryan. She'd heard the agents talking about his possible involvement with Operation Wasp. That also meant he could be thick with the Arroyos.

Bates waved, and she returned the gesture. He pulled his cell from his shirt pocket and pressed in a number — or took her picture. She shuddered. The memories of the night Tigo and Ryan saved her life at the hospital sliced through her. Did she have any reason to be alarmed? Who was Bates calling?

He scooted back his chair and left his plate of food. Surely he didn't plan to start a conversation with her. Two back-to-back confrontations were a stretch. Instead he walked to the door and followed Wyatt outside.

A coincidence?

Kariss stared out the window to see Bates had stopped Wyatt. The two men exchanged a few words, and Wyatt pointed to the restaurant. The men must be acquainted. She let out a pent-up breath.

"You look pale," Vicki said. "Do you know the man talking to Wyatt?"

"Possibly. He looks familiar."

"I don't want to give Wyatt the satisfaction of staring."

Kariss shrugged. "Seemed strange that both men left here at the same time and then decided to have a conversation. He's probably taking Wyatt's side in the little show we gave them."

"A man thing, I'm sure. Sis, where's your Jag?"

"I have it in storage and bought that hot little Prius." She pointed to the parking lot. "It's not a gas hog and has surprisingly good zip."

"I thought you loved the Jag."

Kariss smiled. "I still do. That's why I didn't sell it."

A restaurant worker cleared Bates's food from the table. Outside she noticed the two men shaking hands. Should she tell Tigo about this? Would it make a difference in the investigation?

CHAPTER 37

Saturday morning, Kariss sat in the concealed-handgun workshop. She listened to speakers talk about gun safety, the reasons to have a CHL, and stories from those who'd survived a dangerous situation because they knew how to handle a weapon. Some of those she could use in a book.

She'd chosen to take the workshop first and the shooting portion later. To qualify, she needed to shoot fifty rounds, and she'd never held a gun before purchasing the 9mm.

Tigo arrived midmorning and talked briefly about the FBI, encouraging the participants to get involved in their communities to help fight crime. Kariss wanted to stand and shout she knew him, but she restrained. He reminded the participants of the responsibility of having a CHL and that crime fighting was for those trained in the field of law enforcement.

At the end of the day, Kariss was glad she'd pursued her concealed handgun license and even more glad she'd chosen to take the workshop before the shooting practical. She took the written test and felt good about her answers. All she needed now was to learn how to load and shoot. Hitting a target sounded like an impossibility.

When the class was over, she left the building, mindful of her throbbing shoulder. All she wanted was to pick up something to eat and crawl into bed. While she ordered soup and salad at Panera's, her cell rang. Tigo. He must be in a protective mode.

"Did you make it through the class?"

"Yeah. I think I did fine on the test."

"You sound tired."

"I am. Long day, but it was worth it."

"Do you feel up to the shooting range tomorrow?"

"Tomorrow afternoon sounds good."

"How about I pick you up around two? Not so sure a woman healing from a gun-shot wound should drive to a shooting range. Sounds like you need FBI protection."

"I drove myself today. Are you asking me out?"

He chuckled. "I want to make sure you learn how to use your 9mm correctly instead of developing bad habits."

"You're right. I've never had a date at a shooting range."

"Kariss, go home and take a pain pill."

She hated it when he was right.

The idea of learning how to shoot a gun gave Kariss a headache. One more time, Tigo reminded her to breathe deeply. The shooting range looked like one on a TV crime show: neat and clean. A group of fathers and daughters had walked in ahead of them . . . a wise move on the fathers' part.

"I can't seem to stop shaking," she said. "And I'm embarrassed, like everyone knows I don't know how to do this."

"This is my recommendation." Tigo touched her arm. "If you don't think you could ever shoot anyone, or you'd be too nervous to defend yourself, then this is not for you."

"I want to learn." She rubbed her sweaty palms against the sides of her jeans. "I'll pull myself together."

"You purchased the 9mm for protection, and the first step is to become acquainted with it. Learn to be calm."

"All right. Where do I begin?"

"Hold the gun in the palm of your hand.

It's not loaded, and the safety is on. Get to know every part of it so you feel comfortable." He placed the gun into her hand. "Don't ever point at something you don't intend to shoot. When you're ready, we'll move on to loading it."

The gun felt hard, like a small machine. She expected it to have a mind of its own. "I'd never have made it in the Wild West." She did her best to sound light.

"Handling a gun during those times would have been as natural as cooking on an open fire. Respect its power."

"My dad should have forced me to learn gun safety instead of giving in to my fears. I did enjoy archery. Did well in it. Dad said I had a good eye."

"Owning a gun may not be for you, Kariss. That's why we're here. Owning and operating a weapon is serious business whether it's a gun, a bow and arrow, a knife, or a can of Mace." He stepped behind her and massaged her shoulders, coaxing the tension from her muscles and being careful to avoid the tender spot on her left side.

A jolt of something she didn't want to feel for Tigo swept through her. "Thanks. I appreciate your taking the time to teach me."

"No problem. I've got a stake in keeping you alive."

"My testimony will help you nail at least one of the Arroyos."

"True. But you're a friend, too, and I'd like to keep you alive." His breath tickled her neck.

Should she step away before he sensed what he was doing to her? "You've helped me research my novel, and I really want to do something in return besides bringing you coffee every morning. I want to point him out in a lineup and testify in court."

"Then understand what you're doing now is part of the price." He gave her right shoulder a pat. "Ready?"

"Yes, sir."

"Now let's hold the gun properly as though you were going to aim at a target. Don't put your finger on the trigger until you're ready to fire. Use two hands, one over the top."

"I've seen cops hold a gun like this on TV."

He smiled. "They got that part right."

"Then you put the bullets in a clip?"

"It's called a magazine, and your semi-automatic holds thirteen rounds. I'll show you."

Tigo inserted the magazine and handed the gun back to her. "Focus on the target with both eyes. Line up the sights, the back with the front."

Kariss followed his instructions. "My eyes feel so dry. But at least the earplugs I'm wearing will mute the sound. I bet it'll be loud."

"Blink and clear your mind of everything but the target. Now, slip the tip of your forefinger over the trigger. Pull the trigger gently. Remember to breathe."

She wanted to squeeze her eyes shut, but instead she listened to his voice gently walking her through the process. The gun popped, and she realized how tense her shoulders were.

"Good job," he said. "You have a good eye."

Kariss whispered a thanks. "And I have to do fifty of these for my CHL?"

"Yes. Are you ready to keep going?" He studied her a moment. "I have an idea." He took a pen from his shirt, pulled the collar of her shirt aside, and wrote something on her bandage.

"Did you autograph my shoulder?"

"No. I put a smiley face on it."

By the time she finished the fifty rounds, Kariss realized several magazine loads of confidence. Her aim was good. Better than good. But that didn't answer the dilemma about her ability to pull the trigger if a man wanted her dead.

CHAPTER 38

Monday morning, Kariss was glad to be back at the office. Although the bandage on her shoulder was not a fashion accessory, she did feel a little proud of it, like she carried a medal of honor embellished with Tigo's smiley face.

Some questions about Tigo surfaced, but she needed time to analyze them. Beneath his problem-solving, mastermind exterior was a man capable of deep emotion. His devotion to his mother proved it. And she refused to dwell on how his massage had rattled her.

Tigo peeked around the entrance to her cubicle. "Good to see you back, Agent Walker." His dark-chocolate eyes twinkled. "Maybe someone should license you for a gun."

She wiggled her nose at him. "Very funny. In six weeks or so, I'll be able to protect myself."

"In six weeks, we'll have those bad guys put away. You just use your head, okay?"

She appreciated his concern and thanked him.

Her cell phone rang, and he left her alone. She didn't recognize the caller but answered anyway, wincing a little. Shooting practice yesterday had made her other shoulder tired.

"Hi, Kariss, how are things going in the new job?"

Mike McDougal. What had she ever seen in him? Certainly nothing more than a face. "How did you get my number?"

"Is that any way to treat an old friend? Oh, we were more than that."

"But it was over a long time ago."

"You dumped me for no reason."

Kariss dug her fingernails into her palm. "Let's get the facts straight. You lied to me about needing money for your niece."

"No one believed you."

"You mean no one believed I could be that stupid."

He chuckled, a disgusting sound that sounded like he had sinus drainage. "Read my blog lately?"

She bit her tongue to stop any sarcasm. Mike could do tremendous damage on his blog, since it was read by thousands. "Every

Thursday morning."

"You don't comment."

"You read those?"

"Every single one. Even those who respond like idiots. After all, they're my fans, my adoring public."

She touched her shoulder, feeling the bandage under her shirt. "Imagine that."

"You're not being nice, Kariss. Hurts my feelings."

"You're right. I'm sorry. Just wondered how you found me."

"I remembered you were from Texas City, and I did some searching on the Internet. Called a few of our old friends. Here I am."

"Since you went to all that trouble, this must be important."

"You, pretty lady, are always important." His words were low, seductive. Regret for ever being involved with him washed over her.

"Okay, Mike, what's really going on?"

"I want to interview Xavier Olvera, an exclusive for Channel 5."

"Did you contact him?"

"I went through Gilberto, but Xavier refused. Said he felt like the English newspapers and TV were not doing anything to find his wife."

"He has faith in Univision. After all, their

384

programming with *Aquí y Ahora* helped the FBI solve the death of his daughter."

"But you could get me the interview. He speaks highly of you."

Always the angle. "I can't. I respect Xavier's stand."

"Don't you think you owe Channel 5 the opportunity to continue a gut-wrenching story?"

"Mike, this conversation is going nowhere. I'm not helping you. Xavier Olvera is a friend, and I'll not exploit him. *Aquí y Ahora* has a follow-up this coming Friday. His allegiance is with them."

"Let's discuss this over dinner."

"No thanks."

"I have your address."

"Not any more. I now live in a gated community."

"You're a tough woman, Kariss. Where are you working? Because I've seen the blog posts about your career headed for a shakedown."

"I'm a writer."

"For how long? I'll ignore what I'm reading. By the way, who's the lucky man by your side? FBI . . . That's heavy research." Mike laughed. "I'd like to step into his shoes — or rather your bed."

He made her feel like she needed a shower.

Any attempts to remain cordial dissipated. "We're done."

"You shouldn't blow me off. Readers will see a side of the Kiss of Kariss that isn't conducive to book sales."

"Go for it, Mike. Those who read your blog soon see your vindictive side. I wouldn't lower myself to contradict it."

She disconnected the call, wondering what McDougal Reports would say about her. He couldn't do any more damage than Meredith's recent blog.

Kariss Walker has given the kiss of death to her career. She's decided to write suspense in an over-saturated market in which she doesn't have the skill to run with the big leaguers. That's why the Rockford Literary Agency has chosen to discontinue representation.

How interesting . . . since Kariss had been the one to end the professional relationship. But the devastation to her career had already occurred. Posting a rebuttal to Meredith's post only put Kariss on the defense. Readers of her blog were professionals in the publishing industry. McDougal Reports hit the eyes of fans.

An hour later she left her work area for the employee lounge. A bag of Vitamin M&M's sounded really good. Ever since she'd started this project, her life had taken a definite bend in the road.

No sooner had the thought left her brain than Hillary walked in, and there was no avoiding the assertive agent.

"Hi, Hillary, how are you?" If she gathered up her purse and walked to the door, she might not stop her.

The woman's face brightened. "Just the lady I want to see."

"What can I do for you?" Kariss regretted the words as soon as she spoke them.

"Remember when you told me to take an online course on punctuation and grammar?"

"Yes. Did you enroll?"

"No. Because I felt it stifled my creativity. Stole my voice. But thanks to you, I perused the entire writer website and decided to start over with a new story."

"Wonderful. I'd like for you to reconsider the English refresher. It —"

"Oh no. I'm convinced that I don't need it. An editor can stick in those little commas and fix my verb tenses. But my new story has me up all night writing fast and furiously."

Kariss reached into her purse and pulled out an M&M, popping it into her mouth. "What's it all about?"

"It's a historical novel set in medieval

times during the bubonic plague. One of the rats ends up in time travel to the year three thousand."

"A rat?"

"Yes, but once he's in a futuristic setting, he transforms into a human. A very sexy man."

Oh, please, tell me this isn't so.

Hillary giggled. "I have romance, inner and outer conflict, and a character arc just like you said. Want to know the hero's name?"

"Sure."

"Michelangelo. He paints too. Can't wait to send you the first chapter."

Kariss cringed. "Make sure it's polished. Take your time. I understand your first priority is your position here."

"I'm thinking of resigning."

"Let me make a suggestion. When you earn as much from your writing as you do here, then consider a career change."

Hillary startled. "But I need time to write."

"Try getting up earlier in the morning or staying up later at night."

Hillary's shoulders slumped, then she glanced at her watch. "Great, I'm late for a meeting. You really destroyed my bubble, Kariss. Are you worried I'll take over your spot on the bestsellers list?"

Kariss took a deep breath and walked toward the door. "I welcome the challenge, Hillary."

CHAPTER 39

Shortly before noon, Ryan approached Tigo's desk. "We've got an update on Bates's and Masterson's foreign holdings. Check your in-box. You should have the same report and phone records."

Tigo printed out both attachments, and the two men left the area for privacy in an interview room.

Behind closed doors, Tigo studied the findings. "We already know Bates has a petroleum company in South Korea that manufactures oilfield pipe. He also has a subsidiary located in Chad that specializes in pipe able to withstand extreme heat and pressure — a product that only a few companies ever need."

"Right. Says here the special pipe requires a mineral alloy found only in Chad. That mineral is mined by a company that Masterson owns. This piece is the last step before the pipe's shipped to the U.S. for use in the

Gulf's deep-water drilling." Ryan turned the report over. "Bates wasn't exactly up-front about his relationship with Masterson. Wonder what else he lied about?"

"Probably just enough to keep himself out of hot water. Oilfield pipe might not be the only thing they're importing into the U.S." The width of the pipe had to be a problem in shipping the guns. He glanced up at Ryan. "Would they dissemble weapons before shipping?"

"They'd have to. When the pipe is brought into the Port of Houston, the Arroyos could unload the guns and get them into Mexico. Sounds simple enough. All we need to do is prove our speculation."

"Or find out when the next shipment of pipe arrives from Chad." Tigo drummed his fingers on the report. "Bates said he heard about a shipment of something from Chicago, which could be a way to throw off the investigation. The FIG can research that further."

"Masterson and Bates have a lucrative business going on without smuggling guns. Not much overhead since the guns and ammo are brought right to their front door."

"Shouldn't be a problem to find out when the next shipment of pipe's due."

Ryan leaned back in his chair. "Already

did. August 17. Same as Bates reported."

"Why? Is he trying to eliminate Masterson in the equation? That doesn't make sense. Unless —" Tigo paused to think through what he suspected. "Bates could want more of a cut. I wonder if he has another source in Chad for the mineral used in the pipe. Do you know what other companies extract it?"

"Worth looking into. Bates could stand to make a whole lot more money without Masterson. And what about who's tipping us off about Arroyos' transports into Mexico? Do you think Bates is getting greedy? Possibly looking to the Skulls to find mules?"

"Maybe so," Tigo said. "He could be trying to get rid of Masterson and at the same time muddying the waters with the Arroyos." He stood and walked to the window, where sunlight heated the city. "If he's supplying all the weapons and paying less to get them across the border, he stands to make millions."

"Yeah, and I think Bates is playing us as his ace," Ryan said. "He came to us as a concerned citizen. Gave us the dates of the transfer. The pipe is shipped from Chad after the alloy coating, which means Masterson would be nailed for gun smuggling, and

Bates could plead innocent. With Masterson's record, a good attorney could get any charges against Bates dismissed." He shrugged. "He has proof about coming to us with his suspicions."

Ryan examined the report again. "My guess is that's exactly what Bates wants. But if Masterson suspects a double cross, Bates is a dead man."

"We may be way out there with this, but I've got a gut feeling we're onto something."

Tigo searched through the phone records. "Bates and Masterson are quite communicative. I'd like to have these other numbers checked out." He saw a number resembling one he'd examined earlier. "Hold on a minute while I get Wyatt Phillips's phone records." Once he returned, he compared them to Bates's. "Phillips only has one call to Bates. None to Masterson. That theory just died."

Ryan glanced at his watch. "Linc wants us in his office in ten minutes. We've got footage of Bates and Masterson together."

Upstairs the two men joined Linc. He pointed to his computer screen. "We're fitting a few pieces together, linking Bates's Cardinal Ventures' subsidiary with Masterson's Mining Company," Linc said.

"Do you have surveillance reports?" Tigo said.

"We not only have phone records but both men on film. So much for Bates claiming he didn't talk to Masterson."

Tigo and Ryan peered into the screen.

"This was taken last Friday," Linc said. "They left their offices about fifteen minutes apart and drove to The Woodlands where they met up at The Fountains at Waterway Square. Note how they're on opposite sides of the fountain until Bates receives a call."

"They must have wondered about being tailed," Ryan said. "Who did you use?"

Linc laughed. "An Asian gal who mingled with the teens."

Tigo noted Masterson raising a fist. "Any idea what this is about?"

"Not sure. Our gal wore a wire, but by the time she made it to Bates, the call was over." Linc pointed to the right side of the screen. "That's one of Masterson's bodyguards. A second man stood about fifty feet away, and a third followed Bates to his car."

"Did he get roughed up?" Tigo said.

"No. Obviously Bates and Masterson aren't happy about something," Linc said. "I read the reports. Looks to me like Bates is setting Masterson up — if he lives through it. They talked about twelve minutes, but it didn't get hot until the end. Bates drove back to the Galleria office, but Masterson had lunch at the Waterway Marriott with his wife."

"What do you think?" Tigo said.

"Business partners who aren't getting along. We have additional footage of Bates meeting with two Arroyos on the southeast part of town. Possibly the same two he claimed to see in the parking garage."

"Setting up Masterson," Ryan said.

"We're staying on them," Linc said. "No point in bringing Bates in again. That would only raise flags. Let's stay on him and Masterson. See where it goes. How's the contact for getting you two in position to sell guns?"

"Actually, good," Tigo said. "Cheeky is examining our credentials. Should know soon. Possibly get a buy going about the time of the next gun shipment."

"The Arroyos are heated up. Two more Skulls were found last night. Bullets to the head. Execution style." Linc crossed his arms over his chest. "Watch your backs. I saw Kariss today. Is she ready to make plane reservations and take a vacation out of state?"

"She's not budging. I followed her around Saturday and kept her busy Sunday afternoon. But I'm not a babysitter."

Linc clenched his fist. "Neither do we want her dead."

CHAPTER 40

Thursday morning, Kariss settled into her work area at the FBI office and responded to emails, which were decreasing by the day. She jumped in on writer loops — and most days with good input. Yesterday she'd found a site of suspense bloggers who were looking for a seventh writer to complete a week. She applied and waited.

Ever since Kariss had refused Mike McDougal's advances, she'd read his blog. He edged toward slander against prominent persons in Houston, the state, and the country. Just when she thought he'd forgotten her, trouble brewed. Mom had called her while she was en route to the FBI office this morning and said she'd forgotten to tell her that Mike had phoned the house.

"He said you weren't answering your phone."

"Right. He's a pest. Nasty manners."

"I'm glad I didn't tell him where you lived

because he asked for that too. I told him I could relay a message."

"What was his response?"

"He wants you to read today's blog. Honey, I've read what that man writes, and it's disgusting. I'm surprised someone hasn't flattened him."

Kariss laughed, but the backwash of what Mike could do twisted her insides. "When did you start reading his blog? I didn't think you did much with the computer."

"Since I heard mention of it on TV news. It's usually posted midmorning."

At ten-thirty, Kariss logged onto McDougal Reports.

Sometimes the rich and famous leave their friends behind. It seems money brings on an air of sophistication that discards relationships like old shoes, unless those persons can add rungs to the career ladder. I've run into someone who is one of those user types more than once over the summer, and every time she embraced snobbery like flies take to cow patties. When I attempted to have a conversation with her, she blew me off. And her new muscle-bound boyfriend told me to stay away.

The person in question is Kariss Walker, who is a New York Times *bestselling writer. Prior to that, she performed an outstanding job as news anchor for Channel 5. Those positions have tainted her personality. She's no longer available for old friends. My invitation to coffee was met with stark annoyance. She just batted her long lashes. (And they are for real. Trust me, I know many details about Kariss Walker.) Anyway, my point is she had no time to catch up with an old friend.*

Maybe her readership is about to take a dive.

Kariss clicked on her address book and phoned her lawyer, leaving a message with his answering service. This time Mike had gone too far.

An hour later, she still fumed. Tigo stood in the doorway of her cubicle. Maybe he had a better idea about how to deal with Mike.

"I have a problem."

He lifted a brow. "And you want me to help solve it? Word choice? You're already ahead on this game."

"No." She couldn't hide her grin, despite the problem with the blog. "Remember the obnoxious reporter, Mike McDougal? He just published a scathing blog about me. It's slanderous, and I've got a call in to my attorney."

She turned her laptop his way. After reading it, he whistled. "Once something is written on the Internet, it's there forever."

"Gee, thanks."

"You aren't thinking of refuting it in the comments, are you?"

"I'm not that stupid," Kariss said. "His blogs are usually about political or controversial persons. I imagine my lawsuit isn't his first."

"Don't you think his reputation discounts everything he writes?"

"I think he's read for entertainment, not anything factual. But he has a large following."

"Have you read the comments?"

"No."

He turned the screen her way. "Listen to this one: 'Bet those who've enjoyed Kariss Walker's books will have a different viewpoint.' "

Lately, Tigo had been more of a human being. "Okay. I'll read the others."

"Aloud, please."

She smiled, but her heart wasn't in it. " 'We're tired of people-bashing, Mike. This is the last time I read your blog.' "

"See. The readers get tired of that stuff."

"I feel better all ready." She read the next one. " 'Bring on more! We all know the rich and famous are shallow.' "

"Get yourself a suit of armor."

"While I'm at it, I'll learn how to joust."

Kariss shook her head. "This reminds me why I refuse to read reviews. If they're good, I'm afraid my head will swell. If they're bad, I cry for six months."

She exited the site. Her attorney could deal with Mike McDougal.

Friday Kariss stayed at her condo to help Vicki move in. With her stitched-up shoulder, all she could do was point. Nurse Vicki refused to let her lift a single box.

"But you're the one who's pregnant," Kariss said.

"Daddy moved my household things to one of their storage buildings. All I have are personal belongings — my clothes, books, baby things."

"I'm right here." Their dad came through the door with a box. "I thought when I retired that my backbreaking days were over."

Vicki swung around from the steps leading to the second level. "Daddy, you love doing things for your girls."

"Tell my aching body that tomorrow. I suppose this box goes upstairs?"

Vicki giggled, and it felt so good to hear the familiar ring. "All of it goes up here."

Kariss gave his whiskered cheek a kiss. "Thanks for helping."

"Both of you are worthless. Hope you're steering clear of bicycles."

How awful that she'd had to lie to Vicki and her dad. "It's healing nicely."

"Single women need a man looking after them. Both of you should move home."

Vicki returned from the second floor. Her ultra-thin body had a bit of a pooch. "Oh, you'd love it if we all came back and brought the grandkids."

He laughed. "Until it came time to buy groceries." He studied her. "Sweet girl, you're getting a tummy on you."

Vicki patted it. "Yep, and it's going to get a lot bigger."

"What are we going to call her?" he said.

"Haven't a clue. May have to see her first."

"She'll be beautiful like her mama." His stomach growled loudly.

"We'll do a grand lunch today." Kariss took a small box from her dad. "All the chicken-fried steak and fixin's that you can eat."

"Love those artery-hardening foods," Dad said. "Do they have blackberry cobbler?"

"Desserts are their specialties — chocolate pecan pie, lemon meringue pie, red velvet cake, apple dumplings. You name it." Kariss followed him up the stairs. "What's Mom doing?"

"Volunteering at the church library. She loves those books. I think some kind of book club for kids is going on, so she's putting together certificates and treats for them."

"I thought she was going to slow down, like you. Do more gardening."

"Ah, slowing down means giving up. We'll both work hard till the day we die. Rest in heaven. Mama can plant flowers for Jesus, and I'll work on building another ark."

Kariss ducked into the room designated to be the nursery before Dad got wound up on a sermon. She'd forgotten to pray for Jo-Jack, and he died. But she had been praying for Xavier in hopes he found his child. She rubbed her lower back. Odd thing about faith . . . After the day-care fire, she'd tossed it like a rotten tomato. Claimed she didn't have any until she got into a desperate situation. Lately she'd been in far too many of those.

She had her 9mm, and she could hold that in her hands. Protect herself from those who wanted her out of the way. Kariss shivered. Why think about such things now? Tigo and Ryan were working on bringing the bad guys in. The Arroyos might be fearless, but they were no match for the FBI. She didn't really have to worry. Another day or so and it would all be over.

Late afternoon, Kariss and Vicki were finally alone and seated in the living room. Vicki's eyelids drooped.

"Why don't you and my niece take a nap?"

Vicki closed her eyes. "Not yet. I have all weekend to rest up. At least my clothes are in the closet and drawers. What's left can wait until tomorrow."

"I'll help."

"I don't want to dip into your writing time."

Kariss laughed. "Fat chance of that."

"Why?"

The truth needed to be said. "I don't have an agent or an editor."

Vicki startled. "What happened?"

"Meredith and I parted ways because of my switch to suspense. No one's interested in taking me on."

"What does that mean for your career?"

Kariss shrugged. "I either win or lose. If I don't have a publishing house interested in this book by the time it's finished, then I'll self-publish. Maybe go back to writing women's fiction."

"What do you really want to do?"

"My heart isn't in those books anymore." Her determination rose with her words. "I want to write fiction with lots of action and high stakes. Give my hero and heroine a

time limit to solve a crime then squeeze it."
She caught herself. "Guess I got carried
away."

"We all know you're a gifted writer. This
whole family is behind you."

She sighed. "Thanks. Wish I could convince an agent or editor."

"Give it time. Are you considering going
back into TV work?"

"Nope, sis. The competition is more than
I can handle."

"Isn't this the weekend for the Gulf Coast
Writers Conference?"

"It is. Remember, I didn't plan to go
because of the research."

"But you could have met with agents and
editors."

"Maybe next year. This is what I'm supposed to do now."

"Then I'll simply pray for you."

Kariss shook her head. "Mom and Dad
must have gotten to you."

"God did. I've made too many mistakes,
and He's given me a chance to start over. I
want to raise my little girl like we were
raised."

"And have her resent you?"

"Do you resent Mom and Dad's faith or
respect it?"

Kariss didn't have an answer.

CHAPTER 41

Friday afternoon Tigo studied the squad board. Everything was slipping into place. A sense of satisfaction swept in for a moment, along with an adrenaline rush.

"We have proof that Hershey's still building vehicle units," Ryan said.

Tigo turned from the squad board. "A true craftsman."

"What do you think we should do? He's arranged for us to meet Cheeky."

"He did, and we're grateful. Still, he hasn't given up his side job." Tigo nodded. "Shall we take a ride? Talk about our next move?"

"And we need to pick up our disguises."

"Right. I'll phone Kyowski. Make sure he's there."

Ryan shoved his hands into his pockets. "Love this part of what we do. Taking on a disguise is like being a kid at Halloween."

"As long as we don't get ourselves killed."

"Spoilsport. I'm thinking more like trick *and* treat."

"What do your kids say about you?"

"The same as my wife — hard to get me to grow up."

"That's what keeps us alive and creative. Hey, I need to cash a check at the credit union for Hershey."

They changed into jeans and T-shirts before leaving the office. Tigo drove his new bomb, a twenty-five-year-old Ford. He exited the FBI office onto the feeder road, then sped onto the highway.

"I have a few ideas about Hershey," Ryan sad. "But I want to hear yours first."

"I'm still in problem-solving mode," Tigo said. "Bring it on."

"Idea number one: we could turn around and head back to the office. Ride out what he's doing until this is over."

"I agree. We need to keep him happy until we arrest Cheeky."

"Your turn."

Tigo chuckled. "We've used his daughter as leverage, and he's been good to us. Let's thank him and play dumb about his side business. I'd like to find out if this is his season to wear a wire. I even visited the tech squad and brought one."

"And if he refuses?"

407

"Show the pics of him building and install-ing a unit."

"Tigo, he could pull the plug from our meeting with Cheeky."

"Not if we assure him his daughter has been fully exonerated from the drug theft and an arrest has been made." He glanced at Ryan. "The arrest was in Sunday's paper and in the news."

"Ever get the feeling that God is guiding us through this case?"

"Not really." Tigo understood his partner was a strong believer, like Linc. But Tigo's beliefs about God were based on a deity that created the world, then sat back in his easy chair to see how it all played out. Pray-ing or depending on anything but himself made no sense.

"I think He is."

"Why? God gave us a mind to figure out things. That's what we're doing."

"You solve this case your way, and I'll continue to pray for direction."

"Oh, I caught the sarcasm."

Ryan threw a glance at him. "Didn't mean to come off that way."

"I know. I'm a little touchy about the God thing . . . and dealing with my mother's declining health."

"Is she a believer?"

"The most devoted Christian on the planet. But look at her now."

"Tigo, we all have a purpose. You and I have ours. Your mother has hers. You told me she kept you from turning into a bad guy."

When Ryan didn't add anything more to his statement, Tigo repeated the words in his mind. "What else?"

"Nothing. Just think about it."

Ryan and his faith were confusing at best, and right now wasn't the best time for Tigo to get irritated about a subject that meant nothing to him.

At Hershey's shop, Tigo and Ryan went through the routine of keeping an eye on those standing outside and waiting for Hershey to unlock the door. He had a customer, a black woman with short, tight shorts who was having a problem choosing what kind of firearm to fit her purse. The situation reminded him of Kariss.

Once the woman paid for her weapon, Tigo made his way to Hershey with a box of fifty bullets for his 7mm Remington Magnum.

"What's up? Why are you here?" He blew out a sigh. "You know I'm watched."

"Just wanted to thank you for a good job and pick up a box of ammo." He set the box on the counter.

"I'll know tonight or tomorrow. Looks like things are almost in place for the buy. That's fifty-seven dollars."

Tigo pointed to the box. "It says seventy-five."

Hershey frowned. "Yeah. Seventy-five. I'll text after the meeting."

"Good," Tigo said. "Did you see an arrest was made in the drug theft?"

"I did. Appreciate it. Though we already knew my daughter had nothin' to do with it."

"We have another request."

Hershey eyed him. "What?"

"Wear a wire."

"The answer's no."

Tigo gave him a half smile. "More money in it."

"How much?"

"Another five grand."

Hershey hesitated, then cursed. "Okay. But not my phone. That's the first thing Cheeky takes when we meet."

Tigo pulled out a pin light typical of what was used to look down the barrel of a gun to make sure it was clean.

Hershey slipped it into his pocket. "I don't understand why this is necessary when I've held up my end of the bargain."

"Call it insurance. Like the guys outside waiting on your nod to waste us."

Hershey smirked. "Anything else?"

Ryan had been quiet until this, which was his usual manner. "We're watching you. One slip and your rear's in prison for a long time."

Shortly after Vicki had fallen asleep, Kariss received a call from security that a flower shop van wanted to make a delivery. Working with Tigo and Ryan had made her somewhat smarter, and she wasn't going to let any strangers near her home.

"Just ask the driver to leave them with you, and I'll be right there. Go ahead and sign the delivery slip and tell the driver thanks."

"Yes, ma'am."

She had no clue who'd send flowers since she wasn't seeing anyone, and she hadn't sold a book. Grabbing her keys, she drove to the security gate. There, placed outside the small building were two dozen red roses with baby's breath. Whoa. That brightened her day.

With the aid of the guard, she carefully positioned the crystal vase into the floorboard of the backseat and inched back to her condo. Once inside, she positioned them on the dining room table, their sweet fragrance filling the air.

She lifted the card from the bouquet and opened it.

Vicki,
   I hope these flowers convey my hope for your happiness in your new home. Kariss will take good care of you, and I know you'll be happy. I'm so sorry for the many ways I've hurt you.
Wyatt

Kariss's first instinct was to toss the embossed card in the trash. Vicki would never know Wyatt had sent the flowers. He was up to no good, and this was just a ploy to win her sister over to something that benefited him. His attorney probably suggested it before she filed for child support.

"What beautiful roses. Who are they from?"

Kariss wanted to crumple the card. But Vicki was capable of making her own decisions.

"Sis? What's wrong?"

"They're not for me. They're for you. From Wyatt."

Vicki's eyes widened. "Why on earth would he send me flowers?" She walked to

412

the table and touched a petal. "Can I send them back?"

Kariss saw the torn look on her sister's face, the mix of love, hate, and probably self-loathing for how she'd allowed Wyatt to affect her emotions.

"What would that prove? They're beautiful, and roses are your favorite flower. Accept his gesture and enjoy them."

Vicki inhaled an open blossom. "I'd like to know why. The last time he sent flowers was when he'd been unfaithful."

"I didn't know that."

She shrugged. "I gave them to a neighbor. I wanted him out of my life, but now that will never be because of the baby."

"Sis, you need rhino skin. You still love him despite the many times he's hurt you. The pain isn't going to vanish overnight."

"I keep telling myself that turning all of my affections to this baby will make Wyatt disappear."

"We'll work on it."

Vicki blinked back the tears in her pretty brown eyes. "I'm going to put away a few boxes."

Kariss lifted the vase of roses. "Put this on the lonely table in the nursery. Big and little girls love flowers."

Vicki took them and nodded. "I'm glad

I'm here. You're good for me."

Kariss laughed and planted a kiss on her cheek. "That works both ways."

"Anything you want to talk or rant about or whatever, you can depend on me."

Not about the Arroyos or the mess she was in. Kariss didn't dare tell Vicki about helping Xavier either.

CHAPTER 42

Friday afternoon, Tigo and Ryan picked up their disguises, then said their good-byes for the weekend. Tigo's thoughts were preoccupied with what needed to happen to close this case.

When Hershey gave them the okay, they'd make their sale and nail Cheeky and a list of other Arroyos. In the meantime, Bates and Masterson were under heavy surveillance. Theoretically, they had a sound plan. But between the lines was the potential for too many things to go wrong.

His next stop was the dentist's office — his friend the dentist who never hurt him or made him feel badly for needing laughing gas. After Tigo made a few complaints about the dentist who'd done the root canal, he got numbed up. He leaned back and closed his eyes while the dentist inserted a post where Dr. Nightmare had completed the root canal. Next, impressions were taken for a crown. An hour and a half later, he made an appointment for the permanent crown and headed home. The numbness started to wear off, which made him feel more human. He needed to make a bank deposit, but no way until his mouth moved the way he wanted it.

Once at home, he sorted through mail while sitting beside his mother. His stomach growled, and he reached for a glass of iced tea, pleased that he no longer dribbled down his chin. Normally he liked to cook, but the situation with the Arroyos and the detail to making sure it all happened had him too wound up. He didn't want to eat alone one more night. Of course Natalie would join him, but he couldn't talk work.

In short he was lonely.

He picked up his personal cell phone and stared at it, wondering if his thoughts were foolish . . . desperate. Maybe this had more to do with the novocaine wearing off than reaching out to a friend. He could claim wanting to know about her afternoon or making sure she was safe. Friends stuff.

For that matter, he could call Ryan or Linc to see if their families had plans tonight. Although those situations usually made him feel uncomfortable simply because he had nothing in common with them.

Still staring at his phone, he clicked on the Word Family game. His turn again. He'd beaten her the last game, but she was still one up on him. Studying the letters, he slipped the word *lead* under a previous word, giving him twenty-eight points and Kariss seventeen. He touched Play and Submit.

He thought about her at the office. She had a way of staring into her computer screen as though she were taking a glimpse into someone's soul. Her brown curly hair framed her face, wild-looking yet always in place.

Five minutes later, she texted him.

HOW LAME THAT WE R PLAYING A WORD GAME ON A FRI NIGHT?

He laughed and keyed in his response.

I'M HUNGRY & BORED.

He waited for a response.

LATE DINNER HERE 2. VICKI'S MAKING PECAN-CRUSTED TROUT, SALAD, SWEET POTATO FRIES & ROLLS. SHE SZ U CAN COME.

WHEN?

NOWZ FINE.

WHATZ 4 DESSERT?

THAT'S UR JOB.

He grinned and glanced at his mother's sleeping form. He should stay, but nothing remained of her but a shell. He wouldn't be gone long, and Natalie had his number. "Do you mind?" he said to his mother.

How many times had she urged him to get out more?

I'LL TAKE U & V 4 ICE CREAM.

ITZ A DEAL.

After changing from his grungy work jeans to a more upscale brand, Tigo kissed his mother good-bye and told her he'd be back in a few hours.

Over eighteen months ago, he'd met a woman for dinner. It had gone badly. She'd wanted to come home with him, and he declined. Two reasons: one was his mother, and the second was the woman's aggressiveness. He wasn't sure why the incident crossed his mind now, except the idea of meeting two women for dinner had him shaking. He'd almost rather meet a couple of bad guys on the other side of town.

Kariss would have to see Tigo standing at her door before she believed he'd accepted the dinner invitation. She hadn't been serious, and the idea of him meeting Vicki made her a little uneasy. More like nauseous. What if he slipped and talked about the danger she'd gotten herself into?
  She picked up her cell and pressed in another text.

> PLZ DON'T TELL VICKI ABOUT
> ARROYOS.
>
> K.

Then he added,

> WE NEED 2 LEARN HOW 2 TEXT
> LIKE KIDS.

Kariss laughed.

> WE R FINE 4 OLD PEOPLE.
>
> SZ WHO?

"What's so funny?" Vicki said as she measured pecans for the food processor.

"Tigo says we need to learn how to text properly."

"He's not as bad as you first thought, is he?"

Kariss knew exactly where this conversation was headed, and she didn't plan to dive into those waters. "I respect who he is and what he's done for me. And he's an outstanding agent."

"How did you get hooked up with him to begin with?"

Kariss reached for a bag of mixed greens in the fridge. "Linc put us together."

"I see."

"What does that mean?"

"Maybe Linc had a little matchmaking in mind."

Kariss snipped the top of the bag and dumped its contents into a colander. Just like she'd snip this conversation. "Special Agent Santiago Harris is not my type. And never could be."

"Why?"

"Did anyone ever tell you that you ask a lot of questions?"

"Yep. So why wouldn't you ever be interested in him?"

"He's the problem-solver type. Wants to fix things, and those things have to be done right."

"A perfectionist?"

"More than that. Different. Linc told me Tigo held back from taking a leadership role with his current case. But when he did, he weeded through facts and details and approached it like a bulldog. To him, all the solutions for a problem have to be practical and proven." She sprayed water over the field greens and tossed them lightly. "Which is different from a perfectionist. Worse, I think."

"I see. So your method of creating characters and stories is totally foreign to him?"

"Yeah. I doubt he's ever read a novel. No imagination. If a book doesn't serve a purpose, then he'd not waste his time."

"Sounds like you understand him pretty well."

"Only enough to know he'd drive me nuts. I run on feelings and intuition. He runs on theoretically proven facts."

Vicki laughed. "You've gone to great lengths to understand a guy you aren't interested in."

"Trust me, you'll know what I mean when you meet him." He'd saved her life and acted like a counselor on more than one occasion. But Vicki didn't need to know any of that. "He's not a total pain. Just not my type."

"What is your type?"

"I'll let you know when I figure it out. For sure, the perfect man of my dreams is not Tigo."

Within the hour, the man in question arrived wearing designer jeans and a light blue, button-down shirt. When Kariss invited him in, he carried a box of gourmet chocolates.

"Here I am," he said. "Thanks for the invitation."

"Sounds like your Friday nights are as interesting as mine."

He nodded. "Hey, does my mouth look strange?"

She laughed. "In what way?"

He scowled, but she could tell he was faking it. "Had a dentist appointment this afternoon. Want to make sure I look normal."

"And tell me, Agent Santiago, what is strange and normal for you?"

"Never mind. I shouldn't have asked a writer."

"Right." She bit her lip to keep from laughing again. He could be charming if he put his mind to it.

"I remembered your sister is pregnant, so I brought chocolate instead of wine."

"Wonderful," Kariss said. "Dinner will be

ready shortly."

He sniffed. "Smells wonderful."

"My sister's the cook in the family. I got a pass on those genes."

"I thought one of your novels was about a chef?"

How did he know that? "I did my research and flunked a cooking class."

"Did I hear something about chocolates?" Vicki called from the kitchen. "I want any caramel-cream ones. Bring the notorious FBI agent back to the kitchen. I'm anxious to meet the man who puts up with my sister."

"You have the situation backward. I put up with his fastidious ways." Kariss turned to Tigo and lowered her voice. "She has no idea about what's going on, the mess I've gotten into."

"No problem," he whispered. "Did you see that I'm nine points ahead of you with my latest word?"

"I just played, and you're six points behind."

He grinned. "Not for long."

"I let you win the other game. Now we're down to serious business."

He walked to the kitchen, and she introduced him to Vicki. He lifted the lid off the chocolate box and pointed to one. "That one is caramel filled."

Vicki wiped her hands on a towel and peered over the box. "How do you know for sure?"

"The lid has a diagram."

How like Tigo. And her sister thought the two of them could become involved? If anyone was to play matchmaker, Kariss would be the one to hook up Vicki and Tigo.

Kariss observed how easily he talked to Vicki. He complimented her cooking, and the two exchanged recipes. This was not the Tigo Kariss knew. He asked all the appropriate questions about her pregnancy and even wanted to see the empty nursery. After dinner, Vicki showed him the sparse room.

"Kariss and I are going to paint the walls a pale pink." Vicki's eyes sparkled, and she looked lovely. "It's called Blush."

"And the paint's the kind that won't harm you or the baby?" Tigo examined a rose petal. "Of course not. You're a nurse."

His phone rang, and he snatched it up like a handyman reaches for his screwdriver. "Yeah. What's up?" His facial expressions changed to the professional Special Agent Tigo.

Kariss studied him, and she wondered if the caller was Ryan. Tigo captured her attention, and in that moment she knew the call had something to do with the Arroyos.

"I'll be there within the hour." He ended the call. "Sorry, ladies, I have a situation to handle. Thanks for a great dinner and company. It's rare that I have the pleasure of spending an evening with two beautiful women."

Where had he hidden this gentleman? A second glance at his face showed that he was in think mode, complete with narrowed brows, and she recognized the agent she was accustomed to.

"Thanks for coming," Vicki said. "Glad to meet you. I appreciate your taking care of my sis."

He walked down the steps from the second floor and toward the front door.

Kariss followed. "I'm right behind you."

"Curious?"

"My middle name."

At the door, he turned to her. "That was Ryan. A fight between the Arroyos and Skulls broke out on the southeast side of town. Four men dead. A fifth man, an Arroyo, is listed in critical condition. I'm meeting Ryan at Ben Taub Hospital to question him."

If only —

"No, Kariss. I can read your mind. You're

not going. The place will be infiltrated with gang members, drunk and out for blood. Your buddy, Froggie Diego, will be among them."

She cringed. "I understand."

He appeared to stare through to her soul. "Do I have to tell Vicki what's going on to keep you in one piece?"

"No. I don't want her worried about a thing. She has enough to think about. I know what happens when an Arroyo is after someone."

"Good to hear some common sense."

She tilted her head. "Will you call me later or tell me on Monday what happened?"

"I might. Do you want another tutoring session at the shooting range on Sunday?"

"Yes. I need the practice."

"I can pick you up around two." He gave her a smile and brushed her nose with his finger. "If you learn to cook like Vicki, you and I could spend more time together."

The teasing had returned, along with the charm. "I can speed dial Domino's Pizza in record time."

"Go figure." He left her standing in the doorway.

The urgency to follow him sped through her veins. But the caution factor kept her feet planted inside.

CHAPTER 43

Saturday morning, Kariss woke to the sound of "Great Balls of Fire" on her phone. She moaned — eight o'clock. This was not a work day. Who could be calling at this hour?

The caller ID read "Security gate," so she answered.

"We have a delivery from Brennan's. Looks like breakfast, ma'am."

Just like the incident with the flowers from the preceding night, she hesitated to give the guard permission to let the truck enter.

"I'll be right there." She groaned and forced her legs over the bed. Who was the mystery sender? Probably Tigo.

Ten minutes later, she pulled her Prius up to the gate. The boxes stacked outside security looked like a feast for a dozen. On the top box was a card. Dread washed over her. This reeked of another one of Wyatt's maneuvers to win Vicki over. She tore into the envelope.

Hi Vicki,

I wanted your first morning in your new home to be a celebration. Hope there's enough breakfast for you, our baby, and Kariss. Tell your sister I appreciate all she's doing.

Thinking of you.
Wyatt

This had to stop. Her first inclination was to dump the food into the trash . . . but it smelled so good. And Brennan's . . . Vicki would have to handle this. She stared at the boxes, wondering what delicacies awaited their taste buds. She and Vicki could discuss Wyatt's motivation over this fabulous breakfast. Sort of food for thought.

Beside the delivery boxes stood a huge decanter of fresh-brewed coffee. When she bent to examine it, she saw the two boxes positioned on either side — two crystal coffee mugs from Tiffany's.

Okay, she'd accept this on behalf of her sister.

"Why do you think he's displaying such extravagance?" Kariss posed the question to her sister for the second time.

"I'm horribly suspicious. His idea of breakfast was a martini at ten a.m. with two olives."

Kariss took a generous bite of a strawberry blintz crepe, her second. "Have you thought back through your married life for what he wants? Other than the obvious abortion thing?"

Vicki nodded. "He's working through a list of how best to get to me. Intimidation by having me followed didn't work."

Kariss wouldn't shatter that supposition since Tigo didn't know the identity of the woman at the Galleria. "As our grandma always said, 'Honey goes further than vinegar.'"

"Not when it comes to my baby."

Kariss smiled. "Hey, I'm proud of you."

"Comes with motherhood. Look at how you felt about Cherished Doe. You didn't give up until the right people got involved. We women are nurturers."

Vicki had no idea how far she'd gone to help Xavier. "Yeah, I see where your courage is coming from."

"I forgot to thank Tigo for approaching Wyatt about the Galleria incident. Would you take care of that for me?"

"Already did. Are you going to call Wyatt?"

Vicki nodded. "I won't be ugly, but I am

going to get to the bottom of this." She took a sip of orange juice. "He's bought his way through life, and I'm included in that venture. But no more. I'm not going to abort this baby or give it up for adoption. So he can save his pennies for child support."

"I wonder if Lissa knows about his . . . generosity?"

Vicki's eyes brightened. "Trust me, I'll use last night and this morning as ammunition. She's demanding and possessive. I'm sure if she heard about the flowers and food, she'd have him sleeping on the couch."

"Tell me why they're attending church?"

"That's simple. He has a new trophy. Two of them. I'm sure he's making notes about business the whole time he's there. I'd love to get someone to ask him about the sermons."

"So he's making sure everyone sees him in church and does the forgiveness thing. Then if they have need for a commercial real estate broker, they come to him?"

"Exactly."

"Vicki, listen to me. I've heard you say you're through with him before. Then he manipulates you into doing whatever he wants. Mom and Dad, me, and the rest of the family are here to support you."

"Nothing's going to stop me from providing a good home for my baby — without Wyatt. He cheated on me repeatedly, and he's probably doing the same with Lissa. I could never trust him again. Not unless God sent a lightning bolt."

Once they concluded breakfast and refrigerated the leftovers, which would last them a few days, Vicki excused herself to phone Wyatt. Kariss so wanted to listen in, but she wasn't invited.

Vicki placed a dish towel beside the sink. "I'll fill you in when I'm finished."

"I hadn't said a word about listening in." Kariss took a deep breath. "But I wanted to."

"Don't worry. Taking notes is my specialty, and I'll jot down things while talking to him. I might need them down the road with legal proceedings."

Thirty minutes later, Kariss couldn't wait a moment longer. She stood at the bottom of the stairway leading up to Vicki's suite, as she'd decided to term it. Not a sound resonated. "Are you okay?" she shouted up.

"Yes. Still wondering why he's wasting time and money."

"Can I be debriefed?"

"Sure. I'll bring down my notes in just a sec. In short, he feels guilty about the way he's treated me over the years. Wants to make up for it."

"Did he toss out a dollar figure?"

"Nope. Just useless platitudes about what a good wife I was."

"Note the word 'was.' "

"And he plans to change churches. Says it's too hard on Lissa."

Kariss shook her head. "Pardon me while I throw up. Say, how about pedicures today?"

"Not unless I buy."

"Then I'll flip for lunch."

"Make it dinner. I'll be stuffed until then."

Kariss laughed. She'd treasure these special moments with her sister for as long as possible.

Cheeky swam to the other end of his pool and stepped out. Monika handed him a towel, her string bikini reminding him of their encounter earlier in the day, and he was ready again. "Why don't you go on inside, and I'll be right there."

She gave him an alluring smile and disappeared. Women were his passion, and he usually grew bored within a month or so, but not yet with Monika. Not since Delores had he been this consumed with a woman.

He snatched his phone and pressed in

Paulo's number. He trusted Hershey about as much as he trusted a dog, but the man had brought him a legitimate business proposal, one he needed to rid himself of Bates and Masterson. The paper trail checked out — bank accounts, references, clients. But he knew how all that was done, and this could be a setup. Yet if he found a new supplier who saved him thousands of dollars, it was worth the risk. One way to find out, and that was to have a face-to-face with lots of muscle.

Paulo answered on the first ring.

"Got a Monday-night meeting at the place we spoke about yesterday. I need heavy security."

"Okay. Followed Bates and Masterson. The two argued about something."

"Good. Plays into my plans."

"I think one of them is tipping off the *policía* about our mules."

"I don't pay you to think." Cheeky narrowed his eyes. He knew Masterson had been seen with a member of the Skulls. "After Monday night, I'll decide how to dispose of him." Both men would end up dead. They'd overcharged him long enough, and neither of them had given him the information he needed to eliminate Kariss Walker. Useless.

■ ■ ■ ■

Saturday afternoon at home, Tigo studied the report from last night's shooting on his Blackberry. The FIG had given him more information about the gang rivalry between the Arroyos and the Skulls. He still didn't know what had caused the fight.

The Arroyo who remained in critical condition refused to comment, but Jo-Jack had said the two gangs were vying for the Gulf Coast gun-smuggling market. Although the Arroyos were a larger gang, the Skulls had gained ground by staying under the local law enforcement's radar. They were like snakes, stealing through the night, silent with deadly intent. Tigo was certain Bates and Masterson were selling to the Arroyos. What would be the benefit of supplying both gangs with weapons? More money? Both smuggled across the border, filling the demands of cartels. Could the same cartel be buying from both gangs? Or did the cartels really care as long as they had their assault rifles and ammo? It made sense that if one gang was paralyzed, the other would fill all the orders. He'd find the answers as he wove into Cheeky's small circle of business acquaintances.

A text from Ryan alerted him.

HE'S AWAKE.

ON MY WAY.

Tigo checked in with his mother's nurse
and left for the hospital. The victim had
refused to give his name, but his prints were
in the FBI's database — José Miguel,
wanted for armed robbery and assault in El
Paso.

Ryan met Tigo outside Miguel's room,
where two HPD officers guarded the door.
Inside the man lay awake. IVs and machines
stabilized him after surgery.

"Miguel, I'm Special Agent Tigo Harris
from the FBI, and this is Special Agent
Ryan Steadman. We need to ask you a few
questions."

The man scowled, his glare full of hate.

"Suit yourself," Tigo said. "You're wanted
for armed robbery in El Paso, and we'll send
you back there as soon as you can be
moved. Or we can turn you over to a couple
of Skulls."

Ryan paced the room. "I'd rather Cheeky
found out that one of his boys cooperated
with us."

"Good idea," Tigo said. "Miguel here

435

would be dead by morning."

"What kind of questions?" Miguel spit the words.

Tigo bent over the bed. "What caused the fight?"

"Two gangs. What do you expect?"

"Because we have reason to believe it was more than that. Gun smuggling is big business. Rumors are the Arroyos are losing money, and the Skulls are selling to the cartels."

"You don't know what you're talking about."

"We're being tipped off when one of Cheeky's transports is heading into Mexico. That means the Arroyos are paying for guns and ammo that aren't making it across the border."

Miguel swore. "You paid for bad information."

"Don't think so. Who is setting you up? My guess is the Skulls would pay more for the guns, giving the supplier a bigger profit."

Tigo stepped back, and Ryan walked to the other side of Miguel's bed. "Give us a few names, and we'll make sure the charges are lessened against you."

"Do you think I'm stupid?"

Ryan snorted. "That tells me we're right on. Who's supplying the guns?"

"Only Cheeky knows that."

"How can we find him?"

"Your problem."

Ryan gazed at the IV bags dripping into Miguel's vein. "What happens when these tubes stop pouring meds into your body?"

"Forget it. I'm not telling you anything."

"Think about it." Ryan nodded at Tigo. "Any parting words for our friend here before we leave?"

"His choice. He knows what we can do. We'll make sure this hits the media with his face and name. Make it easy on the Skulls."

They left the hospital with the knowledge that they might be closer to finding out why the Arroyos were out for blood. He was eager to see if Bates's or Masterson's names were mentioned during the gun buy with Cheeky.

"Ryan, what are our chances of Cheeky giving us the names of his current supplier?"

"Zero. Until we earn their trust."

"I want them all — Cheeky, Bates, Masterson, and anyone else who's working with them."

"We'll get them. Patience, Agent Tigo. And time."

CHAPTER 44

Sunday afternoon, Tigo arrived promptly at two. He'd probably waited at the security gate until his Buzz Lightyear watch alerted him to the time. Vicki was sleeping, so Kariss hoisted her shoulder bag, with her 9mm tucked beneath her cosmetic bag, and met him outside.

Tigo looked as calm and together as Friday night, but she knew inside the calm exterior simmered an agent who didn't miss a thing.

"Want to take my Prius?" She dangled the keys in front of him. "It's a fun ride."

"Sure. We could look like the modest couple out for an afternoon of fun."

"At the shooting range?"

"Did you know your zip code contains the largest demographics of CHL owners in the state?"

"Tigo, I'm smarter than that. What about your buds on the southeast side of town?"

He chuckled. "They don't need a CHL. Just cash."

Her mind simply didn't work parallel to lawbreakers. "It won't be long before this lady's packing."

"Your whole county will move."

She laughed and handed him the car keys. This was the same great guy from Friday night. Personable. Teasing. She paused in her reflections . . . Tigo was a friend. Period. Their arguments had been about her safety and her insatiable desire to learn about the role of an FBI agent. Even when he attempted to dissuade her from helping Xavier, he had a good reason.

They walked outside and around the front of her condo to her garage. She positioned her sunglasses and drank in the smells of roses and clean air. She felt protected inside her gated community. Not what she'd experienced in other parts of the city.

Once inside the garage, he opened the door for her. "Did your sister question us going to the shooting range?"

"I told her I thought every woman should have a CHL, especially single ones."

"When are you going to tell her the truth?"

"Maybe never. She has enough problems." She relayed the stories about the rose delivery and extravagant breakfast. "However, she won't abort the baby. He's wasting his time there."

When Tigo didn't respond, she studied him . . . His brow deepened.

"What are you thinking?"

"Just curious about Phillips."

She remembered Tigo's question about him when she'd been on pain meds. "I loathe the man, but I think he's too big of a coward to break the law." Some of his pranks scrolled through her mind. All concerning his lies to cover his infidelity. "I understand motivation can drive a person to do anything. Wyatt's greedy and self-centered. But he's much too concerned about himself, and ending up in jail might damage his face."

"Does he gamble?"

"Too stingy unless it's a sure thing, which makes me wonder what he's up to with Vicki. Do you know something about him?"

"One of his clients is under our radar."

"Who?"

"Now, Kariss. You know I won't give you a name."

"I can try. You might forget you're not with another agent and slip."

He grinned. "I know the difference between a writer and an agent. For the record, an agent wouldn't need a CHL."

"All right. I give for now. What happened when you met Ryan at the hospital?"

"We talked to a patient." The stoic FBI agent had settled into his persona.

"Were you able to get the information you needed?"

"No. He won't betray them."

"What makes gang members loyal to each other? I know they're involved in drugs, sex trafficking, extortion, and whatever else breeds money and power. What is it about gang membership that draws them into a life of crime? I know everything they do is based on their identity within the gang — but why?"

"It's a sense of belonging, a family. Most of them have only one parent or none, and whoever's responsible doesn't give a rip. They've learned survival on the streets, and the way to gain recognition is to be a bad boy. And based on their initiation, their allegiance is for life."

"So if any of them decide to turn witness, they're dead?"

"Right. They know the terms when they agree to help us, and we do our best to protect them. Cheeky's number one man was found dead. In pieces."

She shuddered. "I wonder what he did."

"I could guess, but I won't."

She'd drop the matter because it was obviously out of her control. "What about Candy and Jo-Jack? Weren't they afraid?"

"Money talks, Kariss."

"What a horrible way to make a living." She shuddered, her mind resting on the type of person who'd live so dangerously.

"They live on the streets. Whoever killed Candy made it look like her pimp had slit her throat. Jo-Jack sold drugs for the Arroyos."

Fear crept up her back, sending chills to her fingers. She thought of the thousands of innocent men, women, and children in the city. "Do you think Houston will ever get as bad as the border towns?"

He gave her a half smile. "Not as long as I breathe. That's the commitment of every law-enforcement official who believes in his job."

That's what she feared the most, because she knew he'd do whatever it took to stop Cheeky or any other criminal who threatened the city. Admirable. A hero. The kind of person she loved to write about. But her characters weren't real, and Tigo's commitment meant she might lose a friend.

At the shooting range, Kariss felt more confident than during her previous attempt. She'd been practicing lining up the sights in her bedroom like he'd taught her and hoped her good aim wasn't a fluke.

"Great shooting," he said forty-five minutes later. "I think you'll do fine on the shooting portion."

Satisfaction made its way to her lips. "Thanks to your instructions."

"Your dad was right. You have a good eye."

"I'll surprise him."

"Then you'd have to tell him why you own a gun, and you don't like lying."

He'd gotten her again. "True."

"Would you like some ice cream? I owe you. I was supposed to treat you and Vicki on Friday."

"We'll flip for it."

They drove to a nearby soft-serve ice-cream shop, the kind with two dozen flavors and even more toppings. Kariss waited while Tigo placed their orders. They both wanted chocolate with M&Ms and chocolate chips. Outside patio tables looked inviting, though the heat would melt the ice cream.

Her gaze panned the area, and that's when she saw her. The woman who'd followed her and Vicki now leaned against a motorcycle not far from the Prius. Kariss strained to see her features. She hurried to the front of the line where Tigo stood and grabbed his arm.

"The woman from the Galleria? She's in the parking lot."

He moved out of the line to the glass facing outside. "There's no one out there."

She'd seen the dark-haired woman, and she couldn't have disappeared. "I saw her." Bewildered, Kariss pushed open the door and walked to the parking lot to where she'd seen the woman. Vehicles of all sizes filled the area, and people, young and old, milled about. Yet no one resembled the woman she'd seen moments before.

Tigo was right. Had she become paranoid?

The rumble of a motorcycle caught her attention.

"Kariss, watch out!"

She turned at the sound of Tigo's voice and the touch of his hand. He pulled her away out of the motorcycle's path.

Gasping she watched the cycle speed away. "That's her, Tigo."

CHAPTER 45

Frustrated, Tigo wished he'd gotten more of the motorcycle's license plate number. He'd been concerned about Kariss . . . Ryan's words echoed in his mind. How did Tigo really feel about her? Later he'd analyze it.

All he'd observed about the driver was her black hair and Hispanic features. He released his hold on Kariss. "Are you all right?"

"Sure. Is she working for the Arroyos?" she whispered.

How much did he tell her, and how much dare he allow her to believe? "Could be. But she wasn't armed or you'd be dead."

Kariss nodded, her body still trembling. "Thanks."

He slipped his arm around her waist. "How about ice cream?"

Her pale face didn't match the enthusiasm in her voice. "Good thing I hadn't already eaten it, or I'd be wearing it."

He smiled. Had to like this woman. "Why don't you sit at a table — inside — while I order our chocolate on a waffle cone?"

"Tigo?"

He caught the depth of her brown eyes. This had to stop.

"Don't forget the M&Ms."

He pressed his lips. "Yeah, I know."

"It was her, and she's followed me twice. Not Vicki. If she wasn't hired by the Arroyos, then who?"

"I'm working on it."

"Could she know where I live?"

"In a gated community." He opened the door to the ice-cream shop, and they stepped inside, giving him time to form his words. Once he had her seated at a corner booth away from the glass windows and door, he scooted in next to her. "Kariss, if anyone wants access to your condo, they can get in. Today doesn't seem like a coincidence considering all we know, but at this moment, I can't see a connection."

"Don't lie to me. You said one of the men you're investigating is Wyatt's client. I don't think he's stupid enough to get mixed up with criminal activity, but you posed the same question to me."

Why couldn't she be a little less insightful? He started to stand up, but she grabbed his arm.

"My mind's racing," she said. "But remember when you told me that the Arroyos pay people to drive guns and drugs into Mexico? And you said they used people who didn't have a record and often used intimidation to keep them working?"

He nodded, not sure if he liked where this was going.

"Couldn't that woman be one of those kinds of people?"

"Yes, but highly unlikely. I think your exbrother-in-law is trying to pull something. Perhaps his girlfriend is a part of this."

Relieved that she seemed satisfied with his conclusions, he patted her arm. "If you'll let go of me, I'll get our ice cream."

While standing in line, Tigo honed in on what had just happened. He quickly phoned the FIG and asked for a background on Lissa Montgomery to be sent to his Blackberry.

He and Kariss were midway through their ice cream when his Blackberry signaled him. "I need to see this," he said, glad he was on the opposite side of the booth.

He opened the attachment and read through the document. Everything seemed normal until he noted Lissa's parents' information. *Parents divorced since 1995. Mother remarried Juan Chevez. Two step-brothers and one stepsister.*

"What do you know about Lissa's background?"

"Nothing. Why? What have you found?"

He gave her a grin. "I'll let you know."

She handed him her ice cream while reaching for her phone. "Don't eat mine."

"Are you calling Vicki?"

She pressed in a number. "She'll be up by now."

He started to protest, but the question about Lissa's stepfamily would drive him nuts until he had more information. "Ask about her stepdad and his kids."

"Will do. Hey, sis . . . Yeah, I'm with Tigo. Stopped for ice cream after acing the shooting range . . . No, I'm not another Annie Oakley. I write contemporary not historical . . . Say, I have a question: what do you know about Lissa's family?" Kariss wiggled her nose at Tigo while curiosity nipped at his heels. "Thanks. See you later." She dropped her phone into her purse.

"Vicki has no clue."

Monday morning, Kariss arrived at the office to find Tigo and Ryan in deep discussion. She handed Tigo his venti and hurried

448

to her cubicle. She kept her eye on the hallway and her ears open. The two men walked by toward the hall. Something was going on, and she could feel it down to her manicured pink toes. If this was about the woman who'd tried to run her over with a motorcycle, she had a right to know.

When they returned, she made her way to Tigo's cubicle. "Have you found out anything I should know? Like are the Arroyos behind bars or maybe you learned the identity of the woman who's tried twice to hurt me? Better yet, do you have the man who shot me in custody?"

Tigo lifted a brow, but amusement was on his lips. "Sometimes I think you're in the wrong profession."

"What can you tell me? You know, under the subject of research."

"Not a thing, Kariss. It's all off limits."

She sighed. "I've been threatened and shot while I've been here. That should give me clout." She held up her hand. "Don't mention taking a vacation again. Not going there. Who's Masterson?"

Ryan shook his head. "I'm outta here. Dealing with you has caused me to lose more hair . . ."

"You didn't have any when I arrived." She watched him leave before turning her atten-

449

tion back to Tigo. "I heard you mention Masterson."

"I don't think so. You must have heard wrong."

"Must you always be sworn to secrecy?"

"It's a need-to-know basis, which reminds me — I have plenty to do."

"Tigo, I heard you mention the name of Masterson. And I know you weren't talking about a resurrected Bat Masterson."

"Who?"

"Bat Masterson, the legendary gambler, army scout, sheriff, and sundry other things."

Tigo looked at her, but his gaze was somewhere else.

"What's the matter?"

"I'm impressed. You're a genius."

"Thanks, but what did I do?"

"Can't tell you. Might get you into trouble." He pointed to Ryan's cubicle. "I need to talk to my partner."

"Wait a minute. You can't just leave me. Curiosity will destroy my creativity."

"I doubt that."

"Where are you going?"

"I have a date with Ryan."

"But you just talked to him."

He touched her nose. "Work on your novel while I work on my case. Oh, Hillary is looking for you."

Kariss cringed at the thought of Hillary cornering her again. "I hope you're not serious."

"I did you a favor, so you do me one by stopping pestering me. I told Hillary you might not be in today."

"Thanks. I'll do my best to ask easier questions." She watched him walk away. He'd touched her nose again. A Tigo sign of affection? Now what was that all about?

CHAPTER 46

"The legendary Bat Masterson never entered my mind." Ryan pushed the Up elevator button. "Makes me feel stupid."

"I'm right there with you." Tigo motioned to him about approaching agents. "Yet 'Bat' could be either Bates or Masterson."

"Let's camp on Masterson being the man Jo-Jack told us about. If the Arroyos believe he's charging too much for guns and ammo, his days are numbered. I bet they're looking for another supplier, and we'll fit the bill tonight."

"Then there's Arnold Bates," Tigo said as the elevator opened. "But I'm thinking he might be pushing Masterson out of the game. Working with the Arroyos to cut them a deal. He could lower the price, give the gang a better deal, and still make money."

"One of them is tipping us off about transports. Let's hope we find out more tonight. I'm ready now."

Tigo chuckled. He'd been thinking about this meeting with Cheeky for months. Everything was in place.

Kariss ate a Caesar salad at her desk. She could be working at home, fine-tuning her first chapter and working on the next one, but this office held an alluring fascination. The main reason why she stayed was to listen to agents' conversations. While she typed away in her cubicle, lingered in the break room, or studied the squad board, she learned their opinions, their methods of approaching cases, and their moods.

Her phone rang shortly after one o'clock. A quick glance showed the number was Gilberto's. Probably Xavier.

"Good afternoon, Kariss, I have great news." Xavier's excitement spilled into his voice.

Her stomach did a little flip. "Have you located Delores?"

"I'm a lot closer. My friend says he knows where her boyfriend will be tonight. He's meeting with some of his friends near an apartment complex. She might be with him. I have the address and the time."

"So you're going to approach this man while he's with friends? That sounds danger-ous."

"I have to take the chance."

"Delores isn't stupid. She must know the nursing home is being watched, or she'd have returned to see her grandmother and been picked up."

"If we wait, she could run where we'd never find her . . . or Benita's little brother or sister."

Why did he have to say *we?* "I'm assuming the address is in your part of town."

"Yes, about fifteen minutes from Gilberto's."

"He's going with you, right?"

"He refuses. Says I'm a fool. I told him if I can find Delores tonight, the FBI would be happy, and I can find out what happened to both of my children."

Kariss had seen enough trouble over the past several weeks, and she feared Xavier was walking into more of the same. "Is Delores's boyfriend a gang member?"

"I don't know. I think my friend would have told me."

"Is your friend involved in a gang?"

"No. But he's thinking about it."

Later she'd talk to Xavier about staying away from his new friend. "Why don't you get a couple of agents to go with you?"

"I'm afraid they'd scare away the people I need to see."

That much was true. "Do you have a gun?" The words tumbled out before she thought them through.

"No. But I think I need one. Do you have one?"

"Yes."

"Can I borrow it?"

"Xavier, handing over my gun to you is against the law."

"Then come with me."

"How would I pass for Hispanic?"

"It'll be dark."

"I can't do it, Xavier. Your part of town doesn't like white skin. I've already been shot, remember?"

"True. I'll call you when I learn something."

"How can I talk you out of this?"

"You can't. I have to try."

Could she pass for Hispanic? She had light olive-colored skin. "How long do you think this will take?"

"Not long."

"Can't this wait until I discuss the situation with Tigo and Ryan? They know how to apprehend people."

"You are the only one who can help me, the only one who seems to understand the importance of a child's life. Why don't you come? If anyone asks, I'll say you're with me."

Kariss glanced around her, knowing she should back away. But if she didn't go, Xavier would go alone and he might need help. If she accompanied him, the possibility of danger existed. She rubbed her lower back.

"What are you going to do?" Xavier said.

How could she send him into a lion's den without help? "What time should I pick you up?"

CHAPTER 47

Late Monday afternoon, Tigo and Ryan completed every detail for the night's meeting with Cheeky. They shared an early dinner and drove back to the office to work until it was time to slip into disguise. Operation Wasp was under way. Tigo sensed the adrenaline bumping against the sides of his veins.

Tigo alerted Natalie of his late arrival, possibly into the wee hours of the morning after her shift changed. Due to his lack of phone access, he referred the nurses to his mother's priest and hoped that precautionary step wasn't needed.

In his work space, he turned his attention to Cherished Doe and the reports highlighting the search for Benita's mother. Gathering up the file, he walked to Ryan's work area. "We're coming up with nothing on finding Delores Olvera. She's either back in Mexico or hiding out or dead."

"I'm guessing the director of her grand-mother's nursing home warned her before we positioned agents."

"I should have asked Kariss and Xavier to stay put until we had agents in place." He hated being inept. "I bet the director phoned Delores while Kariss talked to me in the parking lot. Think about it. Delores might have sent the man who shot Kariss."

"Why not get rid of Xavier too?"

Tigo shrugged. "Maybe she has an ounce of decency left and doesn't want to see him hurt." He considered Delores's MO. "She's a strong suspect here, and the fact she took money from him for five years doesn't make her look innocent."

"True. The idea of her getting away with killing her own child keeps me working on it." Ryan's frustration echoed Tigo's. "I understand Xavier's and Gilberto's bitterness."

Tigo leafed through the file. "I've been thinking about the interviews with Gilberto. Remember he saw Delores with a 'bad man.' Why did he say he was bad? By the way he looked? Did the man have a police record? Gang markings?"

"Or did he think the man was bad because he was with Xavier's wife?"

"One way to find out." Tigo picked up his

phone and pressed in Gilberto's number. "Xavier said Delores had done some bad things and had boyfriends. I'd like him to explain his definition of the word 'bad.'"

Gilberto responded on the third ring. Tigo greeted him and posed the questions.

"The man with Delores was part of a gang," Gilberto said. "Arroyo markings. I didn't say to her what I wanted that day because I knew he'd kill me. She didn't have any of the female Arroyo tattoos. As much as I despise her, I can't imagine her going through with the initiation."

Tigo understood. Women who wanted to be a part of the gang were sexed-in, beaten, or suffered whatever means the gang devised that involved pain and terror. "Do you know his name?"

"No. Haven't seen him or Delores since then."

"Do you remember anything about him that could help us run a face recognition?"

"Typical Arroyo. He talked with a lisp, but that doesn't help you."

Tigo remembered the call he received from Candy's phone. That man had spoken with a lisp too. He had to be stupid not to think his impairment wouldn't tie criminal activities to him. "Thanks. She's running with a rough crowd. Is that why Xavier said she'd done some bad things?"

"My brother's angry and hurt. He doesn't sleep at night — always thinking about the past and weighing things she told him. When he learned about Delores visiting her grandmother, he became more obsessed. Always he remembers her lies."

"What kind of lies?"

"Oh, she'd tell him she was going to see her grandmother, but she'd stay out all night. Always an excuse. When she returned with alcohol on her breath, she'd say she had a drink at her grandmother's. The problem was her grandmother's old, and her mind wasn't good. No easy way for him to check up on his wife. Now he knows Delores lied to him."

"Where is Xavier now? I'd like to talk to him about the danger of searching for her when she's been seen with an Arroyo."

"I wish I knew. He left with Miss Walker about thirty minutes ago. They were going to talk about some lead he has on Delores. I told him it was stupid, but he says she has a gun."

Tigo's temples pounded. What was she thinking? "You're right. They could get themselves killed." How many times had he uttered that phrase to Kariss? Did she have to flatline to get the message? "If you hear from them, please contact me."

Tigo wanted to throw his phone.

"What's going on?" Ryan's voice jolted him out of his fear — and worry.

"Kariss and Xavier are out somewhere talking about Delores. He thinks he has a lead. And she has a gun."

"Is she nuts? Call her. Her CHL hasn't been approved, and what she's doing is illegal."

Tigo pressed in Kariss's number and waited until her voice mail responded with a generic message. "Kariss, this is Tigo. I need to talk to you now. Stay away from the southeast part of town. We have reason to believe that Delores may be mixed up with an Arroyo." He turned to Ryan. "Not a thing we can do except wait for her to call. Those two are going to end up dead if we don't find a way to stop them."

"What makes you think Delores is mixed up with an Arroyo?"

"The man Gilberto saw Delores with was one of them. That was three years ago, but she could still be with him. Could be the same man who called me using Candy's phone. Both had a lisp."

"What drives Kariss to help Xavier?"

"I know exactly why." Tigo stared into the face of his friend. "When I researched her background, I learned that when she was in college, she worked summers at a day care. There was a fire, and she tried to save a toddler. Both suffered from smoke inhalation, but the child died. The part of Kariss that walked through fire to save a child has never changed."

"Now I understand why she was so determined about finding Cherished Doe."

"I should have addressed it. Thought she might bring it up."

"Can't blame yourself, Tigo. She makes her own decisions. Hopefully she'll call before we have to leave."

"We won't be answering any calls after we leave here tonight. When I see her again, I'm going to lock her inside that fancy condo and keep the key." That was after he made sure she was alive.

CHAPTER 48

Kariss gripped her 9mm as though it were her best friend and hoisted her bag onto her shoulder. Darkness shadowed her and Xavier as they walked between dilapidated apartments toward a deserted building that held no lights. Angry voices emerged sporadically from the residents. A scream. A child cried. Latino music beat to the steady strum of a Spanish guitar. The smells of poverty and desperation lingered. Oh, she wished Tigo was with her instead of Xavier. She'd made a foolish decision to come here, especially since she couldn't pass as Hispanic in an area where she could get her throat cut . . . like Candy. She'd probably seen her last sunset. The gun in her trembling hands was not metal courage. In fact, she'd broken the law by bringing it.

Xavier believed Delores lived in this crime-seeped, roach-infested apartment complex that should have been condemned a decade ago. He had a lead on a man by the name of Tiny who was supposedly Delores's boyfriend.

Kariss should have warned Xavier about lowlifes here going by different names. Tiny was probably the size of a giant. She should have researched the name, seen if he had a record.

Nothing good could ever come from this section of town.

"Xavier," she whispered. "Let's get out of here. I don't like the looks of this area. If Delores lives here, we can find her in the daylight." And bring reinforcements.

"You go back to the car if you're scared. I've come this far, and I'm not turning back."

She had the gun, and if she left him, he could be hurt. "What makes you think you have the right address?"

"My friend said Tiny would be at this place tonight, and he's expecting me. I'm hoping he can tell me where to find Delores or if he knows about my child."

"What has this man done for you to trust him?" She knew she'd lost her mind, yet still she continued on with Xavier. Why . . . why had she let this go so far?

"He's a good friend. He knows what finding Delores means to me. His wife left him and took their three kids. He hurts too. If I need money, he'll hook me up with the right people."

"Are you crazy? He's probably into drugs or something." She tugged on Xavier's shirt. "Have you dragged me into a nest of drug dealers?"

"Don't worry. I told my friend I wasn't interested. All I want is to find my child."

"We're going to get killed." Logic twisted at her heart. "This is it. I'm leaving. You can come with me or stay here. I've been a complete idiot. You can call Gilberto to pick you up." She whirled around.

"Tu no vas a ningun lado." The low Spanish voice telling her she wasn't going anywhere wrapped a noose around her heart. "You want to see Tiny. We take you to see him." The man ripped the gun from her hands and yanked her purse from her shoulder. His hand dug into the upper part of her arm where the bullet had grazed her. She cried out.

"You escaped us too many times. No more."

In the dripping heat a chill raced up her spine. In that moment all of her fears — the ones that robbed her sleep and the ones she discarded — had come true. They were going to die.

She'd come to her senses too late. Xavier's friend had set them up. These men must be Arroyos, but she couldn't tell in the dark. Surely Xavier had not done this on purpose . . . Would he have sold her out for information about Delores and his child?

The truth paralyzed her senses. Yes, he would. His child meant more to him than anything on this earth.

Tigo had no idea where she'd gone. She'd turned off her phone and hadn't checked messages for hours.

Calm down. Think. She had money. People in gangs could be reasoned with, and money was the key. But did she have enough to satisfy them?

"I'm not interested in seeing Tiny." Her voice cracked.

"Too bad."

"I think you have me mistaken for someone else."

"Shut up."

"Can you let her go?" Xavier's firm voice soothed her. "It was my idea to bring her. She's only trying to help me find my child."

Thank you, Xavier. At least she'd go to her grave knowing he hadn't betrayed her.

The man shoved Xavier to the parking lot pavement. "One more word out of either of you, and you're both dead."

Did God still know her name? Was she ready? She'd become a Christian when she was ten years old, and she understood what it meant. But life had thrown too many wrenches.

God, I don't deserve mercy, but please help us.

Three men pushed Xavier and Kariss between the apartment buildings toward the parking lot. What few people were outside didn't question what was happening. As though they didn't care. Her legs felt like lead, as if they carried her to certain death. Could this be another nightmare and soon she'd awaken? She hoped so.

Or was the impending doom a product of her own stupidity?

They crossed the parking lot and went down a black alley. When they reached a darkened building, the men shoved her and Xavier along the left side and to the rear. A man opened a door and ordered them inside. For the first time, she caught a glimpse of their captors.

Crossbones.

Arroyos.

Just as she feared.

Just as she knew.

The low hum of a voice met her ears, along with a laugh. She stole a look at

Xavier, who displayed no emotion. Was this type of treatment what he expected? After all, he lived in Mexico where cartels had taken over much of the country. Maybe, just maybe, he could talk sense into these men.

They walked down a narrow concrete hallway to an open area where nothing but a few chairs remained. In the dim lighting, four Arroyos stood behind one man, the obvious leader. She couldn't see his face. No women were there, and the knowledge of what these men could and would do crept over her.

Two white men dressed in suits talked to the one who stood out from the other Arroyos. The businessman doing the talking was older, gray haired, with beard and mustache and glasses. The one behind him looked younger, with light-brown hair. What good did it do to memorize facial details? She wouldn't live to give Tigo the information.

"We're ready to do business," the Arroyo leader said in Spanish.

"I can supply a shipment in seven days. Are you ready to deal?"

The businessman spoke with a Spanish accent. What were the two men selling? Drugs? Guns?

"Yes. Where do we make the trade?"

"I'll let you know next Monday."

"How do we know you can be trusted?"

The businessman laughed. "I'm no fool. You've checked out my credentials just like I've checked out your method of doing business. I'm selling my guns and ammo cheaper than your current supplier. I should ask for a deposit, but not this first time. If anything goes wrong, my price goes up." He glanced at Kariss and Xavier. "Who are these people? This was supposed to be a private meeting."

The second businessman pulled a handgun. Another firefight? Kariss sucked in a breath.

"I see you delivered what I asked for," the leader said to the men holding Kariss and Xavier. "Been looking too long for the pretty lady."

"It was easy. Found both of them outside. Said they were looking for Tiny. Just like my man said. Fell right into our plan." The man behind her pushed her forward. Another did the same to Xavier. He'd been lied to by a man he called friend.

"So you want Tiny? He's dead. Shot at a hospital where you were working with cops."

"I'm not a cop," Xavier said, maintaining his stoic composure.

"But she is." The leader pointed to Kariss.

"You witnessed a shooting, and one of ours was killed. That was a bad mistake." The leader eyed Xavier. "I heard you wanted to talk to me about a woman. What do you want?"

Xavier took a step forward. "I'm looking for Delores Olvera."

He laughed low and guttural. "I heard you might want a job, heh?"

"No. I want to find Delores."

"Why should I help you?"

"Why wouldn't you?"

Kariss studied the leader. She'd seen his face on the squad board. He had high cheekbones and a mass of acne scars. A deep dimple sunk into his left cheek. Cheeky Lopez.

"I don't give anything away. You want to know about Delores, then you do business with me. I give the orders."

"I'm looking for my child. Delores is the mother. The child is four years old, almost five."

"Hmm. Boy or girl?"

The last question ground at Kariss's heart. The poor man had no idea.

"I don't know."

Cheeky smirked. "Are you stupid?"

"I was deported before the child was born." Xavier spoke like a man in control.

470

Even in the depths of danger, she mustered respect for the simple man who desperately wanted to find his child.

"Like I said. You're stupid. Maybe she killed it. Told me she killed the other one. Too much trouble."

Xavier clenched his fists. "Maybe she did."

"We'll talk later. You help me. I help you. First I need to take care of the pretty lady."

Kariss shivered, digesting every word.

"She's a friend helping me find my child."

"She's been using you. I said she's a cop." Xavier's eyes flew to Kariss then back to Cheeky. "I don't know anything about that."

Cheeky walked to Kariss, his boots resounding on the concrete floor. He grabbed her jaw and squeezed. "You won't leave here alive."

"That's right." The businessman strode up beside Cheeky. "I know who she is. Sent one of my men to prison. Tried to bring an indictment against my law firm. She's FBI."

"No. You're mistaken." Desperation had sunk to the bottom of her soul. She had no idea what the businessman was talking about. "I'm not *policía* . . . FBI." She nearly choked on the acid rising in her throat.

"Ah, that's why she was at the hospital," Cheeky said. "Check her for a wire. Make sure she didn't bring any friends. Get her phone."

"Look through my purse." Desperation made her physically ill. "Nothing's there to show I work for the FBI."

The Arroyo nearest her tossed her purse to another man, then he searched her. His hands slid over her body, embarrassing and frightening her. When nothing was found he slapped her.

Cheeky turned to the businessman. "Want to do the honors?"

"I do."

She gasped, her knees weakening along with any resemblance of courage.

Cheeky stepped back, and the business-man pulled a gun from inside his suit coat and aimed.

"Please. You're wrong. I'm just here to help Xavier find his child."

"And to our good fortune," the business-man said.

Reality pounded into her nightmarish situation. She couldn't call on God again after leaving Him behind with all the things she'd done . . .

Please.

Xavier protested. Then he tried to stand between her and the shooter. Cheeky smirked and pushed him to the floor beside her.

The businessman lifted his gun.

Narrowed his eyes.

Then drew it back. "I have a better idea."

Cheeky swore. "You haven't the guts to kill her?"

The businessman stared at Cheeky, his eyes narrowed and evil. "No one lives who accuses me of being a coward."

"What's stopping you?"

"I want a little . . . shall I say, entertainment from our FBI friend. As a part of our little agreement I'll return her to you when we conduct our transaction. Unless she angers me. Then I might have to get rid of her myself."

"She's cost me time and money. Chop her up and send her to the FBI as a warning. I'd rather see her blood run now."

"You don't trust me, Cheeky? I'm supplying you with 250 AK-47s for two hundred and forty grand, and you don't trust me to deliver this piece of trash or kill her myself?"

"I have people watching."

"So do I. Would you like a few more references?"

Cheeky hesitated, then nodded. "I'm fine. Just bring her with the guns."

The businessman smiled. "Be on time with the money, and I'll count every cent of it before you receive one rifle."

Kariss sucked in a breath. Time . . . this horrendous exchange of money, guns, and her blood had bought seven days for her to figure out how to survive.

The businessman replaced his gun and shook Cheeky's hand. "Deal. Don't let me down. The Skulls would like my business too. But you impressed me with your operation."

CHAPTER 49

Tigo grabbed Kariss by the arm and yanked her out of the building. She'd nearly blown their cover and lost the case for them. Worse yet, she'd nearly become Cheeky's next victim.

"Please." Kariss's trembling voice displayed her terror.

"Shut up, or I'll finish what I started." He understood the Arroyos were glued to the shadows, and he must maintain rough treatment of her and his Hispanic accent.

"I'm not FBI."

He stopped and smacked her in the face. Not hard, but enough to prove his point with Arroyos watching. "You might be pretty, but your kind is easily disposed of. Let's see how much you fight later," he said in English.

At the SUV, he stuffed her into the floorboard of the backseat with orders not to make a sound. He and Ryan quickly entered the vehicle and sped away.

"Did Cheeky have this bugged?" Tigo said.

"Possibly. I'll check once we're back."

"Doesn't matter. Get the gun shipment arranged and let our people know we have a new buyer."

"You were an idiot to take the woman." Ryan's words punctuated how he'd nearly seen her killed.

"I saw it as leverage."

"Maybe so. But I'd have pulled the trigger."

"I wanted to. The FBI's going to pay for this one. Have you thought about her backup?"

"Not the guy looking for a kid." Ryan laughed. "Didn't know if it was a boy or girl. I studied him. Nothing but a stupid Mexican."

"Let's hope so. Both could have been FBI. That's why we'll contact Cheeky and move the exchange date. Are we being followed?"

"Looks like it."

Tigo needed time to think. The adrenaline still flowed. They were this close to nailing Cheeky and a handful of the Arroyos. His thoughts turned to Kariss. She'd have to sweat it out on the floorboard until they switched vehicles. Then he'd give her the lecture of her life — after apologizing for

476

slapping her. Not exactly one of his finer moments.

Xavier . . . Would he survive this? The man had no reason to doubt Kariss worked for the FBI since that's where he'd met her. Cheeky held the ace in that deal, and Xavier just might do whatever was necessary to get information about Delores and their child. If he refused, he'd be the one left in a pool of blood instead of Kariss.

Tigo drove toward Houston's Northwest Medical Center where they'd left Ryan's car. He kept his attention on the rearview mirror, certain they were followed. After speeding down an off ramp then back onto the interstate several times, he felt assured they'd lost any Arroyos.

Tigo eased the SUV into the hospital parking garage. No one followed, but if the vehicle was bugged, then trailing him was no longer necessary. On the third floor, he pulled in beside Ryan's Toyota.

They exited with flashlights and looked for a bug. There it was behind the left rear tire. Tigo removed it and crushed it with his rented shoes. If Kariss hadn't succumbed to a heart attack by now, then she had guts. In any event, he needed to get her out of there.

She'd nearly been killed.

That's when he realized where his heart had gone.

Kariss had prayed every prayer she'd remembered growing up. She'd added verses along with all the typical promises of how she'd live her life if God saved her from this mess. Back then, her show of piety was to please Mom and Dad. But not now, even if God didn't remember her name.

Was there a way to bribe God?

She thought about Xavier, who was most likely getting initiated into the Arroyos or killed.

Fear set her teeth chattering, made her dizzy. Every day since Nikki had died in the fire, she'd struggled to keep children safe and scatter the accusing voices that tormented her. Taking the job as news anchor for Channel 5 had given her exposure to continue protecting children. But reporting the Cherished Doe case with no closure had only reminded her of her failure. So she'd resigned to write novels. Maybe by putting her efforts in another direction, she'd forget.

The haunting whispers refused to leave her. How could she ever make up for losing Nikki?

She'd volunteered at a women's shelter

and ended up mentoring kids.

She'd supported children around the world.

She'd given away thousands of dollars on behalf of needy children.

Then the idea of writing a novel that showed justice for Cherished Doe entered her mind and wrapped around her heart. On the heels of that endeavor came helping Xavier find his child.

Now she'd be dead in a matter of days, and she'd done nothing to redeem herself for letting Nikki die.

God, I tried to make a difference, she thought.

I'm the only One who can redeem you.

She shuddered. Those weren't her words. Was this the voice of God? Could —

The vehicle stopped. Stage two of her demise. She'd run if given the opportunity. And scream. The younger man regretted the older one's decision to use her as leverage. How did she form the words to convince them that she wasn't an agent? What did the older man mean by stating she'd sent one of his men to jail? Did she have a look-alike somewhere?

The SUV's door opened, and the older man grabbed her arm. "We're moving, little lady." He walked her to a dark green sedan.

Her heart continued to race until she thought it might burst from her chest. Yet that would be an easier way to die. Death by terror had a better ring than what she feared.

God, if it's not too late, I'm really sorry for turning my back on You.

"Inside. We're about to have a little talk." The businessman seemed angrier than before.

Bargaining. Yes. Anything sounded better than what she'd heard back there.

She plopped onto the seat and buckled up out of habit. What was she thinking? She should jump from the car at the first opportunity. The two climbed into the vehicle and fastened their own seat belts. Ever so quietly, she released hers.

"Buckle up, Kariss. You're safe now." The voice was one she knew. Tigo! She gasped. He'd been in disguise.

"Tigo," she whispered, more like a prayer than an understanding. "I . . . I didn't recognize you." Her attention swept from one man to the other, their disguises masking their identity.

"Good. You weren't supposed to." Frustration came through from every word.

She didn't care. She burst into tears, a floodgate of everything that had transpired since she agreed to accompany Xavier. "I'm alive. You saved my life." She sobbed, unable to control herself, and she didn't care how weak it sounded. "How will I ever repay you?"

"Don't ask."

She could feel his anger, but right now she'd kiss him at the first opportunity. "Ryan, is it you too?"

"Yes. It's me." He turned to her from the front seat, lines dug into his forehead. "Before Tigo gets started, I have a few things to say."

She gulped. For a moment she feared throwing up.

"Tonight was something we'd planned for months." Ryan glared into her face. "Do I need to state the risks involved in Operation Wasp? Or the extent we went to with our disguises and paper trail? You nearly blew it all."

She held her breath, almost afraid to let it out. "I'm sorry."

"You're sorry all right," Ryan said. "I can't wait to voice a complaint to Linc about his ludicrous idea to let you write from our files. Your ego might be in good shape, but my wife could be a widow right now and my kids minus a dad."

"I'm sorry."

"You're right." His tone inched closer to a growl. "One sorry excuse for a selfish human being."

"I was trying to help Xavier. See —"

"Don't even want to hear it." Ryan's voice rose. "Your stupid stunt had nothing to do with Xavier. It had everything to do with a fiction writer looking for a thrill to write into her next book. Your idiocy put good people in danger. Xavier is most likely dead. How do you feel about that?"

"You're not being fair." The heat rising in her face had grown into a full-blown defense case. "How dare you size me up and spit me out like a piece of trash. My motives were to help Xavier. That's all."

"Kariss, you're screaming." Tigo's dry tone did nothing to ease her wrath.

"What of it? After what happened tonight and Ryan's accusations, I have the right to scream until tomorrow. You were the ones who refused to help Xavier."

"Calm down. You're reaching hysteria," Tigo said. "He doesn't even know if the child was born."

"But it's a life, and that means something. Did you hear Cheeky? He knows Delores, and she admitted to killing Benita and maybe her other child."

"She's all yours, Tigo." Ryan stared out

the passenger window as the car veered onto the 610 loop headed west.

"I don't want her. In fact, I could let her out right here. In fact, if I never see her again, it would be too soon."

Kariss took a few breaths to calm herself before he made good on his threat. "I appreciate your saving my life. I'm grateful. I was frightened out of my mind." She gasped. "You slapped me."

"I apologize. I needed to look credible."

She understood, only too well. "Thanks. What . . . what do you plan to do about the gun exchange . . . and me?"

"I don't have any problem with the exchange. Cheeky can have you," Tigo said. "What do you think, Ryan?"

"Sure. Give Cheeky what he wants." Ryan's tone indicated his anger had not subsided.

"But I think we can take him into custody before he mistreats you." Tigo didn't miss a beat.

"That's horrible. I won't permit it." The moment the words left her mouth, she realized how ridiculous they sounded. "Guys, please. You have to understand how this happened." Kariss's temples throbbed.

"It wasn't an accident," Tigo said. "You had a gun, which they now have."

"For protection, that's all. I was afraid for Xavier."

"So why did you go?"

She began to sob. "I couldn't bear deserting him when all he wanted was to find his child. I didn't think —"

"Stop right there," Tigo said. "I've done enough of a background check to know why. What happened in that fire was not your fault."

How long had he known? "I think about it all the time. Hear the cries."

"Looks to me like heroism burned a few brain cells," Ryan said.

"I wasn't a hero. I failed. She died."

"Hey, now, I'm sorry," Ryan said, "but you can't live in the past."

"I'm working on that." She stuffed her emotions. Later she'd work through what tonight meant — nearly getting killed, failing again, and hearing what she thought was the voice of God. "Seriously, what are you going to do?"

"Have your obituary placed in the paper and send Cheeky a copy," Tigo said.

She noted her clasped hands in her lap. Still praying. "Will he believe it?"

"I have a better idea," Ryan said. "Let's get the word out on the streets. That'll take

484

care of the Arroyos who don't know how to read."

"Great idea." Tigo palmed the steering wheel. "FBI Agent Sally Seymore found dismembered in parking garage at Northwest Medical Center. Too many pieces to bury."

"Sally Seymore?" If she hadn't been shaking, she'd laugh. "Can't you give me a more professional name?"

Ryan laughed. "Yeah, like Tellie Toomuch?"

They were trying to make her feel better, and she should ease up. Relax if possible. "My car's parked back there."

"We'll have someone pick it up in the morning. Just in case an Arroyo is following us," Tigo said.

"I thought you said we were fine." Panic rose again.

"We are." Tigo glanced at her in the rearview mirror. "Do you really want to pick up your car tonight?"

She didn't want to be alone in a vehicle, worrying about who might be following her. "I can wait." She held her breath. "Do you think Xavier is okay?"

Neither man responded.

"Tigo?"

"Depends on Cheeky's mood. To stay alive, he'll have to prove his loyalty to the

Arroyos. Much like initiation."

"How can we find out?"

"If his body is found, then we'll know. If the next time you see your bud he's covered in gang signs, you'll know then too."

"He wouldn't kill anyone."

"Probably not. There's your answer."

Kariss closed her eyes as Tigo drove toward the FBI office.

Thank You, God, for saving me. Thank You for not deserting me when I tuned You out after the fire. I'm listening, really listening. Tonight was miraculous. Would You keep Xavier safe too?

"Are you going to sleep?" Tigo said.

"No. I'm praying."

"Been there already tonight," Ryan said.

"I owe Him big time for this." Reverence laced her words.

"One of these days I'll look into the God thing," Tigo said. "Promised my mother I would."

Ryan shook his head. "Tonight should have made you a believer."

"Not yet. When Cheeky is behind bars along with Masterson and Bates, then I'll sit on the front row of your church. How's that?"

"Don't wait too long."

The finality of Ryan's advice squeezed her

heart. She'd seen enough blood and too much of the vile actions of cruel men.

"Guys, I have something to say."

Ryan chuckled. "When haven't you?"

"Hear me out. When it comes time to make the exchange, and I know that's when you'll be able to arrest all those involved, use me just like you told Cheeky."

CHAPTER 50

Exhausted, Kariss crawled into bed thinking she'd be able to sleep for the next ten hours, but her mind refused to rest. She'd nearly been killed, and the danger persisted like a horrible disease for which there was no cure. Scenes flashed before her eyes. Tattooed men with evil intent. Dialogue repeated. Worry about Xavier continued. Had he survived? Would he agree to whatever Cheeky demanded? She had no answers.

God had saved her . . . not Tigo and Ryan. What did that mean?

Her cell rang. She hesitated to answer, but she didn't want the sound waking Vicki. A quick glance showed it was Tigo. Dread consumed her but she pressed Talk.

"Are you okay?" Concern filled his voice.

If she had a definition of the word *okay,* she might have an answer. "I think so."

"I want to apologize for slapping you."

"You already did." In the darkness of her

room, she closed her eyes. "You helped save my life. I was so foolish. I'm sorry for interfering with your operation."

"Kariss, you can't save every child in danger."

Instantly her thoughts transported her back to the fire. She heard the cries. Saw the leaping flames. Would she ever be free? Would God take away the guilt? "But I must try."

"Not if you end up dead."

"I'm trying to make some sense of my actions, the poison that drives me to do stupid things."

He sighed. "Try to get some sleep, and I'll call you tomorrow. We'll get this thing figured out."

"I meant what I said earlier. Let me help if the deal requires me in the exchange."

"No, Kariss. We'll stage your death. That's an easy fix. Almost lost you tonight."

His words bordered on endearing, and she wondered if he was feeling the same attraction she did. All of this was more than she could manage. "All right. I'll be there in the morning . . . with your coffee."

"Kariss —"

"Good night." She disconnected the call before he said more. Tigo seemed to understand her inner workings — motivation —

even if she didn't understand herself. Rest would not come tonight. She needed to pray for Xavier and all those involved in stopping the Arroyos.

How strange that, after all the years of growing up in church and youth groups and family devotions, nothing had made sense until now. God had preserved her life for a purpose, and she'd have to keep her eyes open to what He intended. Her gift of writing had come from Him . . . Just like her parents claimed. Yet would He take away the voices? Perhaps they'd always be there.

Would she tell her parents or Vicki about becoming a Christian? No. She'd just show the change.

Tuesday morning before his meeting with Linc and Ryan, Tigo made the necessary arrangements to stage Kariss's death — an FBI agent found murdered on the southeast side of town. He made sure the Spanish stations were included and added she'd been involved in a gun-smuggling investigation. That should keep Kariss safe until after Monday night. If the case wasn't wrapped up then, he'd force her out of town.

"Have you heard from Xavier?" Ryan said

as they walked to the elevator to Linc's office.

"Not yet. HPD hasn't been notified of a homicide." Tigo shook his head. "I hate the idea of him getting involved with the Arroyos, but he might not have a choice. Gilberto is supposed to call the moment he shows up."

"Xavier is a believer. I can't imagine him working for the Arroyos, but intimidation works, and Cheeky had information about Delores."

"I agree. Hopefully we'll know something today. A couple of agents picked up Kariss's car. I'm not going to let her have it until this is over. She can rent another vehicle. Preferably a tank."

"I have a little more info on Bates and Masterson." Ryan waved at an agent down the hall. "We have them videoed together Saturday night. Both men attended the same gala fund-raiser in River Oaks. We have the two talking in private on a back terrace."

"Was anything recorded?"

"No. But neither man was happy."

"Good. Let's hope they got word about our deal with the Arroyos last night. Did you talk to Hershey?" Tigo's head hammered against his skull. The lack of sleep and not eating since yesterday was taking hold.

"Sure did. He's getting the word out on the streets that there's a new supplier in town."

"Linc needs to know more than what our initial report states, and he's not going to be happy with our little obstacles," Tigo said. "I'll tell him. She's my responsibility."

"And Xavier? Are you working on blame overload with him too?"

Tigo's head continued to pound.

CHAPTER 51

August

Tuesday afternoon, Kariss drove home from the FBI office in a rental car, thinking about the day's events. She'd been reflective and stayed inside her work area, pouring over information about the FBI that was open to the public. Earlier she'd told Tigo that he could drive her home, and she really did appreciate his concern. But she'd already been a burden to him. The two men had been gone most of the day, and she hadn't really wanted to see them. Her actions had left her ashamed, and she needed to voice an apology befitting their sacrifice.

Everything in her life mirrored yesterday. The people who passed her on the highway were headed toward their own agenda. She wanted to scream at them, tell them that life could instantly spin out of control. Her escape from death had her shaken, and mixed emotions coursed through her.

She refused to cower like a frightened animal.

Every breath was still a prayer, her thoughts tangled in concern for Xavier and thankfulness for her life.

The bright side of today was life flowed through her. Vicki planned to cook chicken cordon bleu, grilled asparagus, and a chocolate mousse. And Kariss had written more of her novel. Her progress reminded her that a writer did her best work from personal pain.

The peaceful veil over the day had been welcome, a balm to her soul in ways she couldn't explain. Her thoughts focused on her renewed faith . . . Xavier's safety . . . and her gratitude to Tigo and Ryan. She also took note of how she looked at life during times of intense stress. She often became more poetic, her thoughts flowing in symbolism and vivid imagery.

Inside her garage, she breathed in the aroma of dinner, grateful for a loving sister. She entered through the kitchen ready to proclaim Vicki would never be able to leave as long as she cooked like a gourmet chef.

"We're in here," Vicki said.

Lately, her sister had begun referring to herself in the plural. "Dinner smells fabulous. I may never let you leave."

"I could teach you how to cook."

Kariss heard a male laugh — one whose owner she knew. Her spirits dropped to her toes. "Who's with you?"

"Wyatt."

"Vicki, you promised." She straightened her shoulders and walked into the living room. There on her white sofa sat the man who had ruined her sister's life — tried to have the mother of his child abort her baby — drinking one of her Diet Cokes. Vicki sat beside him, and the sight infuriated Kariss.

"In defense of your sister, I was persuasive." He stood.

"Is that so? You can sit, Wyatt."

He resumed his position beside Vicki. "I wanted to discuss our baby."

"I thought you'd already stated your feelings about the matter, and the situation was iced."

His eyes narrowed. "I've changed my mind since we last spoke."

"As if you have a choice."

Vicki stretched out her arm. "Sis, hear him out. We've been talking for the past hour."

Kariss plopped onto a chair opposite the couple. "Don't tell me you're moving in."

"Ah, no," he said. "That wouldn't work."

"At least we agree on one thing." She reminded herself of her new call to follow the

Lord instead of reacting to the man before her.

Vicki's eyes pooled. Another common occurrence with her pregnancy. Kariss chose to ease off a bit for her sister's sake.

"Okay." Kariss pasted on a smile. "Wyatt, what's going on here?"

"I want to take care of my daughter. Be a part of her life." He looked sincere, and his body language agreed with his words. But she knew Wyatt had written the book on manipulation.

"How do you plan to do this? Understand that you've hurt my sister . . . repeatedly. I have no trust in anything you say."

"I feel the same," Vicki said. "Our failed marriage and the conception of this child has wised me up. Empty words mean nothing to me. I want to be shown."

Kariss silently cheered Vicki's insistence.

"That's why I intend to show you I'm serious. I've already seen my attorney and had the papers drawn up so I can take care of the medical costs and provide fifteen hundred dollars a month for child support. In addition, I'll pay for child care when Vicki returns to work." He lifted his chin, the stance Kariss remembered. "Until she feels she's ready to resume her responsibilities, I'll pay an additional four thousand dollars a month."

Wyatt had the funds to do exactly what he claimed, but would he follow through? "And this is in writing?"

He pointed to a manila envelope on the glass-topped table. "It's all right here."

Kariss peered at her sister then back to Wyatt. "I know this isn't any of my business, but have you discussed visitation? In point, your live-in?"

"We're no longer together."

Vicki tossed him a startled look. "When did this change of heart occur?"

Good question, sis. He's feeding you garbage again.

"The day after I met you at the restaurant. She said that if I chose to be a father to your baby, she was gone." He took a drink of the Diet Coke. "I knew the baby was mine. I know Vicki. The idea of being a father appeals to me, but I want to be a good one. I'm not ready for reconciliation or anything like that. Our relationship hit the dust a long time ago."

"Your fault," Vicki said. "Some parts of you refused to stay home. What about the child you and Lissa had together?"

His gaze bore into Vicki's face. "I recently learned *that* baby isn't mine."

"Where are you living?"

"At the present, I'm still in the house with Lissa. And something else too."

Vicki stiffened. "Tell me, Wyatt. As your ex-wife, I have the right to know everything."

"Lissa had her stepsister follow you. I tried giving her a job at the office, but it didn't work out. Lissa had no clue her sister would deck Kariss."

"She followed me more than once." Kariss tilted her head. "That doesn't make sense. If Lissa said she hired her stepsister to follow Vicki, why did she try to run me over with a motorcycle? Vicki was nowhere around that time." She'd call Tigo later on and relay this new bit of information. Someone was lying, and she didn't trust anyone associated with Wyatt.

Vicki gasped. "When did this happen?"

"Never mind, sis. I'm sure Wyatt was made aware."

He cleared his throat. "I had no idea she'd become vindictive, and I'm only relaying what Lissa told me."

Kariss leaned forward. "I have good friends at the FBI, one of whom you've already met. Before you leave here today, I want the woman's name because I'm filing charges."

A flash of anger swept over his face, but

his lips formed a smile. "If it keeps Agent Harris out of my office, then I can give you her name. I mean everything I've said to Vicki."

"I hope so," Vicki said. "Because if I learn this is another one of your schemes, I'll see you in court. My baby doesn't need a father who lies and cheats."

Kariss considered asking him to wear a wire . . .

"I want joint custody and the typical visitation rights," Wyatt said. "Those are outlined in the document."

"I'll read every word." Vicki picked up the envelope.

"I expected no less."

"Now that you're here," Kariss said, "I'd like to talk to you about something that has nothing to do with my sister or the baby."

Vicki stood, her expanding waistline obvious. "I need to finish dinner. Do you need me?"

She detested the thought of Vicki hearing any of the conversation, but it couldn't be avoided with the kitchen so close to the living room. "No." She smiled. "I'm hungry, and I don't want dinner to burn."

While Vicki busied herself in the kitchen, Kariss formed her words. "The day Vicki and I met you at the restaurant, there was another man who followed you outside."

"I remember. Arnold Bates."

"So you know him?"

Wyatt nodded his head. "I let him know when a good piece of property is for sale. But his interest was in you."

Kariss sensed her blood pressure rising. "He asked you questions about me?"

"Said you looked familiar, but he couldn't place where. I told him you were once a TV personality for Channel 5."

Fear churned her stomach. Tigo had introduced her to Arnold Bates as Miss Jenson the day of the interview. Why did he question Wyatt about something he already knew? "What did you say?"

"Saw no harm in giving him your name. I thought he'd seen you on TV, either as a news anchor or from your books."

Wyatt may have added another etching to her casket.

Chapter 52

Wednesday morning, Kariss realized she needed to go home. Her mind stayed fixed on the encounter with Cheeky and fear for Xavier. No one had heard from him.

Her concern for Vicki dissipated when the police arrested Lissa's sister. The bright news was the Arroyos didn't know where Kariss lived. Neither had they sent the motorcycle mama after her.

Her cell phone rang as she checked email one last time before driving home. The caller didn't have a familiar number. She hesitated . . . Looked like a New York number.

"Kariss, this is RuthAnne LeMoy. We haven't talked in a long time. How are you?"

Her heart took a giant leap. RuthAnne had been her favorite editor. They'd been more than professionals — they'd been friends. "How wonderful to hear your voice."

"And yours too. Kariss, I've changed editorial positions, and I'm now working with suspense novels. We want to build our fiction line to include more women writers in this popular, growing genre. In light of recent events, you were the first person I thought of."

Maybe she should pinch herself. Two miracles in one week? "I'm working on a suspense based on an FBI cold case here in Houston."

"Is there a thread of romance? We want to lure those women readers."

"It's a romantic suspense." She hoped RuthAnne couldn't hear her wild breathing.

"Can I see a synopsis and first chapter? I contacted Meredith, and she indicated she was no longer representing you. Who is representing you?"

"No one." Talk about a taste of humility.

"We'll fix that. If you'll get a proposal to me, I'll talk to a few agents. I like working with High Profile Literary Agency. What do you think?"

"Don't they represent several Christian authors?" Only the best in the business . . .

"They do."

"Sounds good to me. I've recently become a Christian, and I want to keep my writing focus there."

"Me too! Isn't it grand how life works out? Once we get the acquisition made, we'll discuss rebranding you. I've already talked to marketing, and we're prepared to invest dollars in the rebrand. You've built quite a social media presence. Nearly fifty thousand Likes on your Facebook author page. Twitter followers and LinkedIn connections aren't shabby either."

"Thanks. Got to keep up with the technology."

"Your hard work has definitely paid off. I remember your first published book."

Kariss moaned. "I rewrote it twice."

"Then it hit the bestsellers list."

"Thanks to your guidance and wisdom. I'll email the proposal this afternoon. RuthAnne, your call has made my day."

"Mine too. Talk to you soon. Bye."

Kariss trembled so much she dropped her phone on the desk with a thud. Her heart beat faster than a butterfly's wings. Thankfulness smacked her in the gut.

"You okay?" Tigo stuck his head around the doorway.

"Yeah. I'm good." Since he'd saved her life twice, he'd been sweeter. Couldn't figure that one out when he should be furious.

Questions bombarded her mind about the weapons' exchange . . .

503

"You look happier than I've seen you for a while."

"Facing death does that to you." She laughed, and it felt good. "An old editor just called to ask me for a suspense synopsis."

"I thought you'd sold this book."

Truth time. "No. I gave my agent the boot when she demanded I continue writing books for women. This . . . this editor just changed positions, and she's interested in my story."

"Congratulations." He jammed his hands into his pants pockets. "I'm glad for you."

"One of the reasons I enjoy writing is the idea of communicating through the written word. I like fiction. It works for me."

"Have you told your parents?"

"I literally just found out. I will in a few minutes." She laughed. "Now my mother can recommend my books to her friends and not be concerned about the company it's being published by. Do you ever read any fiction?"

"Sorry. Mostly biographies, and I download them on my e-reader. Hey, I'm glad for you. What about celebrating tonight, say an early dinner?"

Was she reading too much into this if she thought it was more than friend to friend?

"Sounds good. What about your mother?"

"She'll be fine in Natalie's care." He frowned. "I check on her periodically throughout the day. Run home now and then. Unfortunately, Mom doesn't know anyone's there."

"We don't have to do this."

"But I want to. Give us time to talk."

Talk about what?

His cell rang and broke the moment, if there was a moment being had. Kariss turned her attention back to her laptop and pulled up the proposal for *Shadow Play*, the title she'd chosen for her first romantic suspense novel. The hook was strong. She'd send the chapter, synopsis, marketing plan, and a paragraph about the two protagonists.

"Kariss."

She lifted her gaze back to Tigo, whose face looked drawn.

"I'm sorry, but we'll need to reschedule our dinner celebration."

"No problem. What happened?"

"My mother just passed away. I'm heading home as soon as I inform Linc and Ryan."

"Would you like some company?"

He hesitated, then shook his head. "No need to interrupt your day."

Kariss closed her laptop. "You shouldn't

go through this alone."

"I'm okay. I've known this was coming. She and I planned her funeral several months ago. And the nurses know what to do."

"I'm sure they're excellent and will take care of your mother just like they've always done. But nothing prepares us for the reality of death. Let me help." She pressed a tight smile. "I can follow you."

He nodded. "Thanks. I live in the Spring area."

She slipped her computer into its sleeve. She'd never done anything like this before. But she couldn't imagine going through a parent's death alone. Maybe he had siblings or other close family. But he hadn't talked about them. How sad.

On the way to the parking lot, she couldn't think of a single thing to say. He appeared locked into his thoughts, grieving in his own way. She'd not interfere with his sorrow. Simply be there, a step forward in her faith.

Cheeky studied the spreadsheet that detailed how each section of his business progressed — the amount of money made, the percentage of increase, and who worked the area. Every day he studied what was happening and if his members were doing their jobs. Only Cheeky and his cousin in Mexico had access to the spreadsheet, which was on a network secured by the best money could buy.

He settled back in his chair and smiled. Paulo's work proved his loyalty when he'd taken care of eliminating Froggie's family within four hours. Neat. Clean. Baffled the *policía,* but they recognized the Arroyos' signature. Soon he'd take his place within his cousin's cartel. All he needed was to find two people.

His cell rang. Paulo. "What do you have?"

"Bates is the one informing the *policía* when our mules head to the border."

Cheeky clenched his fists. Bates would pay and so would Masterson. "Good job."

"I have more. The man who killed three Arroyos? He's FBI Agent Tigo Harris. I know where he lives." Paulo laughed. "And he's friends with that Kariss Walker. Found out where she lives too."

"Al fin les pesqué."

"Yes, boss, you've caught them. Want me to kill them?"

Cheeky wanted them dead, but he had another plan that took care of all he needed to prove his power in Houston. "I'll tell you when to pick them up. We'll have a party."

Tigo's emotions felt as if they'd been suspended. He wasn't one to cry, but shouldn't he feel like it? Mom no longer endured the suffering, and for that he was grateful . . . thankful. But he'd miss her — or rather the mother who used to listen and encourage him with endless wisdom.

He glanced in the rearview mirror. Kariss followed close behind. He wasn't sure why he'd agreed to her trailing after him like he needed someone to hold his hand, except he feared being alone. What a statement. The rogue special agent who burrowed his way undercover to stop crime had confessed to needing another human being. Kariss Walker had become a friend. That knowledge kept him from picking up his phone and telling her he'd changed his mind.

Who else should he call? He'd already phoned the priest and the funeral home. A third cousin lived in Dallas and another in Omaha. A few years earlier, he'd tracked his father to Northern California where he lived with a much younger wife. They had three daughters together. At the time, Tigo didn't make contact. But out of respect for his mother, he'd inform his father after funeral arrangements were made.

Upon arriving home, Tigo recognized the priest's car. Natalie would have his mother's body clean and ready for the funeral home to pick up her body. He'd already instructed Natalie to make sure her pink suit was available . . . her favorite. Just like she'd requested months ago. Every time he'd left his mother, he kissed her good-bye, but this was the final one. Emotion bubbled inside him, but he'd grieve privately. Another reason why having Kariss here was a good decision. He must remain in control while confirming arrangements with the priest and talking to Natalie. Still, memories of happier times needled at his impassive resolve.

He waited at his truck for Kariss to walk up the driveway.

"Anyone I can call for you?" Her smile helped him to stay calm.

"No thanks. I've got it handled." They walked to the front door, and he gestured for her to step inside.

Once in the foyer that opened into his living area, Kariss turned to him. "Go tend to your mother, and I'll wait here."

He let her compassion settle into his bones. "I won't be too long. Natalie and Father Upchurch are here somewhere."

"I'm fine."

Tigo walked the hallway to his mother's quarters, the part of the house designated as Francisca Harris's home. She'd overseen the decorating in shades of light green with brown and cream accents and picked out the traditional furniture. The idea was when she recovered, she could enjoy her area in privacy. Her bedroom adjoined a sitting area with a flat-screen TV, a small fridge, a coffeemaker that ground fresh beans, and a microwave. She also had her books, the classics she called friends.

Natalie met him at the bedroom door. The priest had obviously finished because he offered his condolences and left Tigo alone . . . with his mother. Taking her hand, cold and limp, he sat beside her as he'd done so many times before.

"You really look beautiful, and your face is peaceful. Like I know you are. It's over, Mom," he whispered and blinked. "You fought the fight, as you so often said. Now you're in a better place. I know your faith in God brought you through this and to the finish line." He stroked her hand. "Thanks for all you did for me. I know I told you that many times, but it bears repeating. Without your help I'd be in prison. Or dead. You successfully knocked the chip off my shoulder and replaced it with good values. Things that make me the man I am today."

He could almost hear her reminders and swiped at his nose. "Yeah. Yeah. I'll start going to church. Linc's been asking me for a long time. It's not Catholic, but you're the one who said the same God lives in the hearts of all believers who've sworn allegiance to Christ. See, I bet you didn't think I was listening." He stroked her lifeless hand. "I haven't forgotten you wanted me to mentor teen boys, ones at risk. I'll do that too.

"One more thing, that woman I've been talking about? She's headstrong and witty. Pretty too. I can say we're friends. Not sure where it's going, but I want to try. She's made me mad more than once, but when I thought about it, I realized it was because I cared a little. Too many times I wish you'd been able to talk to me about her."

That's when the tears poured like a pent-up dam.

CHAPTER 53

Kariss walked through Tigo's living room, large and tastefully decorated in rich shades of brown and tan, with a cocoa-colored leather sofa and dark woods. Accents of coral and gold caught her eye. A vase looked like it came from the Middle East. Perhaps his mother had traveled there. A wall of windows opened up to a magnificently landscaped yard.

She wandered into a huge kitchen, where the enticing aroma of coffee filled the air. Copper pans hung over the stove, complemented by rich cabinetry, brown and black granite countertops, and a coffee bar. A priest stood with an attractive blonde woman, and Kariss approached them to introduce herself.

"I'm Kariss Walker, Tigo's friend."

The woman reached out her hand and smiled, a genuine gesture. "I'm Natalie, Mrs. Harris's hospice nurse."

The priest extended his hand, a middle-aged man with lots of gray. "I'm Father Up-church." His grasp was firm and his response kind. "I know the name sorta gives me away."

She liked him instantly.

"Would you like coffee?" Natalie said. "We were just about to have a cup. It's fresh. I knew Tigo would want some once he got home."

"I smelled it the moment I walked in. That would be lovely."

Natalie turned to the coffee bar. She reached for two cups, filled them, and handed them to Kariss and Father Up-church. "All the fixings are right here." She gestured to the bar, where every manner of creamer and means of sweetening the coffee were available. "Thank you for being here. Tigo doesn't have much family."

In an instant, Kariss's large family swept across her mind's eye. She couldn't imagine being alone. "Is there anything I can do?" She picked up a small pitcher of creamer and dribbled a generous amount into the dark, rich brew. She stepped away to allow Natalie and Father Upchurch access.

"Consolation is the only thing I can think of," Natalie said.

"What happens with Mrs. Harris now?"

"She's been bathed, and we're waiting for the funeral home to arrive." Natalie glanced at Father Upchurch, and he took a sip of his coffee.

"Are you Catholic, Miss Walker?" he said.

"No. I've attended a wake but not a funeral service."

"The wake will be at the funeral home. The Mass will be at the church where Mrs. Harris holds her membership. From there, the procession will move to the cemetery for a graveside service."

Kariss nodded at the priest as though she knew the procedures for a Roman Catholic burial. She wondered if friends brought in food. Her mother would probably have the answer. "I haven't known Tigo very long, but it appears he's devoted to his mother."

"He's a good man. A good son," Father Upchurch said. "I've been called here before to administer last rites, and he's always been attentive. You're blessed to have him as a friend."

She was blessed in many ways. "Yes, I am. He . . . saved my life. Without his wisdom, I'd be dead." She shivered. "I'm sorry. The happening is still raw, and I've been thankful for every breath of life since then." Offering a smile, she then stared at her coffee. "Today is about Tigo and his mother, not me. I apologize for making it seem so."

"Talking about God's deliverance is always appropriate."

Kariss lifted her gaze to meet his. The priest knew God. More than that — he walked with Him. They had a kinship, and the thought filled her with peace. She turned to Natalie. "He speaks highly of you and the others who have given care to his mother."

"Thank you," Natalie said. "I work the afternoon and evening shift. Every night he sat by his mother's side. Ate his supper there. Worked until way up into the night. Talked to Mrs. Harris as if she were cognizant."

"How very caring." Another characteristic of Tigo that surprised her. She'd seen his gentle side during the times she'd been frightened. Again she considered the complexity of this man.

"And the roses."

Kariss tilted her head.

"Mrs. Harris loved red roses, and Tigo made sure she had a fresh bouquet every five days."

Kariss remembered the way he'd examined Vicki's roses and the compliments. Now she understood his interest. She vowed to be more attentive to her own parents.

"This home and neighborhood is beautiful."

"I agree. Tigo purchased it new when he returned from Saudi Arabia about seven years ago to take care of his mother. The size and layout were perfect, and you can see he keeps it in immaculate condition."

He'd been in Saudi Arabia? That explained some of the accent pieces in his living room. "How long have you been involved with Mrs. Harris's care?"

"Nearly a year. She's been a fighter."

"Are you an agent too?" Father Upchurch took a sip of coffee.

"No, sir. I'm a writer. Tigo has been helping me with research for a novel. I was at the FBI office when he received the call and I asked if I could accompany him."

"He never talks about his work," Natalie said. "Our conversations have been about the care of his mother — and when to expect his arrival."

The new information about Tigo touched her. She'd judged him by his professional mannerisms, his attention to detail and bringing criminals to justice. Later, when this was behind him, she'd ask about his time in Saudi. How commendable for him to return to take care of his ailing mother. A mystery man for sure. At that moment, standing in the kitchen of Tigo's home with his mother's hospice nurse and a priest, Kariss couldn't think of a single trait that didn't fall under the category of an honorable man.

Early Friday morning, Kariss exited the church after the Mass for Tigo's mother. The ceremony had been meaningful, respectful. The attendees were solemn, and there was no music. That aspect surprised her. She expected more of a celebration.

She'd come alone and sat midway in the church. Linc and Ryan had arrived ahead of her and sat closer to the front. The crowded church indicated the number of people Mrs. Harris had impacted positively during her life. Although she'd lived the past two years as an invalid, she'd contributed to many worthwhile projects within her church and community.

Kariss had heard wonderful stories at the wake about how she'd taken care of the poor and the elderly. A good woman who lived her faith. Someday Kariss would ask Tigo more about her. Maybe that would be a good conversation for later, since he'd asked her to stay after the meal at his home. She'd be there for him because it was the right thing to do. Considering he'd saved her from being killed and made sure the Arroyos believed he'd disposed of her body, she'd do just about anything for him. But her presence was more than an obligation or a responsibility. Her fragile faith encouraged her to reach out. She'd always been giving, especially to children. But that came from what happened at the day care. This new devotion came from what Jesus had done for her.

At Tigo's home, the hours inched by until the last person paid their respects and left. The caterer and his servers packaged up the leftovers. Tigo paced the floor like a caged cat, clearly stressed from the day.

"I didn't eat, and I'm starved," he said to Kariss. "The food here had death oozing from it."

"I understand." She'd been too preoccupied assisting the servers to eat. "I haven't either."

"I appreciate how you jumped in and took care of people. Thanks. I owe you." He ran his fingers through his hair, a mannerism she hadn't observed in the past.

"You don't owe me anything. Glad to help."

"I've instructed the servers to take the leftovers. The food would just sit in the fridge and spoil."

"What do you suggest? I'd offer to cook, but it wouldn't be edible."

He gave her a half smile. "We could go somewhere."

"You're worn out, Tigo. Why don't I go pick us up something?"

He looked around as though lost. "Sounds like a good idea. Can't believe how late it is. Anyway, there's an Italian restaurant about five minutes from here. I could call in an order." He picked up a book on grief that someone had left for him. He leafed through the pages then set it aside. "Sure you don't mind?"

"No problem. Just point me in the right direction."

Tigo appeared to labor over the menu, but Kariss recognized the signs of mourning and his need for a time to be alone. She'd linger a bit in picking up the food.

Outside in the starless night, the hot Houston air seemed to wrap a blanket around her. She'd never minded heat and humidity, and her travels across the country to colder and dryer areas made her uncomfortable. Tonight, the heaviness nearly stole her breath away. Perhaps it was the funeral.

She walked down the driveway to her car, which was parked at the curb. Glancing up, she admired the neighborhood. Lights in the windows of well-kept homes and the quiet sounds gave her a sense of peace.

"Do not turn around or scream." A sharp object pressed against the small of her back. The Hispanic male voice with a lisp caused her head to spin. Although he spoke English, she knew without hesitation who'd come for her.

"Takes guts to accost a woman in this area," she whispered.

"Only takes a few seconds to send this knife through you. Walk across the street to the parked car." He nudged her forward.

The car was a Lexus, fitting for the neighborhood but not the man behind the knife.

"Why should I? You're going to kill me anyway."

"This way you keep Tigo alive. He can't save your neck this time."

How did they find out? He'd been so carefully disguised that she hadn't recognized him. Someone had sold them out.

But who?

CHAPTER 54

Tigo checked the time. Kariss should have been back with dinner over twenty minutes ago. Wouldn't she have called if she had been delayed? He pressed her number into his cell. After the fourth ring, it went to voice mail.

"Kariss, it's Tigo. Seems strange you'd be this late. Give me a call."

Ten minutes later, he phoned the restaurant. She'd not picked up the food order.

Snatching his keys and wallet, he headed to the garage and raised the door. She must have had car problems. But why hadn't she called for help? A trace of alarm inched through him. He'd planted all the right seeds for the Arroyos to believe she was dead. Even had a bogus article placed in the paper about finding a dead woman that fit the time and description of the gun deal.

His attention turned to the curb. Kariss's car sat right where she'd parked it after the funeral. He jogged to the vehicle. It was unlocked. No sign of a struggle. But how could he tell much in the dark? He hurried back to the garage for a flashlight.

Moments later, he aimed the light over the area. The grass next to her car had been beaten down, indicating multiple people had stood in the area.

His cell rang. "Tigo here."

"I suggest you listen up," a man said in Spanish. "*Tenemos a tu amiga.* If you want to make sure she stays alive, then do exactly what I tell you."

Tigo scrutinized the vehicles parked around him. All looked like they belonged. A couple of teens played basketball. They might have seen something. "What do you want?"

"We're willing to make an exchange."

"What kind?" Tigo continued to scan the darkness. The Arroyos had spent too much time looking for Kariss and then letting her slip through their fingers to bargain with her life now. "Name your price."

"You for her."

"I'm ready."

"We'll stay in touch."

Fear, such a formidable enemy.

Duct tape sealed her mouth. She tasted

the rising nausea and prayed her stomach would stop its incessant churning. If she vomited, she'd surely choke to death. That would solve it all for the Arroyos.

Her arms were pinned behind her back, and rope dug into her wrists like needles searching for blood. Roaches skittered across the concrete floor, and other quickening clicks hinted at mice . . . or rats.

About twenty feet away, three Arroyos played cards and drank can after can of beer, the ping of each finished container echoing around her as if in time to the strum of a Spanish guitar. They talked about what they planned to do to her . . . Sickening revulsion twisted in her gut.

But the smell attacked her most — dank, musty, and filled with the heaviness of death.

She strained to study where they held her. But her eye was nearly swollen shut. Moving proved painful, and she surmised her right rib must be broken. Piled several feet beyond her were rows of pipe manufactured by Cardinal Ventures.

Even if she were able to free herself, she had no idea where they'd taken her. Some type of warehouse. She'd been shoved to the floorboard of the Lexus — so unlike a few days ago when Tigo and Ryan had ordered her to do the same.

How long before they were drunk enough to act upon their bravado? Or had they already been given their orders?

CHAPTER 55

Back inside his house, Tigo used his secured business cell phone to call Ryan. He quickly relayed what happened.

"I'm not sure when they nabbed her. Some kids across the street were playing basketball. Didn't see a thing."

"Have you contacted Linc?"

"Not yet. What do I tell him? I've gotten Kariss killed?" Tigo wiped his face. "Hey, I'm not being rational here. They want an exchange, and I'll hear from them."

"Tigo, you just buried your mother. I'll call Linc. You contact Hershey."

"Right. I have no way of knowing if I'm being watched, so if you don't hear from me, take over."

"Will do. We'll find her. But you're not making any kind of an exchange."

Oh, yes, he would. "I'll call you back in a few minutes." Tigo ended the call. He walked through his house turning off the lights while he waited for Hershey to answer. But the gun dealer didn't pick up.

Tigo texted him.

CALL ME ASAP.

He shook like an agent in training. Emotional overload.

Mom's funeral.

Kariss kidnapped.

The knowledge of what the Arroyos would do to her.

Helpless to control any of it. His mother would have advised him to pray. So would Ryan and Linc. For that matter, even Kariss had given in to God. But Tigo'd been trained to track down criminals. Depending on something he couldn't see made no sense.

His phone vibrated with a text from Hershey.

CAN'T TALK. W/CUSTOMER.

GET FREE. 911.

Tigo studied the outside darkness through the windows. Nothing moved that he could detect. Where would they have taken her? They'd better not touch her . . . But they would, and so much more.

His cell rang. Linc.

"We're on this, Tigo. Got our best agents scouring the city."

"I'm waiting to hear from Hershey. He'll find out where she's being held."

"Don't go out alone."

Tigo understood what he meant. But not this time. If he got a lead, he was on it.

"Tigo. I know you. This isn't the time to play hero. We all need to work together."

Linc was right. "Okay. I'll call the moment I hear a thing." He slipped his phone back into his pocket.

No updates. No Hershey. And no idea where the Arroyos had taken Kariss. He wanted to leave, but where would he go?

Ten minutes later, his phone beeped with another text from Hershey.

CAN'T CALL. JUST TEXT.

ARROYOS HAVE KIDNAPPED WOMAN. U NO WHERE SHE IS?

I FIND OUT.

Tigo waited another thirty minutes. The Arroyos never wasted time, and they had a prize captive. His phone vibrated.

The Arroyos wanted Kariss and Tigo. There wouldn't be any kind of exchange. Tigo had deceived them, and the Arroyos would make them both pay.

The door opened to the warehouse where Kariss was being held. Men's voices filled her with terror. The time had come. She needed to be brave. God was with her. But the reassurance didn't stop the fear of what would happen between now and when she saw the gates of heaven.

Two familiar faces walked into the shadowed room. First came Arnold Bates, dressed in jeans and an Astros baseball cap and carrying a gun. Walking beside him was Wyatt Phillips, who looked like he'd just come from work. Bates approached the men playing cards. Her ex-brother-in-law strode her way and bent beside her.

"You're such a fool," Wyatt said. "Now I'm getting even." He ripped the duct tape off her mouth.

She gasped, the tape tearing across her face where she'd been struck before, seeping blood into her mouth. "You'll never get away with this. The FBI is on to you."

He laughed. "Don't think so. I've covered

my tracks."

"You scum. You lied to Vicki," Kariss said. "Everything you did was a ploy to keep your eyes on me."

"I had good reasons. Bates offered me a job the same day I met you at the restaurant. He recognized you from the hospital. He knew I was ready to work for some big cash. He'd already done a background check and found out I was your ex-brother-in-law. Fit right into what they needed. Great luck, don't you think?"

Bates walked toward them, and Wyatt stood.

"Wyatt, you're stupid." Kariss spit her words. "They came after you. Don't you see that? Bates recognized me from the FBI office and put it all together."

"Smart girl." Bates chuckled. He reminded her of a neighbor. Tigo had mentioned that very thing . . . "I was at the hospital during the firefight and got a good look at your face. Followed a hunch and paid a visit to the FBI. Never thought finding you could be so easy. Couldn't have our largest buyer handicapped by an FBI arrest. Then I saw you with Wyatt at the restaurant, put two and two together, and everything fell into place." He nodded smugly.

Kariss sensed anger flaring worse than the

pain in her body. She glared at Wyatt. "They used you. You're nothing to these men, and your greed is about to get you killed."

He cursed. "You don't know what you're talking about."

"I don't? What good are you to Bates once I'm dead? Nothing but a witness to get rid of. I bet you haven't even been paid."

Bates aimed his gun at Wyatt. "She's right. And a whole lot smarter than you are."

"I followed your instructions. Did everything you asked." Wyatt took a step back. "How many other people would do that for you?"

"Plenty. You were used. Right down to getting that woman to follow her." Bates sneered.

Kariss cringed. She despised Wyatt, but she didn't want him dead. "You took me outside the home of an FBI agent. This place will be crawling with agents soon."

"We've got it all figured out. Helps to have Cheeky's knowhow in the mix."

"Let me help you." Wyatt's voice quivered. "I can do whatever you need."

Bates shoved the gun into Wyatt's forehead. "You're a fool." He looked at Wyatt as he pulled the trigger.

CHAPTER 56

Hershey called Tigo an hour later.

"Do you know where the Arroyos are holding the woman?"

"I have two locations. One's at a warehouse near the ship channel, and the other's a deserted building on the southeast side."

"Let me have the addresses." Tigo jotted them down. "What else do you know?"

Hershey sighed. "They're using her to accomplish more than one thing."

"What are you not telling me?" Was this about the exchange?

"They'll know where this info's coming from."

Tigo swallowed his ire . . . and his rising desperation. "We can protect you."

"Like Candy and Jo-Jack?"

"They made foolish mistakes. Tried to handle the situations on their own."

"How much money is it worth to you?"

"Fifteen grand." What the FBI couldn't cover, he would.

"If this goes to court, I want protection and a new identity. My daughter too."

"You got it."

"Okay. You've asked about who 'Bat' is. It's Peter Masterson. He's been the Arroyos' supplier for a long time. Lately he's asked for more money, cutting into the Arroyos' profit. Three years ago, he took on a partner by the name of Arnold Bates. This guy's greedy. He plans to get rid of Masterson and take over the business."

"How does this tie into the woman?"

"She's the only one who can identify the Arroyo who was involved in a shooting, messing up Bates and Masterson and the Arroyos. They also want the FBI agent who's gotten too close to their operation and killed a couple of their men. They said they'd exchange the woman for the agent, but plan to kill them both."

"And blame it on Masterson?"

"You got it. Cheeky's not stupid. He knows he's taking a chance with this one, but he's holding another ace."

"What's that?"

"He plans to leave the building and let Masterson handle the situation. They have a new supplier — cheaper than Bates and

Masterson."

"The Arroyos don't need either man. Bates will be killed too."

"Right."

"Okay. We're on it."

Tigo phoned Linc and filled him in. Finally he had all the answers, and all the blanks held names. The part of him that thrived on strategic planning saw Bates, Masterson, Cheeky, and some of his key members at the same place.

"We'll check out both addresses. In the meantime, you stay put and wait for your call."

His cell phone sat in his hand like a bomb threatening to explode.

Kariss watched two of the Arroyos drag Wyatt's body from the building, the agonizing swish fading into the back of her mind. His blood smeared a path to the door, a life wasted in greed. She'd never wanted him dead.

She begged the fog of terror to end, shivering in one breath and feeling the heat of the nightmare in the next. The waiting was the worst anticipation. Prayer . . . Yes, she must pray.

Bates claimed Tigo knew about their demands. Tigo would call Linc and together they'd devise a plan to rescue her. But not at the expense of Tigo's life. No . . . she'd never agree to that.

A door creaked open and shut. Footsteps thudded against the cement and toward the faint light of the room. A tall, dark-haired man appeared in a suit. He swayed slightly.

"Masterson," Bates said. "Wondered where you were."

"Taking care of business." He slurred his response. "Got the woman?"

"We do. Just waiting on you to call Tigo Harris. Cheeky'll be here soon. You're drunk."

"No sweat. I see you took care of Phillips. Passed the boys outside."

"Whined all the way to the end." Bates sneered at Kariss. "Your sister is better off." His words sounded as though he'd done nothing more than applied brakes at a stop-light.

Her gaze trailed after the blood path. "What happened to Xavier Olvera?"

"Cheeky put him to work." He laughed. "He finally found his wife. Delores is in charge of the mules."

So he'd be forced to transport guns or drugs across the border. But he was alive. "What of his child?"

"The boy? Don't know where she has him.

But it will be a while before she lets Xavier have visitation. Got to earn his keep first."

Kariss's thoughts raced. Xavier's search had ended. He'd do whatever was asked of him to see his child. Today it might be transporting illegal goods. Tomorrow it might be stealing. What about the future? Would he resort to murder or gang initiation to have his son? She didn't have an answer. Neither did she want one.

"You'll see him again," Bates said. "He's fond of you. So we're giving him an opportunity to prove his loyalty."

She swallowed the acid rising in her stomach. No point in asking what he meant. Tigo . . . did he have any idea where they held her or what they planned?

No one had mentioned the identity of the new gun supplier. But Cheeky wouldn't tell Bates and Masterson. All of them had different agendas, but each of them wanted her and Tigo dead.

How horrible if they forced Xavier to pull the trigger.

CHAPTER 57

Tigo received the call from an Arroyo shortly after midnight with instructions to drive to Greenspoint Mall alone and unarmed.

"No more games. You're our man, Tigo. Once we have you, we'll let the woman go."

Fat chance of them freeing Kariss. "All right."

"Any signs of cops or agents, and the deal is off and both of you are dead."

"I got it."

"You have thirty minutes."

Tigo called Linc. "Greenspoint in thirty minutes."

"You're wearing a tracker?"

"Got it in a metal button on my shirt. And I'll have my phone until Cheeky takes it."

"The cowboy's hot tonight."

Tigo blew out a sigh. "And I need you hot on my rear."

His mind sped faster than his truck as he

headed south on I-45 to Greenspoint Mall from his home in Spring. Given the time of night, few would be around. And those lurking in the area weren't likely to be upstanding citizens. But Linc had that worked out.

He pulled off the exit ramp and his phone rang.

"Change of plans," the man said. "Drive to the airport."

Tigo didn't like the fact more people could be hurt. "What terminal?"

"I'll let you know when you get closer."

The call ended, and he set his phone beside him. It rang again. Linc.

"We're trailing you. Both addresses that Hershey gave you were deserted."

"I'll call him again."

"No need. Ryan's on it."

"Maybe Hershey transposed a number. He's done that before."

When the call ended, Tigo checked his mirrors. He didn't pick up a tail, but both agents and Arroyos had him in their sights. Once he exited for the airport, another call instructed him to drive to Terminal B.

Another call had him change course and approach Terminal C.

The last call sent him into the parking garage of Terminal C, third level.

He drove by empty vehicles. Where was

backup? His tracker showed every move.

His cell rang again.

"Stop at the end of this row and get out. Arms up."

Tigo did as he was told. The garage was devoid of people. A Yukon pulled up alongside him, and two Arroyos jumped out. The driver lowered his window.

"Pat him down. Take his phone. Look for a wire," the driver said in Spanish.

"Is the woman with you?" Tigo stalled for time.

The driver snorted. "Right." He lifted his chin toward the men. "Find anything?"

One held up his phone.

"Behave yourself and you might see your lady friend. Get him in back."

One of the men tied Tigo's hands behind him and opened the rear of the Yukon. The second man gagged him.

"I like his shirt," the first one said.

"Take it," said the other. *"Él no lo necesita."*

Kariss's back ached from sitting on the concrete floor. Her eye and head throbbed, and her wrists and ankles stung. Exhaustion crept through her mind, but each time she drifted toward sleep, Wyatt's murder jarred her back to reality.

For the first time, she understood what

she'd heard all of her life. Although she wanted desperately to live and she refused to give up, she also understood that living with Jesus meant no more sorrow. No more guilt about failing Nikki. She thought of the little girl . . . Had Kariss really failed or was it the little girl's time to live in heaven? If Kariss survived this, she'd pursue it. If she didn't make it, the problem no longer existed. And for the first time since the fire, peace filled her. How strange when she was at the mercy of a gang.

Cheeky had joined Bates and Masterson — the three men whose criminal activities Tigo had worked so hard to end. Soon they would have him as well. She shoved away the despicable things they'd do to him. She'd read about the torture . . . and the beheadings.

He'd have called Ryan and Linc for help. Yes, she had to hold fast to that thought. The FBI was equipped to stop what the three men planned.

Her prayers seemed futile when no one knew where she was being held.

Masterson cursed. "Hot in here. Why couldn't you have taken her to an air-conditioned location?"

"Shut up," Cheeky said. "You're in my world. Xavier and the agent will be here in a few minutes."

Xavier and Tigo . . . What were they going to do? A mass execution?

Empty moments passed with Masterson complaining, Cheeky threatening to slice out his heart, and Bates confidently observing.

A door creaked open, and Xavier appeared. He threw a quick look her way and frowned. Not a word. Had he hardened in a matter of a few days?

"We have another job for you," Cheeky said.

"What's that?" Xavier stood with his back to Kariss.

"We've picked up another FBI agent. Both of them need to be eliminated. You're the man to do it."

Xavier shook his head. "I won't. I drove your car to Mexico so I could see my son. Then I learned I have to make four more trips there before I can see him. Now you want me to kill good people. I'm finished."

"Delores might bring your son here tonight."

"To see his father commit murder?"

Cheeky grabbed Xavier by the throat. "You'll do what I say when I say it or you're a dead man."

"Then go ahead and kill me. I don't believe I even have a son."

"Ask Delores." Cheeky sneered. "She doesn't know who the father is. Delores wanted to get rid of Benita, and then your deportation let her take care of the kid and you. She got a little nervous and slept with a bunch of us in case the law caught up with her. I liked her and put her to work." He shoved Xavier to where Kariss sat. "You can die with them."

Cheeky's phone rang. He answered, nodded, and dropped it into his jean's pocket. "They'll be here in thirty minutes."

CHAPTER 58

Tigo's gaze swept the warehouse until he found Kariss. Even in the dim shadows, he could see she'd been beaten, but she was alive. Probably raped, but he refused to think about that. He caught her gaze and silently sent reassurance. Xavier sat beside her. How had he gotten involved with this?

"Get rid of the van," Cheeky said to the driver. "Take it to the northeast side and leave it. Call someone to pick you up."

Time . . . Tigo needed time. His shirt with the tracker was in the van. As long as it stayed parked, Linc could find them. He saw the oil pipe stacked for yards and wondered how many of them were filled with guns and ammo.

The Arroyos on each side of Tigo pushed him to Cheeky. Was the FBI in place?

Tigo bore his gaze into Bates. "I was right. You and Masterson are the Arroyos' supplier."

Bates sneered. "Too bad you won't live to tell it."

"The FBI knows. It's just time."

"Something you don't have." Cheeky sunk a fist into Tigo's stomach then stepped aside for his men to take over.

All of them were drinking beer. Masterson struggled to stand. Tigo willed himself to handle whatever happened next — and for Kariss not to cry out. When they were finished with him, they'd start in on her. And it would be savage.

Every second that ticked by brought help closer. But Linc was following the wire on his shirt, now on its way to the northeast side of town. He wanted to look at Kariss . . . No doubt she'd be praying. He should be too — not for himself but for her.

A fist smacked against the side of his face. Lightning pain raced to his skull.

Another fist to his stomach doubled him over. He swallowed a gasp for breath. Two men jerked him to his feet and pinned back his arms.

An explosion of agony burst from his body — his face, his abdomen, his kidneys.

He tasted blood with each blow. Groans escaped him, and it fueled their anger. Bates and Masterson stood back, obviously enjoying the show.

"Enough, before you kill him," Cheeky said. "Bates and Masterson want the pleasure. Put him with the others."

Tigo was dragged to where Kariss and Xavier were held.

"Are you going to video the beheading?" Masterson seasoned his words with hate. "Upload it to YouTube?"

Cheeky laughed. "We've taken care of all those who've gotten in our way. This time it's your turn."

Bates nodded. "I'm going to let you finish them. We'll wait for you outside."

Cheeky motioned to the other Arroyos. "Unless you don't have the guts."

"Hey, what's going on here?" Masterson pulled out one of his guns. He had another one in his waistband . . . Bat Masterson. "Why me?"

"You told me you wanted the opportunity to blow Harris's head off," Bates said. "Now you can do it." He pointed to the three captives and walked away with Cheeky.

The Arroyos would make sure Masterson took the blame for this. And Cheeky would kill Bates outside, after which the Arroyos would dispose of all the bodies — revenge for raising gun prices. Now that they had a new supplier, they no longer needed Bates and Masterson. What irony.

Tigo wondered, *Where was backup?*

"Are you all right?" he whispered to Kariss.

She blinked, her face a blanket of compassion. "Yes. Where's Linc?"

"Just waiting for the right moment."

She held her breath. "You mean he's not here?"

He couldn't tell her the truth. "Patience. What about Xavier?"

"I'll tell you later."

He attempted to look at her, despite the excruciating pain turning his head caused.

"I can help," she said.

They needed more than a prayer.

"Xavier untied me."

Masterson staggered within twelve feet of them, waving his gun. "I owe them thanks. Now I can take care of you myself."

Tigo's body refused to move. His right arm was broken, and he fought to keep from passing out. How could he help Kariss? Her hands might be untied, but he was useless.

Xavier bolted from his position and grabbed Masterson by the knees, knocking him down. The gun dropped and fired, a bullet hitting Xavier in the left thigh. The sound echoed across the warehouse. Kariss scrambled for the fallen gun.

"FBI, drop your weapon."

Masterson ignored the order. He yanked out his second gun and pointed it at Tigo.

A shot rang out from the FBI at the same time that Kariss fired into Masterson's chest. Two bullets took the man down.

CHAPTER 59

One week later

Kariss's phone rang and she pulled it from her purse. She stared at the caller ID. "Can't believe this. Mike McDougal, you're on your way out." She paused for a moment then responded. "Kariss here."

"How did you manage writing the FBI gun-smuggling article for the paper?"

"Skill, Mr. McDougal."

"Want to make a deal?"

"I'm not interested in anything you have to say."

"Oh, you will this one. I'll leave you alone on my blog. Even post an apology for the last tidbit in exchange for getting me into the FBI."

"You have a lot of nerve. I know my attorney filed charges against you for slander."

"Just you wait. My book reviews on your past titles will be up on Amazon before the day is over."

"Go ahead. I could care less about your threats. Your calls are now harassment." She disconnected the call and dropped her cell back into her purse.

"Hope that's the end of McDougal for you." Tigo stood in the entrance of her cubicle, his first day back at work since helping to close the Operation Wasp case and arresting Delores Olvera. His face was still a mass of blue and purple, and the sling around his arm was decorated with Buzz Lightyear stickers.

"Somehow I doubt it, but we can hope." She studied his pitiful face. "I thought we agreed last night that you should rest a few more days."

"Can't keep a good man down."

"You and Xavier have the same philosophy."

"He looks better than I do."

She tilted her head. "You're right. I think he's going to be okay. Truth is he'd go through the whole thing again just to learn the truth about Benita and to discover the little boy is his."

Tigo nodded. "We're working on expediting his papers to keep him here permanently."

"I'm so glad. His little boy looks a lot like Benita — same huge eyes and long lashes.

And he will most likely have his son permanently since Delores will undoubtedly be in prison for life. I'm glad she confessed to allowing Benita to starve to death." She remembered her first glimpse of the long-haired woman with delicate features and cold eyes.

"Xavier's a good man."

"Like you." She hoped he could see her gratitude.

A few moments passed as though he were searching for something to say. "Do you have any idea how good it feels to have Cheeky and Bates in custody along with a few Arroyos?"

"Total satisfaction? So glad I'm no longer looking over my shoulder."

"Thank goodness I remembered that Hershey is dyslexic, and thank Ryan for turning around the numbers in the warehouse address. How's your sister holding up?"

"She'll be all right. It'll take time. The new baby will help her heal."

"Good. She's a survivor like her sister. Hey, congrats on passing the shooting portion of your CHL. Of course for me that happened when you *saved* my life. Your bullet sailed straight through Masterson's heart."

A nightmare she'd never forget. "Here's

hoping I'll never have to use a gun again."

"Oh, and another congrats on officially selling your book. Let's go get Starbucks. I'm buying."

"Looking like . . . that?"

"Why? Are you ashamed of me?"

Never, but she'd not tell him so. "You look like a battered hero."

He lifted his sling and pointed to the Buzz Lightyear stickers. "What's the next step with your book?"

"Once it's finished, which will be in a few months, my editor reads it, then makes suggestions. I take care of those edits, and then it goes to other editors and proofreaders before publication."

"How long does the process take?"

"Approximately a year from the time I turn in the manuscript."

"Long time to wait. So are you going to start another book?"

She laughed. "Yeah. It's in my blood. I have bubblings in my head."

"Back to women's fiction?"

"Not on your life."

Tigo groaned. "Do I want to know the plotline?"

"Same characters. Same setting."

"Any way I can get out of helping you?"

"Do you really want me to find someone else?"

He studied her with the same expression he used to figure out the details on a case. His features softened, and she saw a spark of something that spoke of fragile feelings. "I think we can manage being a team again. Besides, you're up two games in Word Family, and I'm a sore loser."

NOTE FROM THE AUTHOR

Dear Reader,

Although this is a fiction work, Cherished Doe is based on an actual FBI-solved cold case. The first time I heard the story, it attached itself to my heart. Like Kariss, the horror of a murdered, unidentified child would not let me go.

Although the details of the case have been altered, many aspects of the investigation are true. The FBI, Houston Police Department, and the Texas Rangers refused to let the case rest. The idea of calling a joint press conference to enlist media assistance was unprecedented. But the effort worked. Houstonians became involved in finding the identity and the cause of the child's death. The father, who thought he was paying for his child's critical medical care, viewed the documentary on a Spanish-language TV station and made the call to the FBI. Even now, as I write this letter to you, I'm overwhelmed with emotion. I pray this novel moved you to keep your eyes open for potential child abuse and vow, like I've done, to ensure our children are safe and protected.

Thank you for reading my story.

DiAnn

DISCUSSION QUESTIONS

1. Kariss made a decision to follow her dreams. What were the stakes?

2. Tigo had the reputation for being a rogue. How did you feel about his methods of stopping crime?

3. Cherished Doe is based on an FBI cold case that was eventually solved. How did reading about Benita's death affect you?

4. Xavier felt he had nothing to lose. Were his decisions based on logic or feeling?

5. Have you considered the reasons why Delores allowed her little daughter to die? Is there any situation that would justify her actions?

6. Tigo was devoted to the care of his

mother. What does that tell you about him?

7. Do you think Kariss's parents were proud of her success? What was their real issue with her books?

8. Vicki struggled to keep her marriage intact. How do you feel about her efforts?

9. Should Kariss have given up on helping Xavier when danger seemed to stalk her?

10. Desperate people resort to desperate means. Consider the characters in this novel and discuss the lengths and depths they went to to achieve their wants and needs.

ACKNOWLEDGMENTS

Beau Egert; Cathy Nielsen-Barrett; Dr. Richard Mabry; Elaine Cornell; Karl Harroff; Marlon Amell; Shauna Dunlap, Media Coordinator, FBI Houston Division; and J. Victor Moreno. And I couldn't write a book without acknowledging my husband, Dean Mills, for his patience, support, and understanding.

The employees of Thorndike Press hope you have enjoyed this Large Print book. All our Thorndike, Wheeler, and Kennebec Large Print titles are designed for easy reading, and all our books are made to last. Other Thorndike Press Large Print books are available at your library, through selected bookstores, or directly from us.

For information about titles, please call:
  (800) 223-1244

or visit our Web site at:
  http://gale.cengage.com/thorndike

To share your comments, please write:
  Publisher
  Thorndike Press
  10 Water St., Suite 310
  Waterville, ME 04901

AUG 12

RIVERHEAD FREE LIBRARY
330 COURT STREET
RIVERHEAD, NY 11901